REPEATERS

· A NOVEL ·

ERICA FERENCIK

waking dream press
Framingham, Massachusetts

REPEATERS
© Erica Ferencik, 2011

ISBN 9780981574110
LCCN: 2011920210

Printed in the United States of America

Cover design by Judy Blomquist

Publisher's Cataloging-In-Publication Data
Ferencik, Erica.
  Repeaters : a novel / by Erica Ferencik.
  p. ; cm.
  ISBN: 978-0-9815741-1-0
1. Dead--Fiction. 2. Supernatural—Fiction. 3. Psychiatrists--Fiction.
4. Man-woman relationships--Fiction. 5. Love stories, American.
6. Horror fiction. I. Title.
PS3606.E746 R47 2011
813/.6   2011920210

FOR GEORGE

REPEATERS

· ONE ·

Spring came to the square in splashes of color, with careful rows of blood red tulips and banks of showy daffodils. On the north side of the green, a magnolia was bursting with fleshy blooms, its leaves curled like tender green fists. Tucked deep in the knotty branches, a robin sat fatly in her bed of leaves and twigs. Beneath the downy belly of the bird, inside the chalk blue egg tucked below, the nestling's fetal heart – the size of a sunflower seed – beat hot and fierce. The tiny chick dreamed pre-bird dreams of flight and fear; its big eyes pulsed under their purplish skeins of skin; it fit closely inside its jamming shell; it was ready, moments from ready, to break free.

The robin stirred herself, flapped to the edge of the nest where she perched, preened, shook her tail feathers free of a few drops of rain. Only a man's height beneath her, worms nudged blindly to the surface of the soil as if asking to be devoured. The bird cocked her head down at them, then back at her egg: first this way, then that. She made up her mind. With her fierce beak she jabbed at the egg, cracking it open. Yolk spilled around the tiny wet bird as her mother stabbed at it again, ripping at its hot belly. The baby bird opened its mouth once, slowly, soundlessly, before she tore out its throat.

· TWO ·

Doors slammed, stereos cranked louder, cats yawned in windows. The quad was waking up. With a moneyed echo, it came alive with the sounds of students calling to each other as they rushed to classes or the cafeteria for breakfast. Bright, beautiful youth on their way to the future.

The robin, swollen with its meal, flew up and over the three-hundred-year-old brick walls to where the city blistered with traffic and disappointments a four-year education couldn't cure, where the homeless sprawled on benches in clothes heavy with piss, suits marched to cubicles, and subways spewed forth the usual sad salad of humanity. The bird shat a white splat on a newspaper held by an elderly man at a café who'd nodded off as he read, then glided back through a gothic bronze gateway into the quad where it landed on the sill of a wide open dorm window.

Inside the cell-like room, a yellow Labrador dozed next to the narrow bed where Kim Nathanson slept. Fascinated by the bird, he lifted his head from the floor and tilted it, one soft ear grazing the dull linoleum. He glanced guiltily back at his master as he got to his feet and rambled over to the sill with the knowing gait of a dog who never has or ever will catch a bird. The robin had already flown away. Still, the dog stood there happily curious, his glistening black nose twitching with information from the fresh breeze, his long curtained tail swooshing back and forth across his master's face.

"Marty – get away!" She brushed the tail from her eyes, scowling, and rolled over. The dog turned from the window, loped over to the other side of the bed and put his face in hers, tail still churning hard behind him. The stare-down technique.

"Yes, you exist. Okay." Kim rolled away again.

"It's eight-oh-five AM," an automated voice droned from a pyramid-shaped box. She reached over and hit a button on its side.

"You've got to be kidding me." She sat up stiffly, stretched, and smiled to herself. She gathered to her face the roomy man's shirt she wore and inhaled deeply, lost in a moment of the night before, when he'd unzipped her dress and traced her spine with his finger from her hairline, so slowly, to her ass. He held his mouth on her neck and kissed her there, telling her how she beautiful she smelled, how badly he wanted her the moment he saw her, how his desire grew every day. She touched the place on her neck where he kissed her, wondering if he'd left a mark.

She let go of the shirt and reached for her dog. She loved his sweet bony head, his ridiculously cold nose. "We can't be this happy, Marty. It's just not good."

She reached over to her CD player, counted three buttons to the right and pressed the play button. As Ravel's "Bolero" began, building its wave after wave of passionate melody, she got to her feet and held herself, swaying to the music. She was a harem of one for him, dropping scarf after gauzy scarf. Marty wanted to dance too and licked at her knees. She shooed him away.

"God, dog, can't you let me fantasize about my boyfriend for a minute?" She hugged his big body, her long auburn hair falling forward. "Jealous, aren'tcha. Yeah, well, better get used to it."

She pulled the man's shirt up over her head and stood naked in the middle of the spare, mirrorless room. Sunlight poured over her full breasts, narrow hips, flawless nineteen-year-old skin. She brushed her hair which snapped with static and clean, her glittering grey eyes seeing blackness, her body remembering Constantin.

3

· THREE ·

Marty panted in the growing heat as he led Kim across the quad to the science building. Kim's dress flattered her slender frame but looked dated among the fashion-conscious hordes of students swarming all around her. Still, she displayed little of the awkwardness blindness can bring. Her hair was gathered in a smooth ponytail, and her face, adorned only in moisturizer and chapstick, was raised toward the sun.

A student in jeans torn just right wove her way toward Kim. "Kim, wait up!"

Kim gave Marty the command to sit. She felt his tail brush back and forth across her sandaled feet.

"Hi, Marie."

"You going to Jasmine's party this weekend?"

"Oh, I don't think I can."

Marie pouted prettily. "Too bad, should be a blast. Three bands, shitty keg beer, the whole quad will be there. But hey, if you have plans – "

Kim blushed. "Well, I'm not sure about – "

Marie turned to wave at another student at the other end of the quad. "Sounds like you're the one with the hot weekend coming up – well, listen, gotta fly. See you in chem!" She ran off in the direction of her friend.

"Bye, Marie," Kim said to no one.

It seemed to her that since she had fallen in love with Constantin, even though they kept their student/teacher affair under tight wraps, people were coming out of the woodwork to be her friend or just invite her to things. She was obviously exuding some kind of energy that people liked to be around. She wondered if something similar was happening with Constantin, at the same time hoping it wasn't. She'd overheard a comment or two that led her to believe he was as good to look at as he was to touch.

Chemistry was just a ticking clock until biology. She sat in the back row of a cavernous auditorium listening to a lecture on inorganic compounds, wondering if they would see each other that weekend, and what they would do. The weekend before they'd driven to New York City and visited the Bronx Zoo, talking and laughing all the way about life at Barnesdale and just anything at all. She loved the screeching birds in the aviary and wanted to touch every animal he described as they passed by. He drew a picture of each of them in the palm of her hand. For dinner he took her to a restaurant where opera singers sang only yards from their table; the bass notes thrummed in her spine.

Of everything in the world she had heard of or imagined, if she could choose one thing to see for even a moment – such a glorious moment – it would be Constantin's face. She told him this. He watched her face as she touched the rough landscape of his chin, his broad forehead, long lashes over wide set eyes; and felt seen for the very first time.

As she walked with Marty to Constantin's class she caught a whiff of sandalwood someone wore, the incense her first boyfriend Derek used to burn in his room. They'd met at the Stafford School for the Blind where they both had lived for most of their lives. She recalled his birdlike shoulders and soft, eager hands. How convinced she'd been that she had found love, that this was it, this affair of self discovery. How wonderful to be really touched for the first time by a boy, but in the end their world together at the school felt too small and confining. Two blind kids going through puberty are bound to think they're in love at some point, she mused. Of course she compared Derek to Constantin and with a shudder realized once again how precious Constantin was to her, and how much she didn't want to lose him.

· FOUR ·

Constantin Damler sat at his desk gently tapping a pencil against his forehead as he regarded his bright but overwhelmed first-year biology students. He watched as the girls tore their eyes off him and refocused themselves on their books and diagrams, occasionally stealing glances at their handhelds. His thick glasses made his already large eyes seem to almost fill the lenses, while his twelve-dollar haircut did nothing to defuse the irresistible way his preternaturally thick black hair grazed his shirt collar.

A Braille book lay open on Kim's desk. In her hands rested a rubber model of a human heart. As she listened to Constantin speak, she traced the intricacies of the heart with her fingers.

Constantin let the pencil drop on the blotter, sighed, and got up from his seat. Six lanky feet of him strolled around the desk and sat on it, as relaxed as if he were alone in the room. In the first row a redhead flipped through page after page of colorful illustrations.

"Linda?"

She held up her hand to signal "give me a minute" but he gave his head a quick shake.

"Aaron?"

Kim's heart beat hard. She knew the answer and he knew she knew it. Pinpricks of sweat needled her armpits. Marty shifted on the floor, sighed a noisy dog sigh, and lay his head over her foot. She smiled and angled her head toward the rubber heart in her hands.

Aaron pored over his notes and diagrams. "I'm sorry, Professor

Damler, I missed the last class so I'm not quite up to speed – "

"So am I to understand that no one out there..." he watched Kim hold the heart, her face rapt, "...can tell me, after nearly two semesters at Barnesdale University, where only the best and the brightest walk these hallowed halls, what happens during phase two of the cardiac cycle? Can this really be true?"

Blushing hard, Kim raised her hand.

"Kim?"

"The atria relax while the ventricles contract. Since the AV valves are closed while the semi lunar valves are open, blood moves from the right ventricle into the pulmonary trunk, and from the left ventricle into the aorta."

A couple of students turned around to stare at her. A preppy young man sitting behind her made a jerking-off gesture with his hand, prompting stifled laughter here and there.

Constantin glared at the student. "Something particularly funny about knowing the answer to my question, Mr. Alberts?"

He shook his head "no" and looked down, suddenly engrossed by his notes.

Kim's fingers flew over the lines of her book, her mind racing past the details of the pulmonary system of amphibians. Constantin made slow progress toward her as he handed back papers to each student, occasionally leaning down to whisper a comment or two.

Just as he reached Kim, Marty thumped his tail, got to his feet and licked Constantin's hand.

"Sit, Marty, come on." Kim gently pushed down on his head.

Both Kim and Constantin suppressed smiles as he handed back her exam. "Average work as always," he whispered, grazing her shoulder with the back of his hand. She shuddered.

Her finger glanced along the top of the page: 100 points. "I'll try to do better," she said.

He slipped a key into her hand and whispered, "Six o'clock, chicken cacciatore, champagne toast to start."

He walked on. Kim covered her delight with a soft cough as she leaned over to pet Marty and slip the key in her pocket.

· FIVE ·

Lost in thought, Kim found herself halfway back to her dorm before she remembered her promise to have coffee with Carmella, a volunteer at the Stafford School she'd known since childhood. She stopped mid-stride, jolting Marty, and muttered "shit" a few times under her breath. She'd have to catch the 49 bus to Watertown, cross a few busy streets and walk a good half mile to get there, leaving after just a half hour visit to arrive for dinner on time.

Kim had blown off the past two Fridays, their standing date, to be with Constantin, but had not admitted this to Carmella. The excuse was always her studies, knowing Carmella held knowledge and school as sacred and would never question this. When in truth she had spent one of the Fridays drinking margaritas in a downtown bar with him, and the second in bed with him all afternoon. The guilt quotient for a third offense was a bit too much to bear.

Carmella was a five-foot-tall-in-sensible-black-shoes seventy-year-old Italian woman who had once been a personal servant for a rich Italian soap opera star who'd moved to the states in the late fifties. Carmella had come with her, marrying Renato, another Italian immigrant who had his own garage. They'd wanted a big laughing gaggle of babies but tried for years, unsuccessfully, to conceive. At the time, Carmella learned only as much English as she needed in order to talk to doctors about her infertility. Then one day she woke, turned to Renato and said, "I'm pregnant." It was as if her mouth said the words before her brain understood what had come out. Renato laughed and they held each other and cried with happiness, because

9

he knew that when Carmella said something, it was always simply the truth.

In nine months she gave birth to an utterly beautiful, utterly blind daughter. Carmella looked at her husband with a mixture of profound joy and grief as the doctor handed her Christina, pronouncing that she did not see and never would. But the child grew and laughed and filled their lives with joy, and they spent their time learning how to take care of a blind child who would become a blind adult. Carmella took Christina to the Stafford School for the Blind where she learned Braille and where every student and teacher fell in love with her. By the age of seven, Christina spoke Italian and English perfectly, and wanted to be a doctor and move to Italy when she grew up.

On Christina's eighth birthday, there was a mixup. Carmella thought Renato was picking Christina up at school, and Renato thought it was his wife's turn. That day Christina had been given a rabbit in a cage as a birthday present by another classmate's mother. Carmella waited at home frosting a strawberry chiffon cake, while Renato left the garage and headed home early to be there for her party.

At school, Christina waited for parents to arrive at the bottom of the driveway with the other kids and a couple of teachers. The kids crowded noisily around the rabbit's cage while the two teachers stood off to the side, having a good laugh about something that happened that day. As they did so, a young boy, squealing to touch the rabbit, found the door of the cage and slid it open. Christina screamed as she felt her rabbit leap from the cage and into the street, where she ran after it. When the car hit, her small body flew up and over the windshield like it had been shot out of the earth. She died instantly.

At home, Carmella sat and waited by the delicate pink cake. Why did she suddenly feel such despair, an abyss of loss yawning up inside her? Renato pulled into the driveway smiling big and carrying bags of little girl presents. When he opened the screen door and looked at Carmella's face, he knew something terrible, irrevocable, had happened.

There were never any more children. Nothing seemed to ease Carmella's grief except being at the Stafford School. She became a volunteer, eventually specializing in travel training for the blind. How to get from school to work and back, or to a doctor's appointment independently. She trained hundreds of kids and adults how to use the subway, cross the street, negotiate tricky sidewalks and memorize landmarks. Though others were paid for what she did, she refused to take a dime.

She met Kim when she was six years old, a year after Christina's death.

Carmella was working at the school the day Kim's mother dropped her off. She watched the little girl whimper as her mother, remarkably calm, stood by her new Volvo exchanging a few last words with the director of the school. The mother was tall and strikingly beautiful with milky white skin and lots of dark hair piled high on her head. Her daughter, now bawling, had stumbled into the arms of a bewildered looking secretary. The woman signed one last paper and without a backward glance, got in her car and drove away.

Later, when Kim had cried herself to exhaustion and sat crumpled on a stool in the playroom, Carmella cautiously approached her.

She asked her for her name, straining to hear the answer in the girl's almost inaudible whisper.

"Your name is Tim?"

"No, *Kim*." The child wiped her red eyes roughly with the backs of her hands.

"Well, listen to me, Kim, I know you are sad today. This is a whole new world, is that not right?"

Nothing.

"And you are sad to see your mama go, but it is only for the week."

"No, it's not."

"Then the weekend she will come for you, surely?"

"No."

"Well, sometime, she will be back – "

"You didn't hear what she said. She said I better like it here, because she's done with me. She said she's never coming back."

Kim let Carmella hold her close as the tears came flooding back.

· SIX ·

Carmella sat in an armchair across from Kim in the musty living room, her feet not touching the floor. A grandfather clock ticked loudly behind her.

"You know this man how long?" Carmella asked.

"Three months."

"And is he studying the marine biology? Is he in your classes?"

"He's my biology teacher, but he's – "

Carmella gasped. "You're dating your teacher? But Kim, ah my child, that's not so good. You must know this!"

"But he's only twenty-seven, and he's the kindest man – "

Carmella got to her feet. "Kim, Kim, what will we do with you? I must get our coffee." She bustled off to fetch espresso and the amaretto cookies that were Kim's favorite. Kim listened to the click of Marty's toenails on the linoleum as he followed her for a bowl of water and maybe a treat. The squeak and slam of the ancient refrigerator. Checking her watch for the third time in ten minutes, Kim wondered if she would have time to go home and wash her hair before meeting Constantin. She sighed. Probably not.

She wished she could open a window for some fresh air, but knew that Carmella felt cold with the slightest breeze, so held back. The air was further degraded by traces of vanilla-scented incense Carmella burned all day long to cover the smell of a cigarette habit she swore she'd defeated years ago.

Kim heard Carmella and Marty return, and the sounds of a tray being set before her. Carmella reached over and took Kim's hand, drawing it over to touch the tiny porcelain cup and plate of cookies. Kim noted with some sadness how papery the skin felt, and how the hand shook with age.

"Some espresso, a double like you say, and fresh amaretti, okay?"

"Thanks, Carmella." She took a sip of coffee.

Carmella settled herself with her coffee. "I just don't like the sound of this man."

"Look, Carmella, I'm nineteen. I'm not a baby any more."

"He is supposed to be your teacher, not your lover."

"He's both."

"You are in school to make a life for yourself! To learn! All these years of work…"

Kim put the coffee and cookie down. "I'm an 'A' student."

"I just don't like this man."

"You haven't met him. How can you say that?"

Kim heard the chink of a cup settling back in its saucer on the table.

"The signs are bad."

"What signs?"

Carmella saw signs everywhere: in the shapes of clouds, in espresso grounds, in what kinds of birds she saw eating berries in her garden in the morning.

"Just before you came today, I nearly broke my neck on the back stairs."

"What?"

"The landlord, you know, that awful Russian man, painted the back steps. Those steps were rotten. He *knew* that! But he painted over them anyway, and so I took a step down – stupid me, should have gone to the front – and fell right through to the ground!"

"Are you okay?"

"I have a scrape. Tomorrow a bruise."

Kim sighed. "So where's the sign, Melle? I don't get it."

"Something rotten painted over! I know it is rotten and it can hurt me but now that it's painted a pretty yellow, I step on it anyway? If this is not a sign, then what is? And then, one moment later, ding dong and it is you at the door. My heart skipped a beat!"

"You can't make me stop seeing him, Carmella."

"I'm afraid for you. I don't have a good feeling."

"I guess not."

"Always, I've been afraid for you."

"I'm not Christina, Melle, I'm Kim. You're not my mother."

"I'm the closest thing you will ever have to a mother."

"Shouldn't *I* be the one to say that?"

They were silent as they listened to the tinny sound of a television switched on a floor above them. Slowly, Kim reached over to touch her.

"I'm sorry I said that. Melle..." Her hand hung there a lonely moment, trembling, until Carmella gave it a quick squeeze, then pulled her hand away.

"You're right. I am guilty of looking for Christina in you. I thought for years I could see her in your face, but that is not true. You are you, Kim. A brand new soul."

"What do you mean, a brand new soul?"

"It means," Carmella pushed herself to her feet, "that it is your first time here, on this earth, I believe."

Kim gripped the chair tightly, trying to conjure some patience. For years she had listened to tales of Carmella seeing ghosts in the Stafford School, hearing voices from the beyond, reading shadowy meanings into everyday occurrences. At times it was entertaining, at others it just drove her nuts.

"Of course it's my first time, and it's my last time, too, so if I've found someone to love, and who loves me, why should I walk away from it?"

Kim listened to the clink of china as Carmella cleared the dishes. Again she chastised herself for speaking harshly to a woman who truly had been a mother figure to her over the years. But there were times Kim wanted to burst out of her past without a trace, live her new life at Barnesdale where her academic gifts were praised almost daily, and where this new man showed her elements of herself she never knew existed. Forget about where she came from, life as a blind orphan, all the weekends and holidays alone with Carmella when all the rest of the kids had gone home. The piercing loneliness, isolation, and always wondering somewhere inside: what have I done to drive my mother away?

Kim took a deep breath and again flipped up the glass on her Braille watch, though she knew that Carmella was watching her.

"I love you, Kim," Carmella said.

"I love you too, Carmella." Her voice was thin and unnatural.

"Maybe you can bring your young man next week when you come."

"I will. He's been wanting to meet you."

"You go now. He's waiting for you, am I right?"

Kim gathered herself and Marty to leave, slipping his harness over him as he pushed his nose into her hands. He seemed eager to leave as well, leading her quickly to the door, but taking her carefully down the narrow stairs. At the front door she bent down to kiss the tiny woman goodbye, enduring the cloying whiff of drugstore perfume she always wore.

Nothing tasted as sweet as that first breath of fresh air as Kim stepped out onto the porch.

"Next Friday then, with your y – "

"With Constantin, yes. Goodbye, Carmella."

"Goodbye, Kim."

Carmella watched Kim leave, the long willowy length of her. She pictured her at eleven: sitting up till midnight playing chess; at nine: Kim exhausting her with questions about animals, birds, plants, the sky; at six: bursting through the doors of the Stafford School, eyes red from crying. She conjured Kim's mother standing there, shadowy, emotionless, her perfectly cut suit enunciating lavish curves. At that moment she felt a stab of pain in her chest, almost as if she had been punched there, and staggered a few feet to a rocker. She collapsed into the wicker, willing the pain away as she watched Kim turn the corner and step out of sight.

· SEVEN ·

Kim lay in Constantin's arms on a sprawling couch that took up most of the room in his small but comfortable Cambridge studio. Outside, the spring sun had set and the temperature dropped, making things even cozier inside. A half-empty bottle of champagne sat sweating in an ice bucket nearby. Kim pushed herself gently away from him and sat up.

"What's wrong?"

"Nothing," she said. "It's just all so hard to take in." She was unable to stop touching the new ring of gold on her left hand. The smooth yet somehow soft metal, with their two names carved on the inside, along with the date they met. It had already warmed to her skin, as if it had always been there.

"Is the ring okay?"

"I love it. It feels beautiful."

"So do you," he said, stroking her thigh through her thin cotton dress.

"I don't want to keep it a secret any more, you know, that we're together," she said softly.

"As soon as we're married, we can tell the world."

She touched his hand. "This is such a surprise, Constantin. You don't think it's too soon?"

"Oh, come on, don't waffle on me now."

She smiled. "I'm not waffling."

"So you'll be my wife? Say it. I want to hear you say it."

"Are you sure you love me enough?"

"Yes. Do you love *me* enough, Kim?"

She touched his face. "Of course. I guess this is the way life is sometimes – whirlwind, and you shouldn't try to control it."

"Yes, little Miss Scientist, sometimes life overwhelms you. It sweeps you off your logical little feet. Don't fight it, I'd say."

"I won't. I don't. I just – "

"Then stop being so serious, and just love me, okay? Here and now and – "

" – forever."

"That's right. Now I want to hear you say you'll be my wife. I think my head will explode if you don't."

She took the champagne bottle and placed a trembling finger just inside her glass, filling it till the liquid touched the tip. She knocked back most of the champagne. "I'll be your wife," she said softly.

"Then save some champagne for your husband-to-be?"

She smiled and poured herself another glass. "You gotta come and get it."

He took the glass from her hand, downed it and gathered her up in his arms. She shrieked with delight as he carried her into the bedroom.

· EIGHT ·

Two hours later Kim lay in his arms, loathe to wake him but too restless to lie still. She lifted his arm from her shoulders but he woke and drew her to him again.

"Not so fast, babycakes."

"I have to get up."

"Sorry I'm such a lump, but you knocked the wind out of me, as usual."

"Aren't you going to feed me?"

He didn't move. "I guess I did mention something about food, didn't I."

"We can get takeout if you want – "

"No, I want to cook for you. I love cooking for you, because you think I'm a good cook." He kissed her on the forehead. "So, are you going to call your friends and family and tell them the good news?"

"Well, that shouldn't take too long."

"What do you mean?"

She turned away from him slightly. "There's just Adrienne from school, and Carmella, that's it really. But we can call your parents – "

"What about your mother?"

"I don't think she would care."

"It's that bad? Her own daughter getting married and she wouldn't want to know?"

Kim reached toward the bottom of the bed, found his robe and wrapped it around her. She sat up and twisted her hair in a knot behind her head.

"You know what, C? I think I'll jump in the shower before dinner."

He sat up and noted her stiff posture. "Ookay, I must have hit a sore spot. Come on, you know I'm a baboon. Tell me how I fucked up."

She started toward the bathroom, lightly touching the wall as she went. "I told you about my mother."

"You told me she left you at Stafford, but that you kept in touch with her."

"I tried."

"How did you try? I mean, what did you do?"

She reached the doorway, stopped and folded her arms. "I sent her stuff. Little presents I made, my grades, invitations to my graduation, a copy of my acceptance letter to Barnesdale. Totally ridiculous, I don't know why I – "

"So no response, huh."

"Never. Nothing."

"That's really bad. That's terrible." He threw back the covers, got to his feet and padded, naked, over to her. "Are you sure she got everything you sent? I mean, maybe she moved or something – "

"Trust me, Constantin, she's never taken any interest in my life."

He threw his hands in the air in frustration. "But you're beautiful! You're brilliant! You're funny and fun, and kind and cute. And you're all mine!"

He hugged her tight but her body had contracted with sadness. She kept her arms folded. "I don't know why I give a shit any more," she said.

"God, I hate to see you like this, which is why I'm going to – " He grabbed her around the waist and flipped her back on the bed, " – kiss you till you beg for mercy." He kissed her all over her face and neck, tickling her till she began to laugh in spite of herself.

Gasping for air, she cried, "Stop it, you idiot! Feed me, all right?"

He finally let her go, got to his feet and grabbed his jeans. "Let's just risk it and give her a quick call, share some great news with her! She's your only family, Kim. She'll take an interest in this. I'm positive." He smoothed her long hair off her ivory forehead, took her hand in his and squeezed it.

She said nothing. She thought about Constantin's parents, how they had welcomed her into their home and their son's life with such grace and warmth. If only she had more of a family to offer him than a seventy-year-old woman who saw evil portents in rotten stairs.

"She has to know eventually, right?" he asked, standing at the bedroom door.

"I don't think I even have her number any more."

· NINE ·

Waves crashed in great white spumes, then sucked hard at barnacled rocks at the base of a fifty-foot cliff. A modern house built into the precipice rose up another thirty feet, slicing darkly into the star-lit sky, its glass panes reflecting the silver sea below. In the east a pale, swollen moon hung low, as if it were too heavy to lift itself skyward.

In a vast, airy living room with a sunken fireplace and cunningly recessed lighting, painted in pebble grey and every variation of white, Dr. Astra Nathanson, forty, beautiful by any standard, power walked on a treadmill facing a sixty-inch screen television and beyond that, a sweeping balcony overlooking the open sea. Her long dark curls bounced in a pony tail behind her as she watched a newscast about Palestine firebombing Israel and vice versa.

Convinced that the world would never change, as it had not changed in a thousand years, that people would continue to fight and kill each other over how they perceived God, she switched to the food channel. Tuna steak tartar with aioli sauce and capers. Nope, made her too hungry. Click: the travel channel. Elephants thundered across an arid veldt. She recognized the Rift Valley and the Masai grasslands in the distance, and remembered too well the smell of the place, always of something rotting, fruit or flesh, a faint taste of blood in the air, the incessant flies, heat, mosquitoes the size of a child's fist. It had been a harsh life where she had been caught and punished at only seventeen: she couldn't forget that final night running through the black forest chased by screaming elders, poisoned arrows flying at her, one finding its mark. It was another past she did not care to revisit. She turned off the TV.

The wide black eye of the TV mirrored back to her her pale, sweating face and tall, slender frame as she began to run harder on the machine. Turning forty had not been easy for her; it had made her tired and anxious, even though for her birthday she had taken two days off work and treated herself to an exclusive health spa in northern Maine that boasted full body seaweed wraps, gourmet vegan meals and yoga twice a day. For some reason she came back even more exhausted than when she left, and was late for work on her first day back.

She was determined to do her five miles that day, but her knees were objecting and her breath felt shallow, as if her lungs had somehow shrunk overnight. She fought the sensation, staring at her reflection, at the too-slowly changing numbers on the machine, back to the ghostly face. She would not give in to this aging body, one of the oldest she'd ever had. Sweat poured into her eyes, dripped down between her breasts. She would not stop. Four point seven...four point eight...

The phone screamed from its cradle.

"Fuck!" she yelled, running harder, trying to think who might be trying to reach her. In general, she got very few calls, especially at home. She never gave her number to patients, and she had no friends. But she had just joined a new dating service; maybe it was someone calling her back...she peered over at her caller ID. Private number. Shit...four point nine...

It rang a few more times as she turned off the machine and gulped down some spring water.

She grabbed the phone. "Yes?"

She breathed heavily into the receiver, dripping on it, listening. She knew that voice, but from which incarnation? There was simply too much to remember sometimes.

"...Kim?"

She had wanted Constantin close by during the call. He sat on a stool next to her, holding her hand, reading her face. He hoped this was a good idea, in the end. He simply couldn't picture Kim's mother, this woman who would give up and never visit her child.

"I hope I'm not disturbing you," Kim said in a shaky voice.

"Of course not." My God, what did she want? Money?

"You...you sound out of breath."

"I was exercising." Astra took a towel draped over the treadmill and wiped her face with it. "This is really Kim?"

"Yes, it really is."

"Ah...what's new?"

"Well," her throat almost too dry to continue, "it's hard to know where to begin."

Astra walked soundlessly over the lush carpet to the marble-floored, well appointed kitchen, and opened her Subzero. She looked inside it mindlessly, the never-used iron pots and pans all in a row above her head. "Start anywhere, then."

· TEN ·

Astra pulled out a chilled Montrachet and uncorked it as she spoke, pouring herself a brimming glass. With the bottle in one hand and the phone cradled under her chin, she carried her drink back through the living room to the sliding glass doors where she stepped out onto the balcony.

"Do you hear that sound?" she said, looking out at half the water in the world. It sparkled crisply in the moonlight.

"What sound?"

"The sea. Can't you hear it?"

"No, I can't." Kim had no idea what to call this woman. Mother? Mom? Both sounded absurd. She gripped the phone, blanking for a moment as to what in the world she could possibly say next. "Are you in a boat?"

"No, of course not. My house is built on a cliff overlooking the sea."

"That sounds nice."

"It is."

"You're still in Rockport then?"

"After all these years, yes." Completely comfortable, Astra sipped her wine and tried to imagine her now grown daughter. "You're how old, now?"

"I'm nineteen."

Constantin gave her hand one last squeeze. Keeping an eye on her, he started cooking dinner. He gathered chicken, canned tomatoes, onions and basil. Kim stood up, walked into the bedroom with the phone and

Marty close on her heels, and shut the door. Constantin sighed, opened a bottle of Chianti, and poured himself a glass.

Kim sat in bed, inexplicably cold, the covers pulled over her. She picked at an old comforter as she talked. "There's all kinds of technology – "

" – but I mean, marine biology? How can you – "

"You can get anything in Braille, just anything you can think of. Maps, models, I can go online – "

"Well, I never knew any of this. I didn't realize you would be able to do all this. I'm quite impressed." Astra leaned on the railing with her wine, the near-empty bottle close by.

Kim flushed. "You are?" Utterly surprising herself, she welled up with tears. To cover, she feigned a cough.

"You still there?" her mother said.

"Yeah, sorry. Allergies..."

Constantin entered the bedroom carrying a glass of Chianti. He put it in Kim's hand; she nodded thankfully.

"Five minutes?" he whispered.

"Fine," Kim said. He let himself out and shut the door behind him.

"Someone there?" Astra asked.

"Yes, my boyfriend just brought me some wine. But I didn't tell you, I got into Barnesdale on full scholarship, the only one from the Stafford School ever to have done that, and it includes – "

"You have a boyfriend?"

"Yes."

"Well, that must be a help. What's he like? Is he handsome – or should I say, do people think he's handsome?"

Kim took a deep breath. What had she begun here? "I'm told he's drop-dead gorgeous."

"No kidding."

"No kidding."

Astra lifted her leg like a dancer and unfolded it on the waist-high rail, stretching. "Well, aren't you a lucky girl."

"I am."

"So, don't be coy, tell me more about this man of yours. Sounds like you've stumbled on a good one."

"He's my biology teacher – "

"I like him already – "

"He's a terrific person."

Constantin knocked softly and popped his head in. "Dinner's ready when you are. Take your time."

Astra lowered her leg, then raised and extended the other along the rail. "Did I just hear someone say dinner was ready? I'll be right over!"

Kim laughed. "Yeah, he's a great guy. He's been wonderful to me." She got out of bed, still shaking off a chill, and made her way to the kitchen where Constantin sat reading a magazine. Dinner steamed on the table. "I mean, right away we just clicked. I don't want to sound corny but these past three months have been the happiest of my life."

"Corny's okay, corny's good."

"I mean...Mom...can I call you Mom?"

Constantin smiled as he watched Kim take a seat across from him.

"That's who I am, isn't it?" Astra gazed at the sea, still wondering what this person wanted from her.

"I wanted to tell you that I have – I mean, *we* have some news."

"Oh, really."

"We're getting married...I just wanted you to know."

Astra turned toward her vast, silent house; the exquisite artwork, the lush, tasteful furnishings. She poured out the last of the wine. Something pinched at her throat, constricted her chest like a vice.

"Did you hear me, Mother? Mom?"

"Oh, I heard you. I was just thinking, I'm just planning...how can we celebrate?" She took a gulp of wine. "I got it, I know just the thing. Why don't you two lovebirds come up and stay the weekend? Come tomorrow! There's plenty of room." She pressed the edge of the wine glass hard against her lip as she waited for the answer. The pain grounded her. She held her breath.

Kim, smiling, cupped the phone and whispered to Constantin, "C, she wants us to come for the weekend. Do you want to go? I mean, should we go?"

Gently, he took the phone from her. "Dr. Nathanson?"

Astra smiled, picturing him. "Call me Astra."

She stared at the licorice-black sea and concentrated on his voice as he spoke. In her mind's eye she saw a tall man with thick dark hair walking across a college campus with a loose-limbed gait. He was lovely, delicious, just the sort of man she described in her personal ads but never the type who answered them.

She thought of her own daughter finding love when she never had, in all these centuries, and her knuckles grew white as she gripped the receiver.

After giving directions to her home, she hung up the phone, absently running her hand over her forearm. Something felt wrong. She looked down and gasped, then let out a strangled cry. Her wine glass fell hundreds of feet to the rocks, making no sound over the roar of the surf.

Greenish-yellow scales feathered across her forearm. They glowed by the light of the bloodless moon. Whimpering, she yanked at her sleeve to unroll it, then held her arm close to her, as if it were bleeding. She examined her other arm; it was normal. Touched her face: still smooth. Felt her tongue: human. But she wondered about her eyes, had they changed...?

Fight this! she thought, seizing the rail and squeezing her eyes shut. But she couldn't block the images. Flashes of her previous life as a snake bulleted through her mind.

In a way, it was her simplest life.

She killed to eat.

The hum and tick of summer, the smell of hot berries on the vine, a riot of green. Bees furied into flowers, mosquitoes whined. Armless, legless, and four undulating feet long, Astra bellied along the ground, a thousand rings of muscle rippling her through a field of wild grasses. Inside her, a tree frog still jerked its long legs even as digestive juices surrounded it, boiling with acid. Astra felt full, satisfied, sleepy. She nosed through the grass until it ended and she arrived at platter-sized pieces of slate, deliciously warmed by the sun, that sloped down and met the burbling waters of a stream.

Across the water, a young boy fished.

She slithered her length onto the hot rock. Dazed with pleasure, she coiled there and slept.

The boy caught sight of her mid-cast and stood motionless. He propped his fishing pole between two rocks, the line jerking crazily with the pull of the strong water. Keeping one eye on the copperhead, he slipped a hunting knife from his tackle box then made his way, barefoot, across the stream.

He stood only a foot away. With both hands he lifted the knife high over his head where it blocked the early morning sun.

Astra gasped and gripped the rail of the deck as she remembered this death, her body whipping on the slate as her head rolled into the stream, eyes frozen open. Pleading with a god she despised, she conjured her life before she was a snake, stroking the scales on her arm until the skin was smooth again.

She had been a seventeen-year-old kid named Louis running in a gang in East Los Angeles. He dealt whatever he could get his hands on and was a minor league pimp with a stable of three addicted teenage girls who actually brought in enough for him to buy the Lexus he was about to steal. But it didn't feel the same; he wanted that other feeling, that rush of fear, a speeded-up heart. He skittered around the car as he scoped out the night; a jangle of stars, no moon, the headlights from traffic on a nearby highway strobing his face. It was near midnight, the Lexus the only car left in a lot behind a cluster of office buildings. One light shone in a far off window.

All nerves, Louis jimmied the lock, jumped in and hotwired the car. The motor turned over, then hummed, quieter than his own breathing. His face shone with sweat as he glanced up defiantly at the lone lit window.

He tore out of the lot and roared onto the highway. In seconds, blue lights flashed in his rear view as he lit a cigarette. A siren wailed. He picked up speed and took off, leaving the police car behind, but soon the flashing lights and siren were back, brighter and louder than before. He flipped the cigarette out the window and drew a gun from his ratty leather jacket. Red-eyed, he turned to look behind him. The police car matched his eighty-five miles an hour, and pulled up close to him. He could see the officer, a good looking middle-aged black guy. Louis shot him, blasting through the glass and tearing off most of the man's face. The police car spun out and disappeared into a ditch.

He drove to Squeeze's place, one of the girls he pimped. There was something about her he liked, and something he feared. She had a jagged scar across her forehead that he thought might cut down on her customers, but she was the most popular of all three of his girls even though she was the oldest at nineteen. He thought maybe she loved him. He didn't know why he was going there. Something about her calmed him down, and she never once made a comment about his own scar-ravaged body.

He burst into her basement apartment. She was in her slip in bed listening to the radio. She jumped back against the wall and held a pillow over her small, slim body.

"Louis, what the fuck – "

He pointed the gun at her head. "Just shut up, bitch, or I'll blow your head off."

"What the fuck are you talking about? What happened? What did you do?"

"I killed a cop. Now we're both gonna die."

She looked at him, his skinny body a hanger for his clothes, his shaking hands.

"Louis, put the gun down. Sit down." She clutched the pillow tightly to her, as if it would protect her. On a table next to her sat a small bowl aquarium where one lone orange fish swam in swampy water, mouthing at the glass.

"What the fuck! You telling me what to do?"

"I'm asking you to sit down."

He ignored her and pulled a flimsy lace curtain aside to look out. "They'll be here any second and we're both gonna die."

"No one's coming. I don't hear anyone." Slowly, she inched her hand toward a nightshirt on the bed and put it on.

"I didn't tell you you could fucking move."

"Did you come here to talk to me, Louis?"

"I don't know."

"Then why are you here?"

"I don't know."

"Well, if you want to talk to me, you have to put the gun down and sit." She turned away from him and back toward the radio.

"Don't fuck with my head, Squeeze."

She ignored him.

"I'll fuck you up." His hand was slippery with sweat. He lowered his arm. "You fucking whore."

She was silent. With a trembling hand, she tucked a strand of fine red hair behind one ear.

He put the gun down heavily on a night table. "Squeeze."

Still she wouldn't look at him.

"You're gonna pay for this."

She reached out and took a sip from a glass of water nearby.

"You owe everything to me, your motherfuckin' *life* to me."

She looked almost sleepy.

"*Look at me!*" He dragged a chair close to the bed and sat in it. His shoulders sunk in, lost their tension. His voice grew soft. "Goddam you, Squeeze."

She turned to him and reached out to touch his face. He jerked back slightly, then let her stroke his cheek once, gently. It was the first time she had ever touched him in a nonsexual way. She saw tears in his eyes. A cat yowled outside like a cursed soul. No breeze moved the still curtains at the window. A cockroach skittered over to investigate a cough drop stuck to the rough wood floor, its antennae rotating in tiny arcs.

"I know who you are, Louis," she said. "I'm one too."

"What the hell you talking about?" Color rose in his cheeks. He crossed his arms hard across his chest. "You're crazy."

She whispered, "You're a Repeater."

He jumped from the chair and grabbed the gun, jamming it in his pants.

"Listen to me!" she shouted. She got to her feet, dropping the pillow.

"This is bullshit. I don't have to listen to this!" He ran to the door, his hand hovering at the knob.

"We know about you, Louis."

"We? *We?*"

"Word gets around, over the years."

"*What?*"

"We stay away from you, because you're the kind that doesn't learn. Doesn't change. That's the whole reason any of us come back, but it's only once, or twice." She took a few steps back, her eyes widening slightly. "You, Louis, do you even *know* how many times you've come back?"

His voice became a hoarse whisper. "I can't talk to you."

"*Do* you?"

He mumbled something.

"I couldn't hear you, Louis."

"Over a hundred, I think."

Squeeze gasped. "That many lives."

A far off siren began to wail, but Louis ignored it. He looked at his hands as if he didn't recognize them, then stuffed them in the baggy pockets of his filthy jeans. "I don't know how to stop… I – " He looked her in the eyes for the first time that night. "How many times have you come back?"

"This is my third time," Squeeze said. "My last time."

"Why?"

"Because I'm learning about things this time, about how to love. It's slow and things are crazy but I'm not afraid – "

Blue lights strobed the room as a siren whooped. Louis gave Squeeze a long look, grabbed his gun, and bolted out the door.

He jumped into the car and burned down side streets to a road he knew led to the bay. Screeching into a lot behind a diner, he ditched the car and dashed across four lanes of highway to an abandoned warehouse. He kicked open the door and crouched inside with his gun. Light from the highway ribboned across his glistening skin. Recent rain had soaked the rotten floorboards under him. A rat skittered by, then another. There was no higher ground to go to; all the stairwells had rotted out. The ceiling yawned, a hundred feet above him.

Minutes passed and no police lights, no sirens. Still he waited, panting, his eyes wide. He wiped his forehead and dared a look outside. Nothing. He ducked back in. Maybe he had gotten away with it. Maybe no one was coming.

He placed the cold barrel of the gun in his mouth; he tasted metal, smelled lead. Slowly, he pulled it out and turned it in his hand in wonderment.

I could do it, he thought. I want to do it. My lives are getting shorter and more brutal. I feel like an animal, even though I'm not this time.

He held his head in his hands, praying to die this time, to truly die. He was known – they knew him! Other Repeaters shunned him. Of course they would! Look at the suffering and death he had caused. He strained to remember the very first time he existed, hundreds of years ago. Bright lights. A rustling of reeds. A language he no longer understood. He remembered looking up at wide, dark faces, fragments of sky and sun, a warm towelly smell, then his lungs filling with water. He must have been a child when he was killed for the first time. And the rage never left him.

Then the blue lights came, scoping the nightmarish walls of the warehouse. A seagull shrieked as it divebombed from the rafters just past his head and out the shell of a window. Doors slammed closed; he counted six. Three cars. There was a hush, then footsteps echoed outside the warehouse, whispers, maybe seven, eight men. He felt his own physical death coming again and careened with exhaustion, like an insomniac who dreads yet another sleepless night void of healing or regeneration. His loneliness welled in him like a deep black pond. In it floated the corpses of those he had killed, their whitish hands forever reaching for him.

He would come back and he would find someone who loved him, that would be the answer. He would change all this, create something good in the world. And then he could die, and be free.

"Come out with your hands high!" came the voices.

Holding the image of Squeeze in her nightshirt caressing his face, he took the gun, placed it in his mouth, and fired.

· ELEVEN ·

A thin, dirty-looking fourteen-year-old boy sat across from Astra in a matching plush leather chair. He couldn't have looked more uncomfortable if he were sitting on a wooden crate. He fidgeted and scratched his scalp, uninhibited about examining whatever he harvested from under his fingernails and flicking it in Astra's direction.

Astra sat stiffly just a yard away, trying to keep her eyes off the clock behind the boy's head. She wore a turtleneck sweater and skirt. He couldn't seem to stop staring at either her tits or her legs.

"You don't know friggin' shit about me," he snapped. Another bite of fingernail, another eye grope on the thigh.

"That's why you're here, Gerry, for me to get to know you so I can help you."

He shifted his narrow ass to the other side of the seat. "I fooled them all, friggin' retards. And I could fool you, too."

"You 'could' fool me – does that mean you might not bother?"

"Look, I don't even want to be here, okay?"

"You asked for these sessions with me."

"That was back in the beginning." He picked up a heavy marble paperweight from her desk, hefted it, tossed it back and forth from one hand to the other.

"Please put that down, Gerry."

He just stared at her.

This was crazy, she thought, I can't help these kids. I don't even want to any more. Maybe I never did. Let them all do drugs and run away and

36

steal cars and kill themselves, it was fine with her. These days she couldn't even remember what her reasons were for joining this profession. Helping people to help herself? Some kind of horseshit like that.

He slammed the paperweight down on the mahogany desk, snapping her back to attention (they always knew when your mind wandered, when you'd taken a moment away from analyzing their pitiful lives) –

"Look!" he yelled. "I'm tired of being a fake, pretending I'm some kind of nice, goody person, and I don't mean the bad shit."

"So there's nothing good about you?"

"You're not listening to me! I'm not sorry, okay? *I'm not sorry.* I'm glad about those things I did – "

" – glad you blinded your cat? Glad you lit your sister's bed on fire?"

"I loved every minute of it!" he growled. "That's why I did it. Don't you get it?"

Astra stared at him, her pencil shaking in her hand. Her notebook slid off her lap onto the floor. She left it there.

"It felt good, Dr. Nathanson." Left tit eye grope, then the crotch, down to the notebook on the floor. "Aren'tcha gonna pick that up?"

"I'm sure at the time you were doing it – "

"Why don't you shut up and listen to me!"

Perspiration bloomed on her brow.

He went on, a little quieter. "It's like I'm fighting something inside me all the time, something bad that wants to get out. I've got to let it out."

She stared at him a little too long, a gleam of recognition in her eyes. She looked down at the notebook, beating back the ugliness she felt inside her, an ancient rage. She saw the faces of people she had hurt lunge at her, wanting her death, wanting to see her die. The snake's head crowned in the back of her throat and she turned her head away, willing it to go back inside her. The boy watched her, feeling something so much larger than himself in the room, a taste like rust in his mouth.

Astra got up and walked away from the boy, to a window. She gripped

the edge, struggled for a moment; the thing was painted shut. The whites
of her eyes went red in the glass. She would not look at the boy, but she
smelled his fear. The window flew open. She leaned on the sill, gasping at
hot midday air.

Gerry had sunk back into his seat. "You okay?"

Slowly she turned back to him, her face normal, eyes clear, the high
color in her cheeks making her even more lovely.

"Just...warm."

"You're dressed like it's winter or something."

His head now obscured the clock, but she was sure they had gone
over. She looked at her watch, composed herself. "So, I'll see you Monday
at three?"

The boy nodded and quickly gathered himself to leave.

· TWELVE ·

Still in her work clothes, Astra pushed a cart down the dusty aisle of an almost deserted liquor store. The guys who worked there, though they waited on her almost daily and unanimously agreed she was a babe, avoided her eye. There was a cold wind coming from this woman, and no one wanted to have it in his face for long. They imagined she must be quite the drunk, buying four, five bottles of wine every other day, and there may have been some truth to that, but the fact was, this was a woman who needed to relax.

Over the millennia, she had built up quite a tolerance for the grape. It took a bottle of wine or more for that first flush of relaxation to kick in, another to get to sleep at night. She couldn't remember getting a hangover except maybe once in Nepal, how many lifetimes ago she couldn't place, when she drank the local brew of fermented sugar cane and then smoked hashish all night. Now *that* had gotten her a little hazy the next morning, but by noon she was herself again.

As she circumvented a fancy display of Stolichnaya (bottles of vodka in little down vests skiing down an icy styrofoam mountain), she startled a young couple deep in liplock. They parted gluily, affording her a sloe-eyed look as they turned and walked desultorily away from her. She saw the flush on the girl's cheek, the bulge filling the boy's loose jeans. They didn't care, they were just going to move the party, that was clear. The boy's hand grazed the girl's muscular ass, round as an apple in her stretchy capris. Their hands tangled loosely behind them as they strolled toward the chilled beers.

She wanted to touch them, soak up their sexual buzz, take it for her own. To ask them: are you in love with each other? How do you know, how does it feel? Or are you just fucking? It didn't feel like that. It felt like they were onto something good. She gazed after them as they pointed at the freezer, the girl doubling over with laughter at something the boy had said. Do you understand loneliness, she wanted to ask them; not days or weeks but eons of loneliness, until she realized that the girl had been pointing at Astra's reflection in the freezer doors before she started laughing.

Frozen with embarrassment and rage, Astra stood there, staring at herself in the reflection. What was so funny? She looked fine, she thought. Twice their age, but why was that funny? Reddening, she forced herself to look away. She picked up a bottle of Saintsbury Pinot Noir and absorbed herself in the ornately drawn label, where young lovers picnicked and toasted each other on the banks of a lush, elm-canopied river.

· THIRTEEN ·

Though the day had grown overcast, Astra kept her sunglasses on as she drove home. The cliffs and ocean unfolded gloriously to her right, but her eyes stayed front. She popped in a CD of the book *Healing the Wounded Child Within*, smirking as she listened.

"What things do you do regularly to nurture yourself? A few hours spent digging in a flowerbed is calming and nurturing. For others, it's a run in the park, a trip to the hairdresser's, or a matinee. You might want to list all the things you did this week to nurture yourself. Then write down all the nurturing things you'd like to do for yourself, but don't. What interferes with you doing all the nurturing things you would like? When was the last time you nurtured your – "

She popped the CD from the player and threw it out the window.

Gravel crunched under the shining wheels of her Audi as she wound her way up the long drive. Laden with bags of wine, she struggled with the key and let herself in. The red light on her answering machine blinked "2." Her heart flipflopped with the thought that Kim and Constantin had called to cancel their visit. She pressed the button.

A deep male voice: "Astra, Steve. Listen, had a great time with you last week, and I wanna do it again – "

Astra skipped to the next message as she muttered, "Not in this lifetime, you pretentious asshole."

Message number two, a nasal male voice: "Oh, hello, this is Frank Carbuncle from LoveLines. I saw your photo and bio and I tell you, I'm

ERICA FERENCIK

intrigued – "

She hit "delete," marched up to her bedroom, whipped off her work clothes and tossed on her running outfit. Hair in a hasty pony tail, she ran back downstairs and out the door to the beach, where she began running gangbusters along the wet sand.

Thunder boomed in the sky, lightning veining across it like cracks in a blue bowl. She loved running in this weather. She might get killed, this time in a natural way. She wondered what a bolt of electricity slamming into her might feel like, a hot white death. The rain began, and not gently, but like a vast bucket had turned over in the sky. The clouds meshed with the sea like some shapeless dress. She ran faster, recalling an article that said nothing defined the calf muscles more beautifully than running on sand.

Exactly five miles later she squelched up the stairs in her sneakers and peeled off layers of heavy wet clothes on her sea-facing deck. She wrapped herself in a robe and crashed on the couch with her laptop. After checking her stocks – satisfied that her money was still there though not particularly expanding – she turned on the television and surfed from channel to channel. She paused on an infomercial touting the newest all-in-one miracle exercise machine, then clicked off the TV with disgust and stared at the rain slicing into the sea.

· FOURTEEN ·

With the rain still pounding down and thunder rumbling all around them, Constantin and Kim, with Marty in the back, meandered up the rocky coastline of Massachusetts in his ten-year-old Peugeot. Kim reached behind her to stroke Marty's head as the dog slept, unfazed by the violent weather outside.

Constantin downshifted, peering through the grey-washed windshield. "This is weird. It was so beautiful back in Cambridge."

Kim hoped it wouldn't rain all weekend. What in the world would they do with themselves? Actually, rain or shine, she had no idea how it was going to feel being with her mother again.

"Are you okay?" Constantin asked. "Storm freaking you out?"

"Yeah – I mean no," Kim said. "The storm doesn't bother me. It's just that I guess this isn't how I imagined spending the weekend."

"Well, hey, you don't get a marriage proposal every day, or do you?"

She laughed. "Not exactly."

"So you gotta run with it. Be adventurous."

"This fills the bill, believe me."

"Aw, come on, she's just an odd duck, right? We can handle that. Didn't you say she takes care of kids? Maybe she's turned over a new leaf."

"I don't know, C. She's a complete stranger to me. I mean, why is she bothering to see me now, after thirteen years? I don't get it."

"You said you guys had a good talk, didn't you? Maybe hearing your voice jarred her memory about what a wonderful daughter she's been missing out on."

43

"I guess...anything's possible." But she didn't think good things were possible with her mother, as much as she wanted them to be, and the more she dwelled on it, the less she could ignore a blossoming fear, like a rotting lily in the back of her throat.

She sat up rod straight in her seat.

For a moment she couldn't speak.

"C?" Her voice was small with terror. She felt something hurtling at them, a great dark thing full of rage and death. A roar of white noise filled her ears; she could barely hear herself speak. "Constantin!" she yelled.

"I'm right here – "

She gripped his arm. "Where are we?"

"We're almost – "

"Can we go home?"

"You're kidding, right?"

"No, I'm not!"

"We're five minutes away. Less, I think." The wipers at full tilt were useless against the torrents of rain.

"I really want you to stop the car, C."

"We're in the middle of the road! I can't just stop."

"Please, Constantin! Pull over!"

"What the hell is wrong – "

"If you love me, pull over!"

"I can't. There's no shoulder – "

"Do it!" she shrieked, lunging at the steering wheel. She yanked it to the right and they flew off the road into a ditch, lurching to a stop. An ear-splitting crack of thunder silenced their ragged breathing as a shock of lightning halved a massive oak in front of them. The sixty-foot monster, split in two and rimmed in fire, came crashing down only feet in front of their car and across the road.

Constantin stared, slackjawed. "Holy..."

The roar in her ears stopped. She heard only rain falling softly. "Is it over? Are you okay?" Kim panted. Marty cowered in the back of the car, whimpering.

"How did you know?"

Stiffly, she faced front. "You need to listen to me, Constantin, okay? Listen to me when I tell you things."

He looked at her, the perfect profile, the sparkling grey, sightless eyes, her hair wild around her shoulders. "What do you want me to do, Kim? I'll do whatever you say."

He waited, watching her face break into a grimace. "I don't know, C." Her eyes watered and her chin shook. Whatever terror possessed her had been replaced by an almost visceral frustration. Tears streamed down her face. "I don't know what to do," she cried. "I don't know what to say to her. I mean, what's the point? What does she want from me? She doesn't love me, that's clear, so what are we doing here?"

Constantin watched the rain douse the flames on the tree, the wet bark turning velvety in the dusk. "We'll go home right now if you want, we'll do anything you want. In fact, let's just get out of here." He turned the key in the ignition.

She put her hand on his arm. "No, Constantin. Wait a second, okay?"

"Okay." The car idled. Kim lowered the window, took a deep breath of electric air and singed wood. The rain had turned to a ghostly blue fog.

"Let's go to my mother's. I want to see her."

"You do?"

"What the hell, why not? I mean, I have you, I have Marty. What could happen?"

He reached over and hugged her a long time. Her face was damp from crying; her hair smelled like fresh rain. "Don't worry," he said, "it's all going to work out fine."

He revved the engine and mud flew as the car snarled out of the ditch and around the corpse of the monstrous tree, blackened and still smoking in the encroaching darkness.

· FIFTEEN ·

In a walk-in closet where clothes (all size six) were arranged by color, Astra stood in a sweater and jeans, holding a phone to her ear with one hand and flipping through racks of pants with the other. Behind her in a bedroom that echoed with space, outfits were piled high on a bed.

"Yes," she said, her brow delicately furrowed with concentration, "the curried lamb with spring vegetables, potatoes mousseline – that's with the creme fraiche, am I right?...good, yes, the oyster bisque to begin and we'll finish up with English fruit tart – I don't care, rhubarb? Fine, with that liqueur-flavored sauce I love, you know it, right. Four o'clock, no later." She hung up the phone and tossed it behind her onto the pile of clothes.

After trying on several outfits in a three-way mirror, Astra settled on a black velveteen top and black pants, her hair up in a soft chignon. As she smoothed the cloth against her body, she recalled Constantin's deep, calm voice and admitted niceties such as how much he was looking forward to meeting her. The way they spoke of each other made her desperately curious to see them both. How could Kim have done this? Blind, orphaned in all practical ways, how could she have found love? It was too ridiculous.

At a few minutes past four, she poured herself a glass of Pomerol and surveyed several large bags of takeout food spread out on the counter. She pulled out a baking dish and placed it to one side, then opened the container of lamb and spring vegetables, carefully scooping it all in. She did the same with the rest of the food, ladling the soup into a tureen that she'd preheated, the salad into wooden bowls, and the tart in a pie tin that she slid on the warming rack in the oven.

She'd already checked on the food many times and flipped through several magazines, unable to concentrate on anything, when she heard a car turn off the main road. She jumped up and sprinted to the window where she watched the little Peugeot snake around the last curve to the end of the driveway which faced the sea.

The car ticked and cooled, but no one got out. What are they doing in there, she wondered. What are they talking about? She checked her hair again, letting loose a few more curls around her face. She just couldn't picture it; her grownup daughter and this young man who wanted to marry her. She sipped her wine and watched as a woman with long auburn hair, slender and delicate looking, got out of the car. She faced the sea and stood there with one hand on the door. The girl turned out much prettier than I would have guessed, Astra thought. She had started out such a pale, mousy little thing. The driver's side door opened and Constantin got out wearing a dark green rain slicker and jeans.

Now there's the real surprise. Look at him. Just look at that man.

Constantin walked around the car and encircled Kim's shoulder with his arm as they faced the rumbling surf. He said something blown away by the wind, gave her a kiss on the cheek and reached back to let Marty out.

A dog? Had they said anything about a dog? Oh, yes, probably a seeing eye type of thing. Well, he can sleep outside, or in the garage.

They stood for a moment facing the sea, holding hands and leaning in to each other.

Why the hell won't they come in?

She watched them turn and trudge almost reluctantly toward the house.

· SIXTEEN ·

K im's young man was the first through the door, wiping his feet on the mat and smiling at Astra as if he'd known her forever. The warmth of his hand when Astra shook it seemed to buzz up her arm as she watched her daughter take a tentative step into the living room. Kim Nathanson, the product of Astra's attempt to create something to love that would love her back, stood there (still alive! beautiful! engaged!) and still unloved by her. Astra's jaw clenched as she forced herself to step forward and put her arms around her daughter. Show the young man something, that she had a mother's heart beating in there somewhere.

She held the girl close to her for a few seconds, wondering, maybe it's now that I'll feel something, and did not, and inhaled the Herbal Essence shampoo till it caught in her throat and she couldn't breathe. The girl had barely lifted her wan arms to hug her back when Astra took her by the shoulders and held her at arm's length. Time to pull out all the stops, she thought, feeling Constantin's eyes on her.

"Well, look at you, Kim, after all these years! You look wonderful! Constantin, you didn't tell me how beautiful she was."

Astra glanced over at him and almost winked, but caught herself.

"That's why I brought her," he said. "I knew you had to see for yourself."

Kim smiled weakly, her brow furrowing as she tried to decipher the myriad tones in her mother's voice. "Thanks."

They heard a scratching at the screen. Constantin reached behind Kim and opened the door. "Come on, buddy, don't be shy. Astra, this is

48

Marty."

But Marty hung back on the porch, his eyes darting from Kim to Constantin to Astra, and back to Kim. He whined again and pawed at the damp wood.

"Get in here, Marty," Constantin said. "Let's go."

Nothing.

"Marty, come," Kim said, turning toward her dog.

Torn by training, love and instinct, the dog yelped a few times, then let loose a howl at the moon above.

"I've never seen him do this," Kim said, taking a step toward the landing. He licked her hand thankfully and thumped his tail, but when she went back inside he didn't budge.

"He's just mad about being cooped up in the car so long," Constantin said. He slapped his knees. "Okay, Marty, last chance! Get in here!"

Kim turned toward her mother. "Do you have another dog? Or cats?"

"Lord, no. I'm not really an animal...person. Maybe he should stay outside then?" She took a step toward the door, as if to shut it. Marty's whimper lowered into a growl as he glared at her, his long eye teeth bared over red and black gums. She stepped back quickly, squelching her own instinct to attack.

"Marty, stop that. Bad dog," Kim said. She turned to Astra. "I've never known him to do anything like this with anyone. I'm sorry."

"Not a problem. Maybe we should leave him out here till he calms down a bit. Is that all right?"

Astra started toward the kitchen, her dark hair shining in the light. Constantin followed her, glancing around at the elegant living room.

"Don't worry," she tossed back, "I'll give you both the grand tour after we've had a drink or two."

"Sounds good to me," Constantin said, taking off his jacket.

Kim stayed by the door, scratching Marty behind his ears. "What is your problem, big guy? Just come on in the house, okay?" She took a step back. "Come, Marty." But he just lay down on the wet wood and looked at her with eyes full of love. She kissed him on the head and went inside, closing the door gently behind her.

As Astra busied herself in the kitchen with soup bowls and croutons, Constantin led Kim to the sliding glass doors of the deck and looked out at the evening sky.

"You've got quite the view out here," he called back to her.

"Go on ahead out," Astra said, opening wine. "I'll be right there."

"Sure you don't need a hand?" he asked.

"Nope. All set. On the rocks for you, then?"

"You know me well." He smiled back at her, opened the sliders and stepped outside with Kim, pulling the glass doors shut behind them.

Astra dropped the corkscrew twice before taking a deep breath to steady herself. Energy rippled through her. She felt like she could run another ten miles through the night air. She watched Constantin put his arm around Kim as they leaned on the rail. She gathered the drinks on the tray, steeled herself, and headed out.

· SEVENTEEN ·

Astra pointed through the twilight toward a small black island that jutted out of the sea. "Out by there, I saw their backs. They had to be whales. I have no idea what kind."

Constantin sat with Kim on white deck chairs. He let go of her hand as he got to his feet and joined Astra at the rail, peering out toward the island. "Probably humpback this time of year. What color were they? Were they turning over? How many did you see?" He leaned by Astra, setting his drink on the railing.

"I was too far away to see what color they were. But they were turning over on their backs and smashing their flippers on the water. One big one, and one small one."

"Mama and baby, then."

"They were so cute, splashing around," Astra said, watching him. He was close enough for her to smell: clean cotton, soap, the musk of him.

"The mother takes care of the kid for a year," Kim said. "She makes sure her offspring can survive on its own before she abandons it." Her eyes glimmered in the growing darkness.

Astra and Constantin turned back to her. "Oh, have you been studying whales, dear?" Astra said.

"Whales are my favorite animals."

"I'll bet she's a good student, isn't she, Constantin?"

"The best I've ever had. She wrote the most brilliant essay I've ever read on the interdependency of life on coral reefs."

Kim shifted in her seat. "Please don't talk about me as if I'm not here."

"Oh, I'm sorry, dear," Astra said. "I should be asking you about what you're studying and so on. Do you live in a dorm? Do you have roommates?"

"I'm studying biology of course, and chemistry, physics, calculus, and music. And I live in a dorm, but I have my own room, because I have a disability."

"So there's no one to help you..."

"I don't need any help. I have Marty to get around. There's nothing I can't do."

"Even all those years ago I sensed you were a very independent girl."

"I still am. Nothing's changed."

Astra took in her stiff posture, the glint in the grey eyes. "Calm down, dear. No one's attacking you."

"She just meant – " Constantin started.

"I'm not helpless, is all I'm trying to say. I finished at Stafford at the top of my class, and won a full scholarship to Barnesdale. There's no book or computer program that is not accessible to me, there's no place I can't visit, no experience I can't have. I'm blind. That's the only difference between you and me."

"Well, Kim, I guess I can't expect you not to be angry with me." Astra strolled with her wine in a half circle around Kim, as if she were a director studying a camera angle.

"Astra, she's tired – " Constantin began.

"C, I'm right here! I'll let you know if I'm tired!"

Astra considered the man, the way he jumped to her daughter's side. She smoothed a stray curl off her forehead. "How sweet," Astra said. "She calls you C. Do you call her K?"

"I call her BC sometimes. For babycakes."

"C and BC. That's very cute." Astra sipped her wine. She uncorked the bottle and filled her daughter's glass and her own, noticing the flicker of a smile across Kim's mouth.

"Thank you," Kim said.

"You're welcome. It *is* good to see you, you know. I hadn't expected such a radiant being to walk into my house" – Constantin gazed at Kim who beamed – "but it was hard for me way back when. I was having..." (Think of something. You're a shrink, for God's sake) "...emotional difficulties."

Kim's face opened a bit. She looked like an angel in the moonlight. "You were?"

"Well, yes, it's no fun talking about it, but – "

" – I didn't know – "

"Of course you didn't. You were six."

Kim thought back. Actually, she didn't recall her mother acting any differently the weeks before she dropped her off at the school for blind children. Just the usual revolving door of nannies and housekeepers looking after her, then one day she went to her room and everything was gone: her clothes, stuffed animals, toys, everything. She gasped, crying as she read the bare walls with her hands, yanking open empty drawers, gaping closets. Then the sound of her mother's heels clicking down the hallway, the jingle of car keys – her heart in her mouth – what in the world was going on?

"I'd hit bottom, I guess."

(...but her tone was even that day, business as usual, get-in-the-car-we're-going-on-a-little-trip...)

"You needed more than I could give, Kim."

(Even at six Kim was resigned to seeing her mother no more than a few minutes a week: "Your mother is traveling; she's away; she has company." In fact their journey to the school was the longest time they'd spent together in months – almost an hour.)

"I was devastated, but I couldn't take care of you." Astra turned away from Kim and Constantin, lowering her head a bit to convey melancholy. "I was too depressed to move. You had so many needs. I...I..."

"I don't remember much," Kim said.

"To be honest there's not a whole lot I remember either of those days."

"I never saw you, anyway."

"I know. I was a terrible mother. When I wasn't immobilized by my mood, I was trying desperately to get my Ph.D."

(Kim, age five, had long grown used to the sound of her mother laughing and the voices of strange men in the other room, the kiss goodnight from nanny or maid when she longed only for her mother: her exotic perfume, the silly jokes she'd tell.)

"I'm glad you two are talking," Constantin said. "After all this time, however it happened, you two are connecting again here tonight. I think it's great."

Kim loved this man, but he did tend to simplify the emotional world. Hard to shake off years of great parenting, she understood.

Astra looked at him with unabashed adoration. "Well, I agree. I agree that who cares about how we're together again, we're all talking. That's the most important thing. And I don't know about you two, but I'm starving. You guys hungry?"

"Dying," Constantin said.

"It does smell good, whatever it is." Kim shivered in the cool night air as she followed Astra and Constantin back inside.

· EIGHTEEN ·

"This is what, rhubarb?" Constantin said, tasting his desert.

"Do you like it?" Astra looked up from hers.

"Mmm, so tart. I love it."

"You need bags of sugar to make it the least bit edible. Don't you like it, Kim?"

"I never liked fruit tarts. Only chocolate."

"Of course, that's right. So tell me, Constantin, why did you choose marine biology?"

"I know everyone loves the sea – it's almost a cliché – but I'm an adventurer at heart, and I look at the oceans as just great unexplored worlds. Forget about the moon, about outer space. We still haven't explored over seventy percent of the earth – the oceans! There are countless unknown creatures, especially at the greater depths. Giant worms that live on nuclear waste, hundred-foot-long squid – "

"Good lord, have you seen those creatures?"

"Not those, but others. I want to take Kim on a dive soon. We have a sub at Wood's Hole we take down sometimes."

"I'd love to do that. What an adventure." She poured everyone more wine.

"Then you should come with us. We're going down a month from today, on the twenty-ninth."

"Is that an invitation?"

"Sure, I don't see why not." Kim squeezed his hand; he squeezed it back, not knowing what she meant by it. What she *had* meant was that this trip was special to her, and that she would have preferred to go with just him. Constantin went on, "As long as depths don't frighten you. Sometimes they can be worse than heights."

Astra stiffened as she remembered the heave and stink of the slave ship. She was a white man named Victor, in charge of hundreds of starving, suffering East Africans. He sat belowdecks charting the rest of the journey by a sputtering candle that swayed in the growing storm. He had just read in the log the translation of the African port town of Bagamoyo, which was: "throw away your heart." He felt nothing regarding this, but noted in the ledger that three more had died that day.

At that moment, he heard a commotion from the darkness of the lower deck, and looked up to see the wild eyes of a young African man he had whipped only hours ago till his ear hung onto his head by a thread of tissue. The ear was gone; black blood clogged the hole. He had torn it off freeing himself from his neck chains. The slave roared, picking Victor up and dragging him to the upper deck where the slave hurled him headfirst into the fifteen-foot swells of the storm. After the first shock of cold sea water, the dying was strangely easy, like sleeping, and he felt himself leave that body early, looking down at it almost with disdain, at the same time hurtling to a new life half the world away.

"I'm not afraid," Astra said, busying herself with coffee by the stove. "Are you, Kim?"

"Of course not."

Constantin turned to Kim. "Are you okay?"

"Just tired."

"You can go to bed anytime, Kim," Astra said. "The bed's all made up and waiting for you."

"I think I might take you up on that. And I want to go see Marty and give him his dinner."

Constantin helped Kim with her bags in the foyer before they turned toward the stairs. Astra gathered a pile of dirty plates. "Oh! I almost forgot!

I wanted to take you two for a sail tomorrow. Does that sound okay? It's supposed to clear up and – "

"I've never been sailing," Kim said.

"Never?" Constantin said. "You'll love it, won't she, Astra?"

"Do you sail, Constantin?"

"All my life."

"You can be my first mate!"

"Of course, but you're sure you're okay about this, Kim?"

"I guess," she said, laughing, "as long as you strap me down."

"Ah, you'll be fine," Astra said. "We'll take good care of you."

Constantin took Kim to their bedroom, where he gave her a tour of what was where in the room and in the adjoining bathroom.

He held his hand over hers, touching the sink, toilet, bathtub –

"Enough, C, I get the idea. It's a bathroom."

He let her hand drop. "Jesus, Kim, I'm just trying to get you situated."

She rubbed her forehead and sighed. She couldn't ever remember being this tired. "I'm sorry. I didn't mean to snap at you."

"I just wanted to make sure you were okay before I went back downstairs – "

"Aren't you coming to bed?"

"I'm just wired right now. I don't think I could go to sleep. I thought I'd go down and keep your mom company for a few minutes. Maybe knock myself out with one more drink."

Kim turned from him and felt her way back to the bedroom. She took a few steps toward the bed but missed it by several inches. Gently, he put his hand on her back to steer her toward it.

"Whatever. I'm going to sleep. Do what you want."

"Then I'll stay, Kim, if that's what you want."

She sat down heavily on the bed. "No. You know what, go ahead. I think I need to just pass out anyway."

He gave her a quick kiss on the cheek. "Get some sleep, my love. I'll be up soon."

He glanced back at her as she stared straight ahead with eyes that would never see him. When she heard him click off the light she thought of the children's ward at the Stafford School where there was no light or switch, and wanted more than anything at that moment to hear Carmella's voice wishing her good night and sweet dreams. She smiled as she drew back the cool cotton sheets, conjuring her voice, but as she nestled under the comforter she couldn't help imagining what Carmella might say about a sign such as lightning striking a tree only a yard away.

· NINETEEN ·

Astra wasn't surprised when she saw Constantin making his way back downstairs. She had even taken the time to freshen her makeup. Damp curls came loose around her face as she scrubbed out the soup tureen. Constantin watched her for a fraction of a second before announcing himself. "Astra?"

"Oh, hello, Constantin. Was I making too much noise out here? Poor girl must be so tired."

"Oh, no, I'm sure she's far gone by now." He stepped into the kitchen, almost shyly. "I hope I'm not bothering you, but I'm just not tired for some reason, even after all that scotch and wine."

She dried her hands on a towel and headed for the liquor cabinet. "Well, then you need a nightcap, simple as that. Let's see, amaretto, sambuca, Bailey's – "

He watched her turn, her slim arm reaching up. "No, no, just another glass of wine should do me in."

He followed her to the living room where they sat on opposite sides of a black leather couch with their drinks. Constantin, not being a self-analyst, had not realized his attraction to this woman, attributing his excitement to his recent passions: for Kim, for his discovery that he loved teaching, his research; there were plenty of explanations for joy. Now here he sat in this stunning house, this gorgeous woman lounging so close he could smell her perfumed hair, her pampered skin. But it was all copacetic: it was a bonus, in fact. An attractive, intelligent mother-in-law? It beat being related to some kind of shrew. Besides, he felt in complete control.

He knew he would be a fine and understanding partner, an attentive husband, a good friend to his new wife. He couldn't imagine a better future.

Astra watched him settle himself, and waited for him to speak. His big tanned hands around the delicate wine glass, the thick forearms, broad shoulders in a badly laundered shirt. What a completely lovable geek, she thought, turning her best angle toward him as she reached for a chocolate-covered cherry in a gold box on the table.

"I never thanked you for these, Constantin."

He waved his hand toward the box. "Oh, you're welcome. They were just a thought, on the way."

"And how was your trip up? I never asked."

He looked at her and gasped. How could they have forgotten to mention their brush with death? "Good lord, the most terrifying thing happened. A tree was struck by lightning just a few feet from our car. If we hadn't pulled over, we wouldn't be here tonight. That's how close it was."

"Why had you pulled over?"

Constantin looked at her, but she pretended to be absorbed in unwrapping the chocolate and didn't meet his eye. "Kim...she started yelling at me to pull over and I did."

"How lucky for you both."

"Yeah, I guess it was luck. We shouldn't have been out driving in that anyway, should have pulled over at some restaurant and sat it out."

"But you just wanted to get here, right?" She smiled prettily.

"Yup, I'm a guy. Just want to get there, don't ask directions, ignore the apocalypse, and show up."

Astra laughed. Constantin could hear Kim's laugh in her mother's, and he flinched a bit. Was she sleeping yet? Waiting for him to join her? He looked down at his drink.

"That's how you'll get places in life, driving through the storms!" Astra added, reading him.

He looked up at her. "Has Kim ever met her father?"

"No, he left me the day he discovered I was pregnant."

"I'm sorry."

"I could have tracked him down, but what would have been the – "

" – point, exactly. Sounds like you were better off on your own."

"Well, it wasn't easy."

"I can imagine."

"And I have a lot of..." She welled up. Was it the wine? Or was Constantin making her actually feel something? "...regret about what I did, but I was overwhelmed. I couldn't handle all of it – "

In a flash he was next to her, his arm protectively around her shoulder. A gentle squeeze, and he took his arm away but stayed close.

My God, I'm crying, she thought. I haven't cried in eight hundred years, or maybe I have never cried. And why am I crying? It's not about some blind girl asleep in the upstairs bedroom.

Her shoulders were narrow but strong; her red toenails like jewels in a row in her high heeled sandals.

I have to get away from her, he thought, or only felt, and got to his feet. "I can't imagine what you must be feeling, Astra. I'm so sorry."

"It's just, seeing her again...all those years I missed..." God, she was almost starting to believe herself.

He filled her wine glass and sat at his original safe distance on the couch. "But like we talked about on the porch, you're together again. Maybe it'll take some time, but you two can heal, I really think you can. We can come up and visit more, or you come to visit us..."

She took a tissue he handed her and daintily wiped her nose. Looked at him with high color in her cheeks. "Do you really love my daughter, Constantin?"

He met her eye. "I do, Astra, with all my heart. She makes me happy."

She began to cry again; it felt so good, after all these centuries.

"You shouldn't cry about it, Astra. I'm going to make a wonderful husband for Kim. And she loves me too, I know it."

"Of course she does, of course she does."

He wanted to take her hand. He didn't. "Maybe you should get some sleep. Don't try to fix everything tonight."

"You're right, I'm getting a little out of control here." She wondered if her eyes were red, her makeup smeared. "We do need to get started early tomorrow if we're going to sail – "

"What do you mean, 'if'?"

She laughed again. "You're right, we're definitely sailing if the weather lets us."

"You're a wonderful cook, by the way."

"Thanks, I try. But it isn't every day your long lost daughter and her new fiancé visit for the weekend." She sighed and got to her feet. "I better finish up with those dishes, then."

They made their way to the kitchen.

"No, Astra, go to bed. I'll help you in the morning."

"At least let me take out the garbage."

"Let me take care of it."

She smiled and nodded. "If you must."

He reached over to pull up the bag and saw carton after empty carton with the insignia "Givenchy Catering" on it. Holding in a grin, he hoisted the bag and hauled it outside to the trash. It got to him, how she had pretended she made the dinner, probably more than if she actually had.

· TWENTY ·

He woke her early, his hands hot on her breasts, his breath full of sweet words in her hair. She wanted to pout – after all she'd lain there for what felt like hours waiting for him to come to bed the night before – but he was persistent, as if roused by a succubus in sleep, and pressed himself into her never opening his eyes, thinking not of her – not of anyone – but of his own release; he might have killed rather than be denied her honeyed mouth, her delicate waist, the lush sweet place he plunged himself. She put off the pout as her body made its own decision; she swooned, arching into him, a cry escaping her mouth as he covered it, hushing her, but the cry was out; it tore into the morning, out the screened window and to the porch below, where Astra paused halfway through a sit-up.

She held herself there, muscles burning, as the cry left the air rent and bleeding, then jumped to her feet.

She wrenched the glass sliders open and sprinted to the kitchen where she scrambled a serrated knife from a drawer. She ran the knife along the inside of her arm where it left a thin pink line but did not break the skin. Too dull; she tossed it in the trash, then rooted around in the drawer for another. She found a paring knife still in its packaging and began to tear at it with her teeth. I need a goddammed knife to open a knife? she thought, when she heard the upstairs bedroom door open and close and the sound of the shower turning on. She ripped at the package with her teeth; the knife clattered on the granite kitchen island. She stabbed it into the wooden cutting board counter and leaned on it, trying to get her breathing back to normal, when she heard the tick-tick-tick of a cane and light footsteps behind her.

"Mom?"

She turned around and looked at the girl, her heart pounding, her hair worked loose from its braid and wild around her shoulders. Kim stood washed in sunlight, her nipples still hard under a blue silk robe, barefoot on the lush carpet, her cane sweeping ahead of her in a practiced arc.

For just a moment, Astra hated herself for what she felt, for what she did not feel. Then it passed. She remembered what she was living for, this time.

"Are you all right, Mom?"

"Fine, just...getting breakfast a little organized." She jammed the knife into a bulbous honeydew melon and started to cut it in half. "Do you like melon?"

"Love it."

"How about some coffee?"

"I don't drink coffee."

Then you're no child of mine, Astra thought, pulling out orange juice. "Juice, then?"

Worse. "Milk, if you have it."

"I have two percent."

"Doesn't matter. Did you sleep all right?" Kim found a chair and pulled it out.

"Great." She had barely closed her eyes all night. "And yourself?"

"Never better. That's a great bed. Not too soft."

"Bet it beats the dorm, anyway."

"I'm mostly at C's."

"I see."

"Is he...up?"

"In the shower."

"And what does he like in the morning, eggs? Toast?"

"He's a corn flakes kind of guy, actually."

"Oh, well, then I better run to the store – "

Kim laughed. "Don't worry about it, I'm sure he'd love a real breakfast for once. Go ahead and make him anything you want."

"Well, if you're sure. I'll make scrambled eggs with toast, then. I'm not one for breakfast, if you'll remember."

"You were a real night owl. Still are, I guess."

"And you're still an early bird, I see."

"I love the morning. It's when I have all my energy. C would sleep till noon if you let him."

"Well, the salt air must have gotten to him; it's only..." She checked her watch. "...seven-thirty."

"He can't wait to go sailing, that's all."

"Ah, I see."

Constantin appeared in a ratty robe, one pocket safety-pinned on. He combed his wet hair back with his hands as he looked at Astra.

"Speak of the devil," she said.

· TWENTY-ONE ·

The storm had broken the spirit of spring, and summer was there waiting in the wings, grinning and searing. By noon the roads were full of heat tricks, and anyone inland sealed their homes and started up their air conditioners.

Astra, in a long sleeved white cotton jersey and white jeans, hurtled down the highway in the Audi with Constantin in front and Kim and Marty in the back. Marty still wouldn't go near Astra, but followed Kim's command to get in the car that morning. He huddled next to her, drinking in her caresses.

In oversized sunglasses, red lipstick and a white sash tied over her hair and around her neck, Astra looked like a movie star on her way to the beach. Constantin watched her mouth when she spoke.

"We'll grab a picnic lunch at The Daily Landing, and go out for a tour around the harbor. I don't imagine you fish, Constantin."

"I love to fish, but we don't have to today."

"The Daily Landing has gear to rent. Let's rent something in case you get the urge." She smiled flawlessly at him.

Constantin looked back at Kim. "You wouldn't want to – "

"Not in a million years, thanks." She straightened the straps of her simple flower print sundress.

"Oh, I don't think you'll hurt any whales with a rod and reel, dear."

Kim considered this, then asked, "Do you like to fish?"

"Oh, me?" Astra turned into a long sandy drive. "I absolutely love it. The fight a big fish can put up is thrilling. They want so badly to live, you can almost taste it."

Astra walked a few yards ahead of Kim and Constantin, waving at someone she knew on the dock.

The couple slowed their pace behind Astra, who ducked into the restaurant before them. "You've never been on a boat before?" Constantin asked, disbelieving.

"Never had the opportunity."

"Not at school? She never took you when you were a kid?"

"C, my mother never did anything with me when I was a kid. Don't you get that yet? And I'm a first year student at school. I'm not exactly at Wood's Hole yet."

"Of course, of course. It should be that much more exciting then! You're going to love it."

"What if I don't?"

"What if you don't what?"

"Love it."

"We'll turn around and come home."

"Promise?"

"Kim, what's going on in that sweet head of yours? Why would I take you out on a boat to torture you? I'm in love with you, babycheeks."

"But I want you to have a good time too, C."

"I'll – "

"Hey, kids." Astra stood holding open the screen door of the Daily Landing. "I need your lunch orders." The smell of fresh fish frying wafted by them as the door slammed shut behind her.

Kim stood awkwardly on the pier as Astra, then Constantin climbed into the twenty-four-foot Hunter sailboat. She heard Astra laugh at something Constantin said that she hadn't heard, then Constantin's belly laugh, followed by a thud.

"What happened?" The sun beat down on Kim's freckled back and shoulders. It was ninety-five degrees and the air wasn't moving.

"I kind of fell," Constantin said.

Astra laughed again. "And we haven't even left the slip yet."

Kim shifted her weight to her other foot and felt the dock move beneath her. Already she missed solid ground. Marty sat on her sandaled foot, his tail swishing against her ankles. Constantin must have been petting him.

"You guys ready?" he said.

She listened to the water lapping at the dock, the screech of gulls, the clanging of rigging on masts. Two kids ran by her playing tag, but stopped to pet Marty.

"Will he bite me?" a little redheaded girl said.

"No," Kim said.

"Are you blind?" the other girl said, undoing a wedgie as she stared at Kim.

"Yes."

"Then, how can you go sailing?" she asked.

Kim tried to smile. "I have help."

"Run along, kids," Constantin said, reaching for Kim's hand. They scampered off. "You've got to take a big step, Kim, but don't worry, I'll guide your leg with my other hand. You'll be fine."

She let herself step into nothingness (will the ocean really hold me up?) and onto the foredeck where Constantin caught her and lifted her into the cockpit. Marty jumped after her right away, skidding across the deck and landing on the floor of the boat.

Their laughter was drowned out by the sound of the motor roaring to life. In moments they had backed away from the slip. Astra maneuvered them skillfully among the other boats in the marina toward the narrow channel. Kim suddenly felt exuberant and excited, as well as a little ashamed that she'd been so frightened.

"So, you never told me," Astra said as they neared the open ocean, "when's the big day?"

"We haven't decided on the exact day yet, have we, C?" Kim said, thrilling to the cooling breeze the boat's movement created.

"Well, you better set a date. Nobody likes a long engagement."

"A year from today, then. How does that sound, Kim?"

"Sounds good to me." She lay back into him, smiling, remembering the heat of the morning.

· TWENTY-TWO ·

Even well into the afternoon, the day did not fail them. The winds on the open sea were light but steady, and they made good progress out to a fishing ground Astra knew of. After lunch, both Astra and Constantin dropped a line a few times. They each had a nibble or two, but whatever was on there got away each time. They stored the gear and decided to just relax awhile.

Constantin had fallen asleep on a bench in the cockpit, a book over his forehead, with Kim curled up next to him. Astra was buried in a magazine when she felt the wind change. It turned from a dry, onshore breeze to a south-facing, cooler gust that was heavy with fog. She stored the magazine and climbed over to the mainsail. The color of the water had shifted from rich deep blues to a metallic grey, reflecting a weakened sun under gauzy clouds. Astra watched Kim shiver and curl more tightly into Constantin as the boat dipped deep into a trough, then rode up a wave, sending Marty skidding across the floor.

Constantin woke first. "What's going on?" Kim held fast to the seat.

"We've hit some weather, I think," Astra said. A fresh slap of wind lifted her hair eerily off her shoulders. The main luffed and swelled, snapping out loosely. Constantin climbed to the tiller with Astra, who struggled to control the flapping main.

"We should drop the main and go with the jib," he said.

The storm had kicked up from nowhere, a dark bruise on the horizon one minute and all around them the next.

"But we'll be blown out!"

"Just try it!" Constantin raced to the tiller to help her. "Kim, hold on!"

Pale with terror, her wide eyes the color of the sea, Kim gripped the ropes as the boat tipped and rolled over the growing swells.

Astra finally coaxed in the main, but the wind whipped up and pummeled into the jib. The squall had licked up from the east and surprised them, churning the water into rough sculpted peaks that rolled the boat sickeningly deep, then high. From nowhere, a wave rose up like a grey fist and broke over them, soaking them.

Kim screamed as Constantin rushed to her. "Lose the jib!" he yelled back at Astra.

"All right, but we better heave-to!" Astra shouted from the tiller. "Come back and give me a hand!"

"I've got to get her in the cabin!" Constantin gripped Kim hard, hurting her, almost carrying her as he pulled her toward the small clanging galley door. She hit her head on the frame as they fell in, him on top of her, filling the tiny space on the floor. He scrambled to his feet and lifted her on the bed, wrapping her hands around a pole that held up the top berth. "Hold on!"

"Don't go!" she shrieked. "Where's Marty?" The dog had escaped long ago, curled up and whimpering in a berth. Constantin took her hand and placed it on his shivering body.

"I have to help your mother with the boat!" he yelled over the wind, and left her there.

Her knuckles whitened on the pole; she tasted blood in her mouth and wanted to scream. As she rose up high with the boat, her body slid across the floor, then swiveled back around, smacking hard against the side of the berth. She scrambled back on the bed but quickly learned the floor was best because that's where she was going to end up anyway, with Marty flopping over her again and again, scratching at her as he tried to gain purchase with his nails.

She heard the dull shouts of Astra and Constantin above her, and felt the lobster roll she had for lunch come up unbidden to her lips and spill out onto the floor. As the boat flipped up, the warm puddle flew back at her, and she threw up again, crying with fear.

On the deck of the boat, Astra and Constantin screamed at each other in the wind. She had eased out the reefed main when Constantin was in the cabin, and tacked through the wind until the jib backfilled.

He made his way to her, gripping the ropes. "What the hell are you doing? We can't control this boat!"

"Get the tiller tied down!" Astra shouted, soaked through her clothes, her scarf long gone.

He obeyed her, the halyard tearing at his hands as the bow of the boat was forced down, away from the wind. For long horrible seconds they wallowed sideways, a nauseating dip, but the boat righted itself, and they worked with the wind as it keened on them. The mouth of the channel was in their sights.

"You did it!" Astra shouted as she held onto the mast, laughing with delight like some insane mermaid.

He stared at her through the spray, her willowy strong body curled around the main rigging. "You're enjoying this, aren't you?"

"Yes, I am! Isn't it exciting?" Wind whipped strands of black hair, medusa-like, across her face and shoulders.

"Your daughter isn't having any fun."

"Well, I didn't make the storm!"

He just looked at her.

"She loves marine biology? Well, here's a taste of it!"

"So, you can handle it by yourself out here?" he asked grimly, making his way toward the galley door. He didn't wait for an answer.

She shouted, "I'm sorry, Constantin. Is she okay?"

But he was already down below.

· TWENTY-THREE ·

Kim woke to the sound of laughter, a door slamming. It was four in the afternoon, but she was still waiting for her stomach to settle down after the sail. Her skin throbbed against the sheets; even wearing the strongest sunblock, she had burned badly and the aloe Constantin had slathered on made no real difference. A headache drummed at her skull. She felt like she'd been beaten up. She tried to go back to sleep, and not think about where her boyfriend and her mother might be going.

"Let's put it this way," Constantin said as he walked along the rocky shoreline at low tide with Astra, "if an alien civilization came to look at the dominant life form on the planet, they'd be out looking at midwater creatures. I mean, any way you slice it, biomass, numbers of individuals, geographic extent, these are the biggest ecological entities on earth. But we know nothing about them."

"So, you're a sort of ocean cowboy," she said, touching his arm for support as they leapt from rock to rock.

He laughed. "Well, I'd like to be. I'm pretty landlocked these days, with teaching and so on."

"I used to teach, but I got tired of it. All that repetition." She made her way to an outcropping and sat.

He joined her. "There is a lot of that, but to see that light in kids' eyes when they really get it, or get that hunger to learn more, and you know they'll do anything to get the answers..."

"That didn't happen much with me, or just not enough. I got tired

73

of explaining why people are crazy. Sometimes there just is no explanation. Well, there's a medical explanation – "

"So you're burned out?"

She looked at him, the easy understanding in his brown eyes. "Yeah, I think I'm just about there. Hell, sometimes I'd like to talk to someone. I get so tired of listening."

"You must be."

"I feel exhausted, like my soul is exhausted, from knowing too much about how evil people can be." She looked at his tanned bare feet next to her small white sneakers.

"Sounds like you deal with some real screwed up kids."

"Oh, I do. You wouldn't believe what some of them have done."

"I guess you can't tell me, can you."

"No, I can't. Not now."

"What do you mean, 'not now'?"

"Not ever, I guess."

He cleared his throat.

"It makes me feel so alone all the time; it makes me feel invisible," she said, almost under her breath.

"Can't you talk to a friend or colleague?"

"It's not that easy for me. I don't know why. With you, for some reason, I feel like I could say anything, and it would be all right."

He looked at her, then away at the brooding sky. "That's how I feel with Kim, like she'll accept anything that comes out of me – "

" – won't judge you – "

" – puts up with all my crap."

"That must be a nice feeling. I couldn't imagine anything better than being loved like that."

She looked at him, but he stared ahead at waves crashing and lacing back on jagged rocks. "We should go back."

She watched him get up, his muscular thighs tensing under frayed shorts. She wanted to pull him back to her, kiss him for a hundred years.

Instead she got to her feet and ran a bit to catch up with him. "I thought I'd order dinner in for us tonight for a change," she said. "Would that be all right?"

He grinned back at her. "Whatever you like, Astra. You don't have to cook for us every night."

· TWENTY-FOUR ·

Kim had finally been woken by her own misery, the sunburn and headache rousing her from any kind of rest. She got dressed and found her cane, then made her way to the kitchen for a glass of milk. Marty clamored for a walk so she harnessed him and he led her out, down the stairs and along the path that led to the sea.

"Kim!"

She heard Constantin's voice; Marty pulled her toward it.

She felt his arms around her, his dry kiss on her lips. "How are you feeling? Better?"

"Not really. My head's killing me. I couldn't get to sleep."

"I've got aspirin upstairs," Astra said.

Kim flinched slightly at the sound of Astra's voice. "Maybe later." For a strange moment, Astra felt almost as if Kim were looking into her eyes. "C and I are going for a walk."

They headed for the cliff walk, a paved path that was much easier for Kim to navigate. Wild pink roses wove prettily through the waist-high wire fence between the path and a forty foot drop to the sea. Evening clouds streaked across the sky, the humidity slowly lifting.

"You were sort of abrupt back there, don't you think?"

"She can handle it," Kim said, her face expressionless. She listened to his soft footsteps. "Why are you barefoot? Were you two swimming?"

"No. You know me, I hate wearing shoes."

"That's right, you're nature boy. I forgot."

He glanced at her. "You're still not feeling a hundred percent, huh."

"A *hundred percent?* Fuck, C, we were just trapped on a sailboat in a storm and I was tossed around like a sack of garbage and I'm burnt to a crisp! No, I'm not a hundred percent. Try fifteen."

"Fifteen. That's low."

"Stop being an asshole, C! That was a horrible experience for me!"

"I'm sorry, BC. It sucked, but it was a gale that lasted ten minutes, then we had everything under control."

"Longest ten minutes of my life. I knew I shouldn't have gone out on that goddammed sailboat."

"Whoa, Kim, what's going on here? Who or what are you mad at? Me? Your mother? The storm?...Yourself?"

She lifted up on Marty's harness to stop him, resting a hand on the fence. "Shit, all of the above, I guess."

"That's a heavy load, honey."

"So, did you have a nice walk with her?"

"Yeah, she's a nice woman, or at least she seems to be. Smart, hard working. Takes care of screwed up kids. Hell, I couldn't handle that."

Kim tore off a thick green leaf from a bank of rose hips, pinched it in half with her fingernails. "C, is it dark yet?"

"Getting there."

She tilted her head slightly as if listening to the sea. "Can we head home tonight?"

"Well, your mom just went to order dinner."

"She does that every night. She's never cooked a day in her life."

He chuckled. "She orders well, anyway."

"Come on, let's just tell her I'm not feeling well and I want to get out of here. We can stop for seafood on the way home. Maybe not even go home! Stop at a bed and breakfast somewhere, be alone one night before we have to go back. Stay in bed late, doing what we do best..."

He laughed and kissed her. "Kim, that sounds like a blast, but should we really be so rude?"

"Rude? C, my God, the woman abandoned me when I was six. *That's* rude."

"Look, there's no doubt the woman did a terrible thing to you, but she's trying to – okay, not make it up to you, that would be impossible I guess, but maybe heal a little, start a brand new relationship with you. Why are you so closed to that?"

"I'm not closed. I just want to go home. Tonight."

"Will a tree fall on us if we don't?"

"Maybe."

"Let's just have dinner, because look, she expects us to, and then we'll head out, if you still want to. How's that sound?"

"It sounds okay. Thank you."

"No problem."

They started walking again. "Constantin?"

"Yes?"

"Is she beautiful? Is my mother beautiful?"

He hesitated, picturing Astra in the storm hanging onto the rigging, her long wet hair ink black against her porcelain complexion. "Not like you."

"What do you mean, 'not like me'? She's beautiful, but in a different way, or she's not as beautiful as I am?"

"I'd say she's...beautiful in a different way."

"What does she look like? Describe her for me. Does she have a nice body?"

"Jesus, Kim, where are you going with this?"

"Well, does she? What's wrong with telling me?"

"She has long dark hair, and she's pale as a ghost. And skinny. You have a better body, if you were wondering."

"Is she flat chested?"

"Kim!"

"Well?"

"All right, all right, no, she's not, but you're luckier in that department. Now can we drop this? I'm heading back."

She had dinner laid out for them when they returned, watching for them from the deck. She had been watching them the whole time.

· TWENTY-FIVE ·

Nobody seemed to have much of an appetite, especially Kim. Astra began gathering the dinner dishes. "You sure you don't want to get a good night's rest here first?"

"The thing is, we both have a lot of work to do for next week – " Kim began.

"I haven't even prepared my classes, to tell you the truth – "

"Then why not leave early in the morning? I'll get you up at six."

"No," Kim said. "We need to leave tonight."

"All right," Astra said, as she watched Constantin sip a glass of cabernet she had doped minutes before they returned from their walk. "You're the boss. We just have to make sure we make plans to see each other again before another thirteen years have gone by."

"Here here," Constantin said, clinking his glass to hers and smiling.

Kim swung her crossed leg nervously. "Can we pack up now, C?"

"Sure, let's get going." He got to his feet and lurched sideways, grabbing the table for balance. How many glasses of wine had he drunk? He only remembered two, which was not much for him.

"Are you all right?" Astra asked.

"Yeah, I guess I...I feel like I'm back on the ship..."

"We did split a bottle between us – "

"That's nothing."

"You got too much sun today, I bet," Astra said. "That can sneak up on you. You want some coffee for the road?"

"God, no, I can't drink coffee at night. Now *that* disagrees with me."

He slumped back down in his chair and rubbed his eyes. "Kim, your fiancé's a drunk."

She touched his back. "No, you're not. What's going on? How much did you drink?"

"Nothing, two glasses. Look, let's just get our stuff together." He got to his feet and followed Kim, who knew the way quite well by now, up the stairs and to their room.

She sat and listened to him as he opened and closed drawers, tossing their clothes into an open suitcase.

He belched. "Whoops. Sorry Kim, that one surprised me. God, my body feels weird."

"What I want to know is, why doesn't she have a boyfriend, if she's so attractive?"

"Are you back on that again?"

"You can't tell me you don't think she's full of shit."

"Full of shit about *what*?" Man, he felt drunk.

"Everything that comes out of her mouth. After almost three days, I don't know why I'm here."

"Kim, *Christ*, can't you give the woman a chance? She's your goddammed mother, she's goddammed *trying* to begin a new leaf, or whatever that expression is, with you, and you're just not letting her *do* it, Christ knows why – "

Downstairs, Astra opened a can of beef stew and dumped it in Marty's bowl, stirring in a few drops of sodium pentathol, and left it on the landing for him. In a few moments he click clacked up the stairs, sniffed the bowl, glanced through the screen and across the room at her. With a look of ineffable sadness, he dropped his head and began to eat.

Kim had held it in too long, and started to cry. "She never wanted me, and she never will, don't you understand?"

"Do you really believe that?"

"Yes, I do."

"Ah, honey." His head was swimming. He sat down next to her, put his arms around her. "Just remember, I want you, and I always will."

He kissed her hot face, then her mouth, sliding his hand under her soft cotton T-shirt and bra. She laughed a little through her tears as he gently leaned into her, his weight pushing her back on the bed.

"Shouldn't we be packing, I mean she's w – "

"Fuck it, she'll wait." His mouth found her nipple; she groaned to feel his tongue there, his hardness touching her in the right places even through her clothes.

"I guess we could take a few minutes – "

He pulled her clothes off her. "We'll take as long as we want." They both came the instant he pushed inside her, rocking her back on the bed, her head sunk in the pillow, knees at her ears. And then he was gone, unconscious and snoring, two hundred and fifteen pounds of boyfriend on top of her.

"Constantin?...C?"

He snuffled into her, but didn't move.

"Are you okay?"

"Yah, jussleepin', kay? LoveyouBC."

She rolled him off her, laughing. "Guess we're not going anywhere tonight, huh, C."

No answer. She smiled in her eternal darkness.

· TWENTY-SIX ·

When half an hour had gone by and Kim and Constantin had not emerged from the bedroom, Astra crept upstairs. With gloved hands, she began to gather her jewelry, grabbing haphazardly across the case. She opened a few drawers, scattering clothes on the floor, then ransacked the medicine cabinet, flushing the drugs she'd used on Constantin and Marty down the toilet. She caught a look at herself in the mirror, expecting a ghoul, but a stunning dark-eyed beauty looked back at her. This is a terrible inconvenience, she thought, a truly messy thing she was about to do, but she could see no other way to capture the prize. Even now – what was that thump? – the sounds of their lovemaking frenzied her, filled her with unalterable purpose. How many more centuries was she cursed to live without love? She couldn't bear it.

She ran out to her car and tossed the bags of jewelry in the trunk, crept back inside, and waited.

Kim lay holding Constantin for the longest time, loving him perhaps more than she ever had. But her bladder was calling, so she got up and took care of that, then realized dully that she really should, as much as she didn't want to, go downstairs and tell her mother the obvious: they weren't leaving that night.

She wrapped her robe tightly around her, and, skipping the cane, began to make her way down the stairs.

Step by step, she felt her way along the wall to the glass doors that led out onto the deck. She slid one of them open. The fresh breeze from the

83

sea blew in full of salt and life. "Mom?" she said tentatively. "Are you out there?"

Nothing.

She pulled the door shut and started back toward their room, but changed her mind and thought she'd try the kitchen, then give it up. The glass under her hands gave way to the wallpaper of the living room, a doorway, then the lacquered oak cabinets built into the kitchen wall.

She turned to face the middle of the room. Took a few steps away from the cabinets, swaying a little, her bare feet clammy on the cool tile. She smelled leftover salmon from dinner, felt incandescent light on her face. The refrigerator hummed behind her; the kitchen clock ticked in her right ear.

She felt someone there, sitting at the table. A consciousness, watching her.

Her heart slammed at her chest.

"Mom? Are you there?"

Nothing.

"Why don't you answer me?"

Eyes wide, Kim backed up to the cabinets and turned around to face them. Trembling, she started to make her way back, her hands tacky with sweat.

Astra hurtled from her chair and in one graceful movement, wrapped one arm around Kim's shoulders and with the other, slit open her daughter's throat from chin to collarbone. Kim's scream, clotted with blood, ended as the phlegmy howl of a newborn girl began, a tiny thing slippery with afterbirth, the umbilical cord still roping mother to daughter, the violence of birth rorschaching white sheets, the mother's lank hair stringy with sweat as she panted and peered through her legs, praying for normalcy, praying for a healthy baby, a girl would be nice but healthy, please God, oh please God, just show me my baby...as Kim fell back into her mother's arms, quiet now, eyes open.

Blood fountained as it pulsed from her carotid artery, reddening the robe, her hair, her face; a painting gone mad with vermilion. Astra held her a moment, her only child, then dropped her in disgust. Kim's body slipped through her mother's arms, slid down her front and to the marble tiles. Her head thumped on the floor and she stared at the ceiling. Still the blood plumed from her throat in an ever widening circle on the floor.

Astra breathed shallowly and quickly, stepped back from the bright red pool. She glanced around, but there was nothing, no one, only the clock ticking on the wall, the orange eye of the pilot light on the stove, the magazine she'd been reading open on the kitchen table to "101 No-Fuss Grilling Recipes," and a dead woman on the floor.

She dropped the knife next to the body, then stripped off all her own gore-spattered clothes and gloves and stuffed them in a plastic bag, careful not to step anywhere near the corpse. She opened the sliding kitchen door that led out to a long sloping lawn and a smattering of forest, then the main road. She stood there naked, her skin glowing shell-white in the moonlight where she was not streaked in Kim's blood, black where it was. Her breath caught in her throat when she saw a brown lump on the lawn, but relaxed when she realized it was Marty, fast asleep on the grass. Cicadas buzzed in the flower gardens; fat-bodied moths gathered blindly, bumping at the porch light.

Clutching the bag of bloody clothes, Astra crept up the stairs, pausing outside the room where Constantin slept. He was snoring loudly. She kept on going.

In the bathroom she stood over the sink, hands shaking as she took out the stained clothes and cut them into small pieces which she flushed down the toilet, pausing and listening for movement from Constantin's room each time she flushed, until even the bag itself had been sent down into the labyrinth of pipes. She turned the shower on good and hot and stepped in, humming as she soaped herself clean.

· TWENTY-SEVEN ·

A town away in an antiseptic blue hospital room the baby girl still shrieked, even as she was washed of her mother's blood in a warm bath.

"Maybe she'll be an opera singer when she grows up," said the slim, pale nurse as she wiped the baby's eyes clean, cupping the tiny head in her other hand.

"Lucy can be whatever she wants to be," Ellen said. She lay on her side as she watched intently, resting her hands on her now empty belly.

Her husband Tom stood over the raised tub, arms folded, brow furrowed under white-blond bangs. "What's she got there, on her neck? Have you washed her there yet?"

The nurse took a cloth and wiped at the baby's neck, dipping her down and up again in the soapy water. Still the baby screamed.

"Maybe she needs to be held," Ellen said, reaching out for her newborn.

The nurse toweled off the baby and wrapped her in soft blankets, then turned to hand her to her mother.

"Can I see her, please?" Tom asked.

"Come sit with us, honey. We'll hold her together."

As they sat and cradled her, the baby finally calmed down, its little face less flushed. It made small sucking sounds with its mouth. A buzzer rang and the nurse was called away. Ellen and Tom cooed at their baby, remarking on the shape of her eyes (wide set, like Tom's) and her dimpled chin, which was just like Ellen's sister Isabelle's.

86

Tom pulled back the little blanket and they both gasped. A long, raised red mark slashed down across the baby's neck.

"What in hell?..." Tom said.

"Maybe she's still a little dirty." Ellen wiped at the tiny neck. The mark stayed.

"Let's look at the rest of her," Tom said gently.

Ellen started to cry, and rang the bell for their doctor. Tom put an arm around her. Drawing her to him, he kissed the top of her head, never taking his eyes off the baby. Their physician, a good looking Asian man, rushed right back in, clipboard in hand, stethoscope swinging from his neck. He lifted Lucy from her blanket, laid her out on the bed and examined her. He traced the mark on her neck with his finger.

"Your daughter has a birthmark, I'm afraid. But it's absolutely nothing to worry about. You realize these can be removed, right?"

"Well, that's good," Tom said.

"She'll have to be a little older, of course, but you should be happy." He turned her over, palpating her tiny belly, ribs, the alignment of her spine. "You have a normal, healthy child."

Ellen lifted her from the bed and held her. The baby suckled at her gown, and Ellen pushed it aside. Lucy found the nipple, and tasted her mother's milk for the first time. "Thank you, doctor," Ellen said, smiling now. "I think she's perfect just the way she is."

Astra slept dreamlessly, and woke to a perfect summer day. From the angle of the sun across the bed she knew it was past eleven. The house was utterly silent. She wondered how long she would have to wait for Constantin to wake.

Just as she was putting a brush through her hair, she heard the downstairs toilet flush, a door open and close. She put the brush down and applied lipstick as she stared at herself in the mirror. That day she looked twenty-eight she thought, at the outside. She slipped on a port colored robe and sat on her bed for a moment. Closing her eyes tightly, she gathered herself for the fallout of the next few minutes, hours, days.

She cracked open her door and listened for footsteps down the stairs.

"Kim?" His voice from the hallway sounded weak, hungover, a little bit guilty.

She slipped out her door to the top of the stairs and huddled there, waiting and listening to the risers creak as he went down.

Only a heartbeat later, the scream. It sounded like a wounded animal, rising up high, then breaking into gasping sobs. She had done something quite bad, she understood, another unforgivable sin to add to the mountain of unforgivable sins she had committed over so much time and space, but this was the last one, she had sworn this to herself, the necessary one; the only one left between this barren life and a life full of love. She had had no choice. She crouched on the stairs and held her head in her hands, rocking slightly as she listened to him wail, such grief! His agony washed over her and seeped into her as if she were porous, making her understand viscerally the love he had for Kim, and she felt a lump rise in her throat and tears prick at her eyes. Good God, she thought, if he would ever have that much love for her, she wouldn't need another thing in this human life.

She wept for him, because she loved him, and because he was in pain. And it felt beautiful, as if she had been cracked open inside.

In a few minutes she began to collect herself, wiping her face free of tears and rehearsing how she would behave, wondering how long – months, years? – she would have to keep up a charade of maternal grief. She loosened her hair around her shoulders and rubbed her eyes to appear as if she had just been woken by some kind of sound, and had gone downstairs to investigate.

She found him on his knees on the floor holding Kim, rocking her and wailing. Kim's wound had been licked clean by Marty, who lay next to her in a pool of his master's blood. Astra made a chirp of almost genuine shock. Constantin turned slowly to look at her. His face and robe were splotched with her blood, his eyes hollow, the pupils huge and dead. He looked like an old man; she almost didn't recognize him. She screamed, screamed to think this just might not work.

With infinite gentleness, he lay Kim down on the floor, pausing to look at her. He smoothed her hair off her forehead, kissed it, and tenderly closed her eyes before he got to his feet. Then he toppled like a felled tree toward Astra, who caught and folded him in her arms. She drew him, stumbling backwards, into a recliner just inside the living room. They rocked with sobs as she cupped his head in her hand like a newborn's.

· TWENTY-EIGHT ·

For that day and the next, Constantin could not or would not speak. He refused all food and water and was finally hospitalized for shock. Astra was told that though he was given plenty of medication, he hadn't slept. She came to see him the first night, but he turned away from her in his bed. She feared the worst.

In the meantime, there was a funeral to plan and detectives to appease. They arrived in droves, sealing off the house and peppering her with questions.

"You heard nothing? Nothing at all?" asked a hefty blonde woman in a poorly fitting uniform.

"I'm a heavy sleeper. Plus the air conditioners drown out everything. They help me sleep in fact."

"We need a list of exactly what's missing. And we need a report from your son-in-law."

"Well, he was going to be my son-in-law, before this..." and she actually welled up, thinking of Constantin mute in a narrow hospital bed across town, watching Jeopardy with lifeless eyes.

"I'm so sorry, Mrs..."

"Dr. Nathanson." She accepted some Kleenex the detective offered her.

"What sort of doctor are you?"

"I'm a psychiatrist."

"Where do you practice?"

None of your business, Astra thought. "At Greenfield Psychiatric

Institute."

"I see. Well, I'm sorry for your loss. We're going to do everything in our power to nab this guy. We've had a lot of break ins around here, but no...deaths."

Astra stared at the blue chalk outline where her daughter's body had been, wondering if she would have to re-tile her floor. She wiped her eyes, careful to keep her makeup in place. "Thank you, officer."

As it turned out, everything in their power really wasn't much. They pieced together the break in – easy, since Astra never locked her house; the robbery – Astra slept through it, what with ear plugs and air conditioner. It was clear that after taking the jewelry, the perpetrator made his way downstairs and came upon Kim, who startled him in the kitchen as he was on his way out. He killed her and took off, leaving the door open for the dog to come in and basically eliminate the integrity of the crime scene. Astra hadn't even planned on Marty's complicity, but it couldn't have worked out any better, except for one moment with the chief of police in his stuffy, brightly fluorescent office.

"Your daughter was blind?" He raised one eyebrow as he studied the report.

"Blind from birth, yes."

He looked up from his notes, pen poised, his watery blue eyes meeting hers over his reading glasses. "And if you were your daughter, and were surprised by a strange man in your kitchen in the middle of the night, what do you think you would have done?"

"I have no idea."

"Work with me, Dr. Nathanson. We're trying to catch this guy, aren't we?"

"Of course." She gripped her purse on her lap, winding the strap tightly through her fingers. "I think she would have talked to him, maybe."

"Not screamed?"

"She might have screamed."

"But that wasn't your first answer. Why did you say she would have talked to him?"

"Because my daughter was a bright girl."

"Bright enough to think that might be a way out."

"Yes."

"And what do you think she would have said?"

"I have no idea."

"You can't think of anything."

"Officer Schlummer, I wasn't there."

"You don't think she would have mentioned she was blind? That she was no threat to him?"

"She might have. It would have made sense. But who knows? She could have panicked."

He put his pen down. "There could have been no conversation at all, just a brutal murder." The phone rang, but he didn't answer it.

She looked him in the eye. "It's possible."

He considered her beauty; the swell of her breasts under the thin sweater; her clear-eyed composure a day after her daughter's murder.

"Why don't you tell me a little bit about your relationship with your daughter, Dr. Nathanson."

"Call me Astra."

He smiled with his mouth only. "Astra."

"She was a brilliant girl, with only a year at Barnesdale under her belt before..." her voice trembled winningly "...this happened."

"You didn't answer my question, Astra."

She gave him an inquisitive look.

"Were you close to your daughter?"

A hundred answers flashed through her mind. "Yes, very."

"My report says you were estranged, that you hadn't seen her or spoken to her in quite some time."

She looked down and conjured Constantin's wracked sobs as she held him in her arms, her daughter's body stiffening a yard away. Her shoulders began to shake. "Well, you have good sources, officer. I have not been a stellar mother. But I got a call from Kim on Friday telling me she'd met someone and that they were going to get married and I, I had a change of heart, and I decided I wanted, really wanted this time, to be a part of my daughter's life again. And I prayed..." now the tears came "...that it wasn't too late. I didn't know. Would she reject me? Would she refuse to try to have any kind of relationship with me? I wouldn't have blamed her, oh I wouldn't have blamed her at all, but when I saw her standing on my doorstep after so many years, officer, I could have cried with happiness..." and then she lost it, sobbing hard into her lap. The chief got up, walked around his desk, and laid a meaty hand on her shoulder.

"I'm sorry I've upset you, Astra, but I'm just doing my job," he said in a low voice. "Can I have one of our men accompany you home?"

· TWENTY-NINE ·

In a seafood restaurant called the Gull's Nest in Gloucester, a mile south of Rockport, retired couples finished off their rice pudding and lemon meringue pie. By ten they had settled up with the waitress and said their goodbyes to the proprietor, who had the place mopped and locked up by ten-thirty.

The apartment above the restaurant was dark when Ellen and Tom, tired but happy, pulled into the narrow drive with their new daughter.

Ellen carried Lucy to the part of the living room that had been partitioned off with girlie pink curtains, referred to as the nursery for two months now. She nestled Lucy in the bassinet and sat beside her, lost in admiration for her new little girl. She should have been exhausted but she felt buoyant and awake. Lucy gurgled contentedly, yawned once more, and fell asleep.

Tom rested a heavy, sun-browned hand on Ellen's shoulder and she kissed it. "Good work, my dear. She's going to be a beauty, like her mom."

"She's going to be happy, and well educated, and have exactly the life she wants."

"Well if she's going to have all that, I better hit the hay." He bent over and kissed Lucy on one velvety cheek.

"What time do you head out?"

"Call is at four, load up, out by five."

She stood up and went to him. He held her close. "Your family will miss you," she said.

"I hate this, Ellen, but I have to – "

"Another year. I know."

"And the take is getting better. Each time we go out we've been filling the hold before the week is out. I might be back by Thursday – "

" – or Wednesday, like last week."

"Or Wednesday. Good night, Ellen." He cupped her breasts which were swollen with milk, kissed them lightly through her cotton shirt. "I love you."

"I love you too, Tom."

· THIRTY ·

Astra opened the door inch by inch, closing it behind her as quietly as she could. She was pleased to see that Constantin's roommate, a Jamaican man who had been hallucinating and mumbling to himself incessantly, was no longer in the room. His bed was tightly made, as if he had never been there.

She sat in a chair next to him. The TV above his bed was tuned to the world news: the president's diplomatic visits to Cuba, Russia, Spain. Car commercials, pop stars gyrating in a parody of lust, egg substitutes, life insurance. Still Constantin lay on his side facing away from her. She watched his gentle breathing for several moments. Just being alone with him, even like this, gave her some vestige of peace.

She whispered his name. He didn't move. "Body parts have been found in garbage bags behind the Roxy night club in Boston; a drug deal gone wrong is suspected..." She muted the sound on the TV.

She got up and walked around the bed, dragging her chair with her, then carried it, not wanting to make too much noise. His thick black hair was matted and dirty. He lay with his eyes open, but did not acknowledge her.

"Constantin, can you hear me?"

Nothing.

"It's Astra." Her voice cracked unexpectedly. She briefly stroked his shoulder, then pulled her hand away. "It's been a couple days, Constantin. I hope you've been getting some rest. Have you?" She glanced around at the spare, bright room. "Have they been good to you here?"

96

He blinked, but didn't look at her.

"I brought you some brownies...I didn't make them, but they looked great in the store. I've already had two, I'm afraid." She took the gooey tray out of the grease-stained paper bag. The smell of chocolate filled the room. "You do like brownies, right?...I remember, back at the house, how much you liked sweets."

He continued to stare through her. She turned around to look in the direction his eyes were fixed. The blinds, opened slightly, revealed a moonlit, near-empty parking lot.

"Do you want to look outside? Should I open the blinds?" She got up and drew them open. The light from a streetlamp shone in his eyes. He rolled over.

Encouraged by any reaction at all, she brought her chair back to the original side. "Sorry, I didn't mean to blind you." She hung her head as she realized her gaffe. "God, I can't believe I said that."

He blinked hard, but only stared through her as she spoke.

"I came to see you because I can't sleep. I haven't slept since...that morning, and I don't know if you have either. They say you haven't. I never could have imagined such a nightmare, Constantin. I can't imagine what you must be feeling. It's beyond my capacity, I think. They're doing a...thorough investigation and they think they've got some leads. There were a lot of break-ins nearby, so they think it's the same guy. They'll catch him, Constantin. I have such a good feeling about that, and he'll be off the streets and never hurt anyone ever again...and who knows? Maybe he'll get death." Trembling, she reached out and touched his hand. "Maybe they'll kill him."

Then he moved. She pulled her hand away. He curled down deeper into himself, pulling the covers over his head. Underneath, his shoulders began to shake.

"Oh, Constantin, did I say the wrong thing? I do that a lot. Sometimes I don't know what I'm doing. I...upset people, make them angry. I don't even know how I do it sometimes..." She started to cry. "But I just do it. Something's not right about me, but you...you make me feel better. I came here because I can't stay at home. It's where it happened, and you loved her and I loved her and I can't be alone. I'm so tired, and so worried, about you and everything else. I'm a wreck. I've never felt so alone..."

She watched his body shake under the sheets. She was desperate to touch him, in pain that he was not touching her. "Constantin, please don't think I'm crazy, but can I lay down with you a minute, just so I can relax?" Tears streamed down her face and her hands shook so she could barely open her purse to find a tissue. "I just can't relax."

His body grew still under the sheets, and she began to shore herself for rejection. Shuddering with exhaustion, she began to button her jacket. "Well then, I guess I'll just visit tomorrow and you get caught up on – "

The sheets trembled, then lifted. He lay there in his johnny looking at her. He looked thinner than she remembered, his eyes still hollow but with a glimmer, far back in them, like a light deep in a cave.

She kicked off her shoes and climbed up on the bed, curling her back into him. Minutes after he draped his arms over her they were both fast asleep.

In the morning she woke in precisely the same position in which she had fallen asleep. Gently, she lifted his arm off her and laid it along his hip. She crawled out of bed, slipped on her shoes and fixed her hair as best she could in the bathroom mirror. Constantin didn't stir. In all the years that were to come, they never talked about the previous night. She was convinced he didn't remember it.

· THIRTY-ONE ·

Kim's funeral took place on a scorching summer day. Hot breezes carried the scent of strawberries and clover, while dozy bees dipped into heavy, blown-open peonies. The mourners perspired under black as the pastor read a eulogy penned by Adrienne, a shy, overweight classmate Kim had befriended in their chemistry class. Through dark sunglasses, Astra watched Adrienne's pudgy face as she read from a piece of paper torn out of a notebook, thinking: if this is all I'll have to deal with, then I'm home free.

Adrienne blew her nose and continued, occasionally batting a wasp away from her face. "Kim overcame her disability to accomplish great things, even in the short time she spent at Barnesdale. Everyone loved her easy laugh, quick wit, and kind ways that touched everyone..."

Yikes, Astra thought, did she write this on her way to the cemetery?

Next to her Constantin sat slumped but aware, his eyes impossibly sad, hands piled in his lap like dead birds. Beside him his parents – suburban, attractive – sat looking, if anything, confused. Mrs. Damler took her son's hand occasionally during the service, but he withdrew it languidly.

Next to Mr. "Call Me Chris" Damler was a woman Constantin had never met, but was obligated by Adrienne to reach through the Stafford School. A tiny woman in her seventies at least, so short her feet didn't touch the perfectly trimmed grass under her chair. Carmella was her name, and of everyone there, Astra got the worst feeling from her. The woman examined her openly, staring at her a good deal more than the twenty-eight-hundred dollar coffin dressed in a garden's worth of roses, more than

99

the pastor or the boyfriend. Astra stared back through her dark glasses, daring the woman to look away. She didn't, even as Kim was lowered inch by inch into the earth.

After the service, everyone gathered at the Damler's home, a mansion an hour north of Rockport. The Damler's maid, eyes downcast, filled Astra's wineglass before she rushed back in the kitchen to bring out the food. There were a lot of covered dishes: sober meats, steaming casseroles, heavy cheese platters, and plenty of wine on hand. Astra joined Chris Damler in the oversized den where he gave Adrienne a tour of the heads of wild animals he had shot: boar, deer, black bear, fox, moose, and so on. He described in detail the "minimal mounting procedure" used on them, so they looked as though they were "leaping through the wall." Their eyes shone hard as beetles, their mouths open in a snarl. Adrienne followed him dully, sometimes touching an ear or a tooth as she sipped her Diet Coke.

Constantin had wandered to the backyard garden, where he stood drinking a scotch and staring at the sloping hills in the distance. An azure swimming pool framed in jewel-colored tile sparkled nearby. Astra watched him longingly from the kitchen window as she tried to engage herself in Mrs. Damler's chatter.

"It must be very hard, what you do, Astra, your work. Oh, I remember when Constantin was a teenager, he could sure get himself wrapped up in the craziest schemes! He wanted to be an astronaut and would tinker around in the basement – we never knew what he was doing down there, oh my dear, until one day – " Astra watched that old crone Carmella make her way, her cane as gnarled as she was, toward Constantin. She touched his back and he turned toward her. When she reached up to shake his hand, their hands lingered together, until he pulled her toward him and bent down to hug her..." – I'll never forget, he almost blew up the house! We heard this – kaboom! and went rushing downstairs. Broken glass everywhere. Constantin was fine, a little shaken up but still smiling. That's just the way he was. Nothing got him down..." Astra nodded, doing her best to force the corners of her mouth to rise. Constantin and Carmella, hand in hand, walked to a wrought iron bench and sat down, their heads close as they talked.

"An astronaut, that's interesting." Astra quaffed the rest of her wine.

Mrs. Damler's nose wrinkled as she watched Astra drink (sipping her Perrier), then forgave the woman her third glass of pinot grigio in an hour. God knows what sort of poison she'd be swilling if her Constantin had been in Kim's place. "Do you have any other children, Astra?"

"No. Do you?"

"Just our dear Constantin. Oh Astra, I can't tell you how sorry I am. Such a beautiful, bright girl. And they were so in love! I think if I were you I'd still be like Constantin was these past few days...thank God he came out of it. Lord knows how it happened. We visited him, but it was as if we weren't even there. Poor dear..." She started to cry. "Oh, here I go crying about my son, and he's *fine*..."

Astra took her by the arm and led her to the bar where she poured herself another glass of wine. "Would you have a drink with me, Mrs. Damler?"

She didn't see how she could refuse.

· THIRTY-TWO ·

They were well into their cups when Constantin and Carmella made their way back to the main house. Constantin approached them while Carmella poured herself a cup of tea.

"I'd like to get going, if that's okay with you, Astra," he said.

His car was still at her place. She knew he'd need to get it eventually, but assumed he was going to stay with his parents a few days.

"Honey, what are you talking about – "

"I have things to do, Mother. The world doesn't stop because horrible things happen..."

"But you're in no shape to do *anything*, honey, and we thought we'd go for a sail tomorrow to take your mind off things – "

"No, Mom, no pleasure trips yet, pl – "

"Not pleasure, just – "

"Are you okay to give him a ride, Astra?" his father interjected, "because we can take him down by you if you'd like."

"Don't even think about it, Chris. I was headed home after this anyway."

"Oh, son, I just hate to think of you alone at a time like this." Mrs. Damler got up and hugged him tightly. She was a small woman, but she almost knocked him off balance. The chardonnay was kicking in.

Carmella put her cup down and approached the group. Standing, she was an inch or two taller than Astra was seated. She held out her hand to Astra, who shook it slowly as she looked into her eyes.

"I have wanted to meet you for many years, Dr. Nathanson."

"Call me Astra."

"I think I call you Dr. Nathanson."

"As you wish, Carmella."

"Since you are giving rides today, do you mind taking me to the train?"

Astra appraised the tiny woman; the gun metal grey hair tight in a bun at her neck, the faded black purse cinched under one arm. "I'd be delighted."

Carmella sat ramrod straight in the front seat while Constantin lay down in the back. In silence, they pulled out of the drive and onto the main road. Astra turned around after a few minutes to find him asleep with one of her sweaters balled up as a pillow. He looked so crumpled and exhausted and sad.

"It's okay if I smoke, Dr. Nathanson?"

"Just crack the window. It's fine."

She lit up a home rolled cigarette. Astra glanced at it and smiled. "That tobacco?"

"Of course it's tobacco. I'm an old woman. I don't do drugs." She fired it up and inhaled deeply.

"Is that Drum?"

"Yes. Do you smoke?"

"No, well, a long time ago." East Berlin, 1935, in a factory that made shoe soles, she used to spend her breaks on the loading platform smoking with the other women. She could still see the black grit eternally under her fingernails as she rolled one after the other. Three cigarettes was exactly fifteen minutes, and then it was back to the windowless factory floor with her reluctant co-workers.

Carmella stared at Astra. "Most Americans don't know about rolled cigarette. You were born here?"

"Columbus, Ohio."

"I was born in Milan."

"It must be beautiful there." She'd been there hundreds of times.

"It doesn't matter. What matters is I've lost my Kim."

Astra cleared her throat and glanced back at Constantin: still asleep. "*We've* lost Kim, Carmella."

Carmella stared straight ahead. "You remember me, Dr. Nathanson?"

Astra's hands tightened on the wheel. "No, should I?"

"I was there the day you...drop off Kim at the Stafford School."

"What do you mean you were there?"

"I work there thirty-eight years now."

"Well, it is remarkable that you remember me, after all this time." She pulled into the train station, taking the turn a bit too fast. Constantin stirred but didn't wake. They idled in the lot.

Carmella turned to look at him. "He's a nice man, just as she said. She plan to introduce me to him on Friday."

"I'm told you and Kim were very close."

She stared at Astra. "Do you think they catch this person, the one that did this?"

"I don't know. The crime scene wasn't...perfect."

"Interesting that you say 'crime scene.' It is so formal."

"Just trying to distance myself, I guess."

"I see."

Astra cleared her throat and tapped her manicure on the wheel. "Constantin says he'll take Marty."

"That seems right to me."

Astra gestured at a waiting train. "Is that yours?"

Carmella turned to the train, then back to Astra, one hand resting on the door handle. "So you think you are free, now, do you?"

"What are you talking about?" Though the air conditioning blasted full tilt, heat flushed up Astra's neck to her face.

Carmella opened the door, got out, and leaned in the passenger window. "You will come back. Again and again."

Astra lurched to the window, teeth bared. "I am in love," she hissed. She glanced back at Constantin who snored softly. "For the first time, for the last time. It's over."

Carmella stared at her with watery eyes. Her voice was firm and strong. "You've learned nothing, you know nothing. You are a curse on this world." She turned and started toward the train, a tiny woman all in black in hundred degree heat.

Astra jumped back into the driver's seat and slammed the car into drive, racing it up alongside Carmella in the parking lot.

Carmella's head was level with the car window. "You think anyone will believe you, you crazy old hag?"

Her face grimly set, chin up, Carmella kept on in silence.

"I'll kill you, I swear I will."

Shoulders squared, Carmella reached the stairs to the platform, climbed them, and boarded her train.

· THIRTY-THREE ·

Astra took her time turning into her driveway, silently rehearsing different ways of convincing Constantin to stay the night. She pulled up next to his car and stopped, tuning the radio to a classical station. She closed her eyes and eased back on the headrest, giving herself up to a Rachmaninov prelude.

Constantin stirred, then sat up. "That was fast."

She turned around. "You were sleeping."

"It's either I can't go to sleep, or I can't stay awake, nothing in between." He reached for the door handle.

"You know you can stay over, Constantin – "

He sighed deeply, then spoke as if it took all his strength. "I can't stay in your house, Astra, you understand – "

"Oh yes, I do. Of course I do." She touched his hand. He allowed it for a moment, staring at her hand as if it were some disembodied element, then took his away and looked out at the sea. The setting sun rimmed low clouds in strips of orange across a turquoise sky.

He said, "I feel like offering my place to you. I mean, how can you stand to be here either..."

"I live here, for now, so I have to stay here."

He sighed and smoothed his wrinkled clothes with his hands. "I better go."

"Your things are in the car?"

"Yes."

"Are you sure you're okay to drive? I mean, I can put you up in a

106

whole different section of the house. There's a finished basement, with your own entrance – "

"No, Astra, I can't. If I do I'll never leave."

Weeks later she was still analyzing that statement. Did he mean they would be together? Or that he would go back to a vegetative state of mourning and never come out of it?

She got out of the car and opened his door. Every move an effort, he pulled himself up and out of the backseat and stood shuffling through his pockets for car keys. His hair stood up, he smelled a little rank, and his stubble was well on its way to a full beard, but all she wanted was to wrap him in her arms and take him inside.

He reached out to hug her. "I don't know what to say," he said, with a dry sort of sob.

"I don't either."

"I'll say goodbye, for now." He let her go and got in his car, started it and backed up without looking at her.

"Goodbye, Constantin," she said to the sandy clouds his wheels had kicked up.

The moment he was gone she craved his image. Her eyes hurt, her head pounded, she felt sick with loss. She remembered the photographs she'd taken over the weekend, grabbed the camera from the house and jumped back in her car, racing to a nearby pharmacy to have them developed.

She sat down in the store and waited, then got up and paced among the magazines and candy, unable to concentrate on anything but Constantin. The middle-aged woman at the counter who'd taken her camera and memory card couldn't stop staring at her.

"I'm sorry to bother you, ma'am, but are you the woman whose daughter was killed last weekend?"

"How did you know that?"

She showed her the headline in the Rockport Beacon. "Daughter of

Local Psychiatrist Murdered." There were four or five lines of copy, and a picture of Kim. In the picture she looked sighted, as if she were staring straight at the photographer. Astra blinked and looked away, perspiring. She hadn't yet dared to look at the coverage online.

"I just wanted to say how sorry I am. You must be devastated."

"Yes, well I am, actually."

"Do they know who did it?"

"They're investigating, of course."

"I just want you to know that this whole town feels for you, and if there's anything any of us can do, even though none of us knows you real well – "

" – just...there's nothing anyone can do. I need to deal with it myself."

The woman tilted her head and looked at her oddly. "I guess you do, then, I guess you do." She held up Astra's camera. "I don't want to intrude any further, but are these pictures of your daughter?"

"Yes, they are."

"Listen, I'm going to do these next. It'll only take ten minutes or so, okay? Everyone else will just have to wait."

"Thank you."

In five minutes, the woman approached the counter. "What a beautiful girl. I don't know what to say. Take care of yourself." The woman waved Astra away when she took out her wallet and had tears in her eyes as she handed over the packets of photos.

On the living room rug, next to an almost empty bottle of merlot, Astra sat poring over the photographs. How clever she had been to take pictures of him, in the morning laughing and drinking coffee, on the porch sipping brandy, wind-whipped on the boat just before the storm blew in. Carefully, with a small, precise pair of scissors, she cut out her daughter's image from every photo. She cut out images of herself and put them next to Constantin in a scrapbook, painstakingly placing and gluing them together so that in some instances, it looked as if his arm was around her, or that it was she he was gazing at so lovingly. All the images of Kim she put in a small ceramic bowl. She took one (Kim standing on the deck, otherworldly beautiful in her robin's egg blue robe, arm cut off where it had been around Constantin) and lit it from a flame on the stove. The small pile of Kim-faces in the bowl caught fire and burned steadily, till they were a blackened lump of smoking plastic. She placed the bowl in the sink, filled it to the top with tap water, gathered up the scrapbook and lay down on the couch with it.

She placed it on the coffee table so it was eye level with her when she lay down. She touched a photo of him, tracing his hair, the strong cut of his chin, the tuft of chest hair where his shirt opened at the neck, all the way to his belt buckle, where the photo ended. She unbuttoned the first few buttons of her blouse and caressed her own breast, remembering a moment when he had accidentally brushed up against her on the sailboat during the storm. Her other hand slid down into her jeans and under her silk panties. Moaning, she pressed her head back hard on the damask pillows as her hips began to buck.

The smoke alarm sounded, bleating and whooping.

She jumped to her feet and whipped around. Flames leapt from the sink, as if someone had filled it with mounds of dry kindling, soaked it with gasoline and lit it. The heat blasted her back as the cupboards above caught fire. She stood rigid as a row of wine glasses exploded one by one and a line of fire raced along a window frame. Still the flames shot up from the sink, as if blown up from the cauldrons of hell.

Finally she moved, darted to the pantry, knocked aside a vacuum cleaner and old shoe boxes and lunged for a fire extinguisher. Her eyes skimmed over the instructions, the words making no sense at all, saw a red plastic circle and pulled it. Careening out to the kitchen, she sprayed at the flames, knocking them out with the white foaming chemicals until she reached the source of the fire: the little ceramic bowl which still roared with life, as if fed by some hidden well. She aimed at the heart of the fire, straight at it for over a minute until finally it ebbed and died, smoldering still with a terrible reek.

Panting, she wrapped her hands with dish towels and picked up the bowl. She wrenched open the sliding doors, ran out to the deck and hurled the bowl and its contents over the rocks and into the sea. Not waiting for the splash, she jumped back inside and locked the doors behind her.

· THIRTY-FOUR ·

She wore a dark blue suit on Thursday, the day she returned to her office and regularly scheduled clients. Her supervisor, Dr. Ivy Artois, a big clammy woman in her mid-sixties, greeted Astra as she entered the building, almost plowing into her in the foyer.

Wordlessly, Ivy hugged Astra, encasing her slender frame with all that maternal flesh. Astra shuddered and looked over Ivy's shoulder to her office and waiting area, where flower arrangements crowded almost every surface. She watched her assistant's head rise up from behind a bunch of waxy white lilies, phone pressed to her ear, and nod toward her with a look of great gravity.

Eventually, Ivy released her and held her at arm's length, searching in her eyes, Astra thought, for signs of grief. But her eyes were clear and she knew it, and she stared straight back defiantly.

"I can't believe that you're already back here, Astra."

She wanted to shake off the woman's grip but restrained herself. "It does me no good to stay at home and think about it," she said.

"Of course, of course. But don't be so hard on yourself. If you decide you need to take a week off, a month, whatever it is, you just let me know, okay? And you know my door is always open for you."

"Thanks, Ivy, I'll keep it in mind." She glanced at her phone. "I, uh, I have a three o'clock."

Ivy made a "be my guest" gesture; Astra walked past her, down the hall toward her office. Her assistant, Frances, who was constantly on the phone with her boyfriend, recently fiancé, stepped out of her cubicle and came toward Astra, arms outstretched. Oh please, no more hugging, Astra thought, but it was too late. Frances wrapped her arms around Astra and squeezed her tight for a good long time, saying again and again how sorry she was. After more of this than she could bear, Astra peeled the woman's arms from her.

"Please, Frances," Astra said, looking into her moist eyes, "I'm okay. I'm not great, but I'm okay."

"Oh, when I heard about it, well Billy read about it online you know, I just...well I almost fainted. I wanted to call you but you're unlisted and Billy said maybe I should leave you be, you know, to do what you had to do. But are they going to get this guy? Do they have anything on him? I mean – "

"Frances, is my three o'clock here?"

"Yes," she said, sniffling. "She was early this time."

"Well, I better get in there then."

Frances watched Astra open her briefcase, remove a few papers, close it, and take a moment to adjust her high-necked blouse.

"She was very beautiful, your daughter."

"Frances, would you understand if I told you I can't talk about that right now?"

Frances stiffened and began to walk back behind her desk. "Of course, Dr. Nathanson, I'm...thoughtless, you're trying to – you need to – okay."

"What's after my three o'clock?"

Frances flipped the desk calendar open. "You've got Gerry at 4:30, then group at 6. That's it. Listen, if you want to go for coffee between your three and your 4:30 – "

"I don't think so, Frances. I've got a lot of paperwork to catch up on. Maybe some other time, all right?" She turned and disappeared into her office, closing the door behind her.

Ivy walked up to Frances, rested her big elbows on the counter and sighed. "You know, I'll bet it hasn't really hit her yet."

"Maybe not, but I'd be a basket case."

"It's funny, I didn't even know she had a daughter till this happened."

"Me neither."

"She is a bit of an odd bird."

Frances smiled. She wasn't beautiful, but she was twenty-five. "Glad you said that, and not me."

"Takes all kinds to make a world, my mother used to say."

A puddle of a teenage girl all in black with candy pink hair slouched in the overstuffed chair across from Astra, both wrists wrapped in fresh white gauze.

"...it sounds to me like you've just never been there."

"Been where, Melissa?"

She met her eyes with a melodramatic kohl-ed squint. "In love. I mean *really* in love."

"This isn't about me."

"Yeah, yeah, it's about *me*. But how can you help *me* if *you*'ve never experienced true love. It's impossible." She looked away, chewing absently on a chipped black fingernail.

"Why do you assume I haven't experienced love, Melissa?"

"Stop saying my name, okay? I know what you're trying to do."

"What am I trying to do?"

"Make me like you, some shit like that. It's not happening. I'm not liking you. I'm not getting better."

"It's not up to me to make you better, it's up to – "

" – me, blah blah blah. Christ, you people are all alike. Except you're worse."

"And why's that?" She knew this was the wrong path, but took it anyway.

Melissa narrowed her eyes, leaned forward in her chair, and hissed, "because you're a cold fish, I can see it in your eyes. You've never loved a man like I have. Never fucked like I have, until you're red and raw and it hurts but you want more, you want them to rip you in two, like you've finally found your other half and fucking them was like breathing, like the air that you breathe, that's how badly you needed them." She sat back, pleased with her speech. "You would never die for anyone."

"Is dying for someone proof that you love them?"

"Of course it is. It's about passion, something you would never understand."

"Do you wish you were dead today, Melissa?"

"Stop calling me – "

"It's your name. I'm going to use it. Can you answer my question?"

"Yes!" she shrieked. "I wish I were dead!"

"Why?"

"Why? *Why?* Because he left me for my best friend! Are you stupid? Are you thick, deaf, *retarded?* What else do you need to know?" Her voice cracked. She raised a wounded wrist and pressed it to her mouth.

"There will be other boys."

Melissa shook her head and stared out the window. "Why do I bother? Why do I come here. No one understands..."

Astra shifted in her seat, stealing a glance at the clock. Good lord, only five minutes had passed. "Maybe you could think about – "

Teary eyed, she turned back to Astra. "Can I leave now?"

"You just got here."

"This isn't helping me."

"I'd rather you stayed."

"What's the matter? You don't get paid if I bag out early?"

"I get paid no matter what."

"Well, I'd rather go, and I would, but it's too goddamned boring in my room, and my roommate's a pain in my ass. She takes about fifty showers a day. I can't even take a piss."

"So are you trying to tell me that every time a boy breaks up with you

you're going to do this to yourself?"

The girl just blinked at her.

"Do you understand that if you ever are successful at killing yourself, that it's over, that death is final?"

"How would you know?"

Astra shifted in her seat. "What...what do you mean, 'how would I know?'"

"Just what I said. You don't know anything about life after death. It could be beautiful, it could be painless, there could be everyone you ever loved waiting for you, waiting to wrap their arms around you. It could be chocolate cake and orgasms. You don't know."

"It's not...chocolate cake and orgasms. It's just more life."

"What does *that* mean, 'more life'? Anyway, how the fuck would you know? Typical, man, so typical for you to talk about things you know nothing about like you've been there."

Astra felt her loneliness yawn open like a bottomless well. How she wanted to scream and cry to this girl, this child, tell her everything, empty herself of her own truth.

Instead she sighed and looked at her perfectly manicured hands. The knuckles looked knobbier, veins more visible than she remembered. She lifted a stray curl that had come loose from her chignon and tucked it back in, penciling a note on her pad: "fantasizes afterlife is heaven."

"Keeping track of how fucked up I am?"

Astra put the pencil and pad down on her desk and turned to the girl. "So what are your plans, Melissa, after your stay here? Do you want to go back to school?"

"You know what my plans are, *Dr. Nathanson*, and they don't involve living."

· THIRTY-FIVE ·

Marty nuzzled at Constantin, who lay fully dressed in a rumpled heap on his couch, a bottle of scotch and several empty pizza boxes scattered on a nearby coffee table. The dog started to climb up and squeeze in next to him, but Constantin pushed him away and he landed on the rug with a thump. Marty picked himself up, meandered to the window, snuffled at the hot breeze blowing through the screen, gave up and lay down with a noisy canine sigh.

The phone rang every hour or so, but Constantin had turned the message machine off so the trilling went on sometimes for several minutes. The afternoon grew old and the shadows longer in the room, and Marty got up once again to nudge his new master out of sleep.

"Goddammit, Marty." But he pulled himself to a sitting position, dragged on his sneakers without tying them, and headed to the door with the dog at his heels. The moment they reached the pavement Marty lifted his leg and peed, eyes half closed with relief.

As Constantin rubbed the sleep out of his eyes, he felt a heavy hand on his shoulder. The head of the Marine Sciences department, Barry Kindler, stood next to him, hands on hips.

"You don't answer your phone?"

"Why in hell should I answer my phone?"

"Because I'm trying to reach you, and maybe other people are too."

"Well, I'm not available for fucking comment, okay? Didn't I ask for a couple of weeks here?" Constantin started toward the park across the street, Marty happily following.

Barry, a stringy man in his fifties with the nervous energy of a teenager, loped along beside him. "It's been a week – "

" – and I asked for two, so please leave me alone. Can you do that?"

Barry followed Constantin into the park, where they both stood and watched kids shriek with delight as they played a hard-running game of tag, ignoring the elaborate swingsets and jungle gyms. "You can drink yourself to death just as well down at Sully's with me."

"Oh, is it after noon?"

Barry glanced at his phone and answered him before he realized he wasn't serious. "It's four o'clock."

"Look, Barry, I don't want to drink with you. I don't want to drink with anyone but Marty over here, okay? Marty gets me. Marty understands. I don't have to explain anything to him. Christ," he said, his voice thickening, "Marty was there."

"Marty's a dog."

"Wow, you don't miss a trick, do you."

They sat on a bench and watched Marty scamper across the park chasing a squirrel up a tree. It escaped handily, but dropped an acorn it had been carrying in its mouth. Marty sniffed at the acorn, lost interest in the whole thing, then almost guiltily returned to Constantin. He lay down at his feet. "I should really take him back to Stafford and give him to someone who needs him. But I can't, yet. I can't right now."

"She'd want you to keep him."

"She'd want me to give him to someone he can help. I mean, this is a trained – "

"Jesus, Constantin, give yourself a break."

Constantin nuzzled the dog, who gazed at him with utter devotion. "He knows I can see. He's so smart, he knows that. He knows it's okay to take a breather and chase a squirrel."

"Hey, you keep up this drinking schedule, you may need his services after all."

Constantin held his head in his hands. He could smell himself, but he didn't care. He'd worn and slept in the same T-shirt and jeans for three days. He started to cry, his big shoulders shaking.

"Every time I close my eyes, I'm holding her in my arms, or what used to be her." He sobbed loudly. Children looked over, saucer-eyed. "Anything can happen, Barry, *anything*! Do you realize that? You could get a phone call about Sandy, or Mark, and your life could be over, in a second! Everything you love, gone."

"It's not fair, Constantin, I know."

"*Fair*? Fuck fair. I'm not asking for life to be fair, just not so – so random and senseless. She was…she was so beautiful. She made me feel whole, she made me feel like a woman's supposed to make you feel, in every way, in *every* way. You remember her, don't you?"

"I saw her a few times, just in the hallway."

"She was the most beautiful woman I've ever seen."

"Constantin, are you hungry?"

"No."

"Let's get a burger."

"Fucking burger, come on."

"Well, I gotta eat."

"So eat."

"So come with me. You can drink."

Constantin wiped his nose with the back of his hand. "Marty goes where I go."

"Bring the damned dog, then. And tie your shoes."

Slowly, Constantin reached down and began to tie his laces.

· THIRTY-SIX ·

Ellen took off her apron, heavy with change, and tossed it on the counter. She poured herself a cup of black coffee to go, and loosened her colt-red hair from its tight bun.

"You on the run again today, Ellen?" Mike said, wiping down the counter with well-practiced strokes. Jim and Jed, sixty-year-old twins who populated the place from four to close and favored Guinness, lifted their elbows in perfect sync, then lowered them again.

"If you're asking if I have the time to hang around with you drunks, the answer's no."

Mike laughed as he drew the twins their first pints of the night. The owner of the Gull's Nest, Mike had been Ellen's boss since she was a junior in high school, eight years ago.

"When do we get to meet Lucy?" Jed asked shyly.

Jim sipped his draft. "Is she as beautiful as you?"

"She's a hundred times more beautiful. I'll bring her down soon, but I have to help Sally with her now, then meet Tom at the docks." She balled up her apron and headed for the door. "See you tomorrow, guys."

"Seven o'clock, Ellen, not seven-thirty."

"Yeah, yeah. I'll be here." She pushed through the swinging doors into the brilliant sunshine, hoping to be able to get to town and get her hair cut and styled to look nice for when Tom came home before she had to relieve her mother of Lucy. But the second she stepped onto the sidewalk and heard her daughter's signature shrill cry, she knew she'd have to stop at home first.

She walked around the building to their side entrance and trudged up the steep flight, her feet aching after her nine hour breakfast and lunch shift.

The cries were even more piercing when she opened the door. She found her mother, Sally, a handsome woman in her mid-fifties, leaning over the crib with a bottle. Sally eased herself into a nearby rocker and wiped the sweat off her forehead. A fan whirred constantly but the tiny nursery was close and always too hot.

"Did you take her – "

"I took her out, Ellen. I walked her, burped her, she's had – "

Ellen picked up her scarlet-faced, screeching daughter. "Ooooooh, my little darlin's not so happy today."

"Ah well, she wasn't happy yesterday either, or the day before."

"Mom, you can go now, if you're tired."

Sally harrumphed and gathered her purse. "Well, a lot of thanks I – "

Ellen bounced Lucy in her arms. "Mom, I'm sorry. I can see you're tired, that's all."

"Well, you can't exactly be refreshed yourself – what is wrong with that child?"

Ellen laid her back down, adjusted the fan in the baby's direction; still she wailed. "Has she eaten?"

"She won't eat."

"I just pumped before I left, there's plenty – "

"She won't take it, Ellen. I heat it up just right, and she just isn't having it."

"So she's starving, then, that's it." Ellen picked her up again, cradled her, unbuttoned her white waitressing blouse and unsnapped her maternity bra. She caressed Lucy's head, holding her toothless mouth right at her nipple. Lucy grew still, then started up again, shrieking even louder than before.

"Look," Sally said, rising from her chair, "I'm going downtown to get some formula."

The baby was screeching so loud they could barely hear each other. They began to shout themselves. "No, Mom, she'll be fine. She's just – oh, who knows what's wrong."

"The doctor said she was fine, Ellen. No colic, just cranky. I'll be right back."

"No, Mother! I want her to breast feed."

"Ellen, that child hasn't eaten all day. Nine hours!"

"She just needs to calm down. She'll be fine."

"She's starving!" Sally straightened her shoulders, grabbed her purse, and headed for the door. "I'll be right back."

"Mother, no! She needs to – I want her to breast feed!"

The door slammed behind her.

"Mom!" she shrieked. "Come back!" She began to cry helpless tears even as she realized it was no use pressing Lucy, flailing and howling, once again to her swollen breast.

· THIRTY-SEVEN ·

Astra left her office at six sharp, not at all sure how she was going to fill her evening. Her kitchen was still a mess from the fire and reeked of burned wood and melted plastic. A few days of rain had sweetened the summer evening air. She fantasized she was meeting Constantin for a picnic by the ocean; that they would watch the sunset, wrapped in blankets and drinking wine. When the sun had set they would look into each other's eyes and declare their love for each other. Then he would kiss her and pull her down to the sand...

She almost drove off the road thinking of this, shook it off, and got back in her lane again. The closer she got to home, the less she wanted to be there. Suddenly she was hit, laid low, by the heaviest longing she had ever known. A boulder of yearning rested in her belly. She didn't want to go home, she didn't want anything but him. Anything else felt like emptiness, like a mockery of being alive. So this was love, she thought, this sick-as-a-dog feeling. How did I ever want this? Did I actually kill again for this? Compromise this incarnation for this feeling of deadness, of despair? She thought fleetingly of Melissa, the thin wrapped wrists, the firm resolution.

Astra winced, shaking off that particular idea. Who knows where she would come back again, and as who, or what? Stupid, boring teenager. That girl lacked a plan, she thought. She just needed to think things through a bit more. There are always choices; not always easy or convenient ones, but choices all the same. Cheered by the thought, her mood began to lift. Let love give her power, she thought; strength and stamina. The

122

boulder of longing turned in her belly, became limned with sweetness. Such a gorgeous world, she thought. And he was alive in it with her after all, a mere thirty miles away and linked to her forever through tragedy and circumstance.

It was just that, at the moment, he was a little tricky to get to.

She drove right past her house and into Gloucester, turning past the street where Lucy still wailed in her mother's arms, and kept on driving. Down the coast, past historic seaside homes, quaint bed and breakfasts, clam shacks crammed with tourists. She meandered through the outskirts of Manchester until she reached its center, looking for a library she knew of that used to be a church. It was just before seven when she pulled into the parking lot and walked through the Gothic arches and back to what had been the nave. The cool breath of the stone and mortar church wafted over her.

She paused at the romance section with a flash of understanding. For the first time ever, she understood the pull of the torrid covers: full-breasted women with heads tossed back, cinched and helpless in the arms of a swarthy sailor or no-good ex-con (always with hearts of gold). As a man, Astra had felt and acted upon lust; as a woman she had lusted but never loved. Sex had been a necessity like food – get what you need and move on. She browsed for a few minutes, deciding on *Stronger Than Passion*, and *Midnight Train Home* because the man on the cover (escaped prisoner, torn striped uniform) looked a lot like Constantin.

Tucking the books under her arm, she walked past the children's room, study rooms, biography section and tall stacks of fiction to what looked like the sole computer in the library. The librarian, a sweet-looking grandma who looked like she'd worked there forever, raised her head from her book.

"You know we close in three minutes, Miss. Can I help you find something?"

"I'm looking for anything you've got on oceanography or marine biology."

"Of course. We only have a small section on that, but let's have a look-see anyway."

Astra followed her to the back and up some narrow stone stairs where she imagined the church choir would have climbed, robes softly whispering, to sing hymns to the waiting congregation.

· THIRTY-EIGHT ·

Three weeks later, Constantin stood at the whiteboard, marker poised. He seemed to have shrunken, his shoulders sloped and defeated looking, his hair badly in need of a trim. All the students knew of Kim's death and most by now had heard the hushed whispers of their teacher's relationship with her. They waited for him to apply the marker to the board and finish a word he'd begun. A full minute passed before he turned back toward them, eyes downcast. He tossed the marker on his desk, grasped the chair, and finally raised his head to look at them.

"Since your teacher can't seem to...concentrate on the lesson, I guess I can't expect you to. Class dismissed."

The students quietly packed up their books and laptops and began to file out, avoiding his eye. Adrienne, Kim's friend who'd read her eulogy at the funeral, was the last to leave. Constantin had been sitting at his desk making notes in the syllabus for a few minutes before he realized she was still in the room.

She'd cut her wispy blond hair in a short, layered style that did promote her face a bit more than the lank pony tail she usually wore. She was an average student, but every time he walked by the marine lab she was in there, buried under books. Now she gathered them to her chest like body armor, and approached him wearing heels high enough to require thought for each step.

"Mr. Damler, I...I've been worried about you."

He rubbed his forehead and looked out the window at the grassy quad. Frisbee, a couple of his students kissing, an impromptu picnic. Life was going on, no matter what had happened. Realizing suddenly that she'd said something to him, he turned back to her. "I...there's no cause for concern, Adrienne. I'm just having a bad day. You understand."

"Oh, Mr. Damler, I do understand. I can barely eat, or sleep. I can't even imagine what you're feeling."

"Well," he shrugged wearily, "I don't know what to tell you. I'm certainly not at my best." He got up and put on his jacket. He realized how much taller he was than she, and noticed how low her blouse swept over her plump bust. She saw him notice, and was emboldened.

"Would you like to go out for a drink – coffee, I mean, and talk about it? It really helps, I think, to let it out."

He looked at her, and realized with some melancholy what it was she wanted. "Adrienne, that's very sweet of you, and I know she was such a good friend to you, but I don't think that's what I need to do right now. Thank you anyway."

She looked at the floor.

"I hope you're talking to someone professionally about this – it's not good to not eat or sleep."

"No."

"Well, maybe that's something you can think about."

She turned to the window and looked out. "Mr. Kindler's very nice, but he's not you, Mr. Damler. He doesn't bring it all alive like you do, the way you explain things."

"Thanks, Adrienne."

She turned back to him. "So, can we take a rain check on the coffee?"

"A rain check? Sure, why not."

"Will you be teaching on Thursday, then?"

"Of course. Just had a glitch today, a bad day, but I'll be here on Thursday, with bells on."

She made her way to the door, tottering in her heels. "I'll see you Thursday, then."

"Bye, Adrienne."

After she was gone he got up, shut the heavy door behind her and locked it. He went back to his desk, lay his head down on his arms and sobbed.

· THIRTY-NINE ·

Hours later a key turned in the lock, startling him awake. The janitor, Greeley, stood frozen with a mop and bucket. "Oh – Mr. Damler, I can come back..."

Reddening, Constantin fumbled to his feet and began to gather his papers and books. "Of course not. Come on in. I'll be out of your hair in two seconds."

"That's all right, Mr. Damler. Take your time."

It was sunset. Constantin left the thankfully almost empty building and walked to his car, one of two left in the lot. He tossed his briefcase through the open window and was about to climb in when he realized there was nowhere on this earth he wanted to go. Not home, not the lab, not anywhere. Nor did he want anything: food, sex, to teach another class as long as he lived, to do research. Nothing, none of it. Well, there's another version of hell, he thought – to not want anything. To be without desire, or to desire only that which has been taken from you for all time.

He leaned against the car, rubbing his almost fully grown-in beard with one hand, the other mindlessly sifting through change and papers in his pocket. He pulled out a card – his own, but on the back was Carmella's name and address, but no phone. Well, that's where he would go: 45½ Chandler Street, #2, Watertown, Massachusetts. Talk to a person who knew and loved Kim. The longer he thought about it, the less he felt he could do anything else in the world at that moment.

He walked the three miles to Watertown Square in what felt like minutes. When he reached Chandler Street, which bordered a cemetery on one side and a row of modest homes on the other, he almost wished he had a few more miles to go. He stood outside her home, an aging triple decker – all three porches sloped down dangerously – and looked up at the second floor. A light burned in one small window.

He rang the bell that said, "Nardizzi, C.," written with a crooked hand on ancient masking tape. It took a few minutes for her to get down the stairs. She creaked open the screen door and peered up at him, then took a step backwards, uttering a small sound like "Uh…oh."

"Hello, Carmella."

"Who are you?"

He realized he was maybe two grief-filled days away from looking completely homeless. "I'm Constantin."

She raised her hand to her face as if the words had struck her there; then moisture came to her eyes. This was the wrong thing to do, he thought, a selfish thing to do.

"I'm sorry. I didn't have your phone number, only your address. Look, I can leave, I can come back some other time – "

"This is good time. This is best time," she said, taking his hand and leading him into the entranceway. She blinked up at him through thick, smudged glasses and held his big hands with her small ones. "Here, where you stand, is the last time I see Kim alive."

Constantin shook his head and looked past her, down the narrow hallway to stairs that climbed into blackness.

"She was on her way to see you. She couldn't wait to leave her old Carmella and be with you. I knew something then, I felt something. I sent a sign…but it doesn't matter, she's gone now."

"It matters. Everything matters."

"I made spinach gnocchi with pesto. You like that?"

"I don't know what it is."

"Come up. I show you." She took his hand as if he were a little boy and led him up the worn stairs. He couldn't help smiling as he let himself be drawn into her small, dark apartment. Potted flowers and hanging plants crowded every window and completely covered a piano that dominated the living room. She switched on a stained-glass lamp that barely lit up the way to the kitchen. He stumbled over an ironing board but followed his nose to a card table spread with a lace cloth and flanked by two spindly chairs. The room was steamy with boiling pasta and garlicky fumes.

"You sit."

He did so. "I'm starving."

"Looks like you stop eating. Is that true?"

"Yes."

"I stop for two days, then I feel weak, so I eat." She dished out a big plate of gnocchi in pesto sauce and put it in front of him. "If we want to stay alive, we eat."

"Are you going to join me?"

"I eat already. You go ahead. I go get tomatoes from the garden to make salad." She wiped her hands, took off her apron and draped it over a chair, and left the apartment. Constantin took a tentative bite of the greenish doughy lumps, then, as if discovering food for the first time, devoured the entire bowl of pasta in minutes. He stood up with his plate and looked out the window. The old woman was bent over a minuscule vegetable garden that filled the tiny plot that was her backyard.

He was guiltily eyeing what was left in the pot when he heard her footsteps on the stairs.

She came back in the kitchen, her arms filled with fat tomatoes. "Have more," she said, gesturing at the pot of gnocchi on the stove.

"No, I'm fine," he said, and sat down.

She rolled the tomatoes from her arms onto a wooden board and began to slice them. "Have you heard from Dr. Nathanson?"

"No. Why do you call her that?"

"This is her name. I call her this."

"Don't like her too much, huh?"

She spooned the rest of the gnocchi into his bowl. "What mother would do what she did?"

"Well, Carmella, that's true, but we talked about it a little. She was having emotional problems and couldn't – "

"I'm not saying about leaving her at Stafford." She slid the cut tomatoes into a bowl and chose a plump red onion from a bin.

He put his fork down. "What do you mean, then?"

"She's very smart, that woman. I knew it the day I saw her, long long time ago. Smart, but also a monster."

"Carmella, some people can't take care of their own children. It doesn't make them monsters."

"Why don't you see what is right in front of you?" She put a bowl of salad next to him. He ignored it.

"What am I not seeing? Tell me."

She leaned against the stove, looking down at her hands as she dried them on a threadbare towel. "There was no robber that night, Constantin. Only Astra."

"How dare you say...how dare you say such a thing." He pushed his plate away.

"I dare because I see things, I know things." She shook the dish towel at him. "I remember her from before." She turned to the stove. "Ach, you wouldn't understand it. Simple, stupid man."

He got to his feet. He felt like a giant, towering over her. "You don't know anything. You weren't there. You didn't see what I saw. You have no idea how it was."

"You were sleeping, am I right?"

"Look, I better get going."

She followed him down the hallway and into the living room. "I sent you a warning – the tree in the storm – but you kept going – "

He whipped back around to face her. "Jesus Christ, how did you know about – "

"We can do things, even those who have come back a few times – "

"This is insane. I can't listen to this lunacy – "

Carmella grasped his forearm with a shaking hand, looked up into his dark eyes. "She killed her, Constantin."

He turned away, clutching the doorknob. "Carmella, I understand we're both out of our minds with grief. I can barely work, or eat, or sleep, and you want to blame someone, anyone. Maybe it makes you feel better, I don't know. Gives you some sense of order in this fucked up world. But tossing around insane theories does nothing for me, all right?"

A faucet dripped in another room. She cast her eyes down on the thick woven rugs that covered the floor, worrying the dish towel in arthritic hands.

"I'm sorry I swore."

She just shook her head.

"Do you have any children of your own, Carmella?"

"Not any more."

He closed his eyes. They burned with exhaustion. "Thank you for the delicious meal."

"I never see you again. Isn't that so, Constantin?"

He stepped out into the hall and turned toward her. "Carmella – "

She shut the door firmly behind her.

· FORTY ·

Though his stomach was finally full, Constantin left Carmella's apartment feeling worse than when he'd arrived. It was past ten but he knew sleep was not in store for him that night. He caught a bus to the square, intending to get off at his stop, but when it arrived he couldn't bring himself to get off the bus. For company he had a couple of college students making out in front of him and a drunk snoring in the back.

The bus roared down Mount Auburn Street, clattering from stop to stop. A blind man got on with a cane, his pupils swimming uselessly in the milky whites of his eyes. He stood for a block or two hanging onto a strap, then got off. Constantin sat and watched his hands tremble in the blue light of the bus. He sat on them to still them, wondering how he was going to get through the night. He didn't want to go home. Soon the bus descended into the bleakness of Barnesdale Station.

He climbed the urine-stained stairs of the underground bus station, past news stands and clots of teenagers eyeing him as they drank from paper bags. Some were suburban kids who had to get the last train home, almost indistinguishable from the real runaways and street kids. They crowded the subway entrance, clowning around on skateboards, panhandling, hanging out. He walked quickly past them, head down. They stepped aside.

He passed under a stone arch and made his way to the women's dorm where Kim had lived, a dignified brick building at the far end of the quad. He skipped the elevator and took the stairs three at a time in the dank stairwell to the fourth floor, passing a knot of girls in bathrobes smoking

132

weed. They tittered but he ignored them.

He reached her door, number 429, and fumbled at the lock with his key. He was near tears with anticipation, anxiety, and fear; he didn't know why.

Someone said, "Excuse me."

He whipped around. "What?"

The obese hall monitor, Sheila, whistle swinging from her neck, swooshed toward him in one of her trademark big skirts. "What are you doing?"

He gestured at the door. "I'm...I'm – "

"Professor Damler?"

"Yes, that's me."

She looked around. They were alone. "What are you doing here?"

"I'm cleaning up her room."

"Are you all right?"

He wanted to smack her. He leaned on the door, sweating. "Of course. I'm fine."

"Don't you think it's a little late to be doing that?"

He rubbed his forehead. "Late, early, what earthly difference does it make when I clean it out?"

"Well," she harrumphed. "We're waiting for her next of kin to clean out the room. Those were my instructions, anyway."

"I don't really care about your instructions," he said, opening the door and letting himself in. He switched on the light, a bare bulb in the middle of the room.

She followed him, glancing nervously around the dead girl's room. "Look, you have no right to be here, Dr. Damler, regardless of your relationship to her. I'm sorry to tell – "

"Just hold on, I'll prove I have permission," he hissed. He picked up the phone and, weirdly, remembered Astra's number.

Astra sat on her living room floor, surrounded by books on underwater exploration and the life of coral reefs. She was reading an article on the egg-laying rites of sea turtles when the phone rang. She got up to check caller ID.

KIM NATHANSON

She dropped her glass of port, staining the white rug a purplish red. Frozen in place, she watched the stain spread as she listened to her machine pick up.

Then she heard Constantin's voice. "Astra...are you home?" Like a balm, a sweet stirring, a caress of sound.

She exhaled and picked up the phone. "Constantin? What are you doing – "

"Listen, I'm here with Sheila – "

"Who's Sheila?"

"The hall monitor at Kim's dorm. I guess they were waiting for the next of kin – you – to clean out her room. But I'm here now, and – "

"May I speak to her, Professor Damler?" Sheila reached for the phone. Constantin thrust the phone into her hand.

"Would this be this Kim's mother?" Sheila asked.

"Yes."

"This is Sheila, and I'm the hall monitor here at Laurelie Dorm." She turned slightly away from him, fidgeting with the whistle around her neck. "Listen, I was told to not let anyone in this room but you, to...you know, collect your daughter's things. I know that Professor Damler was, uh, close to her but he's acting strange, I have to tell you, and I wouldn't let him in here if I were – "

"May I speak to him, please?"

"Of course." She reluctantly handed the phone back to Constantin, who sat on Kim's bed in a daze.

"What are you doing there, Constantin?"

"Astra, I need to clean out her room tonight. I can't explain it. Look, the thing is, I can't sleep." His voice cracked and he wiped his nose. "Okay, I can't function." Sheila sighed and examined her chipped nail polish. He went on. "I need your permission. Please. I won't throw anything away."

Astra got up and looked out her glass doors at the moon reflected in white slivers on the black sea. "I want to be there when you do it, Constantin."

"Now? It's pretty late, isn't it?"

"It's eleven o'clock," Sheila snapped.

"You sound terrible, Constantin. I'll be there in an hour."

"This is so nice of you, Astra." He looked around the room, red-eyed. "You were probably waiting until you could bear to do this yourself."

"But now you're there and I don't have to do it alone..." She wet a washcloth and rubbed at the wine, but only made the stain worse.

"Right, right. I'll see you when you get here. Drive carefully." He hung up the phone while Sheila glared at him.

"No visitors after eleven."

"She's not a *visitor*, Sheila, she's the mother of the girl who was killed who lived in this room."

Sheila stiffened. "Just keep the noise down. People are trying to sleep." She took a last look around the room, shook her head and pulled the door closed behind her.

· FORTY-ONE ·

Constantin lay down and stared at the ceiling, then closed his eyes and drifted off.

He fell into a deep sleep, slogging in blissful nothingness for a while, before he began to dream. He was back in Charleton, his childhood home, climbing high up on a path that bordered the Deerfield River until he came to the walking bridge called the Bridge of Flowers that connected Charleton to Shelburne Falls. As a kid he used to run full tilt across the narrow bridge with his friends, or fish off it, reeling in sluggish carp or whiskered catfish.

It was just past dusk, springtime, and the bridge was dripping in flowers, although it was too dark to make out colors so they all looked black or shades of grey. White moths as big as children's hands flapped at wrought-iron streetlamps that glowed a flinty green. Cool air floated up from the river. Crows squawked as they flew over him and dipped down toward the falls. Shivering in his thin jacket, he picked up his step to cross the bridge toward home.

A woman wearing a shawl draped over her head carried a baby in her arms. She walked in measured steps toward him across the bridge, which was slung high above coal-dark water. Now steam rose up thickly from the slow river, as if it were generating its own fog. Constantin was about thirty feet from the woman, but couldn't make out her face.

She paused on the bridge, staring at him. The shawl slipped from her head and rested on her shoulders. She was beautiful. He looked at her and smiled, but something was wrong. Her skin looked plastic and her teeth too white, as if she were computer generated, or a hologram. She called his name; he knew the voice but couldn't place it.

He raised his hand to wave at her but she was distracted by her baby, who had begun a thin wail. She looked down at it and arranged its wrap tighter, then glanced up again. Constantin gasped and fell back against the railing. The face of his own mother looked back at him now, her hair thick and wild around her face.

The baby had begun to scream, as if the woman were torturing it. She held the baby up in the air and shook it until its blanket fell away. It was a little boy, its skin glowing in the moonlight, its tiny lungs working shrieks that pierced the night. Constantin ran toward her but the bridge had become endlessly long; he must have run a thousand yards but was no closer to her.

As she watched him run toward her she snarled like a trapped animal. The whites of her eyes went red and her fingernails grew long and sharp, curling until they pierced the baby where she held him. She foamed at the mouth and shook him harder. Blood ran over his swollen belly and down his little legs. Constantin screamed, sprinting across miles of bridge, helpless as he watched his mother turn toward the river and raise the baby high in her arms. Her back was reptilian; a long row of dusky triangle-shaped humps ending in a thick black tail that swished powerfully back and forth across the path, sending up clouds of dust. His mother turned back once more to look at him. Roaring, she hurled the baby toward the river.

And there was silence.

No splash, no sound.

Constantin looked over the railing and saw the baby, so, so far down, floating on a bank of fog above the river.

His mother saw this too, lifted her leonine head, and roared again. Without thinking, Constantin jumped off the bridge and soared down through endless space. As he fell, he looked up and saw her spread enormous leathery wings and lift from the bridge, hover briefly, then dive down toward him.

Astra opened the door soundlessly and let herself in. She walked over to the bed and gazed down at Constantin as he slept. She wanted to fix him in her memory in every possible guise, every light, every mood. She wondered if she had had him as a son, if she would have loved him. Yes, she thought as she watched him turn in a fitful sleep, she would have been a good mother to him.

She sat next to him, reached down and stroked his hair. At her touch he woke screaming and grabbed her wrist so hard he nearly snapped it in half.

"Get away from me!" He shook himself out of sleep and looked at her, but still he gripped her wrist.

They sat there faced off, panting like two animals in a cage.

"What are you doing?" Astra said, finally.

"Oh my God, it's you." He let her wrist drop and fell back on the bed. "Jesus Christ, this is nuts."

"Who did you think it was?"

"Bad dream, Astra. Sorry."

She considered him. "Was I in it?"

He looked at her, the black hair cascading around her face, full red lips, smoky eyes. It was the first time he had seen her since the funeral. "Of course not."

She rubbed her wrist thoughtfully.

"Did I hurt you?"

"You didn't mean to."

She watched him as he took her arm and held it tenderly. "You'll have a bruise, probably." He sat up and combed his hair with his hands. "I think...no, I'm pretty goddammed sure I'm losing my mind."

"Everybody does now and then."

"You must be sick of crazy people."

"I'm not sick of you."

"I can't believe you get a call from me in the middle of the night and you just come over. How many people would do that?" He looked at her again. "It's good to see you, Astra."

"It's good to see you too, Constantin."

· FORTY-TWO ·

Astra had had the presence of mind to bring a few cardboard boxes, so they were able to sort through things and pack them up efficiently. One box for Constantin, one for Astra, and the rest for the Salvation Army or to donate to the dorm or return to the Stafford School.

Constantin kept some of the Braille books, though he couldn't read them; a favorite dress she used to wear; some CDs and her hairbrush. Astra held back her comments on the dress and hairbrush, as she puzzled over what would look good for her to keep. Of course she wanted no part of any of her daughter's junk. Why would the belongings of a poor blind girl interest her in the least?

She knew Constantin was watching her choose what to put in her box. She ended up taking a sweater, some simple costume jewelry, the talking alarm clock, and the model of the human heart Kim had used in class.

By four or so they had cleaned out the room of everything: clothes, computer, stereo, books, old collars for Marty, Marty's bed, makeup, bathroom implements. In the end the room was as it was when Kim moved in: four bare walls, a bed, a bureau, a desk and chair.

They packed up Astra's car and she drove him home. He insisted he would take the Salvation Army boxes over himself, so Astra was left with only her one "Kim keepsake" box in the back seat.

She was quiet on the way to his place, concentrating on how to ask what she was about to ask him. She helped him upstairs with his boxes and he walked her back down to her car. Reaching for the door handle, she hesitated, then turned back around to face him.

"So Constantin, tell me. I know this is an odd time to ask, but do you remember you said you were going to go down in that sub, and that you invited me along?"

"You mean the dive?"

"Yes. It's in a couple weeks, right?"

"Good memory, yeah. You want to go?"

"If I could."

He looked at her quizzically. "Well, sure, if I'm in any shape to go by then, I'll give you a call. Didn't you say you worked Saturdays?"

"I'll arrange something."

"Okay." They hugged awkwardly, the sky behind them pinking with daylight.

Astra drove home exhausted but pleased with her progress. He had given her an odd look when she asked him about the diving trip, but that was to be expected. Two weeks would make a huge difference in his grief process, she was sure of it.

She turned into her gravel drive just as a fingernail of sun glowed on a cloudless horizon. She sat there for several minutes watching it rise and grow to an orange ball just grazing the sea. Sighing, she turned to the back seat to take Kim's box of memorabilia into the house.

Her hand stopped stone cold, midreach. Maybe it was lack of sleep but she could swear something was happening with the box.

Some kind of movement.

Something seemed to be pushing up the lid from underneath, poking at it, dimpling the top and sides.

She blinked hard and looked again.

Still happening. A scrambling sound. Scratching.

What the hell was in there? Only a sweater, junk jewelry, the model of the heart. Crap she intended to toss in the trash as soon as she got home, anyway. She reached back again and started to peel off the masking tape holding the lid on.

She jumped back in her seat, screaming.

The lid burst off the box and shot to the top of the car with the force of millions of maggots that churned inside. They surged over the top of the box in sickening waves, covering the box and filling the back seat in seconds. Frozen with horror, Astra watched the back of her car fill with a roiling sea of larvae that bubbled up and up.

She squeezed her eyes shut, willing this nightmare away, then opened them. Larvae spilled over the headrests, flopping and oozing into the front seat. Shrieking, she leapt from the car and tore up the stairs and into the house, double locking the door behind her. She glanced around frantically, half expecting her house to somehow turn on her, but everything was quiet and in place, just as she'd left it late the night before. New kitchen cabinets sat in a row on the floor, ready to be installed. Books on oceanography and marine life lay scattered on the living room rug.

Trembling, she pulled back a curtain and looked out a window. The white squirming mass had vomited out the car window, now falling in bilious lumps on the green lawn. She gasped and turned away, yanking the curtains closed, her heart drumming in her chest.

With badly shaking hands she pulled out a bottle of Stolichnaya from the freezer, filled a tumbler with it, and knocked it back. She looked at the clock: 6:13 AM. Her first appointment at the clinic was at 8:30. She put the glass down, collapsed onto the couch, and held her head in her hands.

She's still here, she thought. She's come back, somewhere, alive. Like all who are murdered.

She stared at the curtained window and took a deep breath.

"But I'm still stronger," she said aloud.

She got to her feet and brushed her hair back from her face with her hands. I will not play into this, she thought. I will not dignify this illusion with my fear. Clearly this is the work of an amateur, a soul without a body, perhaps, or a soul in a body too young to be truly dangerous.

She stared at the flesh on her hands, willing herself not to slip back. Willed herself to stay human.

Avoiding all windows, she climbed the stairs to her bedroom. She put on her running gear and sprinted back down and out the side door (the one farthest from the car) and to the beach where she ran two and a half miles north (as timed in eight-minute miles on her watch) and two and a half miles back.

At home she took a long, hot shower, luxuriating in the morning sun through the skylights on her bare skin. When she stepped out, she turned rock music on crashingly loud and picked out her favorite suit. She spent extra time on her makeup and hair and carefully packed her briefcase for work. She fixed and enjoyed a breakfast of stone-ground oatmeal with banana, papaya juice mixed with flax seed, soy powder and antioxidants, and a double espresso.

She checked her watch: 8:03. Time to go. Standing at the top of the porch stairs, she gathered herself: her rage, her desire, her pasts – all of them, her formidable will. She started down the stairs and crossed the lawn.

She reached her car and looked down.

Just shiny green grass that needed to be mowed. Eyes averted from the backseat, she reached for the door handle and got in, turned the key in the ignition. The car purred to life. Only then did she turn to look behind her.

The box sat there, the lid taped shut as it had been before. Nothing moved. The floor was immaculate, as always. She put the car in reverse, turned around in the drive, and headed to the highway.

When she reached her building she turned off the ignition and sat for a moment. She turned to the back seat, picked up the box. Holding it fast under one arm, she made her way to a side door which was thankfully unlocked. It led to a dimly lit concrete stairwell. Brushing back cobwebs, she made her way to the basement and the boiler room. She thought she smelled something. Cigarette smoke? Pot? She looked around but saw no one.

Using her jacket to shield her hands from the heat, she opened the furnace. The opening was just an inch too small all the way around for her to be able to shove the whole box in.

She let loose an impressive string of curses. Looked at her watch: 8:31. Nothing to do but do it. Her face shiny with sweat, she peeled back the tape and opened the box. It was all there: the sweater, costume jewelry, alarm clock, the model of the human heart. She tossed it all in, piece by piece, and stood watching it burn.

· FORTY-THREE ·

Rain drummed on the roof as Ellen washed up the last of the breakfast dishes and stacked them on the rubber rack. She glanced at the grey day through the narrow kitchen windows and worried about Tom some more. Worrying about Tom was such an automatic gesture, having taken up brain and heart space every day and night for six years, she was barely conscious of it any more. She would not read and refused to rent "The Perfect Storm." She wasn't, in fact, interested in much at all about fishing; she only wanted him home and with her the brief times he was on dry land, even more so with the baby here. She thought that with Lucy, he would want to be home that much more as well.

The rain let up a bit as she sat drinking her coffee and considering which outfit to wear to go down and meet his boat. She was pleased that she'd gotten the night off, and since she planned to keep Lucy up most of the day, thought she would certainly go to sleep early and hopefully sleep the night.

A crash came from the living room. She slammed her mug down, coffee sloshing on her nightgown, jumped up and ran in the other room. A chunk of plaster, sodden and heavy from the rain, sat in pieces on the floor. She could see the sky through a six inch hole in the ceiling.

"Goddammit!" She ran to grab a bucket from the kitchen and put it under the hole. In a few minutes it was half full. A dark stain of moisture began to stretch across the ceiling.

She picked up the phone and dialed her mother, then slammed the phone down. What could her mother do about this? She cursed her life, she cursed their poverty, then she cursed Tom who had sworn he'd patched the leaky spot where the shingles had fallen off months ago. She watched the bucket fill, chewed her nails, brainstormed what to do.

She ran downstairs to the back of the restaurant where she dragged an industrial sized garbage can to her door. She took off the lid; it was crammed full of stinking bags. After lifting them out and stacking them in a pile, she lugged the garbage can up the stairs, into their apartment, and under the leak.

The whole exercise bought her an hour at most. She picked up the chunks of wet plaster, then dropped them, screaming. A dozen silverfish big as pocket combs scurried out across her hands and on to the floor.

The baby woke and began to whimper. Tom's boat was expected by noon and it was only ten, but she gathered up Lucy and her bottle and toy, tossed on a raincoat and ran out of the house.

It was a mile to the pier. She walked quickly, jostling Lucy. With each step she tried to calm herself. She knew Lucy would pick up on her hysteria, and sure enough, the infant began to wail. Ellen sighed and stopped for a while under a leafy elm where they took shelter on a relatively dry bench. She cooed at Lucy, kissing her sweet forehead, inhaling the baby smell, and held her close. Lucy's mouth formed an "O," made a sucking sound, but made no movement toward Ellen's always swollen breasts.

Ellen felt rejected, in a primal way, by her own child. Every few hours she pumped her breast milk and poured it down the drain. Ridiculous. Spent hard-earned money on fancy soy drinks and formulas the doctor recommended. He said he'd heard of this happening occasionally, and that Lucy was indeed lactose intolerant, but the information didn't comfort Ellen at all. She wished she could talk to Lucy and ask her why she didn't take her milk, if she was indeed her own child?

The rain slacked off to a fine mist as they sat. Relieved that her apartment wouldn't flood if she didn't get home in an hour, she got to her feet and hoisted Lucy to her hip. Lucy had calmed as well, seemingly fascinated by the verdant canopy above them.

They soon left their district of tiny cottages and falling-down triple deckers and turned onto Emily Way, where Victorian homes done up like wedding cakes adorned the street at stately distances. Each had a widow's walk. Ellen was sure the people who lived there had no use for such a thing, while she would have relished such a lookout to watch for Tom's boat.

Soon the road dipped down into the "business" district: a cluster of bars, restaurants, tourist shops, and the lone library, bank and town hall. Cobblestone streets criss-crossed and led her past the town's only Starbucks and to the Raven's Landing, a bar frequented mostly by fishermen and their girlfriends or wives. The air sparkled with post-rain freshness mixed with the smell of fish. Always the smell of fish.

She passed the yacht rebuilding factory and made her way to the public wharf. The closer she got, the less angry she was about the roof; she just wanted to see her Tom, to tell him all about how the week went with the baby, her problems with her milk, the small raise she had gotten just the night before. She wanted to flirt with him, tell him soon, soon they could make love again, but in the meantime they would manage...

His boat, the *Georgia Best*, sat docked at the wharf. She checked her watch: 11:17. She quickened her step until she was only a few yards away, then slowed. Stanley, a deck hand, was tinkering with what looked like a motor he'd dragged to the wharf. But where was everyone else? Hordes of people gathered when any fishing boat pulled in: families greeting their men, contractors emptying the hold of thousands of pounds of fish, and the unmistakable note of festivity in the air that the men had made it home once again, alive.

Queasily, she approached Stanley who looked up from his motor with greasy black hands. He looked so young. She would have been surprised if he was sixteen, the age Tom had been when they first met.

"Ellen, hey, how are you?"

"I'm just fine, Stan."

He got to his feet to make much of Lucy. "Here's the little girl that Tom won't shut up about." He reached out to touch her, then remembered his hands. "She looks just like you, doesn't she? Very cute."

"Thanks, Stan. So you guys have been in a while?"

He looked at her, a shadow passing over his face. He glanced down at the oily parts spread out around him, then back at her, a woman with a two-week old baby. "We got in last night, Ellen."

She blushed hard and kissed Lucy on the top of her head. "Do you know where he is?" She stared at the choppy grey sea.

"I could guess."

"That's all right, you don't have to do that." She turned back toward town. "Thanks, by the way."

He gestured ineffectually. "No problem."

· FORTY-FOUR ·

Her gait, clipped from her fury, slowed as she approached the Raven's Landing. If he was in there, what state would he be in? If he wasn't, where in the world could he be, and with whom?

Even at that early hour, she could hear the sound of male voices and laughter coming from the bar. It was time to feed Lucy again, so she slid the pacifier in her mouth, which she knew would calm her for about a minute. She was beginning to feel like a fool standing outside the bar holding her newborn; finally she forced herself to push wide the swinging doors.

Leslie, the bartender at the Raven's Landing for twenty-five years, was stocking beers in the cooler and didn't notice Ellen when she came in. Roy and his son Craig, both crew on the *Georgia Best*, sat nursing cups of coffee at the bar. Otherwise the place was empty.

"Ellen!" Roy said nervously. "Look who's here, Leslie."

Leslie turned, came out from behind the bar, and embraced Ellen. She was a big, friendly woman who'd seen just about everything over the years and who was known for her diplomacy. She'd lost two sons at sea and had her own problem with the bottle, but thought of her patrons as her family now, and treated them as such. "Look at this beautiful child. Whydja wait so long to bring her down, dear?"

"Oh, you know, work, this and that."

"What happened to her neck, here?"

"It's a birthmark. Look, have you seen Tom?"

Leslie led her to the back of the bar, away from the men. "He's here,

Ellen. He's upstairs."

Tears of rage and shame fell before Ellen could hold them back. Lucy started a pre-howling sort of mewl. "Is he alone?"

"Yes, yes. They all came in late last night and whooped it up. You know how they are when they first get in."

Ellen glared at her.

"I tried to make him at least call you."

"He hasn't seen his brand-new baby in a week. Pig."

Leslie's turn to be silent.

Ellen shifted the baby to the other hip and reached in her bag for the bottle of soy formula. "Do you mind heating this? A minute should do it."

"Right away, hon. You wait here." She took the bottle and headed to the kitchen while Ellen looked out the greasy windows at the rumbling dark clouds in the distance.

· FORTY-FIVE ·

"You should be glad she's too young to understand anything," Ellen said, cradling Lucy as she watched Tom gather his clothes. A bare light bulb swung above her head, illuminating the ragged futon on the floor, small TV in the corner, empty beer cans and cigarette-butt filled ashtrays.

"I've done nothing wrong, Ellen."

"Tom, you didn't come home last night. You think that's right?" Her voice strained with hysteria. "Who were you with?"

"I was alone."

"I don't believe you."

"Well," he said, giving up the search for his other sock, "that's your problem."

"You know I'll find out. I know who to ask. I know who'll tell me the truth."

"You can ask anyone in the bar, Ellen." He pulled his T-shirt over his wide, hairless chest.

"Was it Maddie? She's had her eye on you for months."

"She's married."

"Like that would make any difference to you." Ellen jostled Lucy, who sucked hard at the rubber nipple.

"Those days are over, Ellen."

"And these days are a vast improvement: you just don't bother coming home."

Tom reached out to hold Lucy, but Ellen swiveled away from him.

"You don't touch her. You're not fit to touch her."

"She's my child too." He tried again to take Lucy in his arms.

"No!" Ellen cried. "Stay away from me!" She backed up against the door, her eyes wild. "We just had a baby, Tom, and you work the boat for a week and don't come home the night you pull in? This is *our* baby, Tom, this is *our* new life together, this is what we've worked and planned for, for years! And you just don't come home? What sort of man are you? What sort of life is this?"

"Ellen, don't get crazy. I didn't think you would even know – "

"Don't you have any pride? Everyone knows I just had a baby and this is how you act? What the hell is wrong with you?" She grabbed a small lamp with her free hand and threw it at him. It missed and smashed on the floorboards.

Tom stared at her, then stuffed the rest of his gear into a lumpy knapsack. "I can't talk to you when you're like this." He headed for the door.

"Coward!" she shrieked.

He paused at the door. A timid knock from the other side. "Everything okay in there?"

"Fine, Leslie, we're fine," Tom said in a low voice.

They listened to her heavy footsteps go back down the stairs. He dropped his bag on the floor with a thud. The sound of their breathing filled the room.

"I thought you wanted a child," Ellen said softly.

"Of course I did…of course I do."

"Then you know where to find us." Ellen reached for the door but he caught her arm.

"I got drunk, Ellen. Pure and simple. I got drunk."

"You could have called me."

He looked down at the lamp in pieces on the floor.

"Why didn't you come home to us? Why didn't you *want* to come home to us?"

"I needed a break, okay? Just a little break. One night to get drunk with the crew and pass out in my clothes before I went home and was a good boy again. Can't you understand that?"

"You're a child, Tom. I have two children now. I have two children and a leaking roof and a shitty job and no future with a husband who doesn't bother coming home because he wants to play."

"The roof is leaking?"

"A huge chunk fell out of the ceiling this morning. You can see the sky. Thank God it stopped raining."

"Shit. Shit, I'm sorry, Ellen."

"What? I couldn't hear you. What are you sorry about?"

"You knew I was a fuckup when you met me." He lifted a stray wisp of hair from her forehead and tucked it behind her ear. She didn't move away.

"Oh, so now it's my fault I married you."

"Yes, exactly." Encouraged, he snuck his other hand over her shoulder, down her back and around her waist, pulling her and Lucy to him. "Everything is your fault, even my hangover. Especially my hangover."

"Well, I'm glad we cleared this up."

He kissed her lightly on the mouth. "You're very beautiful when you're angry."

"You're an asshole," she said, but kissed him back hungrily. Between them Lucy gurgled and blinked, her blue eyes wide.

· FORTY-SIX ·

Two weeks later, Astra pulled in to her reserved parking space at work. She sat there a moment, blasting herself with air-conditioned air before stepping out into the furnace-like heat of August. Wavy mirages like thin white snakes rose up from the browning grass, the too-hot-to-touch sidewalks.

In the first week she read three books on oceanography, one on marine mammals, and another on deep sea diving. She was almost pleasant to people at work. She lost three pounds, put subtle reddish streaks in her hair, bought an outfit she thought would be perfect for her day at sea with Constantin: casual yet devastatingly sexy jeans and sweater, earrings to match, a new perfume, and a new sundress should they go out for a meal afterwards. She didn't want him to associate her with how she'd looked before the incident – she wasn't Kim's mother; she was a brand new woman. A woman he couldn't ignore.

In the second week she'd lost a few more pounds, which she hadn't intended, so that a new gauntness threatened her cheeks. Running an extra mile or two didn't seem to tire her, or for that matter help at all when it came time to sleep at night. In fact, she hadn't slept well since the incident with the box, since she'd seen him last.

By Friday of the second week, she was not in a good way. Saturday was to have been the day she went down with him in the sub, but she hadn't heard from him.

Why in hell didn't he call?

From her car she watched bees bury themselves in the nectar of rows of phlox, then fly up, stupid with pleasure and satiety, only to drop into the next flower they came upon. Disgusted with herself, she picked up her cell phone and dialed in for messages at her home even though she'd only been gone half an hour. Nothing, of course. She felt like a neglected girlfriend, a woman who spent her life waiting for the boyfriend to call. She did not like the feeling.

She glanced at her slender, diamond encrusted watch as she clicked down the hallway to her office. It was 8:45. She was fifteen minutes late for a meeting with Ivy Artois, David Davies (couldn't Mom and Dad think of another name?), and Frances. Very unprofessional to be late, but she loathed these meetings. These kids were either going to get better or not, whether or not the staff met to exchange notes.

"Lots of traffic?" Ivy said as Astra took the remaining seat at the conference table.

She wouldn't give in to the dig. "The usual."

"We've already gotten started on Melissa."

"Did she try it again?"

They all stared at her.

"Well, did she?"

"She's under twenty-four hour watch," Ivy said, handing her some papers.

Astra shrugged and pulled notes from her briefcase. "So she's stabilizing."

"She's hording meds and selling them to Candace," David said. "And also, we just found this out, to Candace's brother Jake who visits her."

"Candace is the cutter?"

David uncrossed his legs and crossed them again. He was effeminate, passionate about his job, and brilliant. "Bulimic, cutter, and I think it's going both ways. I think Jake's bringing her stuff as well."

"Great," Astra said. Ivy tossed her a dirty look.

"She tested positive for Quaaludes on Tuesday," Frances said, pencil poised. "Who else has she been hanging out with?"

"Melissa's mom. That's really all I've observed," Ivy said.

"She could use some services herself, in my book." David scribbled some notes on a pad.

"Candace is starting with me tomorrow, right?" Astra asked.

"You have her today, at eleven. Brace yourself." David winked at her, sliding Candace's chart across the table.

Astra opened the folder and sifted through the report, stopping at the photo page. A girl sprawled in a leopard-print bean bag chair leered up at her. Three hundred pounds, purple hair, the expression one of permanent-looking rage compounded with utter intellectual opacity.

Teenagers were beginning to bore her: their narcissistic tantrums, romanticization of suicide, passions that changed daily. But the energy was interesting, she thought, all that energy.

She put the photo of the girl away, then glanced at another handout. "Gerry's being discharged?"

"No more money, no more coverage, nothing," Ivy said.

"But he's...he's – " Frances started.

"A mess?" Astra said, pouring herself a cup of coffee.

"He's dangerous."

"We can't prove that. We can't keep him from going home," Ivy said, still not looking up from his file. "Home visits have gone fine."

"According to who?"

"According to our home visit staff, David." Ivy glared at him.

"You mean Justin, who fakes half his reports because he's too lazy to work a full day? Or Martha, who couldn't spot abuse if someone was spanking her own ass?"

"They've both been spoken to, David. They've both been given the proper warning – "

"You know," David slammed the folder down on the table, "this is why we have kids back here again and again and again. This is why they reoffend, hurt people, hurt themselves. This is why certain sections of the goddammed *Globe* exist. And hell, maybe it's why we all still have jobs, right?"

Silence packed the room.

"Would *you* rather be doing the home visits, David?"

"That's not the point."

"Then what do you suggest?"

"I suggest we hire competent people in the first place. Spend the time or money or whatever it takes to – "

Astra sipped her coffee and watched the daily drama of the Greenfield Institute, West Adolescent Wing. She admired David but it was as if she admired him from a great, sad distance. Why did he care so much? Didn't he know the world never changed, that the likeliness of evil and pain and "reoffending" were one hundred percent? Why bother sticking your finger in the dam when the tide of decay would endlessly spill over?

" – get to the bottom of what's really going on in this kid's house from day to day. You can't keep passing the paper on this one, Ivy."

She looked up at the group, reddened. "I suggest, David, that we conclude our discussions here about the remaining clients and take up the matter of Gerry in private."

He looked her in the eye until she looked away. "That's fine. We'll try it that way for the moment."

· FORTY-SEVEN ·

By ten o'clock the meeting had broken up, and Astra was looking forward to starting a new book on deep sea life before her eleven o'clock intake with Candace. Frances, however, was hovering at her door, red-eyed and wringing her hands.

Astra stood holding her book and coffee, and gave her a questioning look.

"I thought you were great in the meeting," Frances said.

Astra started to brush by her. "Well, I didn't say much."

"Sometimes that's best."

"Are you all right, Frances?"

"No, I'm not. Not at all."

Astra took a sip of coffee and looked at her. Don't make me work for this, she thought.

"I...do you mind if I talk to you, for just a few minutes?"

"Come in," Astra said.

For the first several minutes, Frances couldn't do much more than sob. Why do people come to me with their misery? Astra thought. Can't they see through me, that I don't care about them, that I am, in fact, dangerous? Frances in particular seemed to have an almost perverse inclination to confide in her. Had her own mother been chilly, distant and unavailable? Repetition compulsion exhausted and bored her. Grow up, she thought, do me a favor and grow the hell up.

"What could have possibly gone wrong?" Frances moaned.

"I...I don't know. I wasn't there."

"He took all his stuff, every CD, every sock, all gone."

"Where did he go?"

"He didn't tell me, Astra, he just left! He said he couldn't take the pressure, whatever that meant, that he wasn't ready for 'all this'…the only reason I ran into him at all was because I went home sick yesterday, remember?"

"Mmm."

"I've known him since we were little kids. He's never done anything like this, ever. Do you think he met someone? Do you think that's it?"

Astra glanced longingly at her book. "I don't know Frances. He could have."

This brought on a fresh gush of tears. "Oh my God, maybe that's it. One last fuck before he ties the knot. We were virgins together, you know. He tells me I'm the only woman he's been with."

"You're young, Frances. How old are you?"

"Twenty-five. All my friends are married. I'm the last one."

"Marriage isn't the answer."

She wiped her eyes. "Have you ever been married, I mean, you have…had, I'm so sorry, your daughter…"

"We were never married, no."

"I'm sorry."

"Don't be. I wanted a child, and I got one."

Frances looked off wistfully. "I want a child too someday. I want three."

Astra stole a look at the wall clock. 10:25.

"I won't get over him, Astra. I can't."

"Of course you will."

"Have you ever been in love, Astra?"

"At one time."

"Are you in love with anyone now?"

"Not now, no. Why do you ask?"

Frances seemed to recover a bit. She got up, stretched, walked over to the window and looked out. "No reason. I guess I just wanted to compare notes."

"About what?"

"About being in love."

"Well, Frances, you're talking to the wrong person about that." She organized some papers on her desk in a hopeless bid to hint at the passing of time.

"I just need to know what to do when my heart is broken. There has to be something to do about it. I feel like I'll die without him. I can't believe I got through the meeting this morning." She reached for a box of Kleenex. "You've never felt this way?"

"Like I would die without someone?" Astra felt, to her amazement, a lump in her throat. "You have to wait patiently. Make a plan to get him back. Then follow through, step by step."

Frances turned and looked at her with new eyes. "So look at it like a puzzle, then. Hmm, I like that. I'm going to think about that."

"Take it out of your heart and put it in your mind. Later, when it's safe, when you've got him back, you can put it back in your heart."

"That's brilliant," she said, turning toward the window and the sloping grounds below. "I knew you would have a brilliant idea."

"Regardless of whether *that* is the case, I need to prepare for my 11:00 with Candace, so would you mind grabbing – "

" – her chart. Of course. I'm so sorry, I got carried away." She wiped her eyes and straightened her hair, adjusting her suit jacket as she opened the office door. She ran out, returned with the chart and handed it to Astra.

"I can't thank you enough for talking with me, Astra. I feel much better."

"Glad to hear it," Astra said, sitting down and opening the chart. Frances slipped out, closing the door quietly behind her.

Astra flipped past Candace's photo, the dull eyes glowering up at her, to her chart. Six weeks premature and born at home to an alcoholic teenage mother, Candace was stuffed into a backpack and taken to a state park where she was put in a dumpster. She was found by picnickers who heard her cries. It wasn't known whether she had suffered oxygen deprivation while in the knapsack or in the dumpster, but tests showed brain damage and reduced gross motor function at two years of age. Five foster families had taken Candace in; each had reported an inability to control her bouts of rage and destructive tendencies. One report stated that she had been sexually abused by the foster mother and father, and possibly also the brother. She had destroyed furniture, keyed cars, and most recently forged checks and stolen property. In the last group home she was in, she had come at a staff person with a carving knife. Another resident had pulled her away and restrained her. She had remarkable artistic abilities, however, and was able to draw or paint just about anything from life or memory, though the subject matter was often disturbing or morbid.

Astra flipped through a few of Candace's drawings. A crow with a broken neck, rendered in fantastic detail, on a weed-sprung sidewalk. A woman's hand that looked as if it had been torn off her arm sat in a basket of fruit.

The third was a shockingly realistic portrait of Candace looking in a mirror: shocking because it was as if she were making eye contact with the viewer. She stared at her reflection, one hand holding her tongue out, the other holding an open pair of shears as if she were about to cut it off.

The door opened and Astra jumped. "Candace is here," Frances said, popping her head in. "You also have a call on line two, a Constantin Damler. Take a message, right?"

"No, no, I'll take that call. I'll let you know when I'm ready for Candace."

"All right." She closed the door.

Astra shut her eyes tightly, then opened them. She stared at the phone as if it were a living thing, the red light on line two blinking on and off like a heartbeat.

· FORTY-EIGHT ·

Constantin paced up and down the fisheries lab hallway with his cell phone pressed to his ear. Several of his students said hello as they passed by on their way to classes or lab assignments.

All week he had struggled with his decision of whether to bring Astra down on the sub. He'd been in a cloud of generosity and happiness with Kim when he'd invited Astra to join them a month ago. To take Astra now, when marine science students would have given just about anything for the experience, seemed a little silly, or even strange. Bothering him even more was that out of everyone he knew he *wanted* Astra down with him in the sub, more than any of his students or his usual partner, Barry.

He was on hold almost a minute. In that minute he played it all back in his head as he had thousands of times, that life-shattering weekend, until he saw Astra laughing, soaking wet, on the sailboat in the storm. Instead of Kim's corpse in his arms; instead of her, luminous in her blue silk robe, he saw her mother, eyes glistening as she swayed from the mast, hair coiling down in slippery ropes. He had already begun to take the phone from his ear when he heard her pick up. He listened as she said his name, her voice washing over him like a cool, silvery wave in summer, before he opened his mouth to speak.

· FORTY-NINE ·

Sixty miles off the coast of Massachusetts and nearly fifteen hundred feet down, Astra and Constantin sat inches from each other in a submersible vessel that measured only five yards across. They rested on a sandbar that sloped into the darkness that surrounded the small radius of light from the sub. Except for discussing the animals they saw — bioluminescent jellyfish like great skeletal bells, lantern fish, a see-through octopus and a few small sharks — they were quiet with each other, their faces bluish from the seawater reflected back on them. Constantin let Astra put her hands in the manipulable arms of the sub so she could pick up small creatures from the sea floor.

At dinner in an Italian restaurant in town, Astra sipped her Chianti. She couldn't quite believe he was actually sitting across from her. She wore a tailored navy blue linen dress that played up her small waist and full breasts. But Constantin was quiet, distant, interested mainly in pasta and getting home, it seemed to her.

"You're not doing very well, are you?"

"No, Astra, I'm not."

Astra gestured at their waiter for another bottle of wine. Most of the male waitstaff couldn't take their eyes off her.

"Are you okay to drink more wine?" he asked.

"You're driving, right?"

"Yes, but you need to get home from my place — "

"I'll be all right." She watched him swirl fettuccine on his fork.

"Have you talked to that cop?"

163

"There are no leads, Constantin."

"They have nothing?"

She shook her head.

"That Officer Schlummer is a moron. This small town Andy-of-Mayberry bullshit – "

"Boston detectives are on this, Constantin, not just Schlummer. There's nothing. They have nothing."

He pushed his plate away. "Let's not talk about this."

"We have to be there for each other, Constantin. I'm suffering too." She reached over and covered his hand with hers. He took her hand and squeezed it, then let it go.

"Yeah, I guess we do."

"We need to create our own memories, new memories. We have to comfort each other. Can we make that promise to each other?"

Constantin looked out the window at shuttered office buildings, then back at her.

"I'm alone in that house, Constantin, grieving. I hope someday you'll come by and keep me company."

"Astra, I don't think you understand. I will never set foot in that house again."

"But you won't have to, Constantin. I've already put the house on the market. I can't bear it either."

"Don't take this the wrong way, Astra, but I don't think you're suffering like I am. I know you're her mother, but you weren't close to her."

"Do I remind you very much of her?"

"Sometimes."

"When?"

"You're both stubborn, I think. Determined. Neither of you would ever stop trying to get what you wanted."

On her way home, Astra steeled herself. She had moved too quickly, and would now have to wait – months, maybe – before she contacted him again. But it would give her time to sell her house, move closer to him, and plan her next step.

· FIFTY ·

Six months later, Barry and Constantin sat in a neighborhood bar near their lab drinking beer and watching women walk by.

"Nobody, Constantin? Nothing?"

"Not up for it, Barry. You don't get it."

"Maybe I don't, but you're a young guy. You gotta just push your way through this."

"I am. Slowly."

"What does that mean?"

"It means I'm thinking about someone else, anyway."

"Yeah? Who? That temp in L-Block?"

"Come on. She's an idiot."

"Yeah, but the legs on her – "

"Come on, finish up. I gotta get home and let Marty out."

Barry got up and threw some bills at their check. "So when am I gonna meet this new babe?"

Constantin tossed on his jacket and headed for the door. "Never, my good man."

"Why not?"

He looked Barry in the eye as he turned up his collar against the brisk December wind. "Because it's not meant to be."

· FIFTY-ONE ·

Their courtship was not slow once Constantin gave in to it. His passion, which was still partly grief, fueled his desire for her. He hated himself as he made love to Astra; he got down on his knees and begged Kim for forgiveness before driving to Astra's apartment late at night after long hours in the lab. But he went all the same, letting himself in with a key she had made for him, taking her blindly in the dark like an intruder. She smelled sweet like lilies of the valley, her hair and lips a dark rich feast. He insisted they make love only in the darkness, but encountered no resistance from her. Sometimes her eyes glowed like an animal's as she straddled him, reflecting light from some unknown source. Her nails raked across his shoulders and back. Afterwards he lay staring up at the darkness while she slept soundly beside him.

In the morning he was shy with her, never lured back under the warm covers to explore her in daylight. If he stayed for coffee it was a rare day; he preferred to go home and shower before class. He never made plans to see her at night; he only made a brief call an hour or so before he planned to show up, or just appeared in rumpled tweed, a dark silhouette tossing keys on a chair and slowly, methodically undressing.

The odd fellow teacher or female acquaintance approached him hoping he might be near a point of lessening in grief, but he turned them away with gruff brevity. He had taken on years in his face, the lines creasing under his eyes, across his forehead. And where Constantin looked older, his attentions had softened Astra and made her beauty transcendent. Everywhere, men turned to look at her; they asked for her number at gas

167

stations, convenience stores, in lines at movie theaters. She would listen to their awkward requests with an amused tilt to her head and turn them down pointedly, saying no, thank you, I am engaged to be married.

At first, the romance and passion of Constantin's late night visits were enough to keep Astra happy, but after a few months of this she started to want more.

Early one freezing winter morning she watched as he tried to chip the ice off his windshield with an old CD case from his car. Every morning he would mention he needed to buy an ice scraper, but never got around to it. But he'd never wake her so he could borrow hers. As usual, it seemed to her, he wanted little real interaction with her.

She opened the door and called out to him. Her words felt sharp in the arctic air. "You can use my scraper, you know, dear."

He jumped a little at the sound of her voice. "Yeah – well I turned the car on, so it'll just be a minute."

"And there's coffee brewing, and corn flakes, too. And me."

He didn't look at her, just kept gouging the ice on his windshield. "I gotta let Marty out before school."

"Constantin?"

"Yeah?"

"We need to talk."

She stood on the doorstep, arms folded hard across her chest.

After a few more desultory stabs at the ice, he gave up and tossed the CD case in the back seat. Staring down at the filthy snow, he trudged back into the house.

Barefoot in silver and blue striped pajamas, Astra poured him coffee. Constantin blew on his hands and stole a glance at the kitchen clock.

"I don't want to go on like this with you." She sat at the kitchen table. He stayed standing.

"Like what?"

"You know what I'm talking about. Like I'm some secret you're keeping."

"We talked about this already."

"We talked two months ago. It's been a while, Constantin. Almost four months."

"Has it?"

"I want to be part of your life."

"You are, Astra."

She looked at him, the grey circles under his eyes, his worn winter vest with a duct-taped tear. "Stop being ashamed of me, Constantin."

"I'm not ashamed."

"You were in love with my daughter, who died almost a year ago. It's horrible, but it's true. Nothing can bring her back. And now you're in love with me. You can't help it, I can't help it. Why won't you accept it?"

"I never said I was in love with you."

She narrowed her eyes. "So you're just fucking me?"

"Jesus, Astra, lighten up."

"Well, are you? Do you care about me at all?"

"Yes, I care about you," he said in a monotone.

"You've never once taken me out for a meal, or a movie, or anywhere in public. You've never introduced me to your friends or colleagues. I can understand, for a while, but not forever. Am I just this horrendous secret of yours?"

He was quiet a moment. Then he said, almost in a whisper, "I'm not ready to talk about this."

She got up, took his coffee away from him and poured it down the sink. "Not ready to talk? But you're ready to come over here and make love to me five nights a week? Give me my key back then, and get out of my house." She held out a hand; he watched it tremble slightly.

As if moving under a great weight, Constantin reached in his jacket and pulled out the key. He placed it on the table and walked out of the house, gently closing the door behind him.

· FIFTY-TWO ·

Christmas Eve the temperature never got above ten degrees, and by afternoon a nor'easter had blown in, deadlocking travel and ruining countless holiday plans. Constantin stood at a bay window at Barry and Traci's sprawling Victorian home holding a cut crystal glass of eggnog he had no interest in. He didn't even like eggnog. He had looked around for the rum to have it straight but was told the only liquor in the house at the moment, besides beer, was in the eggnog. So he sipped it every now and then, wincing at the sweetness.

Traci and Barry's extended family – parents, aunts, uncles, nieces and nephews – surrounded him, chattering and laughing. A couple of kids had just unwrapped a remote-powered airplane that they immediately rigged up to fly. Constantin watched the balsam plane fly over the holiday feast and into a fluffy coconut cake.

"Mark! I said the garage *only!*" Traci, a brittly cheerful but voluptuous honey blonde, turned around in a rocking chair by the fire as she discreetly breast fed ten-month-old Alice. Constantin watched the swollen nipple, shining wet by the firelight, briefly leave and re-enter Alice's mouth.

Mark ignored her. He pulled the plane out of the cake, licked off the frosting, and sent it flying again, high above everyone's head. It rattled around the ceiling a few times, its tinny engine revving ridiculously. Barry emerged from a room at the top of the stairs, reached over and grabbed the plane. It sputtered out in his hands as Mark ran up the stairs to retrieve it. Barry held it aloft from Mark as he jumped up and tried to grab it away from his dad.

"Come on, it's mine! Grammy just gave it to me!"

"You go back downstairs and apologize to your mother."

He began to pout and whine, and made one more unsuccessful grab at the plane. "But Dad, it's – "

"Go. Now. Or I snap this thing in half."

Traci smiled, Madonna-like, at Constantin as he watched this family drama. The wind rattled the old panes while a frosty draft leaked through and washed over him. In his pocket he held a gold ring he bought that afternoon. He worried it between his fingers but it held an odd chill, and would not warm to his touch.

"You're not lonely over there, are you, Constantin?" Traci asked. Alice snuggled into her comfortably.

"No, just thinking."

"You think too much. Did you have enough to eat? I'm pretty sure Barry put out the desserts – "

"I'm all set. Just enjoying the eggnog and the winter wonderland out there."

Barry loped down the brightly festooned stairs and patted Constantin a bit too hard on the back. "How about a smoke, old man?"

Traci tossed him a dirty look.

"A Marlboro Light, Mom," he said, glancing back at her as he and Constantin headed for the front door.

They stood on the porch taking long drags on their cigarettes, lit-up snowflakes swirling just out of reach. Dozens of white lumps – cars – lined the road.

Barry rubbed his hands together. A fat snowflake landed and melted on his shiny bald head. "You okay, man? I mean, you're pretty quiet."

"It's Christmas, for God's sake. Of course I'm quiet."

"Do you miss her?"

"Which one?"

"You tell me, man."

"Am I a hopelessly sick, miserable, evil fuck, Barry?"

"Well, I wouldn't say you're hopeless."

They both laughed as they watched a plow roar down the street. "I'm dating...I'm seeing...I'm fucking the mother of the woman I love, loved, who was murdered, by Christ knows who..."

"I thought you quit – "

"I did."

"But you can't stop thinking about her. You sound whipped, man."

"It's not like that – "

"Hey, it's not so bad. Somebody to come home to. Help out with the bills. You even get laid now and then."

"But Kim's *mother* – "

"She's a woman, right? Of the female persuasion? You woulda met someone else eventually. I mean, fuck, you're not gonna win any how-we-met contest, so you're gonna have to let go of that, but – "

"I think she really cares about me, Barry."

"Well, that's good. They're supposed to."

"I care about her too. I don't what it is about her. She just gets to me."

"You sound like me when I met Traci – nuts. I mean good nuts, happy nuts." He poured his eggnog in the snow. It lay there in a yellowy glutinous mass. "This stuff is shit. Why did she dump all the good stuff – "

"Barry, I'm gonna head out."

"What? I thought you were crashing here tonight – "

"No, I gotta get going. I'll dig out my car in the morning."

"Where are you – shit, I know. You devil, you old sonofabitch. She lives pretty close, doesn't she? Okay, Santy Claus, at least come in and say goodbye to Traci."

"Nah, I don't want to disturb the party. Just tell her thanks, would you?"

"If that's what you want, but at least take your coat, lover boy." Barry stepped into the foyer, grabbed Constantin's jacket and handed it to him. He tossed it on, pulled up his hood, shivered, and turned toward the palace of whiteness.

"So will I get to meet this woman someday?"

"Just say the word, Barry." He stepped down off the porch and waved. "Merry Christmas."

"Merry Christmas, my friend."

· FIFTY-THREE ·

His footsteps were soundless in the drifts, his shoulders hunched against the cold. Christmas lights glowed under cottony snow. Picture windows framed families gathered in their homes. Constantin thought that maybe he loved Astra; that love could possibly be the name for this new sense of emptiness he carried with him now. All he knew was something about Astra quelled the endless loneliness in him, something no one else had been able to do since Kim died. He was comforted by her strength, her passionate conviction of her love for him, even though she had made no effort to contact him these last two weeks. He knew she was waiting for him.

Though his hands were warm, the small gold ring he kept in his pocket still felt icy to his touch. He reached her street and stood on the corner, gazing at her bungalow a few houses down. Her lights were on, her car in the drive. A small, tastefully decorated Christmas tree filled one window.

He untied a red ribbon from her neighbor's mailbox, took out the ring and tied the ribbon in a bow through it, then put it back in his pocket. Walking up her drive, he thought he saw a shadow flit across an upstairs window. He rang the bell and held his breath. He could still change his mind.

But the door opened as if Astra had been standing there the whole night. She wore a velvet green pant suit and held a glass of sherry, as if she were entertaining guests, but he saw or heard no one else. She only looked at him and smiled, with more teeth than he remembered, then stepped back to swing the door open wide.

Five years passed. Their wedding was small, private, attended only by Constantin's parents (who were shocked by this turn, but adored and trusted their son) and Barry and Traci. Constantin felt he was a good husband; he paid attention to his wife, listened to her, bought her thoughtful gifts, came home at night. He moved into her house, abandoning his small, cozy bachelor apartment almost with relief. He still pictured Kim there lying naked in his bed, her long auburn hair scenting his pillow, her limbs entwined with his.

Marty came to tolerate Astra, but would never obey her command. He shadowed Constantin everywhere: at his office, school, the lab, even on boats on research trips. Constantin became more absorbed with his work than ever before, spending sometimes entire weekends at the marine lab in Woods Hole. He had begun to specialize in whale communication systems, and needed access to sensitive technical equipment there. He invited Astra to come with him now and then, knowing that she would only occasionally agree to spend the weekend in a fisheries lab.

But she loved him embarrassingly well. When he came home depressed or down about his work, she buoyed him with superlatives about his intelligence, the importance of his research. She was vigilant about her weight and her exercise plan, keenly aware of the fourteen year age difference (not in her favor) between them.

Their habit of making love only in the dark continued. In addition, Astra never slept naked; she always wore a camisole or T-shirt. Constantin thought it rather sweet that his wife was shy in this way, at the same time he was struck one evening, on his way home from office hours at school, that he had never seen his wife completely naked. At first it had been *his* obsession – insisting on the dark. He explained that it was an odd habit of his, but the truth was he couldn't face the fact that he was actually making love to Kim's mother. But now, after so many years, he was ready to see her. The thought mystified and aroused him, and he pulled in their driveway that night determined to see Astra full in the flesh.

After dinner they drank wine and watched a movie on TV. Astra sat by him on the couch, watching him as he drank four glasses of wine as opposed to his usual two. He put his arm around her and pulled her close.

"Are you okay, Constantin?"

"Never better." He kissed her gently, stroking the hair off her face.

"You seem – "

"It was a long day." He kissed her again, stroking her breast under her silk pajama.

She pulled back from him. "So you don't have to correct papers?"

He got to his feet, lifting her off the couch and kissing her. "I don't have to correct a damned thing." He took her to their bedroom and laid her down on the bed. She smiled and cocked her head.

"Was it the Italian food that did this to you?"

"I'm not sure." He pulled off his shirt and pants and lay next to her as she reached over and turned off the light.

"No. Keep it on."

She breathed heavily in his ear, but didn't move. He reached past her and turned the light back on.

"But I like the dark," she said.

"Only because you're used to it, because that's what we've always done." He untied her pajama bottoms and pulled them off. She stared at him, unblinking.

"I need the darkness," she said, and flicked the lamp off again. She turned away from him.

"What do you mean you 'need' it? I need to see you."

"You see me."

"Shit, Astra, I've never seen you. Think about it, in five years I've never seen my wife naked. Isn't that a little *strange*?"

He reached over and began to unbutton her pajama top. She lay there apparently willing, but in the darkness her eyes were like saucers, her body rigid with concentration.

ERICA FERENCIK

Second button, third, fourth; his hand trembled there. He felt
something, a kind of buzzing energy that froze him in place. Her breath
came shallow, her heart beat in her ears.

He undid the fifth button.

She leapt from the bed with an inhuman snarl. "I said *no!*" she
screamed, and stood at the window, facing away from him. Panting, she
buttoned up her top, willing herself to calm down.

"My God, Astra, I only want to see you." He flipped the light back
on.

"Trust me, you don't."

"What in God's name are you talking about?"

"There are things on this earth...you wouldn't understand, Constantin."

He lay back and sighed. "Try me, Astra."

She folded her arms tight across her chest and gazed out the window
at a silver elm, its leaves flipped upside down in a brisk wind that seemed
to whip up from the ground. A storm was coming. "I'm a little bit older
than you, dear."

"Don't be condescending, okay?"

"I'm not." She rubbed her forehead with the palm of her hand. "It's
not easy being an older woman married to a younger man. It makes you
very self-conscious. Your skin changes, your hair, how you put on weight,
everything is different." Rain pelted at the window. "I had no idea it would
be like this."

"Be like what?" he asked more gently.

"Be so hard. To lose your beauty. Your power. To age. I mean, I've
never done it before."

"What did you say?"

To cover her gaffe, she started to cry. Constantin rustled himself from
the bed and came to stand behind her. He put his arms around her and
rested his head on her shoulder.

"Don't you know how beautiful you are? You must, you *must* know. Your age means nothing to me, Astra. It's actually very sexy."

"Sexy older woman – that's always such a lie." She sniffled a little into a lacy handkerchief. As she did so, she glanced down her top. The skin on her torso was smooth and clear.

"Come on, stop crying. I'll leave you alone, my vampire lover."

With a coy smile, she turned to him, opening her pajama top. He lit up. Laughing, he caressed her. She led him to the bed, sat him down and straddled him, stroking his glossy hair back from his brow. Kissing him hard, she pushed him down against the pillows at the headboard.

He let her kiss him, then lifted her up and snapped off the light. With a whisper of violence he pulled her toward him and flipped her on her back. He cupped her ass and sighed.

"Thank you, my sweetheart," he said, filling her quickly with himself.

A fterwards he slept, his arm leaden across her shoulders. She lifted it off her, pulled on his workshirt and stepped out to the bathroom where she flipped on the overhead light. Staring at herself in the mirror, she slowly opened the shirt, all the time willing her skin to stay normal, smooth, unmarked. A little trick she had always been able to perform but lately there had been surprises…in the shower…changing rooms in clothing stores…on the beach…the shock of the past rising up on her skin.

She locked eyes with herself. Seconds passed, a minute, two; she became dizzy, pain stabbed at her skull and still she stared, praying, commanding her body to obey, for her skin to stay unblemished and beautiful. Sweat gathered at her skull and dripped down between her breasts. She began to shake; she gripped the sink to still herself. Her image doubled in the mirror, quadrupled, until all the Astras blurred together and she swooned and fell back against the door, sliding down to the cold tile. With great effort she lifted her head off her chest and tried to open her eyes. The bolts holding down the toilet swam into focus.

Already knowing she'd lost the fight, she reached inside her shirt and felt the skin on her torso. It wasn't right. Already it was changing. Gagging, she pulled herself to her knees and threw up in the toilet bowl. She cried as she cleaned herself, needing some sort of plan but bereft of one. She had gotten away with it this time, but in the end she knew it would never again be safe to show him her body in the light.

· FIFTY-FOUR ·

Cake was everywhere: on the walls, the furniture, on the floors and ground into the already frayed and stained rug. Ellen never learned exactly who was the inspiration for the food fight, but suspected six-year-old Richard, the son of her friend Emma whose family owned the grocery store in town. Amy and Mistelle, mothers of Grace and Ruby, crowded around the kitchen with Ellen drinking coffee and enjoying a few moments before the inevitable cleanup.

Richard and Evan, Emma's twin boys, had splintered off from the girls and were zoning out on video games, cake still in their hair and sticky little hands, while the girls had escaped to the back porch with their new dolls and doll clothes.

Lucy, Grace and Ruby sat in the twilight, dolls and their rainbow of clothes spread out on the unstained wood of the porch. Cold rain slapped at the windows but the girls paid no attention; they were completely absorbed in their game.

"But it's *my* birthday," Lucy said, wide-eyed and virtuous with childish logic. Her silky red hair hung down her little back in two tangled plaits. The scar crossed her neck harshly, vivid against luminous white skin.

"Yes, but on your birthday you're supposed to be nice to guests," Grace said, holding a doll-sized wedding dress just out of Lucy's reach. Smears of chocolate frosting decorated her nose and forehead.

"You're always supposed to share, Lucy, no matter what day it is," Ruby chimed in, locking her arms across her sparrow chest.

"It's not fair!" Lucy lunged at the dress, snatching it out of Grace's

181

hands.

"Give it back!" Grace screamed, and pounced on the much smaller Lucy, fists flying. "You're sposta *share!*"

They both caught hold of the dress and tug-of-warred with it until a fluffy little sleeve ripped off in Lucy's hand. She held the tiny white scrap out in front of her, evidence of profound misery. "But it's my *birthday*," she sobbed, and got to her feet.

She ran into the kitchen and crawled into Ellen's lap, bawling.

"Honey, what is it?"

Lucy held out the little sleeve.

"Who tore this?"

"Grace."

"On purpose?"

"Yeah, she tore it off."

Ellen picked up her daughter and held her as she cried, sharing exasperated smiles with Amy and Mistelle. With resigned sighs, they pushed themselves away from the small kitchen table.

"I knew it was too peaceful," Mistelle said, turning to stack the dishes.

"But wasn't it a great ten minutes?" Amy said as she soaped a sponge to clean frosting off the floors and walls.

"Come on, Lucy," Ellen said. "Let's go see your friends." She carried her to the porch where Grace and Ruby were playing dress-up with the dolls like quiet little angels.

"Grace? Ruby? What happened?"

"She wouldn't share the dress like she promised," Grace said calmly, adjusting a cheerleader outfit on a Barbie.

Ruby looked up from combing a raven-haired Barbie with a little yellow comb. "Even if you're the birthday girl, you don't get to act mean."

"You girls having a little trouble sharing?" Ellen looked at Lucy who stared at the floor, her small, sticky arms loose around her mother's neck.

No one said anything.

"Does anyone have any ideas about how we can share today?"

Silence.

"Well, I do. Each of you is going to get five minutes with an outfit, and then you'll have to switch with each other. I'll go grab the kitchen timer."

"That's stupid," Grace said.

"It's stupid but you've all shown me you need help, that you can't do it on your own." She bent over, put Lucy down, and picked up the one-sleeved wedding dress. "Now, I'm going to go sew this. And set the timer, all right?"

Lucy sat down, red-eyed, and sullenly pulled a cowgirl outfit from the pile.

Ellen turned on her heel. "Five minutes."

· FIFTY-FIVE ·

Lucy held the cowgirl outfit and sniffled. For a couple of minutes the girls played in silence, the rain tapping at the thin roof of the porch the only sound.

"It was *my* wedding dress," Lucy said, her mouth still in a bow-pout.

"Shut up, Lucy." Grace's chubby fingers strained to button a tiny jacket.

"I never even invited you. Ellen did," Lucy said.

"Ellen? You mean your mother?"

"She's not my mother."

"You're so stupid," Ruby said. "Of course she's your mother. She takes you to school, right? She makes your lunch, right?"

"Yeah, but she's not my mother. My real mother lives in a big house by the sea."

"You're weird, Lucy," Grace said, sitting her Barbie on a little pink motorcycle.

"I am not."

"Your mother's right here, in the kitchen."

"No, she's not."

"Then who's the lady in the kitchen?" Ruby asked, head tilted.

"I...I don't know. A nice lady."

Grace stared at Lucy a second, then opened her mouth wide. "Mommy!" she shrieked. "I want to go home!"

The three women stumbled in from the kitchen, not sure which little girl had screamed.

Ellen stood in her dirty apron, hands on hips. "What is going on out here? Can't we get through five minutes without somebody yelling?"

"Lucy says you're not her mother."

"What?" She turned away. "Dammit, Lucy," she said under her breath.

Lucy played with the fringe on the cowgirl outfit and stared miserably at the floor. Mistelle put a hand on Ellen's slender shoulder. Amy looked totally confused.

"She said what?" Amy asked.

"Don't...don't encourage her. The stories she comes up with."

Ruby looked up at all the silent, sad-looking adults, her angry friends, and started to wail at the top of her lungs. "I wanna go home! Take me home, mommy!"

Mistelle bent down and picked her up; her Barbie fell with a clunk to the floor.

"Ruby, don't be such a baby," Grace said, getting up and wandering back to the living room where the boys sat still transfixed by the TV.

"But she says her mommy's not her mommy," Ruby sputtered in her mother's arms. "Are you my mommy, or not?"

Ellen shook her head as she blinked back tears of frustration. Mistelle stroked her daughter's hair and said, "Of course I'm your mommy. I'll always be your mommy."

Mistelle and Amy started back toward the living room, leaving Ellen alone with Lucy.

"Another day ruined by this nonsense."

Lucy was silent.

"You promised me, Lucy."

"I'm sorry," she said softly.

"Ellen," Mistelle called from the other room, "I think we're going to hit the road."

"Be right there!" Ellen called brightly. "Lucy, come on and say goodbye and thank you to your friends."

"I don't want to. They hate me anyway."

"They don't hate you, Lucy. Now, come on."

Lucy looked up at Ellen with sorrowful eyes. "I really, really don't want to."

Ellen shook her head and started toward the doorway. "All right then, don't."

Lucy listened to the murmurs of her friends as they gathered their coats, the tinkling laughter of the mothers as they said goodbye, the sound of the heavy front door closing, and her mother's footsteps clattering back out to the porch. The whole time she just stared at her doll.

She felt her mother towering over her. "You promised me you would keep this stuff between us. In fact, you promised you would never talk about it again. Don't you remember that?"

"Yes."

"What nonsense did you tell them? About being blind? That you never met your real daddy?"

"No, just about...that you're not my mommy."

"Jesus, Lucy." Ellen started to cry exhausted tears. She kneeled and lifted up her daughter's heart-shaped face by her chin. The face she'd kissed for six years now, the glittering blue eyes that sometimes seemed to look right through her. "Do you know how it feels to hear you say that? Do you have any idea?"

"I guess so."

"Then honey, why do you say it?"

"Because it's true. You're nice, and I call you Mommy because you want me to. I call you Mommy so you won't get mad. My real name – "

"Lucy! Your name is Lucy!" She got to her feet and whipped off her apron, balling it up in her hands. "I'm your mother, all right? Ever since you could talk you've been coming up with these crazy stories. Whatever you make up for your own fantasy world stays in your fantasies, do you understand? Like make-believe friends, like...like cartoons, or Disney

186

World, Cinderella, Pinocchio, all those stories we read together, all right? Okay, honey?" She kneeled down and looked at her daughter, whose face held a sadness beyond her years. "So you look at me, and you tell me right now, honey, right now, that I'm your mommy, okay? You tell me that. I need to hear it." She wiped her reddened eyes with her sleeve.

Lucy looked down at the Barbie in her hands, the cowgirl outfit complete except for the cowboy hat just inches from her fingers.

"Tell me, Lucy."

She sighed and looked up. "You're my mommy."

Ellen cried and pulled her close. Lucy stared past her shoulder, unblinking, at the damp night. "Thank God, thank God," Ellen said. After a few moments she let go of Lucy and stood up, brushing off her skirt almost self-consciously.

Still wiping tears from her cheeks, she began to pick up toys and toss them in a wooden chest already bursting with dolls, dollhouses, and board games. Without looking at Lucy, she said, "So, do you like your presents, honey?"

"Yes."

"How about some cocoa, before bed?"

"Okay."

"Well, cheer up then. It's your birthday."

· FIFTY-SIX ·

Ellen wandered off to the kitchen. Lucy listened to her hum a tuneless tune, then heard the radio news click on. She put the doll down and did what she had started to do a lot lately.

She shut her eyes and touched her scar. Waited for the story. There were never any pictures, but there were voices, smells, sounds, and feelings.

For a while, there was nothing, just the tinny radio voices from the other room. Soon that faded to a sort of static. Then she heard it. Short, heavy panting. Trembling, she reached out her hand. A dog's head, velvety smooth, bony. With both hands she stroked the long silky ears, smiled as it licked her hand and nudged her with its cold, wet nose. Abruptly, a leather loop wrapped around one wrist yanked her to her feet. She stood on the porch, alone, eyes squeezed shut, one arm taut and outstretched. An ocean breeze, full of fish and salt, blew across her face.

The dog wrenched at her and she tripped forward, tried to stand up straight but it pulled harder until she was jerked – stumbling – then running across the floor. She ran the length of the porch till she smacked into the wall and fell to the rough planks.

She heard the radio snap off. "Lucy?"

The dog was gone; his smell, touch, all gone. Breathing hard, Lucy snapped her eyes open. Just the rain pattering on the roof, the sharp smell of electricity in the air. She saw nothing.

"Lucy, answer me!"

She looked down, up, toward the sound of her mother's voice. Only blackness. Terror caught at her throat but she couldn't scream. Finally, she was being punished for her secret world, her other world.

Her mother's footsteps grew louder as she ran to the porch. Lucy blinked again and again; only blackness greeted her. Whimpering, she reached out her arms.

"Lucy!" Ellen shrieked. She knelt down and gathered her up. "What did you do to yourself?"

"I fell, and now I can't see!"

"What are you talking about? Where did you fall?"

"Mommy, did you turn out the lights?"

"Of course not! What's wrong with you?"

Lucy buried her face in her mother's sweater, inhaling the familiar smell of sweat and fabric softener. "Please turn on the lights!"

"They're on, Lucy!" Ellen ran with her into the kitchen which was flooded with overhead lights, and pulled her away from her shoulder.

Lucy blinked and stared up at the lights. "It's dark, like nighttime, only darker."

Ellen sat Lucy on the kitchen table. Lucy tried to blink back the darkness, but couldn't. She smelled coffee grinds and orange peels in the garbage next to her. Her small, clammy hands clenched and unclenched the edge of the laminated kitchen table. With trembling fingers, Ellen gently pulled down the lids of her child's eyes.

"Oh my God, I don't even know what I'm looking for." She waved her hands in slow motion inches from Lucy's face. The pupils were large but her eyes stayed fixed. "You can't see me, honey? Don't play games! Tell me!" She gripped Lucy's small shoulders.

"I won't say it ever again, that you're not my mommy. You're my mommy."

"I know, honey, it's okay. Listen, I'm going to get your coat, and we're going to go see the doctor, all right?"

"All right."

"I'll be right back."

"Don't leave me alone!"

"I won't, I'm right here, honey. Just listen to my voice."

· FIFTY-SEVEN ·

Hours later, Ellen angled her rusted Dodge Dart into their narrow drive. Lucy was fast asleep in her seat, the bluish light of the moon paling across her face. Ellen had probably been this tired before in her life, but she couldn't remember when.

She glanced upstairs; a light burned in the bedroom. After leaving countless messages on his cell phone, she had finally reached Tom on his way back from the bar. He wanted to come to the hospital immediately, but she was already on her way back.

Lucy snored softly in her ear as she carried her up the poorly lit stairs. As she fumbled for the key, she heard Tom's heavy boots thud across the floor.

He looked so ashen and terrified when he opened the door that she almost forgave him not being there when she needed him. The overhead light fell on his white blond hair and across his forehead, creating dark crescents under his eyes. He reached out to take Lucy, but Ellen shook her head "no." He let his big arms drop to his sides, and stepped back to let them in.

Wordlessly, Ellen carried Lucy to their bedroom. She laid her in the middle of the wide bed, covering her with a frayed quilt she had made long ago. She slipped off Lucy's little sneakers and kissed her forehead, loving more than ever this child who mystified her, terrified her. Lucy nestled into the down, never once waking.

A hulking shadow of a man, Tom stood in the doorway holding Lucy's favorite doll. He stepped into the room and laid it next to her. Ellen didn't move from Lucy's side. Tom put his hands on his wife's shoulders and helped her stand, then walked with her out of the room, softly shutting the door behind them.

Tom held her as she cried. She smelled the liquor on him and didn't care as long he cradled her and stroked her hair. After a while he gently pulled her away and held her at arm's length, his rough hands cupping her shoulders.

"Tell me what – "

"You weren't here – "

"What's wrong with her?"

"She can't see, and they don't know why. They all looked at her, Tom, four, five doctors, one after the other."

"She can't see? What do you mean, her vision is blurry?"

"I mean she's blind."

Tom shuddered, as if loosening himself of what he had just heard. "Did she fall? Was she playing? Where were you?"

Ellen stepped back and straightened her shoulders. "Where was I? Where was I? I was in the kitchen, cleaning up after your daughter's birthday party. Where were you?"

She jerked open the freezer door, pulled out a tray of ice and yanked back the handle; the steaming ice popped out onto the counter and on the floor. As she rummaged for gin in a cabinet, Tom got tonic from the refrigerator and two glasses.

"I was at the bar," he said, pouring the tonic. "Watching the game. I'm evil. We've been over that. Tell me what's wrong with Lucy."

"Like I just told you, they can't find anything wrong with her. Then we went to see a shrink. A child psychiatrist."

Tom doused the glasses heavily with gin. "And what did he say?"

"That it's all in her head. That it's all some hysterical reaction to something – "

"To what?"

"I don't know." She sipped her drink and folded her arms under her breasts. "Then they asked about you."

"What do you mean?"

"What kind of father you are, things like that."

"And what did you tell them?"

Ellen sipped her drink and looked out the window at the triple decker across the street, the shadows of another family playing across the curtains. "The truth."

"Don't play games, Ellen. What did you say about me?"

"That you're never home, and when you are, you're useless."

"I bet that cleared things up. That it's my fault my daughter all the sudden can't see."

She turned back to face him. "They asked if you hit her."

"You're the only one who spanks her."

"You're never around when I have to discipline her."

"Damned if I do, and damned if I – "

She fixed him with her light blue eyes. "I'm asking you, Tom, if you've done – noticed anything lately that would upset her. That would traumatize her like this – "

"No."

"Think, okay? *Think*! There must be something – "

"I don't need to think. I love my daughter."

Ellen stared at him, her lips a pale line.

"I think I know what you're asking me, Ellen, and it's making me sick. It's making me literally sick."

Tom sat down with his drink in a rickety kitchen chair. He sighed and sifted through a pile of bills without seeing them. "Maybe you should take a look at yourself, Ellen."

"Please – "

"I've heard how you talk to her sometimes. Telling her she's full of silly ideas, that she's spouting nonsense. She's six, but she has her own thoughts. She knows her own head."

"You don't know what she says to me, the horrible things she says to me, that I'm not her mother, that you're not her father – "

"It's a fantasy. She's got a crush on Mistelle. You know that, don't you, Ellen? She fantasizes that she's her mother because – "

"Why?"

"I don't know. How should I know."

"What is it about me that – "

"She's got a big imagination. Those drawings she does, the weird creatures, castles on hills, flying demons?"

"Do you think that's why this happened? She imagined something she didn't want to see, and made herself blind?"

"Honey, I don't know, I'm just trying to think of what – "

"Oh my God, maybe that's it. All her stories are real to her."

Ellen finished her drink and smoothed her hair as she approached Tom. She touched his hand briefly. "I want to go be by her, put my arms around her. Can we both do that, and go to sleep?" Her voice trembled. "I just can't take any more of this tonight."

Tom fell asleep right away, his heavy arm across Lucy and Ellen, but Ellen lay sleepless, staring at the darkness until dawn outlined Tom's rough features and Lucy's small form, her hair still in pigtails, her doll hugged close. Ellen slipped from the bed, pulled on a flannel robe, and made coffee. It was 6:30. She had to be at work in an hour.

She sat with her coffee, her hair shining and loose around her face, her shoulders drawn tight with fear. She would wake her gently, accept what needed to be accepted, do what needed to be done. Lucy needed her, no matter what.

She went back into the bedroom and watched Lucy sleep, then slipped under the covers next to her. She touched her daughter's velvety forehead, traced her thin eyebrows with the tips of her fingers. Watched the tiny pulse at the side of her neck; the dry, half open lips. Prayed.

She tried to sound light. "Lucy, honey, it's time to get up. Time to get ready for school."

Lucy stirred, rolled toward Ellen. Her eyes fluttered open, the lashes crossing like insect wings.

Ellen watched consciousness seep into her daughter's face, then recognition. Lucy's eyes swept across her mother's face, then focused on her eyes. Her little brow furrowed. "You look tired, mom."

Choking with sobs, Ellen pulled Lucy into her arms. "Oh my God, oh my God."

Tom stirred, then came to his elbow and smiled as he watched them before pulling his family close.

· FIFTY-EIGHT ·

Seven years went by.

Astra, now fifty-six years old, sat in her office examining in a hand mirror a new growth of grey shocking through the hair at her temples. The scars from her face lift had finally healed, but she wasn't sure she liked the results. Her chinline was sharper but so was her expression, which had become one of eternal expectation. She tried different faces in the mirror, noticed a few more spidery veins along her nose, and made a note to talk to her doctor about dermabrasion.

No longer a size six, she wore a ten and loathed herself for it, trying every diet she came across: all celery, all fruit, high protein, liquid, everything she knew as a physician was ridiculous but tried anyway to shed the fifteen extra pounds she wore. Knee surgery had kept her from running for the past several years, so she had started swimming before work in the morning. She hated squeezing into her swimsuit in the predawn darkness, slogging through thirty laps staring at a red line on the bottom of a pool for an hour, avoiding the touch of goggled, froggy old men who would slide into her lane without fail. How disgusting it is to grow old, she thought; she hadn't missed a thing in the past. What a gift to die at thirty.

Except for Constantin. He was her gift and her salvation, her reason for this lifetime, for all her lifetimes. She never forgot that. Now forty-two, he was tenured, passionately involved in his research, and teaching more than ever. Working late, bringing work home – this was the norm. Unavoidable, he told her. Necessary to publish to stay in the game.

But part of her was sure it was her. The wider circumference of thigh, the thinning hair, the new age spots on her hands every day, it seemed. She couldn't let it go; the way he holed up in his lab on nights and weekends, coming home so tired he passed out on his desk surrounded by books on obscure marine life and slides and samples of who knew what. It seemed like every night she had to go downstairs and nudge him awake just so he'd come to bed with her.

And in bed he slept turned away from her, facing a book he inevitably brought with him, his glasses still on, crooked against the pillow. Every month or so he would reach for her in the night, but there was no talking, no words of love, only a brief grope and release, and it was over. Some half asleep apology about getting to bed earlier, spending more time with her, but it never happened.

Tonight would be different, she thought, gathering herself to leave Greenfield where she had, over the years, become Director of Adolescent Programs. There was a Christmas party in Constantin's department. She couldn't wait to arrive on his arm in a smashing new dress, the doctor wife of the tenured biologist. He would have to be proud of her then, wouldn't he?

She shopped for hours at malls, tiny boutiques and haute couture shops looking for the perfect dress. She was fawned over at the pricey shops, yawned at in the malls, lied to in boutiques. She bought the sexiest dress she could find: ankle length, high necked but cut close to the body on the bias, slit up the back.

The Christmas party was held at the marine sciences lab. Under harsh florescent light, a two-foot tree, decorated with a few pieces of old tinsel and a desiccated blowfish for a star sat in the corner next to discarded microscopes and a file cabinet. Graduate students in jeans sat sprawled on a couple of sway-backed couches drinking beer and whispering dirty jokes to each other. The department secretary, Cindy, an overworked but attractive single mother made her way in with a plastic tray of cheddar cheese and Triscuits. The students jumped up and swept aside lab equipment so she could set it down.

In the doorway, Constantin took off his and his wife's coat. He gasped when he saw her dress. "Astra, what are you wearing?"

"Do you like it?"

"It doesn't matter if I like it – this is just a...you know, Barry and Traci and some students. Didn't I tell you?"

"You just told me it was a Christmas party, Constantin," she said, sweeping open and sashaying through the lab doors. "Aren't you proud of me? Don't you want to show me off to your friends?"

An hour later, they drove in sullen silence through the wintry night, the broken windshield wiper flapping each time it crossed in front of Constantin.

"Goddam this thing – " he sputtered.

"So get it fixed." She pulled her fur coat closely around her.

Constantin glanced over at her. "Put your seatbelt on."

"No."

"What do you mean, no? I'm driving on solid ice. Put it on."

"It doesn't matter. None of this matters. You just don't know."

"You really are a trip sometimes, Astra. Now put on your goddammed seatbelt."

"Are you ashamed of me, Constantin?"

"Don't be ridiculous."

"I saw you winking at that woman – "

"Her name is Cindy – "

" – about my dress. At least I have the decency to dress up for parties. Is that a crime?"

"Of course not. You looked fine."

"'*Fine*'?"

"You looked beautiful."

She crossed her arms and stared straight ahead. "Those farty fish professor friends of yours were a bore."

Constantin drove in silence, his face rigid.

"They barely spoke to me."

"You could have tried speaking to them."

"I'm not interested in those geeks."

"Those are my friends, Astra."

"And what am I? Aren't I your friend?"

"Astra, don't be childish. There's room in the sandbox for everyone."

"I just don't want to hang out with your boring friends."

"Just what is in your craw tonight?"

"We never spend any time together." She looked out the window. Her reflection stared back, bone white, surprised. "Don't I interest you? Don't I satisfy you?"

Constantin downshifted noisily as he navigated a steep hill. "Of course you do. Look, I've been busy. I'll make more of an effort – "

"Why do you have to make an effort? Why is loving me an effort?"

"You need to get out more, Astra, get a hobby, make some friends."

"I don't need any of that nonsense. I have you. I love you. I can't help it that everyone is a bore but you, my love. I worship you. You know that."

"I never asked for that."

"You never asked for it, but you got it."

The car fishtailed, barely reaching the crest of the hill.

"Pull over, Constantin."

"What? Why?"

"You'll see, my love."

She grabbed the wheel and turned.

"What are you, nuts? Let's just go home."

"I said, *pull over*." She yanked the wheel out of his hands. They turned into a piece of dark farmland, finally stopping in a swirl of powdery snow.

Constantin breathed heavily, staring at his wife in disbelief.

"Look, Constantin, look at the night. The stars the same as they've been for thousands of years, and we here on earth spinning out our lives as if they mattered. As if anything mattered but love, the love between two people meant for each other. I want to die with you, Constantin, die in your arms, so your love can follow me, warm me, comfort me through to the other side – ”

“Astra, you’ve had too much to drink – ”

“Constantin…” She sat back in her seat and opened her coat. She was a shroud of blackness in the seat, a negative imprint. Her hair coiled darkly on the headrest like eels crawling out of a bucket. Her voice turned gravelly, strange. There was no moon that night; its face turned away.

“I’m going to take us home.” He turned the key in the ignition, but she grabbed his hand with a strong, icy grip.

“No, you’re not.” She slipped the car keys in her pocket. “You’re going to make love to me.”

He stared ahead at the frozen corn field, the stalks like skeletons under shrouds of snow. “Give me the keys, Astra. We’re going home.”

“I wouldn’t hear of it.”

“What did you say?”

“I said, my silly boy, you will fuck me now.”

“Don’t be – ” But she was on him, kissing him hard, writhing against him. He hardened in spite of himself, but pushed her away. She climbed back on him, her torso still but her pelvis grinding into him as if she had no spine. He watched her body move in disbelief.

“Come on Astra, cut it out!”

“Say you love me, Constantin.”

She kissed him again, but this time her tongue felt strange, raspy and narrow. He tried to pull away but she held him there against the headrest. She felt as strong as a man.

Finally she finished her kiss and pulled away. “I said, say it, Constantin. I need to hear you say it,” she hissed.

She yanked her dress up around her hips; her naked pubis glistened underneath. She flipped open his belt, unzipped him, freed his swollen penis and fit it in her, falling forward on him, her hair surrounding him, suffocating him, her hot strange breath filling his ears.

"I love you," he said hoarsely, slamming into her, turning and laying her all the way back on the seat where she meshed with the dark leather except for her shell-white face. He squeezed his eyes shut and lifted her with his hips till she groaned.

"Look at me and say it," she said, gripping him with her viper-strong legs.

But he was in his own world and not hearing her, until she grabbed him by the shoulders with her still freezing hands. "Look at me and say you love me."

His eyes snapped open almost against his will.

"I love you," he blurted, staring at her face in the velvet darkness. But she had changed; something about her eyes – what was it? A trick of light? They were small and yellow, glowing slits like a reptile's. But his orgasm flooded him and he moaned and shut his eyes again.

When he opened them she was Astra again. She lay beneath him weeping fetchingly, her eyes hazel and thickly lashed as always. "You said it," she said, gently stroking his hair. "And darling, I believed you this time. Come on," she said, gathering herself. "I want you to take me home."

· FIFTY-NINE ·

Lucy was a beautiful sixteen-year-old girl.

Under her teenage melancholy, the dew and spark of youth graced her lush skin and shining red hair, intelligent eyes and graceful limbs. She loved gymnastics, especially the balance beam. Walking on the beam she would stretch tall and straight, losing herself to something bigger that guided her through a kind of darkness. The squeak of the chalk on wood, the respectful silence of her teammates; it was a meditation. She never considered falling; she never fell.

Off the beam was a different story. Though she tested much higher than average, she was diagnosed with attention deficit disorder and prescribed Ritalin. She knew she couldn't concentrate without it, but after a few months of the accompanying exhaustion and headaches, she flushed the pills down the toilet every morning instead of taking them.

Her grades took a dip along with her confidence. Already a loner, she kept even more to herself, trying to understand where she fit in the world. How would she ever grow up, how would she ever become something, when she felt another force inside her almost as strong as her own. She could barely talk to other kids because she didn't care about the football game, about clothes, about who hooked up with who, what grades she got. She was a stranger in her own life.

Which was not what her guidance counselor, Mr. Breadloaf, wanted to hear. He glanced at her hair, breasts, legs, and pushed up his wire rim glasses with a meaty hand. "Well, dear, regardless of all this, this...about how you *feel*, don't you think you should be thinking about college?"

She stared at him, imagined him at home, sucking up online porn while his wife worked nights in the clinic, picked up her scruffy backpack and left. Taking a sharp turn out of his office, she headed for the back door of the school through the gym.

She chose the long way home, passing a trio of teenage girls who stood smoking in the frigid air. They dropped sizzling cigarettes in shallow puddles, tossed back their hairstyles, and sneered at her as she walked by. Lucy knew they thought she was a snob, but had no idea how to change their minds.

She wasn't a jock, or an art freak, chess club geek, goth, or preppie. Nothing fit. Drugs were available but frightened her deeply. Who knew how much more terrifying and bizarre her inner life would be with drugs? The one concession to beauty she made was to keep her hair long, just past her waist, but it was more to cover the scar on her neck or hide behind than anything else.

She liked boys but they bored her, almost as much as the girls. At least she saw less pretense in boys, found them easier to talk to than girls, their bravado charming in a juvenile way. There seemed to be no hidden, labyrinthine agenda to deal with, beyond the fact that they wanted to sleep with her. And the girls resented her for the fact that, in their eyes, she didn't even try and the boys still wanted her.

She loped down the hills of Gloucester, past homes built in the seventeen and eighteen hundreds painted in turquoise or mint green. Her town lived off its quaintness – the bed and breakfasts, white steepled churches, seafood restaurants with lobster traps hanging from the ceilings. It lived off the men who risked their lives at sea, as it had for centuries.

As Lucy passed the Crow's Landing she almost went in to see if her father was there. He had left Ellen five years previous, just after Lucy's brother Peter was born, for a woman who'd run a now closed video store and who also spent all her spare time at the Crow's Landing. Tom and Shelley lived in a rundown apartment a few doors down from the Landing.

Their wedding was in two weeks. Lucy was invited but didn't want to go; she thought Shelley was a phony and believed her mother when she said their affair had been going on for years, though Tom denied all of it.

But she missed her father, so she stopped at the corner and put down her backpack, stalling for time to make her decision by pretending to look for something at the bottom of the bag. Anytime, he'd said, just drop by if you see the truck. His truck was there, but so was Shelley's Toyota. Lucy hoisted her backpack and kept on going.

The farther she got from the bar and her father's place, the better she felt. She loved her brother Peter more than anything in the world, and couldn't wait to see him. He was five and a lot of work, but he cheered her up. There was something about him that grounded her; his little weight, his sweet smell, his thousands of questions about the world that made her laugh, made her think. (How DID that man get in that little box? Why IS the sky blue? Why AM I so short?)

Lucy had Peter duty from when she got home from school till ten o'clock, which was when Ellen got back from the restaurant, which she now owned. The divorce had done that much for her, though she still worked twelve hour days: replacing the cook who was sleeping off the booze or the newest waitress still in bed with her boyfriend, or just doing her regular shift as a manager. Lucy had her old room, and Peter slept in his little bed in Ellen's room.

A few blocks from home, Lucy heard a voice behind her.

"Hey, Luce! Wait up!"

It was Ian, a boy she actually did like a little. She looked down, letting her curtain of hair cover her neck, a gesture that had become second nature.

"What are you doing here, Ian?"

He caught up with her, an easy six feet of gangly teenage boy. But he had a sweetness about him, a way of listening Lucy found rare in most other kids. "My dad lives up here, I was just going to visit him."

"I just visited mine," Lucy said softly.

"Cool. He's a fisherman, right?"

"On the *Georgia Best*, with Michael and all those guys."

"So did you cut out early from school, or what?"

"Yeah, I just – "

"Don't worry, I won't say anything. I blew off the whole day, myself."

"Wow."

He hooked his thumbs in the belt loops of his jeans and looked away. "So, listen, I was thinking about asking you to the prom, if, you know, you're free and no one else has asked you."

"The prom."

"So you're going with someone – "

"No, I'm not. It would be fun to go with you."

"That's great, Lucy. We'll have fun. Can I walk you home?"

She shrugged a shy smile, and he snuck his hand in hers as they turned a corner toward her house. When they reached it, Ian pulled her gently toward him to kiss her, but they stood right in front of the restaurant, so Lucy led him behind a patch of dense bushes.

It was a good kiss, long and sweet. Dizzyingly long. She closed her eyes tight and opened the door, let the blackness wash over her, let her memories unfurl like heavy dark flowers. Everything changed. The air turned dense, cloying. A man, bigger and stronger than Ian, held her, stroked her hair, her breasts. She wanted him, was hungry, starved by the memory of him. Swooning, she tugged at his belt buckle –

"Jesus, Lucy," Ian said, embarrassed but trying to stay macho. He pulled her off him and wiped his mouth. "I mean, we're outside and everything."

"I'm sorry." She blushed deeply. "I don't know what I'm doing sometimes."

He walked her around the house to her entrance in the back where they awkwardly said their goodbyes. Lucy paused in the doorway, watching him walk away, wondering if she was losing her mind.

· SIXTY ·

S till in a daze, Lucy climbed the stairs and let herself in.

Afternoon cartoons blared from the TV. Ellen kneeled next to Peter, who sat in the center of a kaleidoscopic jumble of toy trains, trucks, action figures, books, Play-Doh, crayons, and Legos. She held up what looked like half a dump truck. "How do you expect me to find the back of this, Peter? Do you have to take everything apart? Can't you just *play* with a toy?"

"I like to see – "

" – what's inside. I know, I know." Ellen tossed a few more toys in a box.

Peter noticed Lucy in the doorway and couldn't stop a little smile. "You're in trouble."

Lucy shook her head and went to the kitchen where she dumped her knapsack on the table and opened the freezer. No more fudgsicles, of course.

"Why do we keep the good stuff where he can reach it?" Lucy said, slamming the door.

Ellen turned off the television and slipped on her waitressing shoes. "I thought we had an agreement, Lucy. If you're going to be late, you call. Is that so hard?"

"I left my stupid cell phone at school."

Ellen looked at her daughter, who was an inch taller than she and still growing.

"I'm sorry, Mom. I lost track of time."

206

"You know Andrea needs to get home to her kids. Why do you do this?" She twisted her hair in a bun and clipped it expertly.

"I already said I was sorry."

"Look," she said, with a nod toward Peter, "he needs a snack, and he's been a little monster all day. I don't know what's gotten into him. And no more TV, and bed by eight at the latest."

Lucy drank from an orange juice carton and nodded.

"And I'm sorry I'm leaving you this pile of dishes. I got so busy – "

"It's all right, Mom. Just go to work, okay?"

But she was halfway to the door. "Thanks, Lucy. You know where to find me."

"Yeah, yeah." They exchanged a little smile before Ellen kissed Peter goodbye and left.

Lucy walked over and sat down by him. "Watcha doin', little buddy?"

Peter's red curls fell into his face as he concentrated on fitting together a plastic train track. Lucy wondered if she had been this cute when she was five. Impossible.

"I'm not a little buddy."

"Yes, you are."

"No. I'm just Peter."

"Okay, just Peter, you gonna be all right while I do some dishes?"

He looked up at her and rolled his eyes, affecting all the sarcasm a five-year-old can muster. "Yeah, I think so."

"Good, then – "

"But I want TV."

"You heard what mom – "

He got to his feet and turned it on. "But this is my favorite show."

"They're all your favorite show."

He grinned at her and crawled up on their worn out couch. "And for snack I want Ritz crackers with squirty cheese."

Lucy laughed and got up. "You little monster." She gathered the snack, spraying five little rounds of crackers with blobs of cheese.

"I'm not a little monster, I'm Pete – "

"You're Peter. Yes, I know." She smiled as she handed him his plate.

"Thank you," he said, already riveted by some raucous cartoon.

"You're welcome."

She started gathering his toys, then gave up and went to the kitchen. He would just recreate Peter-World as soon as his show was over anyway.

Sighing at the mountain of dishes in the sink, she turned on the faucet and squirted dish detergent on a sponge. She reached for a pile of silverware which she mindlessly started soaping up, letting herself drift back to the walk home with Ian, the unexpected invitation; how much she liked him. The way he pulled her aside for a kiss, and how she had responded, as if he were someone else, someone whose touch and smell put her in a frenzy of remembering the other time, the time when she saw with her hands. Her secret other life she would never, ever share again, but that she had to understand, somehow. She washed the silverware without seeing it, dazed by this remembered man's touch, his voice, his laughter like warm honey. Bitter smell of the ocean, cool sheets, bare wooden floors. A place where something happened, a place from where she never went home. Something terrible just out of reach.

She rinsed a plate, a fork. A soapy butcher knife lay at the bottom of the sink. She washed it with trembling hands as she looked at her reflection in the metal. Her white, moon face, the long red scar on her neck –

All went black.

Shrill TV cartoon voices chattered loudly.

She blinked, looked up, down, to either side. Black as if she were buried alive.

She gasped for breath, gripped the edge of the metal sink.

"Stop this," she whispered hoarsely. "Oh please God, whatever this is, stop it." Still she clutched the knife. She squeezed her eyes shut, reached up with her other hand and, shaking, touched her eyes to make sure they were closed. "When I open my eyes again, I will see, I will see, I will see..." she whispered to herself. "There will be light, and I will see my home. The dishes, and Peter watching TV."

She opened her eyes.

Nightmare blackness. Her breath caught in her throat, turned shallow and harsh in her lungs.

The TV noise faded, bit by bit, till it was replaced by the wet tick of a kitchen clock over a pall of yawning silence.

"Peter?" She stepped back from the sink. "Are you there?"

Just the tick of the clock and cool tackiness of marble tile under her suddenly bare feet. No more braided kitchen rug. Her shoes were gone. Her jeans and sweater – gone. She wore something slippery, silky, tied at the waist. The air humid and thick.

She took another step back. The floor creaked.

"Quit fooling around, Peter, I know you're there." Her voice began to break. "Help me, Peter, somebody."

But she knew he was gone. She could feel it. She traced the heavy, sharp blade of the knife with her finger.

"What's happening to me? Where am I?"

The clock ticked louder, thumping along with her heart. With arms outstretched she touched a refrigerator, a modern stove, a granite counter. A kitchen, but not their kitchen.

She took a few more steps backward, then stopped and held her breath. Someone was in the room with her, watching her, listening to her.

Terror licked up her spine.

She knew she was going to die.

· SIXTY-ONE ·

Get away from me!" She lunged out with the knife, but felt the presence move behind her, heavy as a bag of sand, liquid like mercury.

Hot breath on the back of her neck.

She whirled around with the knife to cut whatever it was in half. But it had moved to the far side of the room. She could feel it – whatever this thing was – enjoying the game, relishing her helplessness, her fear.

"Who are you? Say something, goddammit!"

It took its time before it came screeching at her, skimming across the tile and slamming into her, knocking her backwards on the floor. But still she clutched the knife, slicing at the air, until freezing, strong hands wrapped around hers, grappling for the blade.

"I'm going to kill you!" Lucy shrieked.

A faraway voice called, "Lucy!"

A voice she knew, from somewhere...

"Lucy, let it go! It's your mother, it's Ellen! Give me the knife!"

Lucy shouted over a roar of white noise. "No! She'll kill us all! She's here, she's in the room! You've got to hide Peter!"

Lucy blinked.

She saw Ellen in her black and white waitress uniform, sweating and crying as she wrestled to free the knife. A red stain gathered and blossomed on her white cotton sleeve. Lucy watched her mother's mouth distort in horror as she fell back on the kitchen floor. Her face was dirty and scratched, hair loose from its bun, eyes wild.

210

"I can't – " Lucy started, "I couldn't see...and then – "

Sound rushed back: TV blaring, her mother's ragged breathing; Peter, red-eyed, whimpering, cowered against the wall a few feet away.

"Mom, your arm. I hurt you." She turned to her brother. "Peter, oh Peter honey, are you okay? Did I..."

He dropped his jaw to wail and crawled into his mother's lap. The stain was spreading to her shoulder. She didn't seem to notice it as she held tight to her son.

Lucy looked into her mother's eyes and dropped the knife, backing up quickly on her hands like a crab till she knocked into a kitchen chair. For several seconds they crouched on the floor like animals. Lucy glanced all around her: yes, their kitchen floor with their tattered rug, their table legs, her sneakers and blue jeans.

Her family who looked at her in terror and disbelief.

· SIXTY-TWO ·

Ellen wandered down the hall in her wool coat, speaking in hushed tones into the phone. "Tom, it's not something that's just going to go away – I know she's a teenager but it wasn't like that. You had to be here to understand...I'm not being that way, dammit. Look, we'll pay for it, okay? We've got to figure out a way."

She glanced at Peter curled in her mother's lap with a bowl of popcorn. With a quilt from the bed wrapped around their shoulders, they watched TV with sad eyes. Behind them, facing the back door, Lucy sat at the kitchen table, her silhouette bulky in her big down coat.

"Uh...hold on." Ellen called to the kitchen. "Lucy! Do you want to talk to your dad?"

Not turning around, Lucy shook her head.

"Daddy!" Peter cried, nearly flipping the bowl of popcorn as he jumped out of his grandmother's lap. "I wanna talk to Daddy!"

Lucy stared out the window in silence as they followed the icy highway south into the city. The world looked incredibly ugly to her that day. Filthy, snow-covered hills merged with a grimier sky. A fine grey sleet raked across the windshield as they passed an endless parade of McDonalds, Burger Kings, and gas stations.

Since the event of yesterday she had had no more memories, or fear of them, but felt strange in her own body, like she didn't fit in it any more. Getting dressed that morning she avoided the mirror entirely, brushing her hair as she faced the wall.

Though the car was warm, she still felt cold and pulled her hat farther down over her ears and sunk deeper in her seat.

"Why do you wear that thing?" Ellen asked, glancing at her as she drove.

"What thing?"

"You know what thing."

"I'm freezing to death, okay?"

Ellen shook her head and put the heat on high. "Look, I know you don't want to do this, but I think you have to talk to someone."

"Maybe I'll find someone who believes a word I say."

"I believe *you* believe what you say – "

"Then you think I'm fucking crazy – "

"Don't you swear at me young lady – "

"This is such bullshit – "

"I said stop swearing!" Ellen's hands tensed on the wheel.

"Is that all you care about? Is that all you can get emotional about? My swearing?"

"Oh, don't be such a teenager for five minutes, all right?"

Lucy slid even deeper in her seat.

"I thought we got through this when you were six years old," Ellen added.

"You will never understand what's happening to me. *I* don't understand it."

"Maybe not, Lucy, but we're going to try, get you some help."

Lucy was silent under her hat.

"Are you warm enough under there?"

"Yeah. So...does your arm still hurt?"

Ellen smiled and looked over but still Lucy stared at her boots. "Just a little twinge now and then. I'll live."

· SIXTY-THREE ·

Astra finished her notes on her eleven o'clock patient, an obese, manic depressive fourteen-year-old boy. She powered down her laptop, dropped a few papers and files in her briefcase and snapped it closed. The afternoon looked good: first a little lunch in the cafeteria, the gym and personal trainer at two, hair and nails at four, then buy the ingredients to make homemade pizza for herself and Constantin when he got home at seven.

Her assistant, Steven, interrupted her on her way out. "Dr. Nathanson, don't you want me to fill you in on tomorrow's schedule?"

"I don't know," she said, turning toward him. She was still a remarkable looking woman; regal and lush in a deep purple, tailored pant suit and black turtleneck. "Can't you just email it to me? I'm kind of in a rush today."

"No problem," Steven said. "I'll do it right now."

"Thanks. I'll see you in the morning."

"Have a good afternoon, Dr. Nathanson."

Astra climbed the three flights to the cafeteria and took a tray in the crowded lunch line. Steam rose from chafing dishes of stewed meatballs, macaroni and cheese, franks and beans, roast beef and cabbage. She smiled pleasantly and nodded to a few of her colleagues as they ordered from the steam table. As she made her way around the sandwich bar and toward the cooler for her light yogurt and apple, she noticed a slim young woman with waist-length red hair and an older woman, possibly her mother.

Astra poured herself some coffee as she listened to the girl order a

BLT. Had the haunted look of a cutter, but maybe not. Sad around the eyes, probably depressed. Astra had some slots open; she wondered if this girl would be assigned to her.

Just as Astra was about to excuse herself to reach for the Sweet n'Low, the girl flipped her hair back from her face, revealing the vicious slash of a scar across her white throat.

Astra's hand stopped midreach.

Out of the corner of her eye, Lucy noticed Astra's hesitation. "Excuse me," she said. "Am I in your way?"

Astra tried to say no, but only stuttered, shook her head "no" and walked away. She never looked her in the eye.

Thinking the woman had been repulsed by her scar, Lucy pulled her hair forward and stroked it thoughtfully. Ellen had seen the woman's startled expression and quick exit as well, and gave Lucy's narrow shoulders a little squeeze.

"I think it went well this morning, don't you, honey?"

Lucy glanced behind her at the swinging door the strange woman had just disappeared through. "She didn't pay for her food," she said quietly.

"Oh, she probably works here, probably has an account or something."

"Mom, I want to have this removed." Lucy traced the length of the scar with the tip of her finger.

"I know you do, but it's not covered by insurance because it's cosmetic, so we'll have to – "

Lucy turned to her mother. "I want it gone. Ian invited me to the prom and I want it gone by then. I'll pay for it myself."

"That's only a month away, honey."

But Lucy had turned back to the counter, picked up her BLT, fries and Diet Coke and started toward a cluster of tables and chairs.

Astra walked briskly down the hallway, still carrying her yogurt and apple, briefcase slung hard over her shoulder. She consulted her handheld a few times, as if quite late for something, and was a few yards from the exit when she heard a woman's voice behind her call her name.

She looked longingly at her bright red Audi in the snowy lot, then forced herself to turn around.

Arlette, David Davies' perky new assistant-intern, held the office door open with her foot as she leaned out. "Dr. Nathanson?"

"Yes?" Astra shifted the yogurt and apple in her hands.

"Sorry, were you leaving?"

"What is it?"

"If you have a minute, Dr. Davies would like to have a word with you."

Astra started toward her. "Of course."

Arlette held the door open wider for Astra to enter. "He said if I saw you I should grab you, so here I am, grabbing you!" she said with an awkward giggle.

Astra followed her into the office, a hundred reasons whipping by in her mind why David, now her boss, would want to see her. There had been a section-wide meeting just that morning, with all bases covered, in her opinion.

Arlette gestured at David's door, but it was closed. Astra knocked softly, still holding her coat, briefcase, apple and yogurt.

"That's not much lunch," Arlette said, smiling.

"It's my...lunch," Astra said, a headache blooming in the back of her skull.

Finishing up a phone call, David opened the door and motioned for Astra to come in and sit down.

"Anything you want's fine, Kevin. Whatever you make I eat, you know that," David said, laughing as he walked behind her and shut the door. "All right, see you later."

He hung up and smiled at Astra as he reinstalled himself in his overstuffed leather chair. She had opened her narrow briefcase and was trying to maneuver her food into it. Neither item fit.

"That's not much lunch," he said, watching her.

"Well, I've a busy afternoon ahead of me, so – "

"So, how is Constantin?"

"Oh, he's well. Working a lot as usual."

"Interesting guy. Fascinating guy. What an amazing field he's in. Is he out on the water a lot these days?"

"Well, it's winter, so not really...how's Kevin?"

"Wonderful as always, cooking me up some wacky French-Thai dish tonight. I said just go ahead and make whatever. You're the cook, I'm the dishwasher."

Astra smiled pleasantly, her lunch still on her lap.

"Listen, the reason I had Arlette drag you in here was that I had an intake on a new patient this morning." He extracted a thin manila folder from a pile of them on his desk and leafed through the contents. "Presents depressed, had an episode of hysterical blindness yesterday, sounded genuine, at least according to the mother. Very interesting case."

Astra cleared her throat. "How old is she?"

David looked up at her. "Now, that's interesting. How did you know it was a 'she'?"

Astra coughed and reached for a Kleenex on his desk. She forced a chuckle. "It's the usual, right? Girls present depressed, boys angry."

He turned back to the file. "True, true."

Astra began to notice how David hadn't aged well at all. The only hair left on his head was a grey donut, like a monk's cut, combed carefully behind his ears. It was clear he'd given up on the gym years ago, around the time he'd moved in with Kevin.

He leaned back. The chair made a leathery "poof." "So, can you take her on? How's the schedule look?"

"Oh, I'm pretty full, every day – "

"Except for Thursdays?"

"Today? Well, Thursdays are my half day, you know I've had this schedule for quite some time now, David, and – "

"What's the problem, Astra? One more hour, one more patient? You're down one anyway, since Margaret was discharged…"

"Well, we all know it's never just an hour. There's follow up, and group, notes and so on – "

"Astra, are you okay?"

"Of course I'm okay."

"Are you sure? I mean, you looked upset when you came in here today. You can tell me. My God, how long have I known you?"

Astra laughed a little. "Too long, I'm afraid."

"Eighteen years we've been curing teenagers, with words, drugs – "

" – and time," they both said, laughing.

"It's a wonder we're not nuts ourselves," David said. He watched her another moment, then put his feet up on his desk. "So, what do you say, Astra? One more client? I'd give her to Helen but she's swamped and so's Franz, and I'm – "

"It's fine, David. I'll take her. Would Thursday starting at two work for them?" She got up, brushing off her coat, though it was spotless.

"Probably, but I'll clear it with them tonight."

"What's the girl's name?"

"Lucy. As in 'I Love'."

"Lucy," she repeated, her hand on the door. "Well, you have a nice night, David. Enjoy the French Thai food."

He gave her a little wave. "You too, Astra. My best to Constantin."

Arlette glanced up from her typing to chirp, "Good night, Dr. Nathanson!" but Astra had already slipped by her desk, tossing her yogurt and apple in the trash as she passed.

· SIXTY-FOUR ·

Lucy pushed away her empty ice cream dish as she watched Ian finish his banana boat. She reached up to touch the bandage on her neck where the doctor had removed the birthmark a week before. The skin was still tender there, but she couldn't wait to wear her hair in an updo at the prom. Only another week and it would be "smooth as a baby's bottom," or so the doctor had promised her.

She stuffed her hands in her jacket pockets and stared out at the winter night. Blue moonlight reflected off freshly fallen snow. "So, you didn't feel it?"

He looked up. "What?"

"When we were kissing, how I changed."

"I don't know if you changed. I just know you really got into it." He gave her a tentative smile, but she wasn't having it.

"That's because I became who I used to be, and I thought you were someone else, someone I can almost remember."

"Jesus, Lucy, I don't know about that."

A posse of teenagers, three boys and two girls, jumbled noisily into the diner, strolling down the aisle where Lucy and Ian sat. The girls wore tight jeans, cheap jewelry and thin coats, even though it was below zero outside; the boys strutted behind them, artificially bigger in puffy down coats. The girls ignored Ian and Lucy, whereas the boys chucked Ian on the shoulder and grinned at Lucy. Thankfully, they settled at a table far in the back.

Lucy's eyes welled up as she looked helplessly around the diner. "Ian,

I gotta be able to tell somebody this stuff. Somebody who doesn't think I'm nuts, or who wants to give me drugs or talk me out of it. Or tells me it's some stupid teenager thing."

"You can tell me whatever you want."

She leaned forward, her hair a rich curtain sweeping the table. "I can? How can I know you won't run off and be like the other kids whispering about me in the halls at school? Or those jerks over there? I mean, I could tell you stuff, and you could dump me."

"I won't, I swear."

"Then you have to promise me you'll tell me some secret about yourself, that you haven't told anybody, ever."

He finished the last of his ice cream and sat back in the booth. "I guess I can do that."

She pulled a napkin from the dispenser and started tearing off little bits.

He fixed her with his pale blue eyes. "So tell me, Lucy. Believe me, I've been through some totally weird shit in my life."

She stared at the napkin as she shredded it. "I was killed. Someone killed me. And I came back."

Ian glanced behind them. The cluster of teens huddled over shakes and sundaes, oblivious to them. He leaned forward in the booth. "How...how were you killed?"

"I don't remember."

"Who killed you?"

"I have no idea."

"Then why do you think you were killed?"

"Because I go into, like a trance. Like when I was kissing you. And don't make jokes."

"I won't. What happens in the trance?"

"My body feels different. I touch my hair, it's rougher, wavy, I'm wearing something slippery, maybe a robe or a long dress. I get to a certain point, and I just, I come back."

"Back where?"

"To being me, Lucy."

"Who do you think you were? I mean, who is this person in a robe?"

She spoke in a hoarse whisper. "I don't know. I'm a woman, but I'm older. And it's always dark, which doesn't bother me, until the end when I know I'm going to be killed. Then I'm scared."

"So you were blind."

Lucy looked up from her napkin, her fingers frozen in space. "I was blind."

"You just said it was dark."

"But I never thought – I was *blind*. Oh my God." Tears came to her eyes.

"Why are you crying?"

"Because you're helping me."

"What else do you remember?"

"There's a dog sometimes, who pulls me."

"Maybe it's a seeing eye dog."

"Maybe it is." She wiped her eyes on her sleeve.

"What else?"

"There isn't much more, just the part I almost remember, but not quite." She looked at him with red-rimmed eyes. "I'm so tired of holding this in. I'm always depressed, like I've lost something. Or there's some part of me that's lost and wants to come back. God, I don't even know who's real any more – the woman who died, or me, Lucy? Or maybe I'm both people?"

She cried freely now, facing away from the booths in the back and toward the sweating windows of the diner. "Do you think I'm crazy, Ian? Do you want to break up with me? I would, I would if I – "

He took her hand and held her cool fingers. "Come on, Luce, I just told you I've been through some weird shit. Don't cry, okay?"

"Do you believe me, anyway?"

"Yes."

"The doctor at the nuthouse thinks I'm crazy. I could see it in his eyes. 'Do I have these dreams often?' I must've said fifteen times, they're

221

not dreams. They happen when I'm awake."

"Guy sounds like a fucking idiot."

"What should I do, Ian?"

He reached in his jeans pocket, pulled out a few crumpled bills, flattened them on the counter with chapped hands. "If you were blind, maybe you went to a blind school, like that place in Watertown. Maybe you should go there."

"Why?"

"Figure out who you were, maybe remember more things. Be a detective, sorta."

"But I'm so afraid."

"You're afraid anyway, right?"

She straightened her shoulders in her coat and looked at him. "Now you tell me. Tell me a secret you've never told anyone before."

Ian zipped his coat and pulled on his fisherman's hat. Pieces of badly trimmed blond hair stuck out from under it. He rubbed his hands together as if they were already cold. "I will, but on the way home."

She smiled for the first time that night and sunk deeper in her seat. "No, you won't. You'll tell me right now."

"Come on, Luce. I need a walk."

"Why, so you can have time to think of something?"

A sly smile crept over his face. "Oh, I don't need time for that."

"What, then? And remember, something you've never told anyone, ever."

He shook his head and looked out the window. "Promise you won't dump me?"

Lucy rolled her eyes.

"I've had a crush on you since third grade. Can we go now?"

Laughing, Lucy got to her feet. "I like that secret."

· SIXTY-FIVE ·

Afternoon sun cast long shadows across the courtyard where Astra and Constantin walked. They chose their way carefully on the icy sidewalk, passing students laden with backpacks and bundled against the brutal cold.

"It was nice of you to meet me for lunch, Astra," Constantin said. "Do you have to go back to work?"

"Of course. It's Friday."

"Oh, well your schedule changes so much, I – "

"My schedule hasn't changed in a year."

He looked at her drawn face under her black fur hat. She flipped up the collar on her matching fur-lined coat with quick slim hands. He thought she looked oddly bloodless, her painted on mouth the only real color on her face.

He pulled on his gloves as they crossed behind the library. "Did you like your salad?"

"It was pretty ordinary. How was your pizza?"

"Great."

"Even with, what was it, bacon and pineapple? You like the strangest food."

"I just like food."

"Lucky for me, with my cooking."

But Constantin had stopped paying attention. He stood in front of an ivy-veined dorm where half a dozen students stood chatting on the steps, their brightly colored hats and scarves sharp against the brilliant blue sky.

He rested his hand on the railing and stared up at a window on the fourth floor.

A hand lifted a curtain, a face looked out. A young woman with long wavy hair gazed down at them. The curtain dropped. Constantin gasped and put a hand over his heart.

Astra took his arm. "My God, Constantin, are you all right?"

"Fine, fine. I always get this way, you know, emotional, when I pass by here."

"Why?"

Constantin looked at her. She really meant the question. "Astra, how can you say that – why? Don't you know where we are?"

"Christ, Constantin, I really have no idea what you're talking about, but I do know it's too damned cold to stand around here talking about whatever it is – "

"This was Kim's dorm. Tell me you remember *that*."

She looked up at the window. The curtains rippled but the figure had disappeared.

"Of course I remember, but it was a long time ago and all these dorms look exactly alike. How am I supposed to keep track of – "

Constantin turned and walked away.

She ran after him, slipping in the snow. Finally she caught up with him, grabbed his arm and yanked him around. Her voice was nearly a growl. "Don't you ever walk away from me again."

He watched her pupils grow large, though she faced the lowering sun. "Sometimes I can't believe what you did to her."

"What are you talking about?"

"You know damned well what I'm talking about. Never visiting her, never calling her. Even after you said you were...better."

"Don't make me relive this, Constantin. I told you, I felt too guilty about what I'd done to have a relationship with her. Why are you doing this to me? I thought we had a nice time at lunch. We talked everything out, and now – now you're blaming me for things so far in the past..."

He looked away and past her, toward his office.

She shook him, her pupils huge. "Look at me, please, dammit! Constantin, do you still love me? Please tell me you do. I need to hear it."

Finally he looked at her. "You always need to hear it, Astra. Ten, twenty times a day. It's never enough, is it? I never love you enough, or do it right. Why is that? It's tiring, Astra. You're wearing me out."

Speechless, her eyes welled up and spilled over. With a coughing sort of cry, she threw her arms around him and sobbed. He tentatively touched her back, avoiding the stares from students and faculty who passed by. She didn't cry often but he was somehow unmoved by all this emotion.

Eventually, she sloughed off him and looked at his impassive face.

"So you think I'm a bad person?"

"No, I – "

"You think I'm evil?"

"Wh – "

"You have no idea, you know that?"

"Stop it, Astra. People are staring – "

"I don't give a fuck about *people*. I give a fuck about you, and what you think of me."

"I think I should go – "

"It's a good thing I love you, Constantin. Trust me. You've never been so loved, and you never will be."

He pulled his hat low over his eyes, turned away from her, and began to walk toward his office. Soon he left the cleared sidewalk and took a short cut through foot-deep drifts across the quad. She watched him go but didn't move, standing still as death next to her daughter's dorm, her form a black cutout against the snow.

· SIXTY-SIX ·

Lucy waited in one of the stalls in the girl's bathroom. She leaned against one graffiti-ed wall, listening.

"Mr. Hardnet – hardass – should go screw himself. *I* wasn't talking, *you* were talking."

"I was answering *you*, dumbass."

"True."

Giggles. The snap of makeup cases, sound of zippers, a heavy sigh. The smell of piss and lemony perfume. Lucy pictured the merciless assessments in the mirror: face, hair, figure. Never good enough. She smoothed her hands down the front of her oversized flannel shirt and watched a pair of booted feet leave the stall next to her. Hiss of a lit cigarette in the toilet and the stall door slapped shut. With a clattering of platform shoes, they were gone.

She smiled to herself. Today was the day she'd been waiting for: the day she could remove the bandage from her neck. That morning, before school, she'd been too nervous to take it off, but as the day wore on, she found it harder and harder to wait.

She unlocked the stall and stepped out, quiet as a cat in her well worn sneakers on the cement floor. A high, gated window sifted gauzy afternoon sunshine that lit up her coppery hair. Dust motes glittered. She brushed her hair in long staticky strokes, staring at herself in the cracked silver mirror. With quick white fingers, she twined her mass of hair into a shimmering knot behind her head and fastened it with a silver clip. Still she stared at herself, as if she could see inside to some secret behind her

226

eyes that stared back at her.

Tentatively, she reached up to her neck and lifted a corner of the bandage free from the skin. She squeezed her eyes shut, then opened them, and peeled the rest of the bandage off.

It was gone.

Her eyes widened. Sixteen years she'd carried this mark, this ruddy shadow of a slash across her neck that she'd hidden, ignored, explained, covered, hated.

Gone.

She stepped closer to the mirror. With a trembling hand she reached up to touch the flawless luminescent skin, smooth and cool as the inside of a shell. Her hand lingered there as she watched her pulse beat at the hollow of her neck, delicate as the heart of a baby bird.

Lucy tossed her books in her locker and slammed it shut, spinning the lock before she turned toward the gym. Kids changing classes passed to either side of her as she made her way down the hall, head down, winter coat clutched under one arm.

She was about to duck into the girls' locker room when she heard someone call her name.

"Lucy, hold up." Ian caught up to her and gestured toward the cafeteria, a few doors down. "Don't you have lunch? It's fourth period."

"I've got to go somewhere."

"Well, where?" he said, grinning.

"That place we talked about."

"The blind school? You're going now?"

She nodded, glancing behind him.

"I thought we were doing that together."

She slipped on her coat. "I can't. I need to do it alone."

"But what if you, I don't know, flip out?"

"I'm not going to flip out," she said angrily. "I can control myself."

"C'mon, Luce, think about it. It could be bad. Just let me come with you."

She looked at him and shook her head. "It's harder when you're with me. I need to let myself feel whatever it is..."

He held up his hands and took a few steps back. "Okay, okay, I gotcha. I'll call you tonight."

"Fine."

"Your bandage is off."

"I know."

"Well, you look nice. That's all I wanted to say."

"Thanks."

He turned with a little wave. As she watched him walk away, blending into the stream of kids on their way to lunch, she hoped she was right about going alone.

The bus to Cambridge seemed to make endless local stops before finally lurching into Watertown Square. Lucy checked her phone: 1:33. She had less than an hour before she had to catch a bus back home and take care of Peter. By that time her mother would have gotten the call that she'd skipped school, so there'd be that to explain as well.

In front of her, a compact, steel-haired old woman sat erect in the middle of her seat, cane at the ready. She held her chin up and tilted her head as she listened to the sounds around her: a girl flirting and laughing with her boyfriend, a young man tapping on his laptop, a middle-aged businessman snoring, his face pressed against the cold-fogged window.

When they reached the square and the bus paused at the stop, the old woman got to her feet and stood waiting in front of Lucy for the rest of the passengers to get out, then carefully made her way off the bus. Lucy thought if she just followed her, she would surely find the school.

But it wasn't easy to be subtle. The woman's progress was quite slow on the narrow walk, so finally Lucy spoke up.

"Excuse me, but do you know if the Stafford School is nearby?"

The woman stopped, turned back toward her and raised her head, her dark sightless eyes fixed on something far beyond Lucy. Only then did Lucy realize how tiny she was – well under five feet.

"I'm going there, young lady. Are you blind?"

Lucy watched her lined face listen for an answer. "I'm not, no."

"You sound not so sure." She smiled, a hundred fine wrinkles livening her face.

"I'm sure...I'm not blind."

"Why don't you walk with me, then. I'll show you the way."

"Sure, all right." Lucy reached down for the woman's arm.

"No, let me take your arm, and I direct you." She reached up her thin arm in its worn wool coat. Lucy tucked it under her elbow and continued in the direction they'd begun.

"Why aren't you in school?" the old woman said.

"I needed to go see a friend, at Stafford."

"Which friend? What is the name? I know everyone there."

"Oh, she's new. Her name is Helen."

"Your age, this girl?"

"Exactly my age."

"Blind from birth?"

"Yes."

"I know no Helen, blind from birth."

"We're best friends."

"I believe you, but there is no Helen at Stafford. No one your age. And you must not visit much with her, because you don't know how to walk with a blind person. You took my arm. That's wrong, blind person takes *your* arm." She stopped and gently patted Lucy's hand. "Tell me, why are you really going there?"

Lucy smelled food and looked up. They stood outside a diner called the Do Walk In. She was suddenly dizzy with hunger.

"Because I'm trying to understand something."

"What?"

"It's impossible to explain."

"Oh, young lady, I'm eighty-eight years old. You don't think I may understand this thing, whatever it is?"

Lucy watched the woman look past her as if examining the moon or sun. "I remember being blind."

· SIXTY-SEVEN ·

The lunch crowd had thinned at the Do Walk In, but waitresses in turquoise uniforms and white aprons still moved with lunch-rush energy as they clattered dirty plates into bins and wiped down tables. Lucy and the old woman sat across from each other in a weathered naugahyde booth. She stared at a menu but couldn't focus on the words. The woman's shoulders barely cleared the linoleum table. She sat with her hands neatly folded, black gloves still on.

"You must eat anything you like," she said. "It's my treat."

"Oh, you don't have to do that," Lucy said. "I have money." She reached in her pocket and felt two bills. She knew they were ones.

"You missed lunch at school?"

"Missing lunch at school is no loss, believe me."

A heavyset waitress with a kind face and hair in a blonde bun paused at their table. "Hey, Carmella," she said. "How are you?"

"Is that Debbie?" Carmella lit up.

"It sure is," she said, wiping a few crumbs off the table.

"How are you, dear?" She reached her small hand out and Debbie took it and squeezed it.

"I'm just fine. Is this your granddaughter with you?"

Lucy smiled shyly, shaking her head.

"No, she's a new friend."

"I'm Lucy," she said. "It's nice to meet you both."

"Lucy," Carmella repeated softly.

Debbie looked back and forth between Carmella and Lucy. "Well, you look related. Maybe it's the smile. Anyway, what can I getcha today?"

"Coffee and a couple of the little chocolate cookies for me," Carmella said.

Lucy shrugged. "A BLT."

"Something more, Lucy?"

She glanced at a sunbleached photo of a steaming bowl of clam chowder on the wall. "And clam chowder, please."

Debbie nodded and turned toward the kitchen.

"This is so nice of you," Lucy said. "But I don't understand why you want to take me to lunch."

"Like I tell you, I know some things." She took off her gloves and lay them side by side on the table. "Tell me more about what you remember, about being blind. Is it a dream?"

"No, I'm awake."

"When does it happen, this remembering?"

"When I'm upset, or excited." Lucy blushed. She looked around anxiously, but the only people left in the place were a couple of burly men in down vests at the counter, far out of earshot.

"What else happens?"

"I'm someone else, at the same time I'm me," Lucy said. "Sometimes I'm with a dog. I can smell him, I can even hear him pant. He pulls me, leads me, and then I smell the sea. I...I'm in love with a man with smooth hair and a rough chin."

"How do you know this?"

"I'm not sure I want to tell you."

Debbie dropped off Lucy's lunch and Carmella's coffee and cookies, taking a moment to guide her hand to the cup.

"You two enjoy your lunch now," she said, bustling off.

"Don't worry, Lucy," Carmella said. "I have loved before. You are a young woman. It's your time now."

"But why do you want to know these things? I met you on the street and now I'm telling you these things about me – "

"Does it feel right to talk to me, Lucy?"

Lucy stirred her chowder. "Yes."

"Then tell me. How do you know this man you love – loved – has smooth hair and rough chin?"

"Because when I was kissing my boyfriend, Ian, he turned into this other man, in my mind, anyway. It sounds so crazy, I know. And...and then I remembered having him inside me, and I wanted him again, it was like I had missed him for so long and suddenly I was holding him, I'd found him! But it was only Ian. And how could I remember sex, if I've never had it? But I remembered it."

With trembling hands, Carmella sipped her coffee. "Do you remember this man's name?"

"No."

"What else, Lucy? Is there more?"

"Yeah, but it – it's not good for me to talk about it." She ate a small spoonful of chowder.

"Most important things are hardest to say. Don't you think that's true?"

"I guess. Okay, it's like this: I'm in a room, a kitchen, some strange kitchen. I'm wearing a robe. I think it's a robe. It feels cool and slippery and I have bare feet."

"Why are you in this kitchen?"

"It feels like I'm looking for someone but I don't remember who, or even why. And then I feel something in the room, something watching me. And I'm terrified. Then I, I sort of snap out of it, and I'm me again."

"Lucy, I must ask you something, and you must promise not to be afraid. But you must tell me the truth."

"I'll try."

"Do you have a birthmark on your body, a long mark across your neck?"

Lucy gasped, then whispered hoarsely, "Who *are* you?"

"Do you, Lucy?"

She pushed her food away. "My God, how did you know?"

Carmella's eyes welled up and she reached her hands out to Lucy, who held them for a moment, the skin papery and cool. "Oh, my darling," she choked, "my darling Kim."

Lucy looked around. Debbie glanced over at them but kept wiping down tables and straightening chairs. The men huddled over their coffee and sports section.

"Who's Kim? Carmella, maybe we should stop talking – "

Carmella let go of Lucy's hands and reached in her purse, pulling out a package of tattered Kleenex. "You must be patient, dear. You can think I'm crazy old lady but listen, first, I beg you. Promise me you stay a little longer, no matter what I say."

"A few minutes. But I've got to get home to babysit or I'm in big trouble."

Carmella dabbed at her wet face. "Do you understand, dear, who you are? What you are?"

"What are you talking about?"

The tears kept coming, but she didn't seem sad. Her face was open and elated. "Some of us, when we die, Lucy, we don't really die. We go to another body. We're called Repeaters. You are a Repeater, and your name was – "

"*We*? You're a Repeater?"

"Yes. This is my third time."

"And how many times have I – "

"I knew you when you were the blind girl. When you were Kim."

"That was my name? But why did I come back?"

"Repeaters come back if they have not learned how to love, or if they die with violence." Carmella dabbed at her eyes again; cleared her throat. "Are you eating your lunch, dear?"

"No."

"It's not good? We'll get you something else."

"It's good."

Carmella reached for Lucy's hand; she let her take it. "You have to let yourself *remember*, Lucy. Remember everything. If you don't, you slip back to what you were – "

" – is that what I'm doing, slipping back?"

"If you resist, Lucy, you go back to what you just were. For you, this is Kim. You must try not to be afraid...when was first time you remember anything?"

"When I was a little girl I knew that my mother wasn't my mother. She got so upset when I talked about it. And sometimes I would slip back. She didn't believe me, ever."

"She pushed the knowledge back inside you. It works for a while, then it doesn't. Then the body remembers, and the body tells the mind."

Lucy pushed her food away and sat with her head in her hands.

"This is all so crazy. I feel like a freak. What am I going to do?"

"You are not a freak, Lucy." Carmella lowered her voice to a whisper. "Repeaters are everywhere."

Lucy placed her trembling hands flat on the table to still them. "I don't believe you."

"Yes, you do, dear."

"All right – so if it's true, what do I do?"

"You must first remember how you died. Remember who killed you. You know, don't you? I think you do."

Lucy watched the squiggly-worm pattern on the linoleum table blur with her tears. "Look, the birthmark, the scar, it's gone. I got rid of it. I borrowed the money from my dad. I don't have to think about it any more. I'm not hideous any more – "

"You are not hideous – "

"And I won't, and I can't think about it. You don't understand, whoever you are – "

"You must think about it, Lucy, this...this is not going away, this thing that happened to you – "

"So tell me, then, if you know! I can't stand this any more!"

Carmella sat back in the booth, looking even tinier there. Her voice was thin. Lucy strained to hear. "The moment I saw her I knew who she was, what she was – "

"Who?" Lucy's face was swollen with tears.

"We are all afraid of your mother, Lucy, your real mother. She has repeated so many, many times, only evil is left in her. She killed you, Lucy. She cut your throat – "

"No!" Lucy blurted. "That's impossible! Did you *see* it? Were you there? You're blind yourself!" She pushed herself out of the booth and stood there, panting.

Carmella reached out for her, her small arm shaking. "Lucy, don't leave!"

She took a step back. "Stay away from me!"

The two patrons at the counter turned to stare at them. Debbie looked up from where she stood at the cash register, fingers poised at the keys.

Lucy leaned down and said in a harsh whisper, "How can you say that? How do you know that? You *are* a crazy old woman!" She grabbed her jacket and mittens and tossed on her backpack.

"Lucy, listen to me! You're a Repeater – you have powers! All of us do, but you must work to find them, control them – "

"Look, this is insane."

Carmella struggled to make her way out of the booth. "Please stay, Lucy. This is life and death – "

"Thanks for the lunch. Goodbye."

Head down, Lucy ducked out of the diner and into the raw winter afternoon.

· SIXTY-EIGHT ·

Shoulders hunched in her thin jacket, Lucy climbed the hill to her home. Tears had long since frozen on her face, and her hair had come loose from its clip and fell wildly around her shoulders. As she trudged along she stared at the frozen ground, unseeing. Every so often she reached under her scarf to touch the smooth clear skin of her neck. It comforted her. She imagined that it had always been this way, that all the rest had been a bad dream.

Passing the sparsely filled restaurant, just a few locals that night, she crossed around to the back and climbed the steep stairs to the apartment. At the door she took a deep breath and turned the key. As she did so she realized she hadn't once thought about an explanation for where she'd been all afternoon, never mind for skipping the last half of the school day.

She let herself in. The smells of cooking, Grandma Sally's rosewater perfume, and moist heat surrounded her. Peter jumped off his hobby horse and came running toward her like a forty pound bullet, his face covered with Spaghettios, yelling, "Yahoo, Lucy's home!" She caught him in her arms and couldn't help but laugh and come to life a bit with his sweet warmth and weight in her arms.

He grabbed her nose and held it. "You're cold like an icicle."

"I know. You gonna warm me up?"

He nodded, then turned with a somber expression behind him. "Mom and Grammy are real mad."

Both women stood, one a larger, older version of the other, hands on hips, staring at her. Silhouetted by the kitchen light, their faces in shadow.

The TV droned on mindlessly in the living room.

"I watched a hundred and one, no, a million and one, no," Peter giggled, "dalmatians!"

"That's nice, honey." Lucy gently put him down. He ran off to the kitchen and climbed back on the hobby horse, creaking back and forth. Lucy took off her knapsack and dropped it on the coffee table, then started to unbutton her coat.

Feeling their eyes on her, she turned to look from her mother to her grandmother and back. "So go ahead and scream at me."

"I'm not going to scream at you," Ellen said in a trembling voice.

"Well, that's good," Lucy said, unwinding her scarf.

"Because you're going to do all the talking. You're going to tell me why you left school today, and who you were with, and what you were doing. And you're going to tell me the truth."

Lucy crossed the living room into the kitchen on her way to her room. "I have my own life. I don't have to tell you everything I do."

The kitchen air was thick with the smell of meatloaf and mashed potatoes. Sally sighed, untied her apron, and laid it over a chair.

"You're sixteen years old – "

"Almost seventeen – "

"And you will tell me where you were this afternoon. I already know you were with that boy."

Lucy turned and looked at her mother's red face, her hands worn from dishwashing and twenty years of restaurant work. Peter made kissing sounds and hugged himself, then rocked with giggles.

"Peter, you spied on me!" Lucy said.

"Come sit with me, young man," Sally said. Scowling, Peter got off the worn wooden horse and followed her into the living room where he crawled onto the couch and into her lap.

"You were with that boy, weren't you, Lucy?"

"He has a name, you know."

Her mother took a step toward her. A gentleness softened her face. "You took off your bandage."

Lucy turned her head away.

"Let me see." She folded Lucy's collar back and took a small sharp breath. Lucy flipped the collar back up and took a step into the shadow of the hall.

"You're too young, Lucy. You know that, right, honey?" She started to cry in an exhausted way. "We haven't even really talked like we should, because I thought, didn't think it would happen – "

"Ma, nothing happened, okay?"

"Don't lie to me!" she cried, then covered her mouth. More quietly, "Don't lie to me. I called his home. His mother said he wasn't home yet either."

"He doesn't even live with his mother."

"His stepmother then. Just tell me, Lucy, were you careful?"

She looked at her mother's tear-stained face. "Yes, we were careful."

"Oh, thank God. Thank God."

"Can I go in my room now?"

"Fine. I'm too angry to talk with you any more tonight anyway."

Lucy shook her head and ducked into her room, closing the door behind her. Ellen went to her door and stood there a moment, her hand hovering at the doorknob, but she let it drop and walked away toward the light of the living room.

· SIXTY-NINE ·

As if shedding a heavy, painful skin, Lucy took off her clothes; the worn flannel shirt and cotton undershirt, jeans soaked at the cuffs with slushy snow, sodden socks and half-frozen sneakers, and piled it all by the door. After drying herself completely, she pulled on thick wool tights, a clean T-shirt, and an oversized nightgown.

Her simple narrow bed with its collection of stuffed animals and threadbare quilt never looked more inviting. She thought of lying down and just going to sleep, even though it was only seven at the latest, when she was struck with an impulse to pray.

She had only been to church a few times, since Ellen was a lapsed Catholic and only took her and Peter on Christmas and Easter. Even those few times they kneeled on the hard pews in church she had never really prayed, only bent her head and closed her eyes, letting her mind wander as it pleased. She understood what prayer was, but something in her resented being told when and where to do it.

But now she kneeled on the braided rug next to the bed, pressed her hands together and let her chin drop to rest on the tips of her fingers, her face lit only by the glow of a reading lamp.

She didn't believe in God, the wise-looking man with the long flowing beard, but she believed in something powerful beyond herself, beyond human and animal life. Whispering hotly into her hands, brow furrowed delicately, she prayed to that something, prayed that this day had not happened, or if she couldn't have that, prayed that this old woman was some sad and crazy being who needed to tell stories, a lonely deluded stranger she'd run into at a bus stop. She prayed that her fits of blindness and terror would end, swearing that she would bring up her grades and participate more in school like her mother wanted her to. Make friends, pay better attention to her appearance. Think about college. She would do it all, if only this hell would end.

As she kneeled there engrossed in her thoughts, rocking slightly back and forth on her knees, she didn't hear her doorknob turn or her door pushed open.

Footsteps approached her slender, curved back.

Still she rocked, prayed.

"What are you doing?" Peter said.

Lucy spun around. Peter stood in the middle of the room holding a plastic tray of steaming food.

"I lost...I dropped something under the bed, so I was looking for it."

"What did you drop?"

"A barrette."

Peter continued walking with his tray to Lucy's night stand where he reached up and set it down. He wore pajamas with Goofy printed all over them, and slippers that looked like little fire engines. "Oh, you always lose those."

Lucy got off her knees and sat on the bed. "You brought me some food." She pulled her hair back and tied it with a rubber band she rummaged from a drawer.

"Yeah, there was leftover. Mom said to bring it."

"Thanks, Peter." The smell of meat with thick hot gravy and buttered mashed potatoes made her dizzy. "Do you want some?"

He pulled himself up on the bed next to her. "No. I ate at dinnertime."

He watched her as she devoured the food.

"So, are you still sick?"

"What do you mean?" she said with her mouth full. "I was never sick."

Peter looked down at the rug, the spot of light there. "When you cut

Mom's arm. She said you were sick. That's why you did it."

Lucy swallowed hard. "No. I'm not sick any more."

"Well, that's good." He pulled at a thread on his pajama bottoms. "You coming home tomorrow after school, or not?"

"Of course I am, Peter." She took a long drink of milk. "There was something I had to do today."

"Yeah, I know," he sighed. "Kissy kissy face."

"No, that's not true. Something important."

"What?"

"I went someplace to get better. To stop being sick." She shrugged and lifted up the palms of her hands. "And it worked. I'm better. See my neck?" She turned toward the lamp so he could see.

"It's gone!" he gasped. Then more quietly, "It's like magic." He ran his hot little fingers across the place the mark had been. "A magic trick."

"Except it's real. That's the good part."

Peter pushed himself off the bed and slid to the floor. "I'm going to watch my ghost show."

"Don't get too scared."

"Naah, they're nice ghosts. Grammy said they were." He reached up for the doorknob. "By the way, your boyfriend called."

"When?"

"Just a minute ago."

"Why didn't somebody tell me?"

He hesitated, then decided on the truth. "Mom told him you were asleep."

Lucy shook her head as she ate the last bite of sugar snap peas. "You want me to tuck you in later?"

"That's okay. Mom can do it."

"Kiss me now, then."

He let go of the knob, ran to give her a quick wet kiss, then sprinted out of the room without another word, slamming the door behind him.

She imagined him gunning down the hall and into the living room where he would watch, wide-eyed, his weekly show on ghosts that haunt New England towns from the safety and warmth of his grandmother's lap.

· SEVENTY ·

Lucy woke early the next morning, a good half hour before her alarm was set to go off. For a few minutes she lay staring out her window. The day before and all that had happened felt like a strange dream.

The morning was not much brighter than the night. A steady sleet pattered at the window. She got out of bed and patiently brushed out her tangled hair, wincing each time she combed out a knot. She heard Peter's squeals of laughter and his rapid footsteps as he ran down the hall past her bedroom, then the slam of the bathroom door.

When she heard it creak open and his return footsteps, she ventured down the hall toward the bathroom, yawning.

The overhead light bulb snapped on and swayed back and forth over her head. She rubbed a small circle in the steamy mirror and glanced at herself before rummaging around for her toothbrush and the nearly squeezed-flat toothpaste. She settled for Peter's bubble gum flavored kind, even though her mouth never felt clean after she used it.

As she brushed with one hand she used a washcloth to wipe the rest of the steam off the mirror.

Her hand stopped halfway through a wide arc across the glass.

The toothbrush fell out of her other hand, clicked on her bottom teeth, and clattered to the tiled floor.

It was back.

Longer, deeper than before, an angry red furrow from her chin to her clavicle.

Saucer-eyed, she grabbed the sink to steady herself, her mouth an "O," pink toothpaste on her lips. She gagged and dropped her head toward the belly of the sink, focusing on the rust stain in the shape of India she could never scrub off, and shut her eyes. Opened them again.

The stain, the sink, a smear of pink toothpaste on the rim.

She lifted her head to look in the mirror again.

It was still there.

Reflected in the glass, in the dim hallway, a shadowy figure of a woman slipped by, moving as if on a cushion of air. The figure came back and hovered at the doorway, staring.

Lucy screamed and pounded at the mirror, but it would not break.

Ellen stepped in the bathroom. "Lucy, what are you doing?"

She grabbed her daughter's wrists and tried to hold them but couldn't. Flailing and howling, Lucy beat at the mirror with her fists until it shattered. Pieces of glass fell splintering into the sink, the floor, all around her feet. Shrieking, she kept hammering, now on the bare plaster wall.

Blood coursed from her wrists and hands, spotting the walls, ceiling, tiles, everywhere as she pounded, shards stuck and hanging from the flesh of her arms.

She pounded in the darkness, howled in darkness.

Ellen fought to hold her but Lucy turned, her eyes now a glittering grey, a triangle of bloody glass in her hand. She spun in circles, crying, holding the glass at arm's length.

"Don't touch me! Get away from me! I'll kill you!" Lucy screamed. Ellen jumped away and pulled the bathroom door shut, falling backwards into the hallway.

From inside the bathroom Lucy keened and moaned as if possessed, banging at the wall where the mirror had been. Peter stood shaking at the doorway to the kitchen.

"Go to your room and lock the door!" Ellen hissed. "And don't come out till I tell you!"

Still he stood there.

"I said, go! *Now!*"

He turned and sped down the hallway and out of sight. His door slammed shut.

Ellen crouched in the dark hallway, frozen in the odd position she had landed, blood spattered on her light yellow nightgown and pale face. She listened with every fiber to her daughter wailing and crying, tearing at the walls as if she were lost in some hellish labyrinth, not just a bathroom with a door and a handle.

Lucy's cries weakened, the pounding slowed, and a dull, rhythmic sobbing began.

"Lucy," Ellen said hoarsely, crawling to the door.

The sobbing continued.

"You've got to let me in." She pushed herself to her feet, gasping at the blood smeared on her hands, her nightgown. It showed black in the dim light of the hall. She pulled a two inch piece of glass out of her thigh and dropped it on the floor, shuddering. "Lucy, I'm coming in."

Her palm slippery with blood, she struggled to grasp the doorknob. She pushed the door but something was blocking it.

"Lucy, move. Get up."

The sobs grew quieter, but stayed rhythmic, like a heartbeat, like a mantra.

Through a one-inch gap, Ellen peered inside the bathroom and saw the bottom of Lucy's feet. They were glossy with blood and studded with pieces of mirror. She leaned into the door, feeling it push a body across the tile. She stepped inside.

A riot of red on white tile, Lucy lay curled in the fetal position, rocking side to side as she moaned. Her face, arms and hands were covered with cuts, her nightgown torn almost completely off, her eyes open, unseeing.

"Lucy," Ellen breathed. She crouched next to her, not knowing what to do, how to touch her, whether to startle her from this hypnotic state where she at least appeared to be calming down. "Lucy? Can you hear me?"

Lucy stopped rocking. She blinked and focused on the base of the toilet inches from her face. Her forehead creased with sudden awareness. She whispered, "Ellen...is that you?"

"Yes, I'm right here, honey." She stroked her daughter's forehead, pulled a shard of glass from her hand.

Lucy turned to look at her. "Did I hurt you?"

"No, I'll be all right." She began to cry, wiping a bloody hand across her cheek.

Lucy's eyes were wide and unblinking. "You've got to help me. I remember now. I remember everything."

· SEVENTY-ONE ·

Four days later, deep into a frosty winter afternoon, Ellen knocked at Lucy's door with a tray of soup, toast and tea. Her hair was combed back in a dour bun and she wore her waitress uniform.

There was no answer.

"Lucy, come on, open up."

A dull voice from inside the room. "It's open."

Ellen let herself in and winced at the sour smell of closed-in air, of Lucy who hadn't bathed for several days. She lay in bed facing away from the door toward her window, her long hair in stringy ropes across the pillow, quilts piled high on top of her. Unread magazines, school books and novels lay on the floor near her bed, along with unopened boxes of candy, cookies, and junk food.

Nothing had enticed her to get out of bed.

Not even the bouquet of yellow roses Ian had sent her on the night of the prom, two days previous. Ellen knew they were from Ian because he delivered them himself, but the small envelope wedged in the dying flowers was unopened, unread. Ian had asked to see Lucy, but she had refused.

"I brought you chicken noodle, honey, and some of that sesame toast you like." She set the food on the floor next to the bed and sat at the foot of it.

"Thanks."

"You gonna eat something?"

"No."

Ellen looked sadly at the piles of stuff on the floor. "You going to go to school tomorrow?"

"No."

"Yes, you are," she said softly.

Lucy didn't answer.

"You're going to get up, take a shower, and go back to school. And at three o'clock, we're going to see Dr. Nathanson."

"Dr. Nathanson can kiss my a – "

"You're going, Lucy." Ellen started to pick up dirty clothes and old trays of food.

"I don't need any doctors."

"What do you need, then?" she said harshly.

"You wouldn't understand. You haven't yet and you never will."

"Lucy, you're going to be seventeen next month, and you sound like a ten-year-old."

"Ellen – "

"What is this 'Ellen' crap. Call me 'Mom'."

"Okay...Mom, I need to go to sleep."

"You've had a week of sleep."

"I need to think."

Ellen got up and brushed off her spotless apron. "You can think in school tomorrow. And you can think in the doctor's office, and you can keep on thinking tomorrow night when you catch up on a week of homework."

Lucy said nothing.

"I'm going to work now."

"Have a good night at work."

Ellen harrumphed and walked over to the door. "And for God's sake, spend some time with your brother. He's...he's not over this one. And don't fill his head up with nonsense."

Lucy listened to her door close and her mother's receding footsteps down the hall.

After an hour of dreamless sleep, Lucy woke to the sound of her door opening and closing, and Peter's shuffling steps in his fire engine slippers. A long clattering noise.

She turned over in bed and saw him standing in the middle of her room in a circle of toys he'd dumped out of his toy box. Pushing a few of them aside, he plopped down next to a pile of train tracks and toy soldiers, Elmo dolls, dump trucks and Legos. The tray of untouched food sat nearby.

Lucy pushed herself up to one elbow. "Peter, do you have to play in here?"

"It's stinky-poo in here."

"Then why don't you – "

"Grammy's asleep. I got scared."

Lucy watched him as he set up blue soldiers on one side of the floorboards, and green ones on the other. Carefully he lined up tiny blue and green cannons behind tanks and tufts of plastic trees and bushes.

"You play war too much," Lucy said.

"You should get out of bed," Peter said.

"Why?"

"I need someone to be the blue guys."

"Why not the green guys?"

"Because I'm green. They're my toys."

Sighing, Lucy pulled back the covers and swung her feet to the floor. As if drunk, she dropped her head in her hands. "Oh, all right."

She slid down to the floor near him, sitting with her knees drawn up.

"Do you understand what happened on Monday?" Lucy said softly.

He scrambled around in his pile of toys and pulled out more blue soldiers. "Okay, this is what you do," he said. "First you line up your guys."

"So you don't want to talk about it, Peter?"

He looked up at her. "Talk about what?"

"What happened in the bathroom."

"Mom said you got sick again. I was scared."

"I was scared too."

"You're not lining up your guys."

She began to line up the little blue infantry men along a floorboard a couple of inches away. He watched her a while, his red curls shining in the light of the reading lamp.

"Not all your guys. The ones with the big guns, they stay back in like, holes – "

"Foxholes?"

"Yeah, foxholes, where no one can see them. They almost never get killed. Unless there's nuclear bombs."

"Peter?"

"Yeah?"

"What do you think happens when you die?"

He looked at her, her exhausted eyes, hanging hair. "I don't know, I never died." He moved his men slightly forward with a pudgy hand.

"But what do you think happens?"

"You bleed. Ladies cry. You don't move, and you stare straight ahead."

"That's all true, but sometimes, something else happens. Sometimes, when you die, you're reborn into another body."

"Really?"

"Really."

"Come on, you're not doing it. Put your guys with guns in the foxholes."

"Okay." She did what he asked.

"Well, how come Grandpa Purdy didn't get reborn. How come he stayed dead?"

"He may have come back in another body, maybe somewhere far away. Or maybe he stayed dead, because he didn't need to come back. Didn't have anything else he needed to do."

"So take your guys, and fight with me."

Peter picked up two of his soldiers, one in each hand. Making whirring and shooting noises, he knocked over two of Lucy's blue ones. Mimicking his noises, she knocked over four or five of his men.

Peter sat back on his haunches. "Well, that's not fair."

"Do you understand what I just told you, Peter?"

"Only one guy gets to knock out one guy."

"Peter, look at me."

He did so, still clutching his soldiers.

"I lived before. My name was Kim. I was blind and I studied biology. I died when I was nineteen."

Peter's face changed as he listened to her; his mouth turned down and he reddened. Gasping, he opened his mouth and began to bawl, flopping his arms in frustration at his sides.

"No, Peter, don't cry," Lucy said, leaning toward him. But he pushed himself up by his hands and threw down his men, then kicked them, scattering the pieces all over the floor, under the bed, into the bowl of cold soup on the tray.

"You don't even want to play! You just want to tell stupid stories!"

Lucy held out her arms to him, her eyes welling up. "Come here, Peter. I'm sorry."

He kicked some more pieces around, stomping his way to the door. "If you," he started, choking on his tears, "aren't really you, then you're not my sister!" His voice rose to a shriek. "So stay away from me!"

Lucy jumped to her feet and ran over to him, sweeping him up in her arms. She inhaled his sweet, clean, little boy smell. His small chest heaved with tears.

"Peter, I'm sorry. I shouldn't have told you those things. It was wrong. Completely wrong, okay? I feel so alone, and that's why...but that's not right."

He sobbed on her shoulder, his arms tight around her neck.

"I'm your sister, okay? Always and forever, and you're my brother, no matter what, always and forever."

"But you were some – "

"Look, Peter, sometimes grownup people say dumb things. Or don't say things right. Just because they're big doesn't mean – "

He pulled back a little and looked her in the eyes, wiping his nose on his pajama sleeve. "You're not a grownup, you're a teenager."

"That's absolutely right. I'm not even a grownup."

"But I'm still your brother, always and forever?" he whispered.

"Always and forever."

He pulled a piece of lint off her nightgown, then smoothed it with a sticky hand. "I'm hungry."

"What do you want?"

"Peanut butter and banana on toast."

"You got it, kiddo." She kissed the dense smooth curls on top of his head as she opened the door, and, still carrying him, walked out to the hall and toward the kitchen.

· SEVENTY-TWO ·

L ucy got out the bread and found one last banana in the fruit basket, then searched for peanut butter in a cabinet over the sink. Peter ran over to the couch, then skipped back into the kitchen.

"Grammy's snoring."

"Well, she's tired. Looking after you isn't easy."

The phone rang, but Lucy didn't move to answer it.

Peter had strapped on his plastic six guns and was bouncing on his hobby horse.

"Aren't ya gonna answer it?"

"I don't want to talk to anybody right now."

She pulled a chair over to the sink and climbed on it, still rummaging. Finally, the answering machine picked up and Ellen's cheerful outgoing message played.

A hesitation, then a voice. Lucy pulled out the jar of super crunchy peanut butter and listened.

"Hello, this is Dr. Nathanson calling to confirm an appointment with Lucy tomorrow at three..."

Lucy dropped the peanut butter. The glass jar smashed on the linoleum. Peter jumped off his hobby horse and rushed toward the mess.

"You broke it."

"Be quiet, Peter," Lucy said, her eyes wide.

"...appreciate a half an hour with Ellen, so let's make it 2:30. If this won't work, then please give me a call. Otherwise I'll see you both tomorrow."

"My God," Lucy whispered hoarsely, hanging on to the doors of the cabinet. "It's her."

Peter looked up from where he sat next to the pile of peanut butter and broken glass. "Now I can't even have my sandwich." He reached over and pulled a chunk of glass from the gooey pile.

Absently, she glanced down at him. "Peter! Don't touch that." She climbed off the chair and went to the answering machine on the kitchen counter. Her head clouded with rage as she watched the red light blink on and off. She pushed "play" and listened, again, to that voice.

Peter had started to cry in an exhausted, dry-eyed sort of way, but it took Lucy a while to hear him. She pressed "play" again, touching the machine with the palm of her hand. The sound vibrated there, informing her, like an electric current lighting up this memory, then that: tastes, smells, years of yearning. She reached up and touched the scar on her neck; it throbbed with fresh pain. She played the message again, fearlessly, letting the voice inside her like a rasping sword, the sound of her future and her past. A headache bloomed in the back of her skull, spreading down her neck and to her arms. She played it again, and again, until her whole body was washed over and through with pain and clarity.

"Stop doing that!" Peter yelled, yanking on a pant loop of her jeans as she stood over the machine. "You already heard it a million times!"

She turned to look at him. "You're right, I have. I don't need to hear it any more." She reached down to pick him up. "Why are you crying again?"

"Because I want a peanut butter – "

"Ah, okay, then why don't we take a trip to the store? Maybe get some ice cream too?"

He smiled through his tears. "Strawberry?"

"Whatever you want, honey. And let's get Grammy some vanilla, too."

The next morning arrived clear and quite cold. Ellen salted the steps before she sat with her coffee and newspaper, watching Peter eat his Fruit Loops. The bathroom door slammed and the water pipes banged to life. She glanced at her watch: 6:30. Lucy was up and taking her first shower in a week.

"Peter, did you wake Lucy?"

"No."

Ellen got up and padded down the hall in her slippers. She stood outside the door and listened, then knocked timidly. "You need some clean towels in there, honey?"

"No," Lucy said. "I have one, thanks."

Smiling, Ellen walked back to the kitchen and gingerly started to stack the breakfast dishes. "Come on Peter, you've read the back of that box a hundred times. You've got ten minutes to be dressed and ready for school."

· SEVENTY-THREE ·

They arrived at Greenfield right on time, but Lucy found herself walking less and less purposefully down the long corridor toward Dr. Nathanson's office.

"Come on, Lucy, we're already late."

"You're meeting with her first, right? And I'm starving, so I think I'll grab something at the cafeteria and meet you there. Is that all right?"

Ellen looked at her quizzically. "You don't have any funny plans, now, do you?"

"Come on, Mom. I missed lunch."

"Three o'clock."

"Three o'clock."

Lucy watched her mother walk through a set of swinging doors, then turned and headed for the cafeteria where she bought a grilled cheese sandwich and considered coffee, but decided her heart was pounding hard enough.

She made her way to her appointment: fourth floor, corner office. For a few moments, she stood outside staring at the big block letters that read, "Dr. Astra Nathanson, MD."

The door was surprisingly heavy and the air in the waiting room still and thick. No one else was there except an assistant who sat at a desk with a lone Fica plant. A half dozen framed photos lined the inside of his cubicle. As Lucy meandered past, a certain photo caught her eye: a dark-haired woman and a tall, good looking man standing next to a Christmas tree.

"Are you Lucy?" the assistant asked, shuffling papers away.

"Yes." She listlessly shook the hand he offered her, never taking her eyes off the photo.

"I'm Steven, Dr. Nathanson's assistant."

"It's nice to meet you." She pointed at the photo. "Who are those people?"

"That's Dr. Nathanson, of course, and her husband, Constantin. Great guy. He's a marine biologist."

She picked up the photo and held it. "This is Constantin?" Her eyes filled with tears.

Steven reached for the photo, but she made no move to hand it back. "Do you know him?"

She gently placed the picture back on Steven's desk. "I thought I did, but no. What time is it?"

"You have about ten minutes. Why don't you have a seat?"

Ellen dabbed at her eyes with a dusty piece of Kleenex she'd rescued from her purse. Astra: cool, collected and impeccably dressed in a black wool suit, held out a fresh box of tissues.

"I didn't plan on, you know, crying like this, Dr. Nathanson, I want you to know."

"We can't plan our emotions, Ellen."

"No, no, you're right."

"You can take off your coat, if you like."

Ellen got up and slipped off her dated winter coat, sat back down with it folded double in her lap. "I just get so cold all the time, I forget it's on."

"I see. So you were saying...?"

"All this about I'm not her mother, I think that's the most hurtful part. She calls me Ellen, like I'm some stranger, or...or a classmate or something."

"That must be quite painful for you. Have you asked her why she says these things? Does she have an explanation?"

"Oh, dear. You don't want to know, the stories this girl comes up with! And what she did four days ago!"

"What was that?"

"Well, she went crazy. But the most bizarre thing happened that set her off. She got a birthmark removed from her neck, and it was gone, or at least she'd covered it up with makeup, that's what *I* think happened. Then she went to sleep and the next morning said it had come back, but of course she'd just rinsed off the makeup and there it was, as usual. Anyway, she went nuts! She smashed the mirror and said horrible things to me..." The tears started to flow again.

"What did she say, Ellen? Remember, I'm here to help you, help both of you."

"She threatened to kill me."

Astra rearranged the pleats of her skirt under her, her face flushing slightly. "Did she try to hurt you?"

"No, not on purpose, anyway. She wasn't really there, Dr. Nathanson."

"What do you mean, 'wasn't really there'?"

"She has these fits, I mean even when she was a little girl she would go blind, or that's what she said, and start screaming. Oh, it was just awful."

"Tell me more, Ellen, about what happens during these fits. Does she call you by a different name? Or herself by a different name?"

"Well, no. She's traumatized by something – "

"What in her past do you think she might be remembering?"

"Nothing bad. She's had a wonderful childhood. I mean, I'm divorced but she sees her father, now and then. He's out a lot. He's a fisherman."

"I see. So she's never mentioned anything about him that was at all inappropriate? Or another male figure in her life? A boyfriend? Neighbor? Family friend?"

"Dear God, no."

"I hate to say this, Ellen, but we almost never know everything our child has seen or experienced. It's just not possible to be everywhere they've been. Something may have happened to her that's too traumatic for her to share with you, or even with herself."

Ellen cried freely now. "I tried so hard, but I've been alone. And I have my boy, Peter. He's only five."

"Don't put the blame on yourself. We can't control everything. Lucy may also, unfortunately, be showing early signs of schizophrenia – "

"Not that! She's not schizophrenic – "

Astra flipped opened a folder. "I do see some family history – "

"My grandfather. But that can't mean – "

"There is a tendency for the disease to run in families. But I'm not diagnosing her, Ellen. I haven't even met her yet."

"Of course, of course."

"But these seizures – fits, disturb me. Sounds like she may need to be on an antiseizure medication, along with a few others."

"'A few others?'"

"Your daughter is a teenager, Ellen. It's a rough time. And for some kids, it just happens to be even rougher. We don't know why, much of the time. But we do know, in most cases, with proper therapy and treatment, they get through it." She looked at the wall clock. "It looks like it's her turn, now, Ellen."

Ellen got to her feet. "Please help her, Dr. Nathanson. I love her so much."

"I'll do my very best, Ellen, I assure you."

· SEVENTY-FOUR ·

The clock read 3:01.

Steven sat behind his wall of photos, tapping away on his computer. Lucy stared at the pages of *People* magazine without comprehension.

The door opened. Ellen, still wiping her eyes, walked out to the waiting room in her plastic, salt-stained snow boots.

Still Lucy stared at the letters on the glossy page which read, "Stars Strut Their Stuff at this Year's Emmy's."

A swish of satin lining on pricey wool, the click of heels on hard wood.

A flawlessly manicured hand crossed the page, obscuring the words, the snapshots of daring Hollywood fashions. The hand trembled slightly, but the voice was strong, deep – and horribly familiar.

"Lucy? I'm Dr. Nathanson."

Lucy stared at the hand. She closed her eyes against an impulse to bite it, inhaled the heavy, sweet perfume she had known as Kim, and exhaled.

She lifted her head. "Hello, Mother."

Astra kept her face composed as she looked into the glittering grey eyes of her reincarnated daughter, but her body shrank back into her clothes and she dropped her arm to her side.

"I'm Dr. Nathanson, Lucy, not your mother."

"Whatever you say." Lucy put the magazine aside.

"Well," Astra turned to Ellen, "we'll be forty-five minutes or so. There's a cafeteria in the building if you – "

"Oh, we've been there, Doctor. I'll see you at three forty-five. And again, I can't thank you enough."

Astra turned on her heel and strode into her office. Lucy followed unhurriedly into the spacious room. A flowering plant hung in the window; books lined one wall of built-in shelves. The top of Astra's mahogany desk was brutally neat and the sidetables shone as if freshly burnished.

Lucy stood watching Astra rummage around in a drawer.

"Did you lose something?"

Astra kept her eyes on the contents of the drawer. "No – it's just – I need a fresh notepad. Ah, here's one." Feeling Lucy's eyes on her, she looked up and gestured briskly. "Why don't you have a seat."

Lucy sat in the wine-colored chair, stroking its fat leather arms. "So this is where your psychos sit until they're cured. Very nice."

Astra finally located a pen and sat opposite her. She cocked her head to one side and rested the pen on her cheek. "Is that what you feel you are, a psycho?"

"No, but that's what you're going to say I am, isn't it?"

"Of course not. Listen, why don't you tell me a little about what's been happening in your life recently."

"There isn't much to tell. Just that every now and then I go blind and remember who I really am. What really happened that day, Astra."

"Lucy, we met three minutes ago. I have no idea what you're talking about."

Smiling slightly, never letting go of Astra's eye, Lucy pulled a rubber band out of her pocket, swept her hair off her shoulders and gathered it into a pony tail. She folded back the collar of her mock turtleneck. The angry scar pulsed at her neck. "Does this ring a bell?"

Astra stared at it a moment, then down at her pad where she scribbled something. "You're suggesting – "

"I'm not *suggesting* – "

" – that I have something to do with your scar?"

"It's a birthmark," Lucy said in a low voice. "Or that's what I've been told all my life."

"Well, then it's an unfor – "

"But we both know it's not a birthmark, don't we."

"So tell me, Lucy, how do you know I'm responsible for this scar, then?" She cleared her throat.

"I know because I stopped being afraid. And I met someone who told me the truth about who I am."

"Really. Who?"

"An old woman. Someone I owe an apology to. Someone I need to find."

Astra's eye twitched. "What old woman?"

"Her name is Carmella. She knew me before. She took care of me, like a mother. Like a real mother."

"And what does that mean to you, Lucy, 'a real mother'?"

"Someone who doesn't cut your throat, for starters."

Astra shifted in her seat, scribbling furiously on her pad. "And?"

"Someone who doesn't dump you when you're a kid in some institution. Someone who takes care of you, spends time with you, things like that. I'm sure you'll be able to find some literature about it if you really look."

Pinpricks of sweat gathered on Astra's forehead. "Is your mother like that? Is she good to you?"

"You are my mother."

"Your mother, Lucy, is outside in the waiting room."

"That woman out there? She's been very nice to me, all my life. Unfortunately, she's not my mother. Unfortunately, you are."

"Lucy, you do realize how this sounds...?"

"The truth is ugly sometimes."

Astra crossed and uncrossed her legs. "All right then, let's take a little time to talk about your father. Your parents are divorced, is that right?"

"You know, it's good to finally see you. I never knew you were so beautiful. Other people told me, of course, but it's good to see for myself. In fact, I'd like to see a picture of myself someday, from before. Maybe you've got an old photo lying around, you know, for sentimental reasons."

"Thanks for the compliment, Lucy, but let's get back to – "

Lucy waved her hand. "My dad, my dad. I heard you. I've got nothing to say about him. Since of course, he's not my real dad either."

"So...let me see if I've got this. Your father is also not your father? This is getting complicated – "

"You never did tell me much about my real father. God knows what you did to him."

"All right, let's move on. Your mother tells me you – "

Lucy leaned forward in the chair, her face inches from Astra's. "What I really want to know is: how do you like fucking my boyfriend?"

"Lucy, sit – "

"Huh? Is he good? I hope so, because I remember he was great. Took his time, you know. A slow hand. Crazy, crazy lovin', all the time. Is he like that with you? Or maybe he was in the beginning but not so much any more? Time marches on, doesn't it? And there was that nagging problem of me – Kim – the woman he really loved, in his mind all the time. I'll bet he fucked you with his eyes closed, is that it? Is that how you guys got over it?"

"Are you finished?"

"Nope. Just a few more questions." Lucy sat back in the chair and folded her hands on her lap. "Is he ever sad about me? Does he talk about me, ever?"

" – this is – "

" – and tell me, Astra, how does that make you feel?"

Astra swiveled in her chair and slapped the pad of paper on her desk. She took off her glasses and wiped them with a Kleenex; took another and dabbed her forehead with it. "Well, Lucy, it doesn't look like we're getting anywhere today, does it?"

"Oh, I don't know. I think we've done very well." She smiled brightly and glanced around the well-appointed room. "I think we've covered a lot!"

"But it is three forty-five, and I have another patient, so – "

Lucy pushed herself out of the chair and stood up. She looked even younger than her seventeen years with her slight build, puffy down vest and worn out sneakers. Jamming her hands in her pockets, she gazed out the window at the gathering dusk, the snow-covered parking lot. "I just want you to know, Astra – Mom – that I'm not going away this time." She turned back to face her. "In fact, this time, you might want to watch your back."

"Are you threatening me?"

Astra's phone rang. She answered it with a snap of her arm. "Yes. Just one minute." She hung up. "I have another – "

Lucy made her way to the door. "Yeah, I got it. See you next week."

· SEVENTY-FIVE ·

The moment the door closed behind Lucy, Astra exhaled and collapsed into her chair. How had this happened? How had she been so careless? She'd done nothing to investigate the clues years ago: the burning photos, the box overflowing with maggots! But even though it had been clear Kim had come back, what were the chances she would be reincarnated in a neighboring town?

Astra flipped open Lucy's chart. Date of birth: May 30, 1994, Gloucester, Massachusetts. The next town over from Rockport, where she had killed her. She recalled Kim's innocent face, then the pall of dread when Kim realized she wasn't alone in that kitchen...

The phone rang again. She snatched it up. "I just need a few minutes for notes, Steven, please. Missy will have to wait."

A brief hesitation on the other end. "I was just calling to let you know that it looks like Missy's a no show."

"Oh." She got to her feet and walked to the window. "All right. Then do me a favor." She pulled aside the heavy curtains. "Check on Dr. Davies' schedule, can you? Is he free right now?"

"Looks like...hold on...he has no one right now. Don't know if he's in, but – "

"That's all right, Steven. That's all I needed to know." She clicked off the phone but gripped it tightly in her clammy hands. She gazed out at the parking lot where two small figures, Ellen and Lucy in a bright red hat, trudged through the snow. How ridiculous I am to worry, Astra thought. What the hell can she do to me? No one will believe a word of any of this.

And she's just a kid, for Christ's sake.

Just as Astra was about to turn away, Lucy turned and looked up at where Astra stood, frozen in the bright frame of the window. Ellen kept on walking toward the car. Lucy smiled up at Astra, blew her a kiss with a mittened hand, then ran to catch up with Ellen.

Astra jerked the curtains closed.

She scrambled to her desk and pulled out her purse from which she extracted a hand mirror.

She held the mirror up to her face.

Her eyes closed sideways, her pupils dark slashes. Her tongue: forked, thin and black as an eel, slipped out of her mouth and flicked through the air. She sucked it back in and gasped, clasping her hands over her mouth.

The hand mirror made a tinkling sound as it broke on the hard wood. Sobbing, she sank to her knees and held her head in her hands. "No, no, no...I will not *I will not* slip back. Please, God no, I can*not*..."

Her hands felt strangely cool. She pulled them away from her face.

Brown and yellow scales banded her hands and wrists. She watched as her fingers sucked back into her hands, which were disappearing into her arms...

"No!" she moaned, falling to the floor. "She can't do this to me! She won't do this to me! I'm stronger than she is, please, this can't be, this can't *be*..."

A timid knock on the door. "Dr. Nathanson?"

She cursed under her breath and somehow got up to her knees, clicking the deadbolt lock closed with her teeth. Her sleeves hung down from her shoulders, empty, her bracelets and watch scattered on the floor.

"Is everything all right?"

"Fine, Steven. You can go home now."

A pause. "But it's only four o'clock."

"I said, you can go home. Go...home."

"Okay, I'll see you tomorrow. Have a good night."

She panted, listening to him go to his desk, gather his things, and leave, shutting the main office door behind him.

She hovered at the door, her tongue whipping in and out of her mouth, her head slowly flattening, hair in clumps on the floor. Her arms vanished into her suit as her feet left her shoes and shot up into her legs. Falling forward, limbless, hissing, she writhed out of her clothes and slithered under her desk.

Hours later Astra woke with a choked scream. She scrambled from under the desk and gasped for breath.

She forced herself to look at her hands.

Covered with real skin again. The blood red manicure flawless and shining. Her wedding ring glittered a few feet away on the oriental carpet. Naked, weeping, she crawled over to it and picked it up, kissed it, and slipped it back on with shaking hands. Reached into her mouth and touched her tongue. Human. She pulled herself to her feet and looked at her reflection in the window. Her eyes were her eyes again.

Whimpering, she put on her clothes, not bothering with her panty hose which she crammed in her purse. Again and again she ran trembling hands over her hair and body, making sure she was all there.

Satisfied, she stuffed papers and files into her briefcase, grabbed her coat and ran to the door, stepping inches from the crinkly brown and yellow husk of snake skin coiled under her desk.

· SEVENTY-SIX ·

"You're saying she actually *threatened* you?" David asked, tilting back in his chair.

"She said I should watch my back. That's a quote." Astra sat ramrod straight across from him, her coat and briefcase perched on her lap.

"Yikes. That's not good." He pulled a pencil from behind one ear and made a note on a pad of paper.

"No, it's not."

"Does she seem dangerous to herself?"

"No. She seems dangerous to me."

"But that mark on her neck – "

"She was born with that – "

He raised an eyebrow.

"Look, David, she thinks – she really believes – that I'm her mother, and that I killed her."

"So she's projecting the whole kit and kaboodle on you, then. I wonder if she would do that with any female doctor she was assigned to. What do you think?"

"That's probably true. It's clear to me she should be seeing a male doctor."

He wrote another note in his pad. "She actually accuses you of killing her? How?"

"Cutting her throat."

"Like your daughter was killed."

Astra glared at him.

"I'm sorry, Astra. You don't need to be reliving that with this girl."

"No, I don't." She looked away, as if she had become tender.

"Look, I'll see what I can do. I'll talk to Lucy, too. See what she wants to do."

"Oh, I'm sure she'll want to stay with me."

"Why do you say that? If you killed her, so to speak?"

She paused, reading him. "Isn't it obvious? I fit the mold of whatever fantasy evil mother she's conjured, and she gets to punish me."

"I still need to talk to her."

"I won't work with her, David. It's not good for her, and it's terrible for me."

"I must say, I've never seen you refuse a patient. And I've sent you some real doozies. But you know the deal, Astra. I start you with someone, there are expectations..."

Astra glanced at the back of her hand. Perhaps it was a trick of light, but she thought she saw five or six scales shimmer at her wrist.

"Astra?"

She snapped her head up. "Yes?"

"You really are upset about this, aren't you."

"Yes, I am." She pulled on her gloves and got to her feet.

"Then I'll just refer her out. Kendall has a few spots."

She slipped on her coat. "Thank you, David."

"You're welcome."

"And listen, I can't make it in tomorrow. I need to take it easy for a day."

He sighed and got to his feet. "That's fine. But just one day, right?"

"Just one day."

He walked her to the door. "Then do me a favor, and do something nice for yourself, will you?"

She smiled. "That's a great idea. A little pampering. Thanks for understanding, David."

Ellen pulled into her driveway and turned off the ignition. Both she and Lucy looked up at Ian who stood outside their door. He hopped back and forth from one foot to the other in the blistering cold.

"Is this all right?" Ellen said, turning to Lucy. "Do you want to see him?"

"Yeah, sure."

Ellen rolled down her window. "Hi, Ian."

"Hey, Mrs. Duggan." And more shyly, "Hey, Lucy." His nose was red and running from the cold. "I wanted to see if you wanted to go into town and hang out or something."

Ellen turned and gave Lucy a little smile. "Be home in two hours? Seven sharp?"

"Thanks, that'd be great."

Ellen got out of the car and Lucy slid over to the driver's side. Brightening considerably, Ian thanked Ellen, loped around to the passenger side and got in.

"Remember, you promised Peter you'd take him to – "

"Burger King, I know. See you at seven."

Smiling broadly at Ian, Lucy backed out of the drive.

· SEVENTY-SEVEN ·

They parked at the Overlook, a makeout haven for high school kids on a rocky ledge that jutted out over a metal grey sea. High, dark cumulus clouds rumbled over each other, releasing hard lines of rain in odd patches over the water. They sat far from each other, each tucked in their own insufficient winter clothing. Lucy turned the heat all the way up and directed it toward their feet.

A match fired blue in Ian's cupped hand as he lit a Marlboro. He took a deep drag and cracked his window. A rope of smoke escaped his lips and snaked through as he watched the cigarette destroy itself in his chapped, red fingers.

"That's quite an amazing story, Lucy."

"It's not a story, it's – "

"Oh, I believe you. I mean, wasn't I the one who suggested the whole blind school thing? That it might make you remember something?" But still he didn't look at her.

She stared at the sea. "Why do I feel like you're having trouble with this?"

"I guess, to be honest, I think it's pretty amazing that you, you know, actually met someone you knew in a former life."

"So you don't believe me – "

He turned to her. "Lucy – "

"That's all right. I don't blame you. Shit, when I really think about everything I've told you, I wouldn't believe me either." She stretched the sleeves of her sweater to cover her hands, and rubbed them together.

"She said you were a – "

"Repeater. She knew about the scar, even though she was blind."

"But the scar was gone then, wasn't it?"

"She knew it had been there." She sighed heavily. An enormous gull landed on the hood of the car and stared in at them with shiny black eyes, a purple strand of fish gut hanging off its hooked beak. "Let's just head back. I have to take care of Peter, anyway." She reached down to turn the ignition but Ian put his hand over hers. She let her hand drop. With a great heave of wide wings, the bird launched itself from the car, its long taloned feet hanging down.

"Don't get mad, Lucy, come on. I just want to know one more thing: how did you know Dr. Nathanson was...who she was?"

"Her voice. I told you that already."

He took a hard drag of his cigarette and lowered the window another few inches. "So by a woman's voice you knew that this was the woman who killed you in your former life? I don't know, Lucy."

"What do you mean, 'you don't know'?"

"You're gonna be mad if I say something."

"I'm already mad."

He let his hand rest on the cool hair that flowed over her shoulders. "Maybe you're just angry, you know, at your own parents, and you sort of need someone to take it out on. I've done that with my dad – "

"So you think I need someone to be mad at?" Her eyes welled up with angry tears. She pulled back her scarf, revealing the jagged line at her neck. "*Look* at this thing!"

He drew his arm away. "You're still beautiful."

"That's not the point! It came back," she cried. Her voice lowered to a whisper. "It came back because I didn't pay attention to what this has been trying to tell me since the first time I looked in a mirror."

"What has it been trying to tell you?"

She looked at him for a long beat. "It's none of your business."

"Jesus, Lucy. Why are you doing this?"

"I thought I could trust you."

"You can. Look, I missed you on prom night."

She absently began to braid a small section of hair. "What did you do?" she asked in a small voice.

"Stayed home. Watched TV with my sister."

"The flowers were pretty. I never thanked you."

"That's all right."

"Sorry, I couldn't...I wasn't...that was a bad night."

"Your mom said you had a seizure."

"Whatever."

"I think you should keep seeing that doctor."

She looked at him. "Oh, I will."

"Or maybe some other doctor, then, right?"

"I don't get it, Ian. You believe me one day, then not the next. I thought you were my friend."

He took a last drag of the cigarette and flicked it out the window. "I want you to promise me something, Lucy."

"What?"

"Promise me you'll call me every day. Just to tell me you're all right."

She looked in his pale blue eyes, and wished she felt for him whatever sweet things he felt for her. "I can't do that."

"Just a quick phone call to let me know you're all – "

"But Ian," she said, shaking her head in frustration as she leaned over and started the car. The engine grumbled to life. "You don't get it at all." She backed evenly out of the gravel lot. "I'm not all right."

· SEVENTY-EIGHT ·

At seven o'clock the next morning, another dark winter day, Astra stood at her kitchen counter in a black and silver striped silk robe. One by one she cracked three eggs in a bowl, tossing the shells in the sink and shuddering each time the slimy whites touched her fingers. She stood staring at the three yellow eyes in the china blue bowl, trying to remember what came next.

She listened as the water for the shower shut off, and for the hum of Constantin's electric razor.

Oh yes, just milk, and then the bread. She pulled out a half-empty carton of light cream, which would have to do, and poured the contents over the eggs. Possibly too much, possibly not enough. Hard to tell till the whole thing was done.

She placed a frying pan on the stove and turned it on high, scouted out a loaf of stale French bread and started cutting it in small rounds. This too didn't look quite right. She threw the rounds in the egg mixture and mashed them with a fork.

Constantin came out of the bathroom wrapped in a towel, wordlessly padded into their bedroom and shut the door.

The mystery was: how long to keep the bread soaking in the eggs? She reached high up over the stove and pulled out her only cookbook, *The Joy of Cooking*. Appetizers; Breads and Pasta; Cakes and Pies; Fish; Shellfish; Poultry and Beef...

Something was burning – the pan! It must be time to cook the French toast, she reasoned. She stabbed the soggy rounds with a fork and managed to drop five or six into the pan. The eggs spit and crackled, searing to the aluminum where she had forgotten to put – butter! She jerked open the refrigerator and yanked out a tub of whipped butter, spooning up a hunk of it and dropping it amidst the sizzling lumps of egg-bread.

She heard the sound of Constantin's loafers on the tiled floor as she struggled to jam a spatula between the pan and breakfast.

He glanced at the stove as he looped his tie into a knot. "What are you doing?"

She tossed him an annoyed look. "Making your breakfast."

"That's nice of you, but I have that meeting with the department at seven forty-five. I told you last night. Don't you remember?"

She flipped them over. They were black circles, yellow on the inside. "I guess I forgot."

"Don't you have an eight o'clock this morning?"

She slid the pan off the stove and rested it on the cooling rack. "I'm not going in today. I don't feel well."

"What's wrong?"

"I have this terrible headache, and I've been so exhausted lately." She turned toward him, pouting, and reached up to put her arms around him. He gave her a quick kiss and quicker hug and gently pulled away from her.

"Well, get some rest today. I'm sorry I can't stay for breakfast." He looked at the steaming pods in the pan. "It probably tastes better than it looks."

"What time will you be home tonight?"

"Oh, eight or so." He pulled a heavy winter coat over his tweed jacket.

She stepped toward him, seductively stroking his tie. "Let's go Christmas shopping and then out for dinner."

"I said eight, Astra."

"I heard you, I just thought since we haven't done anything together in a while – "

He picked up his briefcase and put one hand on the doorknob. "Don't the stores close at eight?"

"It's Christmastime, Constantin. Stores are open till midnight."

He flipped up his collar and peered out at the slushy roads, the snow-heavy sky. "Well, I'm not, I guess. Open till midnight."

"Do you still love me, Constantin?"

His shoulders sagged. "Don't start that, Astra."

"I asked you a simple question. Why is it so hard for you to answer it?"

He looked at her, and for the first time in a while, actually thought about the question. About how, years ago, her trying and failing to pull off a French toast breakfast would have been funny and sort of sweet. Now it felt tinged with desperation and sadness. It felt utterly disconnected from whatever good feelings she swore she had for him. He looked at the angry, angular way she stood with her grim mouth and arms akimbo at her hips and tried to remember the last time they had laughed together. He couldn't.

He forced himself to look into her eyes. "Of course I still love you, Astra."

She turned stiffly away from him. "Well, you better get going. You don't want to be late."

He opened the door and stepped out on the porch. Rock salt crunched under his feet, the air a cold slap. "All right, then. See you later." He shut the door gently behind him.

Astra stood with her arms straight down at her sides, staring at the closed door, then went back to the kitchen. She picked up the pan of now-hardening eggy disks and took it into the den with her.

She stood at the picture window and watched Constantin scrape the ice off his car window with yet another old CD case, even though she had given him countless ice scrapers over the years. As she watched his strong wide back lean over the windshield she began to eat the French toast from the pan with her hands. At first she took just a few tentative bites, then she ate it all, ravenously, barely pausing to chew.

· SEVENTY-NINE ·

Ellen bustled into the kitchen in an orange terrycloth robe, her wet hair wrapped up in a towel. Lucy, dressed and ready for school, stood at the counter making sandwiches.

"Wow, you're ahead of everybody today, honey," Ellen said as she rushed by clutching a wrinkled shirt. "I have to iron this for work and get Peter going. Do you mind making his lunch too?"

"Already did it."

Ellen paused to look at her daughter. "Thanks, Lucy." She took off the towel and started to dry her hair. "I'm so glad you like this doctor. I'm so proud of you for going." She reached up and hugged Lucy tight. Still holding the long serrated knife she was using to cut the sandwiches, Lucy stared blankly at the dull flowered wallpaper behind her mother's shoulder. "Everything's going to be all right," Ellen said. "I just know it."

Lucy stood enmeshed in the hug until she was released, gave her mother a small nod and smile, and went back to cutting the sandwiches. Ellen found the iron and set it up on the board, then went to Peter's room.

When Lucy finished she rinsed off the knife. It hung in her hand, dripping into the sink.

"Peter," she heard her mother say from the bedroom, "you can*not* wear your Tigger pants to school…"

Lucy dried the knife and slipped it between some notebooks in her bookbag. She reached in her jeans pocket and pulled out a piece of paper where she'd scribbled, "14 Emmerly Court." She stuffed it back in her pocket, tossed on her jean jacket and down vest and slung her bookbag over her shoulders.

"Hey, Mom," she called, hovering at the door. "I gotta go. I'm gonna be late."

"Bye, honey!" Ellen called. "Have a great day at school!"

Chin tucked into her scarf against the cold, Lucy trudged down her street until she came to Western Avenue, Gloucester's main drag. Donut shops with steamy windows dotted the street. Cars sliced by in the slush. Snow began to fall; fat pretty flakes that melted on her nose and cheeks but rested like delicate ornaments on her long saffron eyelashes.

She looked left: the bus she took to school lumbered up over a hill and began to make its way down toward her stop.

She looked right. A downtown bus, bigger and sleeker but still filthy, crawled up the hill. She sprinted across the street, her bookbag slapping at the small of her back. Breathlessly, she climbed aboard the downtown bus, fishing for change in her jeans pocket.

"Excuse me," she asked the driver, a small, bony man dwarfed further by the enormous wheel of the bus. "I'm trying to get to Cambridge. Davis Square."

He didn't look at her as he pulled away from the curb. "Last stop. Fifty-five minutes."

Ignoring the eyes of the commuting crowd, Lucy made her way to the back of the bus.

· EIGHTY ·

It was snowing heavily by the time she arrived at the street. She pulled her hat down low over her eyes as she made her way to number fourteen. The house was smaller than Lucy had imagined, a modest colonial tucked in a grove of firs at the end of a cul de sac. One car remained in the driveway next to a set of tire tracks in the snow that arced out to the street. The knife hidden in the sleeve of her thick wool sweater had warmed to her skin. As she approached the house she carefully flexed her wrist to feel the sharp point against the back of her hand.

A light burned in the second floor window on the far right side of the house. The rest of the windows were dark, empty eye sockets. Suddenly she missed home, Peter, Ian, Ellen, even school. She ran and hid behind the evergreens that surrounded the house, flattening her back up against the clapboard. A squirrel, taken by surprise, ran over her foot and paused a few feet away in the snow, its jaws working over an acorn it held in its little paws. Lucy bit her lip, shut her eyes and crouched down, summoning her memories, her will, her rage. They did not fail her.

She drew herself up and made her way along the side of the house to the back where a Currier and Ives lawn sloped down to a frozen stream bordered by a low stone wall. Soundlessly, she climbed the few steps to a deck and stood by a glass door, breathing shallowly, her hand trembling so hard she could barely grasp the cold copper knob. With terrible slowness, she turned it.

It was unlocked. She exhaled.

The door swung wide, then stuck halfway open on a doormat. Warm air rushed out at her. She listened till she thought her head would break open. Nothing.

Then: the clang of pipes, and water running through them. The sound came from over her head. Someone was upstairs, in a bathroom, maybe washing their hands, maybe taking a shower, a bath. The water kept running.

Emboldened, Lucy stepped on the doormat and pushed the door shut behind her. She stepped silently across the Mexican tiled kitchen floor. The smell of eggs, something burned. A blackened frying pan and spatula rested in the sink. The water above her ran steadily.

Bookshelves filled with texts on psychology, marine science, and philosophy lined the richly furnished living room. Sprawling leather couches formed an L-shape on the oriental rug. A treadmill sat in an alcove facing a small television.

Lucy turned a corner to find a graceful curving staircase. She was about to set foot on the first step when she picked up a mounted photo of Constantin from an antique desk.

He stood on the deck of a sailboat, smiling broadly next to a three foot tuna that hung on a gaffe next to him. The water looked rough, the sky overcast. Listening constantly for the running water, Lucy flipped the frame over and slid the photo out. She slipped it inside her shirt, put the empty frame down, and started up the stairs.

As she neared the second floor landing she peered down a hallway. Light poured out of an open doorway. Her back hugging the wall, she inched her way to it until she was less than a foot from the opening. She stood frozen, every cell in her body listening. The smell of soap, shampoo. Steam wafted into the hall, pillowing out and dissipating in the colder air like ghosts.

Over the churning sound of water she heard someone sloshing into a bathtub, then the squeak, squeak of two faucets turned off.

Drip, drip, drip.

The sound of a body easing into bathwater.

A contented sigh.

Lucy's heart beat so loud she couldn't hear anything else. She pulled the knife from her sleeve and clutched the handle in her fist.

Drip, drip, drip.

Lucy ran screaming into the bathroom where Astra sat in the bath facing away from her. She lunged over Astra's head with the knife pointing in an arc toward Astra's belly.

Without turning her head, her body still except for one smooth movement, Astra reached up and caught Lucy's forearm and twisted it with a horrific cracking sound, sending her flying like a rag doll over the tub and through the air. Lucy crashed into a wicker vanity that smashed under her weight.

Whimpering with pain and terror, Lucy scrambled to her feet.

She looked at the woman in the tub.

Astra sat immersed in voluminous clouds of Victorian rose scented bubbles, her curly black hair combed luxuriously around her neck and shoulders. Both arms rested lazily along the rim of the antique tub. Above it, a narrow shelf held perfumed soaps and shampoos in fancifully shaped bottles. A cup of jasmine tea steamed on a saucer nearby.

"It appears that you, young lady," Astra said, taking a sip of tea, "still have some issues to deal with."

"How did you – ?"

"Please. I heard you walking down the street."

Lucy got to her feet but stumbled backwards. Doubled over, she cradled her hurt arm. A small white bone jutted through her sweater which quickly reddened with blood. "Jesus Christ," Lucy whispered hoarsely, "you broke my wrist."

Astra yawned and settled the cup down on the china saucer. "As much as I'd like to, you know, help you sort out all your acting out, your hallucinations, your impulsivity, obvious depression and probable bipolar if not schizophrenic tendencies, I am trying, as you may notice, to take a badly needed and might I say well deserved..." She lifted her leg and began soaping her calf, "...*day off.*"

Lucy glanced at the knife which had come to rest inches from the front claw of the tub. She fell on it and with her good hand raised it high over Astra who gazed up at her impassively. Lucy gasped for breath, eyes wild. Drops of blood from her wrist sizzled on the frothy white bubbles, pinking the oily water in small circles.

Astra looked down at the blood, than glared back up at Lucy. Her voice was a low growl. "Get back."

Crying, bleeding, Lucy stumbled a few steps back. Still, she held the knife high.

Gripping the sides of the tub, never losing eye contact with Lucy, Astra stood up.

· EIGHTY-ONE ·

L ucy screamed.

Horrific scars marched across Astra's chest, torso, and pelvis. Soap bubbles slid off, exposing pockmarks from bulletholes, long ridges from knife cuts, ropey burn marks circling her neck, great purple welts that criss-crossed her belly and glistened in the overhead light.

"Do you really think you can kill me, Lucy? *You?*" She shook out her absurdly beautiful hair. Her eyes grew dark as beetles. "Just look at me! Do you have *any idea* how many times I've been killed?"

The knife shook uncontrollably in Lucy's hand.

"I've been stabbed, shot, suffocated, strangled. I've been burned at the stake, crushed between granite slabs, ripped apart by wild dogs. And you think you frighten me, with your little bread knife?"

"No," Lucy cried. "Please stop."

"I come back, don't you understand? Just like you did. I'm just like you, Lucy."

"You're nothing like me!" Lucy shrieked. "Nothing!"

"Stop that, Kim." She took another sip of tea and sat on the edge of the tub. "Like mother, like daughter, isn't that how it goes? I think you should count yourself lucky that you can see what's in *your* future." She gestured at her hideous scars. "Not every daughter gets a chance to – "

"Shut up! *Shut up!*"

"Look, it's not like we have a choice, Kim. We're Repeaters. We come back. Forever. Which is, in my experience, a very, very, *very* long time." Astra closed her eyes and raised her hands. "But it's not all bad. Coming back gives you certain powers. For example, I don't have to wear these all the time..." She made a low, inhuman growl. The scars began to disappear, sinking into her skin.

Sobbing, Lucy sank to her knees, the knife still in her hand. "Why do you bother? Why do you bother with life?"

"Oooh, a little philosophy on my day off. A little history. I can handle that. I guess you almost deserve it. Almost." She reached for a towel and draped it over her shoulders. "It was like this: I had you – I wanted you at the time. I thought it would be the ultimate way of being loved. Isn't that what they all say? Nothing like the bond between mother and child? Well, I didn't feel it. I felt nothing."

Lucy cried soundlessly, the blood from her wrist pooling on the tile.

"No, that's not quite the right word," Astra went on. "I felt...disgust. And I didn't love your father. He was just some way of having you, a weak fairy that loved me. And you, you loved me too, pathetic little thing that you were. And you still do, don't you?"

Lucy said nothing.

"Otherwise, why are you here? What else could you possibly want from me but my love?" she sneered. "To be fair, you were interesting for a while, but then you started to become just like your father – weak, demanding, in a word: boring. Plus that blind thing was a real pain. I hadn't expected that at all."

Lucy drew herself up, snatched a towel off a rack and wrapped it around her arm, never letting go of the knife. "Why did you kill me?"

"Because for the first time in ten centuries, I fell in love. But you already know all that, don't you?"

Lucy stared at her. Before her eyes, the scars began to reappear on Astra's body, rising from the depths of her, puckering and branding her flesh, slashing fresh red ribbons across her torso from the inside. Following Lucy's eyes, Astra looked down at her body. Astra paled, her expression frozen for just a moment. Their eyes locked. Lucy caught a flicker of fear, almost helplessness, in her face. But Astra turned away as she snatched up her robe and slipped it on. With a sneer of annoyance, she stepped onto a towel and sat down in a wicker chair next to the tub, crossing her long legs with casual grace.

"I got so tired of being hated, each and every time. I was bad news, I guess, but I swore that this time I would be a good person; I would have love, I would deserve love, and it never happened – not until that day, after eons of loneliness, that I met Constantin. That weekend you came up to see me with him. Can't you see how expendable you were? It was fate – Constantin and I were fated to be together! Our wedding photos are downstairs. Did you happen to notice them on your way in?"

Lucy shook her head no.

"And he loves me, Kim. He always will. He loves me like he never loved you."

Lucy glanced at the door. "Why don't you kill me?"

"Don't tempt me." She sighed, flipping her hair free from the collar of the robe. "Unfortunately, it wouldn't look good, trust me."

"Hard enough the first time, was it?"

Astra got to her feet, tied the robe tight, and took a few steps toward her. Lucy backed into the broken vanity. The air was thick with loathing. "It was a breeze, actually."

"Don't come any closer to me."

Astra took another step. They stood less than a yard apart. "This is my house, little girl. It's called breaking and entering, self defense – "

"Get away from me!" Lucy shrieked, swiping the knife in a wide arc. Astra leaned back, missing the blade but losing her balance. She slipped in a soapy puddle and fell back on her hands as Lucy tore out of the room, down the stairs, out the door and into the night.

· EIGHTY-TWO ·

Lucy sat in the passenger seat staring straight ahead as Ellen took a right on Lincoln Avenue and headed down the hill toward the high school.

Face grimly set, Ellen reached down and flipped the radio on, searched briefly for a station, then just as quickly turned it off.

"I don't know, Lucy, it's like I can't believe a word that comes out of your mouth any more."

"I fell off the balance beam, Ma."

She turned sharply toward Lucy. "You weren't even at school yesterday! Don't you think I called? How stupid do you think I am?"

Lucy looked down at her sneakers and shut her eyes.

"Let's try this one more time. How did you break your wrist?"

"I fell."

"You fell, how? Look at me, dammit."

Lucy turned to her. "I fell off a curb. I tripped running for the bus."

"Is that what happened?"

"Yeah."

"Really, you fell off a curb?"

"Yeah."

"Then why couldn't you tell me that last night at the hospital? Why did you have to make that up about the balance beam?"

Lucy looked back at her feet. "I wanted you to think I was in school."

"Jesus, Lucy." She turned into the wide circular drive that led to the school. "What am I going to do with you?"

"I'm sorry. I don't mean to be such a pain."

"You're not a pain, Lucy, you're my daughter and I love you. I'm just worried. Every day it's something." She held a lock of hair that had fallen into her face. "See the grey? This wasn't here last week."

Lucy gave her a weak smile.

"Give me a hug, and get in there."

Lucy hugged her, holding her hurt arm away from her body.

"I'll see you out here at two-thirty for your appointment."

Lucy shook her head. "Oh, no, I'm not going to that."

Ellen sank back in her seat, exhausted. "You're going."

"You can be out here at two-thirty, Mom, but I won't be here. I swear."

Ellen looked at her evenly. "Then I will simply come in the school, take you by the arm, and drag you to this car. Do you understand?"

"Yeah," Lucy said, opening the car door and getting out. "I understand." She slammed the door and walked toward the school without a backwards glance.

C ast hidden under her denim jacket, Lucy stood among throngs of students that broke around her as if she were a stone in a rushing stream. Opening her locker with her good hand, she noticed another student coming toward her, a popular girl with her leg in a cast. Her cast was covered with signatures, well wishing poems and colorful doodles, whereas Lucy's stayed blank. Hearing her name called, the girl hobbled off on her crutches.

It was 2:30. Lucy sat in math class, the last class of the day, completely absorbed in finding the unknown in an algebra problem. The girl with the leg cast sat a few seats ahead of her, giggling with a boy who sat next to her.

Absently, Lucy put her pencil down and reached up to touch her scar. Something warm and wet oozed from it.

She pulled her hand away. Blood covered her fingers. With a sharp intake of breath, she reached behind her chair for her scarf which she pressed against her neck.

She pulled the scarf away. Already soaked through.

Wordlessly, she jumped from her seat and ran out of the room and down the hall toward the girl's bathroom. All the while, she felt the blood pulse out of her into the scarf, inhaling the rusty horror of it as she ran.

As she burst through the doors of the bathroom, she became dimly aware of shouting, people running behind her. She ducked into a stall and sat, head dropped forward woozily in her hands. The door opened. Someone took her by the arm to lift her to her feet but she shook herself free, stumbling out of the stall toward the door. A gauzy weakness flooded her brain and limbs. The darkness spread like curtains closing on both sides of her vision until there was only the comforting shabbiness of the girls' room door and her bloody hand pushing it open.

Then her whole world went blank.

· EIGHTY-THREE ·

Lucy opened her eyes. Above her, Astra's face, a great swollen moon framed with a black mane of hair, floated back and forth, the mouth making words that played too slowly for Lucy to understand. She strained to listen, to comprehend the globs of sound; she lifted her good arm up but it was so heavy she almost passed out from the effort. She let it drop down to sheets drawn tightly around her, a thin coarse blanket. She shivered uncontrollably; her hands, her feet too cold to feel. Her tongue swollen in her mouth like a fat pupae. She moved it and pushed out sound but knew it was nonsensical noise. The Astra face swarmed closer, huge over her, blurry then clear again, the mouth gigantic and red, the teeth obscured, then revealed and glistening, smiling. Lucy felt her eyelids held open, then let go. The moon face was gone.

Lucy willed her eyes to open again. Ellen's face floated by, smaller, the eyebrows meeting in a tent of concern, the mouth moving more quickly. Cool hands touched Lucy's cheek, forehead. Her head gently lifted, a dixie cup held to her mouth, something sweetish and cool slid down her throat.

She shut her eyes again.

Everything went away.

Until she felt a hand creep along her arm and a deep jab in the crook of her elbow. She opened her eyes wide and saw Astra sitting on the edge of the bed. More words piled out of Astra's mouth. If she could only understand this slower than slow language. Smacked with the rush of the drug, her eyelids drooped down.

Lucy forced her eyes open one last time, made herself remain conscious. She watched Ellen hand Astra the knife Lucy had taken from home.

"...found it in her bag."

"Then it's clear," Astra said. "She must have cut her own neck."

"My God, please tell me that's not true," came Ellen's voice, soft and far away.

The drug led Lucy into a velvety darkness.

Five hours later, thirst and a full bladder stirred her from her chemical peace. She lifted her head, heavy and pounding, from the flat pillow and propped herself up with her good arm.

Where in the world am I, she thought. The light from a streetlight striped through half open blinds over her flimsy hospital gown, tied in two places in the back by someone other than herself, she didn't want to think who. She pushed off the bed and went to the window. A snowy parking lot half filled with cars.

With bare feet on a cold floor, she padded over to the bathroom, which, with all its gizmos for wheelchairs and bathing, was almost as big as her room.

She did a double take at herself in the mirror. Dank, unwashed hair fell over her face and down over her johnny and thin chest. Her eyes looked hollow and huge, with great dark circles underneath. A wide bandage angled down across her neck; her wrist throbbed viciously.

She looked around at the spotless white porcelain, the container of urine specimen cups, the "ring for emergencies" rope next to the john, and started to cry tears of frustration.

She felt, more than ever, like a motherless child.

For several minutes she let herself cry, hitting her thigh with the fist of her good hand. She turned on the faucets full blast, cupped her hands over her mouth and screamed until her throat was raw and there was nothing left.

Then she threw water on her face, toweled off and left the bathroom.

The heavy, windowed door of her room swung open soundlessly onto a dimly lit hallway. At the far end of it, a nurse sat reading at an L-shaped cubicle lit by a desk lamp.

The nurse looked up, startled, as Lucy approached her. She was small-boned, with sharp features and badly made up lips like a child's drawing. She flipped her book shut and got to her feet. She wasn't much taller than Lucy.

"Are you all right...Lucy, isn't it?"

"Where am I?"

"Well," she gestured rather helplessly, "Greenfield."

Lucy took in the endless hallway of closed doors just like hers. "Are you the only doctor here right now?"

"I'm a nurse, but if you want to see Dr. Nathanson, I'm afraid you'll have to wait till morning. Dr. Strand is on call. He's very nice. Would you like to speak to him?"

"No. I just want, well, I can't find my clothes."

The nurse took off her glasses and laid them on a chart. "It isn't policy to – you're a patient, and you need to be here."

"But I'm fine. I feel fine. Do you have my clothes?"

"Yes, but you need to be here, Lucy."

"So you won't give me my clothes?"

"No. I can't."

"That's crazy. They're my clothes. Well, I'll just leave without them, then."

"I don't have the authority to let you do that, Lucy."

Lucy peered all the way down to the end of the hallway through a much larger set of doors to a well-lit corridor. "I don't need your permission."

"But Lucy, you can't leave."

Lucy started to walk, then run down the hallway, her naked heels pounding on the sickly green linoleum, her cast banging at her rib cage. Cold air snaked up the back of her johnny. She felt she'd run for miles by the time she finally reached the massive doors that led to freedom. She grabbed the handle and yanked so hard she pulled a muscle in her shoulder, crying out in pain.

It didn't budge.

She banged on the door with her fist, screamed, "Let me out of here!"

The nurse began running toward her, followed by a large orderly.

She banged some more. "Open this door! I'm not crazy! Please!"

Beyond the door, doctors, patients and families walked and mingled, some less than a foot from her, but no one could hear her, or if they could, they never turned their heads.

· EIGHTY-FOUR ·

Six weeks later, Lucy sat in a circle of teenage girls in a sterile room where three of the walls were plastered with inspirational posters of sunsets and birds in flight over moonlit canyons. Chore charts, job wheels, medication and recreation schedules took up the rest of the wallspace. The fourth wall was all glass.

There was Michelle, fifteen, her slender wrists freshly wrapped. Rows of scars marked the tender flesh of her forearms. Natanya, fourteen, stared out the window with heavy lidded eyes as she rocked gently in her chair. Kat, thirteen and over three hundred pounds, folded her arms tight and high over her belly and sneered at Misha and Marsha, African American twins who had a pact with themselves and sleeping pills. And there was Lucy. Everyone had one eye on the wall clock.

Astra sat closest to the door, legs crossed, eyebrows raised. "That's very good, Lucy."

"What do you mean, 'that's very good'?"

"It sounds like you're starting to be truthful with yourself."

Lucy stared at her with glazed eyes. "I guess it's about time, right?"

"Ass kisser," Misha said with a note of jealousy, not looking up from examining her long ropey braids.

"You don't agree that's the first step, Misha, being honest with yourself?"

"It's just not my friggin' problem, I guess," she said, snickering along with Marsha, her mirror image.

"So what, anyways?" Kat said, turning with reptilian slowness toward

294

Lucy. "We all tried to kill ourselves. That's why we're here, isn't it?"

"Natanya," Astra said. "Do you want to add anything to this?"

"No," she said, still staring out the window at the sloping grounds.

"She's in witch-world," Michelle said. "I wouldn't bother her. She might put a spell on you."

Natanya turned to Michelle. "It's not about spells, it's about earth, and goddesses – "

"Bitch world, is more like it," Misha said.

"All right, young ladies, none of that sort of language in group. Are we – "

Lucy brightened. Behind the glass wall, Ellen and Peter stood in their coats and hats, waving at her and smiling, Peter stuffing what looked like a cookie in his mouth. All the girls turned to see who was visiting, each in her own private way reacting to the fact that these visitors were not there to see her.

With a rigid smile, Astra waved at Ellen and Peter who enthusiastically waved back.

"May I go see them, Dr. Nathanson?" Lucy asked politely.

She turned her watch face up on her bony wrist. "We still have five minutes, but all right. This once."

Lucy smiled and got up. "Thanks."

"Meds first, don't forget."

"I won't."

She pulled the door shut behind her and turned around to Ellen's woolly embrace.

Peter hugged her leg. "Happy birthday! We brought you a cake!"

"Peter!" Ellen said, letting go of Lucy and stroking her hair. "That was a surprise."

"There's chocolate chip cookies too."

"Not the way you're going at them, young man."

The three of them turned a corner to a common room where a

chocolate frosted home-made cake sat next to a platter of cookies. "Maybe when the girls get out they'd like to join us?"

"Sure," Lucy said.

They sat on benches next to a low table smeared with dried paint. Peter swiped a gob of icing with his finger.

"Enough, Peter," Ellen said. "You're going to be sick."

"I don't care."

"So, Lucy," Ellen said, taking off her hat. "How do you feel?"

Lucy looked at Peter. "I feel fine."

"Fine?"

"I mean I feel good."

"Things have been going well with your therapy? Your doctors? What about Dr. Nathanson?"

"She's been great."

"I thought you didn't like her."

Lucy shrugged. "I guess I was a little angry when I first met her. I wasn't being honest with anyone about what was really going on with me."

"Oh, honey, I'm so glad to hear you saying these things. We miss you so much, don't we, Peter?"

He smiled through a mouthful of cookie. "Yeah. Sometimes."

Ellen began cutting the cake with a plastic knife. "I'm sorry there's no candles, but they said no matches or anything sharp allowed on – "

"Yeah, I know," Lucy reached out to Peter. "Com'ere, Nugget."

He crawled on her lap and pushed a piece of cookie in her mouth.

One by one, the girls from group wandered into the common room. Kat grabbed a cookie and a hunk of cake, took a seat and began eating in silence, staring at Lucy and Peter. Nantanya held back, politely taking her piece when Ellen offered it to her.

"Happy birthday, Lucy," she said softly. "I can't wait till I'm seventeen."

"You'll be lucky to make it to next week," Misha said, taking her piece.

"Shut up, Misha," Kat said, reaching for another frosting-heavy slice.

Astra breezed in, files in hand. Ellen jumped up to offer her a seat.

"Dr. Nathanson, would you like some cake?"

She looked at the cake, the roomful of girls chewing. "I think I'll pass, Mrs. Duggan –"

"Call me Ellen, please."

"Ellen – besides, we have a meeting with Dr. Davies that I'm sure Lucy wouldn't want to miss."

Lucy got up and set Peter on his feet. "I'm ready when you are, Dr. Nathanson."

Ellen, Lucy and Peter followed Astra down a series of hallways to Dr. Davies' office. While Ellen took Peter to a corner of the waiting room and set him up with crayons and drawing paper, Astra grabbed Lucy by the collar and roughly pulled her aside. They were well hidden behind a rack full of coats. Her nails dug into the back of Lucy's neck.

"I know what your plan is, Lucy, and it won't work," Astra hissed.

"What plan? I have no plan."

"Sometimes, young lady, you act as if you simply don't remember what I'm capable of."

Lucy slapped her hand away. "Get your filthy hands off me."

Just as Lucy stepped away from Astra, Dr. Davies turned the corner of the hallway carrying half a sandwich and a carton of milk.

"I'm so sorry," he said. "Lost track of time. I'd lose my head if it wasn't screwed on." He motioned Lucy and Astra into his office. "Hello, Astra. Hello, Lucy. Your mom here?" He noticed Ellen bent over Peter and his toys in the far corner of the waiting room. "Oh, there she is. That your little brother?" He took a bite of sandwich.

"Yeah," Lucy said.

"Cute kid. Well, listen, this shouldn't take long. Just a few simple questions."

· EIGHTY-FIVE ·

Lucy sat on her hands, eyes on the floor, Astra's stare burning into the side of her face. "Well," she said softly, "I think I had a lot of anger toward my mom."

Ellen welled up. "I try, I really do, but with Peter and all my – "

"I'm sorry, Ellen, but we need to hear from Lucy today," Dr. Davies said. "We can talk later on, if you wish."

"I'm sorry," Ellen mumbled into her Kleenex. "I'll be quiet."

"So, Lucy," Dr. Davies prompted, "keep on with what you were saying. And remember, we're here for you. All of us." Astra stared at her blood red nails.

"I guess I feel like I've worked it through here, my anger at Mom and at myself, about the divorce and all of that, with Dr. Nathanson, and group, and everything. I feel much better. I miss my family and I want to go home. And I'm not a danger to myself any more."

The room was silent except for a ticking clock.

Astra asked, "Do you mean that, Lucy?"

"Can we trust you not to hurt yourself any more?" Dr. Davies asked.

"Yes, you can. It was a one-time thing, a horrible mistake."

Dr. Davies pulled a form from his drawer. "This is a contract, Lucy, and it's not just a piece of paper. It really means something. Your signature is a promise to us, to your family, to the world, and to yourself that you won't ever hurt yourself again. Do you feel ready to sign it? Don't feel pressured, I want you to be honest with all of us." He handed her the paper and a pen.

Without hesitation, Lucy signed the paper and handed it back to him. Tearfully, Ellen hugged her as Lucy stared at Astra over her shoulder.

Astra closed the door behind Lucy and Ellen. She stood staring at the door, her arms rigid at her sides.

"Okay, Astra," David said. "Tell me what's up. I've known you long enough – "

She whipped around, steadying herself with a white-knuckled grip on the leather chair where Lucy sat only moments before. "I can't believe you can't see it."

"See what?"

"She's – she's faking everything."

"Faking being well? I don't know, Astra – "

"Just two weeks ago that girl was in tears in my office, swearing she couldn't wait to get out and 'try it again.' She was despondent, she was hysterical – "

David held up his hand. "I hate to sound cold, but that was two weeks ago. A lot happens in a teenager's life in two weeks."

She walked around the chair and sat down. "It's just not enough time, David. Can't you see? She's not ready to leave here. She's got a history of depression, self-mutilation, seizures, delusions – "

"She's responding well to meds, there's complete compliance with a promise to continue at home. She was terrific with the other girls, or so I'm told."

"She completely flew off the handle in group last week. Just lost it."

"We all lose our temper now and then. Look, Astra, we're here to help these kids. Why are we always so surprised when we actually do? When they leave here better than when they arrived? Who cares if it took six months, six weeks, or six minutes? We did our job."

"She'll be back, David."

"And if she is, we'll take care of her."

Astra shook her head.

"I don't mean to sound critical, Astra, but I hope you haven't become too involved emotionally in this one. Got to keep our distance, for professional reasons as well as our own sanity. Listen, you're a wonderful doctor, but you had a tremendous loss, one I can't even imagine going through."

"This isn't about that, David."

"Well, maybe it isn't. I just think we should pat ourselves on the back every once in a while, don't you?"

Lucy followed Peter who ran up the stairs to where Ellen stood with her key in the lock.

"There's a surprise for you, and you'll never guess it," Peter said, grinning.

Lucy stood with her backpack and laundry bag filled with her belongings. A low growl came from the apartment, then a joyful squeal as Ellen opened the door.

A yellow Labrador puppy with a big red bow tied to its collar scrambled out the door and leapt into Ellen's arms, licking her face, its whole body wagging hello. She handed it to Peter, who fell back laughing on the carpet while the puppy covered him with kisses. Lucy knelt down and picked him up.

"His name is Sherman," Peter said. "He's your Christmas present."

Lucy's eyes watered with happiness as she held Sherman's wriggling body. "He's adorable. Thank you so much."

"He doesn't know you yet," Ellen said, "but he will. He's not house trained yet, either." She stepped over a small yellow puddle on the kitchen floor. "In fact, would you guys walk him? I think he's trying to tell us something here."

A warm spell had melted the top layer of snow to the consistency of brittle candy on the sloping lawn behind their house. Lucy and Peter collapsed with laughter as they watched Sherman skate and slide until he butted up against a birch tree at the bottom of the hill. Sherman looked up helplessly as Peter ran down the hill after him, his little boots crunching into the snow. He lifted up the puppy and hugged him.

"Come on, Peter, you have to let him do his business," Lucy said, standing at the top of the hill in the twilight.

"You mean pee and poo?" he giggled.

"That's exactly right."

"You mean number one and number two?" He was cracking himself up.

"You're such a smart little nugget. Now leave him alone a minute."

Peter put the dog down and stopped in his tracks, holding his hands behind his back in a parody of waiting. As if he knew this was his window of opportunity, Sherman squatted and burned a yellow steaming hole in the snow.

"Good boy, Sherman," Peter said. He looked up at Lucy. "You're supposta praise him. Say 'good boy.'"

"Good boy, Sherman."

The second he finished, Sherman tried to scramble back up the slope, but couldn't get a grip on the ice.

Peter looked at Lucy. "Can I get him now?"

Lucy nodded while Peter ran off and carried the puppy back up the hill.

"He's so smart, he doesn't even need a leash. Do you like him?"

"I love him, Peter. How could I not love him?"

"So, are you better now? Mom said you were better, but that you still need to take medicine for your brain."

"I'm much better. And you shouldn't worry about my brain."

"And you'll want to be home more because of the puppy. I mean, now you have me *and* Sherman."

"Peter, listen to me a second, okay?" Sherman scrambled out of his arms and Peter chased him in circles around a tree, its branches casting elegant shadows on the white bank of snow. She grabbed her brother when he came close enough that she could. "Are you listening, Peter?"

"Yeah."

She took him by his little shoulders and looked into his blue-grey eyes. "I just want you to know that no matter what happens to me, that I love you more than anything."

He blinked. "What's gonna happen to you?"

"Nothing. But I know it looks like I don't care sometimes, when I don't come home right on time, or when I...I lose control, but I do care. About Mom too, and Dad, and now Sherman. Do you understand?"

"Can we go to the store with Sherman?"

"You want to show him off to Mr. Ezbeke at the 7-11?"

"Yeah, and I want some Snickers ice cream."

"Fine, let me get the keys. I'll meet you at the car."

Peter whooped with happiness, picked up Sherman and ran toward the car.

· EIGHTY-SIX ·

After school every day for a week, Lucy took the bus to Cambridge and wandered around the campus and marine science building, but each time she couldn't bring herself to do anything but roam the halls. She watched students changing classes, read poster boards about roommates needed, laptops for sale, study groups, and quad parties. After an hour or so, she'd get the bus back home, staring into space.

But on Friday she woke up determined. After school she ran to catch the bus to the city. Scouting a seat at the back, she pulled out the now dog-eared photo of Constantin, the one she had stolen from Astra's house. When the bus groaned to a stop in the square, she wrapped it carefully in a piece of notebook paper and slipped it in the back pocket of her jeans.

She navigated the crowded sidewalks and crossed the street into the quad. Elegant brick buildings surrounded her; students swarmed by on their way to class or a café for coffee or a beer.

Lucy stopped a studious looking girl rushing out of the marine science building and asked if she knew how to find Constantin Damler. She said she'd never heard of him and hurried away into the quad and the deepening winter dusk.

With damp palms and a fluttering heart, Lucy approached the somber brick building. As she pulled open the heavy double doors, she realized she hadn't thought this through one bit, even with all her trips there that week. At that moment she couldn't think much beyond some scenario such as: he would see her, recognize her and take her in his arms. There was no Plan B.

It was clear she had arrived while most classes were in session. The halls were hushed, with only the occasional student drinking from a fountain or rushing late into class. They all looked around her age but more sophisticated in some way she couldn't put her finger on. A studied casualness, hair cut just so.

She passed classroom after classroom filled with students bent over books and laptops, or sitting back in their chairs, deep in thought. Methodically, she walked down one side of the hall, then the other, peering in at the teachers. A teaching assistant handed out booklets in a lab. A young woman in a crimson suit pointed to graphs on a whiteboard. A bald man in a plaid shirt gesticulated; the whole class broke up laughing. It made her lonely. She wished she could have heard what he said.

She felt herself losing her nerve. The clock in the hall said 4:45. She was supposed to be home fifteen minutes ago. Still, she climbed the stairs to the second floor.

She walked the length of the corridor, her squeaky sneaker footsteps the only sound, and had just turned around to come back when all the doors seemed to open at once. Laughing, talking students spilled out of classrooms on both sides of her. So many clogged the way in front of her that she was forced to come to a full stop in front of the last classroom on the right before the stairs.

It was there that she saw him. He stood at the front of a classroom near a whiteboard, deep in conversation with a student, a thin, long-haired boy with a whisper of a mustache and the bearing of someone eternally embarrassed. Lucy watched Constantin make a few gestures as the boy nodded vigorously, then he drew something with great sweeping arcs on the board – she was at the wrong angle to see just what – but he had evidently made his point. The boy smiled and picked up his books. Constantin set his marker down, folded papers in a briefcase and, trailed by the student, left the classroom.

Constantin's shoulders passed inches from her face. His scent – like fresh snow and tangerines, wafted by her. She followed close behind him and the student, unable to take her eyes off him. Her hands tingled from the memory of him, the cool, smooth hair, the angles of his face and breadth of his shoulders; she could almost hear the warm honey of his voice and deeper channel of his laugh.

But as students splintered off into groups or left the building, she held back a bit, until Constantin and the student entered a stairwell and climbed out of sight. She watched them reach the third floor, hesitated, then ran up after them.

Bursting through the third-floor doors, she looked either way. Everyone had disappeared.

She gambled and took a left and saw his office. On the door were his name and office hours in raised, blocky letters. She reached up and traced the letters, stunned by the sense memory.

The door swung in and Constantin leaned out. "Can I help you?"

Flushed, she unzipped her bookbag and pulled out a pen and paper. "No, I was just getting your office hours for later, some other time."

He laughed a little. "I'm free now, if you like. And I know my classes can get pretty big, but I thought I'd met all my students. Which class are you in?"

Her hand fluttered to her forehead, then down to her hair which she draped across her neck. "I'm not in any of them, but I'd like to be, if there was room."

He held the thick oak door open wide for her. "Why don't you come in. I'll figure out what I can do for you."

She followed him down a short narrow hallway into a tiny study, its walls filled with books up to the ceiling. They covered the floor in teetering piles while neatly stacked papers marched around the perimeter of the room. His desk, armchair and a classroom chair opposite filled whatever space remained. A casement window with an untended ivy plant on the sill looked out over the yard.

On one corner of his desk sat a model of the human heart. Without thinking, Lucy picked up the heart and examined it, closing her eyes as her fingers traced the chambers, the brilliant workings of the organ. Just as quickly, she opened her eyes and put it back on the desk.

He had been watching her intently. "What's your name?"

She offered her hand but still couldn't meet his eye. "Lucy."

His big warm hand encased hers. "Nice to meet you, Lucy. So tell me, what year are you in? And please sit down." He gestured at the student chair mercifully free of books and papers.

"I'm not really enrolled yet."

"Not enrolled?"

"I'm a high school student and I was very interested..." She finally looked at him and was overcome. She hadn't counted on this memory of love, how it would flood her brain and body with desire and confusion.

He smiled, a whisper of concern at his temples. "You want to see what it's like to be in college? Is that it?"

"Yes, I'd like to audit your class if I could."

"Lucy, I'd like nothing more, but you still have to be a student here to do that. Did you know that?"

"No."

"What school do you go to?"

"Gloucester High." She looked out his window at the ice-glazed tree limbs, the black silhouettes of students crossing the quad alone or in pairs. She felt helpless.

"Doesn't your school offer AP biology, or chemistry?"

"I want – need something even more advanced."

He pushed some books aside and tapped his laptop to life. "Have you gone on the web? I'll bet in the library alone you could find enough to keep you busy till you get to college. I can suggest different books depending on which field – "

"Listen, Dr. Damler, I'm not here about school."

He stopped fidgeting and looked at her. "I didn't think so, for some reason."

"Then you understand?" she said in a trembling voice.

"Understand what?"

"Dr. Damler, do you believe in reincarnation?"

His hand went nervously to his collar, half of which was caught under his sweater. "Well, no. Not in the least, actually."

"You need to listen to me. You need to forget about science for a minute."

He gave a shrug. "This is – "

"Just for a minute, Constantin."

He stared at her. "We should probably stick to formalities, Lucy. Call me Dr. Damler."

"Dr. Damler, then."

He pulled at his collar again, but it was buttoned down. "I wish I did believe in reincarnation. It's quite a romantic concept, actually, that souls can be reborn, but I'm a realist. When the body dies, the person dies." He put a hand through his thick, greying hair and looked out the window. "Sad but true, I'm afraid."

She leaned forward in her chair. "But what if I told you, Dr. Damler, that I am the reincarnation of someone you love, or...loved."

"If you told me that, I think I might ask you to leave."

"But why?"

"Because I don't – Lucy, is it?"

She nodded sadly.

"Because, Lucy, I don't have time to deal with whatever problems you have that have contributed to this delusion of yours. I'm a science teacher, not a shrink."

"Don't you want to know who I am?"

"You've just told me that." He got up and pushed his chair under his desk. "Shouldn't you be getting back home to Gloucester?"

She got up and reached down for her bookbag. "You really don't want to know, do you. Maybe it's easier for you if I never came here." They stood a few feet apart. "But I did come, and I am here, and I'll come back again."

"It would be wonderful for you to get through high school and come to school here, if that's what you mean."

She looked up at him, searching his face for some spark of recognition. She found nothing. "I thought you'd be braver than this, Constantin. I thought you'd at least want to know who I am."

He held the door open for her. With measured steps, she walked into the hallway and turned back to face him.

"I'm Kim, Constantin."

His expression changed from annoyance to shock, to a strangled sort of hope, then anger. With hooded eyes he said, "Get back in here."

She came back into the entranceway, inches from him.

"Who told you about Kim?" he said roughly.

"No one had to tell me, I – "

" – you have no right to harass me with my personal life."

"I'm not – "

"I've seen you, Lucy, I've seen you around campus. How long have you been following me? Are you a former student? If you have a crush on me, that's fine – just say so. It's all right. I won't be angry. Is that what's going on?"

Lucy looked down at the threadbare runner. Students and teachers passed by out of the corner of her eye. "No."

"Listen, Lucy, liking someone is one thing, but stalking them, using their personal history against them, well that's another. Do you understand?"

She lifted her face to his. Quick as a cat, she got on her toes and brushed her lips against his. For a moment, she tasted the future, the past.

He turned his head away and said, "Get out."

Well after he shut the door behind her, and long after he watched her lanky figure cross the quad and trade the campus for the bustle of the square, he stood motionless by the window holding his fingers against his lips where she had kissed him, as the night came on and the moon rose high over the gate separating Barnesdale from the world.

· EIGHTY-SEVEN ·

Astra and Constantin sat in the far corner of a posh French restaurant decorated in dark paisley walls and velvet curtains. Fantastic purple lamps shaped like trumpet flowers hung down from the ceiling, barely lighting the room. Astra wore a snug aubergine dress, her hair in a dramatic upsweep, while Constantin looked professorial in his preppy shirt, natty jacket, and baggy-in-the-knees corduroys. They silently tucked into their forty-dollar entrees.

Astra snapped her fingers at a passing waiter, pointing at her empty wine glass. The waiter nodded but made no eye contact, turned, and disappeared behind heavy drapes into the kitchen. Constantin concentrated on his filet mignon, cutting it into small, even pieces.

"Why do you have to do that?" he asked, not looking up from his meat.

"Do what?"

"Snap at people like that. Waiters." He gestured with his knife.

"Don't do that with your knife, Constantin, and I wasn't 'snapping,' I was ordering another glass of wine."

"Well, you don't have to snap your fingers at them. They're not performing seals."

She took a long sip of Perrier and considered him. "What's the matter with you tonight? Can't you be nice? It's my birthday, after all."

He gestured again with his knife. "Sorry, I guess I had a weird kind of day. This girl I've noticed hanging around campus came to see me – "

"Who?"

"I don't know, this girl, this crazy girl came into my office today and asked me if I believed in reincarnation, of all things." Constantin studied her briefly, then went back to his meal.

The waiter brought the wine; Astra nearly yanked the glass out of his hands.

"And do you?"

"You're supposed to say 'thank you.'"

"I'll say it with a tip."

Constantin shrugged.

"So do you believe in – "

"Don't be ridiculous. I'm a scientist. Death is the end, we know that. You know that." He took a big bite of meat.

Astra shifted in her chair and reached back to check her hair with a nervous hand. "What did she want from you, this girl? Did she tell you her name?"

"At first she said she wanted to audit some classes, but then I got the truth out of her which was – and this happens once in a blue moon, you know – that she has a crush on me. I got rid of her, in a nice way."

Astra took a careful bite of her Caesar salad. "And she didn't tell you her name?"

"Why is that important? I'm sure I took care of it."

"I like to keep track of all your admirers, dear."

"Well, if it's that important to you, Lucy. I think that's what she said."

"Looks like you've still got the old charm, right, Constantin?"

He smiled wanly. "I don't know. You tell me."

· EIGHTY-EIGHT ·

Astra canceled all her afternoon appointments, got in her car and headed north toward Gloucester. Grey sleet slanted across the windshield as a Bach violin sonata boomed from her stereo. Soon she found herself driving past stately Victorians toward the center of town.

After briefly cursing herself for leaving the directions she'd printed out on her desk at work, she stopped at a gas station. A short, swarthy man pulled himself out from under a flatbed truck on a low cart to answer her sharp, "Excuse me." She stood primly on one of the few spots on the garage floor that was free of oil as she asked for directions to Gloucester High school, and for a map of the town. He gave her what she wanted, wiped his greasy hands on a greasier rag, then watched her walk back to her car, her high collared black leather coat cinched tight at the waist.

Still listening to the sonata, she drove to the school, a single story, L-shaped building, and sat in the parking lot staring through the glass of the well lit entranceway.

For two hours she didn't move, never taking off her coat or even her long black gloves as she watched for Lucy. When she caught sight of her she turned her head just once with a snapping movement like a hawk that has spotted a mouse in a field. Lucy was walking alone, her hair in a long braid down her back, an oversized bookbag slung over one shoulder. Astra watched her pass through the glass corridor and disappear inside a perpendicular section of the building.

Finally, at 2:15, Astra picked up her cell phone and called Ellen.

"Mrs. Duggan?"

"Yes?"

"This is Dr. Nathanson. I hope I'm not interrupting anything."

"Oh dear, no, just putting my son to bed. He's got a little flu, I think."

"I'm so sorry to hear that. Listen, the reason I'm calling is that, as you know, Lucy seems to be doing well, but something very strange has come to my attention."

"What do you – "

"She's been stalking my husband."

"*What?*"

"Ellen, I think it would be so much easier to talk about this if we spoke in person." Astra started her car and swung out of the lot onto the main road. "I happen to be in Gloucester visiting a sick relative, and I've got a few moments before I have to head back to the office. Are you free right now? I thought we might have a private chat before Lucy gets home from school."

Ellen looked in on Peter. The color bloomed high in his cheeks but he'd finally stopped coughing and fallen into a deep sleep. She was thankful his fever had gone down but knew he was exhausted and expected him to sleep through the night. His favorite DVD, Road Runner, played rather loudly near his bed, but he didn't seem to be able to fall asleep without the television on, and especially liked to play Road Runner or Bugs Bunny cartoons over and over when he was sick. It seemed to comfort him. Sherman was curled in a tiny, contented ball, snuggled in the crook of Peter's bent knees.

Ellen threw on an old coat over her waitress uniform and ran down to the restaurant where she grabbed some fresh coffee and muffins, rushed back up and laid the food out on a chipped tray in the living room. She was just rearranging the throws over the furniture to cover the worst of the holes when she heard footsteps on the stairs and a knock on the door.

"Please come in," Ellen said, opening the door wide for her. "Make yourself at home." She fluttered around Astra, who kept her coat on and accepted a cup of coffee as she took a seat in the chair closest to the door. "We just got a puppy – I don't know if Lucy told you – and on top of Peter's toys, this place is impossible to keep picked up."

"Oh, I understand completely," Astra said, sipping politely. "This is delicious coffee."

"Thanks, it's just the coffee from our restaurant downstairs." She settled on the couch. "Do you have children of your own, Dr. Nathanson?"

Astra cleared her throat. "I had a daughter, but she was killed."

Ellen paused as she broke a blueberry muffin in half and looked up at Astra. "I'm so sorry. How did she die, if I may ask?"

"She was hit by car, playing in the street. She was six years old. I was at work and she was with her sitter, who was watching television with her boyfriend."

"I don't think I would ever get over that. And the sitter, how could you ever forgive her?"

"Well, you have to go on. You can't harbor hate. It just eats away at you. The grief is enough."

"That's true, but still, my God." She put the rest of her muffin down on a paper napkin with the insignia of the Gull's Nest on it. "So please, tell me about Lucy."

Astra shifted in her chair. "My husband told me last night that Lucy has been coming by his place of work. He's a teacher at Barnesdale – "

"So *that's* where she's been going every afternoon after school. That girl cannot tell the truth to save her life." Her voice quivered slightly. "I'm sorry, Dr. Nathanson, go on."

"Astra, please call me Astra."

Ellen smiled weakly. "Of course, Astra."

"To put it bluntly, Lucy threw herself at him yesterday, claiming – and you know her wild theories – that he was her lover in a former life – "

Ellen slapped her knees. "What nonsense, years of this – "

" – and that she was determined to get him back."

"Who would believe this?" Her voice broke. "Who would believe this about our lives?" She got up, mindlessly gathered a Tonka toy and dropped it in a box, then sat back down. "I'm so sorry about all this, Astra. My daughter has been invading your life in this bizarre way, and I had no idea."

"She said she would do anything to get him back, even hurt me."

"She *threatened* you?" Ellen's voice rose. "I can't handle this any more. She needs...I don't know, I don't know what she needs."

Astra sighed convincingly. "At this point, I'm not sure either. Has she been compliant with her medications?"

"I think so. I make sure and remind her to take them before school, and at night."

"But are you sure she's taking them? She could be – "

The door opened and Lucy stepped in.

Her face turned ashen when she saw Astra. She seemed to shrink back into herself. Mute, she looked from her mother to Astra and back, walked into the kitchen and took off her bookbag, setting it down on the kitchen table. She took a can of Pepsi out of the refrigerator and popped it open. The only sound was the fizz of the soda pouring into a glass.

· EIGHTY-NINE ·

Ellen looked at Astra, who held her gaze. "Lucy, I don't remember your saying hello to Dr. Nathanson."

Lucy took a long swallow of soda. "What's she doing here?"

"You know exactly what she's doing here."

"I don't want to interrupt your bonding session. I can see it's going pretty well. Coffee, muffins…when's the wine coming out?"

"We're not *bonding*, we're talking. Dr. Nathanson has gone out of her way to – "

" – find out where we live – "

Ellen whipped around in her seat to face Lucy. " – to come out here and talk about this in a calm, rational way."

"This is my home. She has no right to be here."

"I *invited* her here, Lucy. This is my home too. She is a welcome guest. Now I want you to get in here, sit down, and talk to us like a human being."

Lucy took another drink. "I have nothing to say to either of you."

Ellen jerked herself up off the couch and stormed into the kitchen. She glared at Lucy, her face flushed with rage. Her voice was exhausted and gravelly. "You will go in there right now and talk to that woman. She came a long way, out of her way, to settle this. You should be grateful."

Lucy gave her mother a long look, saw the strain in her eyes, the cords standing out on her neck. She put the glass of soda down on the counter. "All right, let's get this over with."

Lucy walked over and sat at the far end of the living room. Ellen rolled her eyes and sat back down.

"Now, I can understand how Lucy must be feeling," Astra said sweetly. "Here she comes home from school and – surprise, surprise – her therapist is here! I just want to say I dropped by because I thought if the three of us talked this through, we could work it out right away. I must admit I was quite concerned when my husband told me what she had done."

"Of course you were!" Ellen said.

"Whatever she said to you is a lie," Lucy said, looking at the floor.

"Don't you dare sit there and talk to us like that."

"*Us?* I'm talking to you," Lucy said, daring a look at Ellen, who turned away, disgusted.

"Look, I'm sure she feels put on the spot – " Astra started.

"Regardless of how anyone feels," Ellen said, getting to her feet, "I have to get to work" – she looked at the kitchen clock – "fifteen minutes ago."

Lucy felt Astra's eyes on her. The hair on the back of her neck stood up.

"Don't leave me here with her," Lucy whispered to her mother as she passed.

"Don't be ridiculous. You two need to talk." She put her fists on her narrow hips. "You and I, young lady, will have another discussion when I get home tonight, you can count on that."

She went to Peter's door, cracked it open and looked in on him. Satisfied, she pulled the door closed and turned to Lucy. "Your brother's still sick. He's in here sleeping with Sherman, so don't bother him till I get home, all right?"

"Fine."

As Ellen stood at the threshold of the apartment in her ratty winter jacket, Lucy became suddenly aware of their poverty; Astra's tailored leather coat and expensive boots next to her mother's rubber salt-stained ones.

"I can't thank you enough for coming by, Astra."

Astra turned to her brightly. "Why don't we connect at some point tomorrow afternoon – I'll give you a call?"

"That would be great. Any time before three." Ellen smiled, gave her a brief wave, Lucy a dark look, and left.

Lucy and Astra stared at each other as they listened to her descending footsteps on the stairs.

· NINETY ·

"Sorry to hear your little brother is sick. I thought he was very cute."

"Get out of this house."

"You seem to care very much for him."

"He's my brother."

Astra leaned over and set her half-empty mug of coffee on an end table. "Your mother, on the other hand, is not the brightest bulb on the tree."

"I'm going to call the police."

"Go ahead. By the time they get here, I'll be gone," she said, smiling sweetly, her eyes dead and shiny. "Besides, I only came here to talk to you, ferret out any further plans you may have to destroy me, and let you know what I'll do to you if you try to carry them out." She yawned delicately, covering her mouth with a still-gloved hand.

She got up and strolled over to a box of toys near the Christmas tree, a yard away from Lucy, kicking a piece of train track out of the way with her pointed boot. "Your mother seems a bit overwhelmed with...motherhood." She traced a bright green ornament with the tip of her finger, felt a dry branch. "What a sad little tree. Did you pick it out? Tell me, was it the cheapest on the lot? Was it all mummy could afford?"

Lucy got to her feet and crossed her arms hard over her chest. "You need to get out of here, now."

"Is that all you can say to me, darling daughter? If I leave, how will we ever become close? How will we ever truly get to know each other? Isn't that what you want? Isn't that what you're so desperate for, really, with all your games and lies and acting – some of it not bad, I'll admit – " She turned toward her, backing Lucy into the wall behind her. "I mean, what's it all for, really, but to win a mother's love?"

Lucy stumbled backward into the kitchen, grabbing at the counter for balance. Astra followed her, casually picking up and putting down knick knacks and family photos.

"So what's it like, Lucy, to be a freak who can't stay in one incarnation? Somebody who's half someone, half someone else?"

Lucy looked around. No weapons in reach: a plastic bowl filled with fruit, a half gallon of milk, a couple of dirty spoons. The blinking lights from the Christmas tree colored Lucy's face red, orange, green; red, orange, green.

"It must happen to you too, the slipping back."

Astra picked up an apple and took a bite, grimaced, and tossed it in a wastebin. "I can control it. You can't." She sashayed over to the kitchen knives stuck in a wooden block; stood stroking their handles, one by one. "You still haven't told me, Kim."

"Told you what?"

"Your plans. Your poorly thought out, infantile, hysterical plans that will only backfire and make your miserable little life even more hopeless and pathetic." Astra pulled out a heavy butcher knife. "Mummy was supposed to put these away, wasn't she?"

Lucy's peripheral vision dimmed. She gasped, clutching the counter behind her.

"If you tell me, Lucy, I'll put this back. Maybe you'll live, maybe you won't. Maybe your dear brother will live. Maybe he won't."

As if she were inside a drawstring bag looking out, Lucy's vision shrunk to a hole of light, the edges burning like embers. Then there was nothing.

Blackness.

The squeak of leather.

Footsteps.

Lucy panted and clawed at the air. "No...no you can't – " She knocked over the bowl of fruit. Overripe apples and pears fell to the floor with sickening thuds as Lucy groped her way around the table. She felt a chair, knocked it aside, then another. She reached the third and stopped, kneeling, and reached out to nothingness.

The sounds of Road Runner crowded the air, the syrupy animated voices.

"Goddamm you, where are you?" Lucy whispered.

A door opened; the volume on the DVD player turned up. A door closed.

"Tell me where you are," Lucy said, crying.

A cold, strong hand caught her at the neck, slammed her into the wall and held her there.

"Did you miss me, honey?"

Lucy's heart banged at her rib cage, her eyes watering in the darkness. She couldn't speak.

"Because I. Missed. You." With each word, Astra knocked Lucy's head against the wall. "I *love* these spontaneous visits, don't you? Don't you, Lucy? Speak up!"

Astra spit at her face, and let her go.

Lucy slid down the wall, falling sideways over a kitchen chair. Coughing and sputtering, she scrambled to her feet and stumbled forward.

Completely disoriented, she stood halfway into the living room, facing away from Astra.

Astra hovered just outside Peter's door.

Crying and panting, Lucy took a few more steps into the living room. "Where are you, you bitch!" She smelled pine, reached out and touched the brittle branches of the tree, a hot bulb. Yanked her hand back.

The sound of Peter's door opening. Cartoon characters cackled at the top of their lungs; Road Runner music filled the room.

"No, not Peter! You leave him alone!" Lucy whipped around, sprinted toward where the music seemed to be coming from and fell headlong over the coffee table on her barely healed wrist. She rolled on the rug, howling in agony.

"Beep beep!"

Lucy got to her knees, the pain exploding into a thousand white sparks in her brain.

The sound of Peter's door shutting again. Muted movie music.

"Peter...Peter, run!" Lucy cried hoarsely. "Astra, leave him alone! Take me! I'm the one you want!"

Using the couch, she dragged herself to her feet and stood there swaying, blue eyes brilliant bright, face shining with tears and streaked with dirt.

She took a few steps forward and felt linoleum under her feet. Gasping for breath through her tears, she placed her hands flat along the wall, making her way to Peter's door.

It was open.

Astra stood half a yard away; Lucy could smell her sickly sweet perfume.

"What have you done to him," Lucy cried, gripping the edge of the open door. She reached out with shaking hands. "Give him to me."

A gurgling howl of pain, of something dying.

Lucy smelled hot blood; heard it drip on the floor. She stumbled forward and slid in it.

"Give him to me!" she shrieked, falling to her knees, her arms outstretched.

The movie ended.

A hideous silence.

Something exhaled for the last time.

Then the limp weight of a body in her arms and the click of

high-heeled boots stepping briskly around her.

"You're next, Lucy."

The apartment door slammed shut.

Lucy held the dead thing in her arms, unable to move, unable to comprehend, until she heard, slicing through her skull, the high keening scream of a young child.

The sound tore at the curtain of her blindness; her vision opening from the middle, out.

Peter stood framed in the doorway of his room in his fire engine print pajamas, howling so loudly she could see his tiny tonsils vibrating in the back of his open mouth, eyes squeezed shut in horror, his small chest heaving for air.

Lucy forced herself to look down.

Sherman, opened from throat to hind leg, his still warm entrails spilled onto her forearms, lay motionless in her arms.

· NINETY-ONE ·

A month went by.

Nights, days blurred together in a haze of medication, confusion and disbelief. She was assigned another therapist, a stumpy older man who sat and talked at her for an hour twice a week about her rage, the divorce, and ultimately forgiveness for her "act of violence," but all she remembered of the event was Sherman's soft puppy body torn apart in her arms. My God, is it possible she had done this? Her thoughts, memories, were not in order, like objects scattered in a room.

Three times a day Lucy was given her "happy shot" as she'd heard it referred to by the staff. The night time shot was especially potent, knocking her out sometimes until noon the next day. If she refused it, an orderly would hold her down and jam the needle in her hip. She would wake up in the same position ten hours later, clutching her thin pillow, eyes gummy with sleep, her pajamas still pulled halfway down her rump. The effect of the shots seemed to grow stronger as well, and last longer as time went by. There were some days she was conscious barely long enough to eat and wash herself. Her room had a tangy smell, of old socks and bad breath. Sometimes she thought she had a roommate, then she would wake and the lump in the neighboring bed would be gone, sheets pulled tight. There was so much she couldn't hold onto.

Outside, the worst winter in fifty years raged on; its shifting mountains of snow and shrieking winds enclosing her ever tighter in the ward.

During the rare times she was awake and lucid, Lucy forced herself to observe her surroundings for some way to escape. Ellen visited once a

324

week but had long since stopped believing anything Lucy said, deferring constantly to Dr. Nathanson and her "kindness and years of experience with these things."

Even after a good deal of investigating, it seemed impossible to get out. Nurses and orderlies far outnumbered the patients, and they'd been well trained in thwarting all kinds of escape attempts over the years. But Lucy waited, and she watched.

Every day, three times a day, the ward door was unlocked for an enormous food cart to enter with steaming dishes, and to leave with empty ones. On Tuesdays and Thursdays there was soup, in ten gallon tureens, loaded onto the back of the cart behind the plates. Between the tureens and the plates was a narrow space, just big enough for a skinny teenager to hide.

Lucy stared at the oversized puzzle pieces until their edges furred and the table became a mess of color and shape. Across from her sat Selda, a volunteer with painted-on eyebrows and a permanent smile. She wore a cardigan with a snow scene knitted into it, reindeer scampering across her chest and over one shoulder.

Lucy reached out a thin arm over the middle of the table; it hovered, then dropped down with a thud.

"Oh, come on Lucy, you did the whole thing practically single-handed yesterday! I know you can do this."

Lucy focused on Selda. "I'd like a piece of cake, please." She gestured at a birthday cake in the back of the room leftover from a resident's party that morning.

"Well, you're not crippled, young lady. Why don't you get up and get some yourself?"

"I'm just so tired. Do you mind, Selda, please?" Lucy gave her a weak smile.

"Oh, dear, since you're being so polite today, I suppose I could. Maybe even take a little piece for myself," she said with a giggle.

Selda got up and ambled to the back of the room where brightly colored streamers were already starting to come down from where they'd been scotch-taped to the ceiling. Lucy kept her eyes on Selda as she reached in her big crocheted purse, pulled out her wallet, and slipped it in the back pocket of her farmer jeans.

· NINETY-TWO ·

The noise in the ward never stopped. Hysterical adolescent laughter from the hallway, a moan from the room next door, the constant announcements over the speakers. Occasionally the clattering sound of patients strapped on gurneys headed for electroshock, their eyes hollow and dark. Uncirculated air reeked with a stew of disinfectant, plastics, rubber, and urine, a strangling smell so bad at times Lucy had to breathe through her nose to keep from vomiting.

She slept through four o'clock group to save her strength. The sound of the dinner cart banging open the ward door woke her, the usual nausea and disorientation washing over her as she forced herself into consciousness. She pushed herself off the pillow, made herself sit up, went to the bathroom.

Splashing cold water on her face, she gathered herself. In the mirror the scar across her neck drew a ragged purple line. With trembling fingers she touched the length of it to force herself into visceral memory. Her face drew tight as she recalled her last visit from Ellen, who said that after they buried Sherman in the backyard one frigid winter evening several weeks ago, Peter announced he never wanted to see his sister again. She hadn't seen him since.

She pulled on all three of her pairs of socks, her falling-apart sneakers, and the only sweater she had over a thin shirt. Her winter coat and boots were locked up somewhere.

She lingered as long as she could in her room before going to dinner, then found a seat at the very back of the dining hall, right next to the food cart. Long after everyone else had finished and wandered away to watch TV or go back to their rooms, she stayed at her table, pretending to be engrossed in a magazine. Two cafeteria workers who spoke little or no English bustled around her, emptying trays and wiping tables.

Lucy's hands began to sweat as she read about "How to be a Boy Magnet" in Teen Beat. How would she ever do this thing? She could only sneak onto the cart when both workers were in the kitchen, and before the orderly came to take it away. Finally, one worker backed into the kitchen with a bucket of dishes while the other remained, bussing tables only yards from her.

Lucy stared at a dessert dish that had the tracings of blueberry pie. She picked it up and walked over to the worker, a small, moon-faced woman with a gold tooth.

"Could I get...some pie, please? I mean, I never got any pie."

The woman looked at her, rolled her eyes and started to walk away.

Lucy took a few steps toward her. "It's just...I'm still so hungry, could I...?" Her brain too fogged to let her finish her sentence.

The woman turned back and gave Lucy a once over. She saw an extremely skinny hollow-eyed girl, one who'd given her no trouble in the past. "Okay, okay," she said smiling, gold tooth flashing, and held up a finger to say, "I'll be right back."

She disappeared behind the swinging kitchen doors.

Lucy stared at the cart, heart speeding. This was it, a twenty-second window, at most. She darted over to it and slipped between the tureens and stacked plates. There was barely enough space for her, and she had to crank her neck at a strange angle to fit her head under the trays. The stink of industrial food gagged her, Manhattan clam chowder and macaroni and cheese-caked dishes inches from her face.

She watched the bottom third of the kitchen doors burst open and a pair of chubby legs in waitress shoes squeak to a stop a yard from her. "Hello, girl?" The doors swooshed shut. "Pie for you, girl!" The feet turned this way, then that, then approached her. A blueberry pie-stained apron filled her vision. Then a harrumph, followed by a plate clattering into a plastic bucket that rested on top of Lucy's head, the sound nearly drowned out by a string of Portuguese curses.

The feet walked away. "Hey, Hermione!" the woman called, clapping twice. "Dinner is done!"

· NINETY-THREE ·

Lucy barely breathed as the cart was rolled on to the elevator, the wheels squeaking and grinding. Cold pea soup dripped onto her forehead and dribbled down her face. She stayed motionless, staring at a huge pair of black sneakers as she and the orderly sank six floors to the kitchen, deep in the bowels of the building.

She was ferried down a cement-floored hallway, turned sharply, and rammed through a set of double doors. Her cart came to a stop, nose-to-butt with a line of carts that hugged one wall; on the other, dishwashing machines opened and closed with ear-cracking booms. Steam thick with bile and old lasagna hung in the air. Lucy huddled for several minutes, listening to the laughter and chatter of employees as she tried to place where they were in the room. Every few minutes her cart was pushed up closer and closer to the machines, until hers was next in line to be emptied. She couldn't wait one more minute.

She squeezed out on the wall side, froze, and listened. The talking, laughing continued. Still in a tight crouch, she turned and scuttled past the carts along the slimy floor, bursting through the kitchen doors to the fetid dark halls of the basement.

Eyes wide, she looked up and down the hall. Only the echo of laughter, dishes banging from the kitchen, a distant radio. Her ragged sneakers untied, she ran toward a glowing red exit sign at the far end of the hall where she scrambled up a flight of stairs, nearly fainting at the top with exhaustion. A clock said 6:06. Next room check and injection time, usually by Astra herself, was at seven.

She stood in the middle of an echoing dark hallway of closed offices. Far off through double doors at the end she could see a parking lot where fresh snow fell on the few cars that remained. Shivering, she hugged herself, leaning against a wall. Faint with relief that she had gotten even this far, she realized she had no real plan of what to do next.

Blinking back tears of panic, she crept along the hallway, trying to open the door of each office she passed. Locked, locked, and locked again.

Several offices down, a door opened and a woman stepped out. A tall, slender silhouette with shoulder length dark hair. Lucy stayed in the shadows, not breathing. The woman paused, put down a laptop bag, buttoned her coat and put on her gloves. As she bent to pick up her bag, Lucy turned a doorknob. Unlocked. She slipped in and went flat against the wall, listening for the woman's footsteps out the door and into the night.

Lucy sat crouched against the wall in the shadows, her breath ragged. She crawled over to a desk where a phone sat with a dozen glowing buttons. With violently shaking hands, Lucy called information and the Stafford School. She sank down under the desk, eyes shut tight.

Please God, she thought, let Carmella be there.

Carmella had been tucking in some of the younger students for bed when she got the call.

"She says it's urgent," the receptionist said from the bottom of the wide mahogany staircase. "Stay there. I'll bring the phone to you." She climbed the stairs, placing the phone in Carmella's hand.

She knew. Her eyes glittered with the knowledge. "Lucy, where are you?"

"I'm at Greenfield somewhere, the place – "

"Can you get out?"

"I snuck out," she whispered hoarsely. "I wanted to say I'm sorry, that I believe you –"

"There's no time for that right now. I understand. You were afraid."
She turned and walked back toward the children's ward, fingers grazing
the handrail that lined the hallway. "You were right to be afraid."

Carmella's voice sounded so sweet to her; here was someone who
understood everything, who cared about her. She started to cry, wiping
her nose on a filthy wool sleeve. "I still need to know some things,
Carmella. You said when we met that we have powers." She glanced around
the room, her eyes finally adjusting to the dimness; she could make out
another table, chairs, a basket of dried flowers, a calendar. "Tell me how
to use them. Please, I need to know."

"The more you come back, the stronger your powers will be. This is
your first time, Lucy, so you have some, but Astra is very, very powerful."

"She's going to kill me again, Carmella."

Carmella paused in the hallway, her gnarled hand gripping the soft
wood of the banister. "You have to fight her, Lucy. Try to understand,
why does she come back? What is her worst fear?"

"She's not afraid of anything!"

"She slips back more easily than you think. The walls are thin for her
too. Don't be fooled."

"Will you come back again, Carmella?"

"No, I am done."

"How do you know? You can't know – "

"Because I have loved you with all my heart, Kim, like my own child."

"I love you too, Carmella. I wish I – "

"You can't know everything right now. It's too much. Just remember:
do not become what has shaped you. Do not become her."

Lucy's eyes stung with hot tears. "Please, Carmella, I don't understand
what you're saying – "

"It's all right. Now you must get out of that place. Escape! She knows
you're gone or not?"

"No, I don't know, she will soon – "

"Come to me at Stafford. I can hide you here. Do you have money?"

"Yes, some – "

"Get out of there, Lucy. Run. Now!"

"Okay...goodbye."

Lucy hung up the phone with great gentleness.

The clock on the wall said 6:48.

She got up and ran out of the room, down the hall, and into the winter night.

· NINETY-FOUR ·

Lucy stumbled into the slushy parking lot and came to a halt. Her breath rose in puffs to the velvet winter sky. She felt exposed in the lights from the building, unable to think. Nearby, a car door slammed. Not looking back, she sprinted across the lot and between several looming brick buildings, breaking through snow almost to her knees. The stolen wallet bounced heavily against her thigh in her jeans pocket.

It was some time before she came to a road. A winter wonderland of houses twinkled with colored Christmas lights, everyone home and happily preparing dinner. She walked in the street, shivering, wondering if she should knock on someone's door – but to ask for what? Protection from being killed again by her mother?

Her sneakers and three pairs of socks were sodden by the time she reached the end of the road which intersected a much busier one. A spitting kind of snow had begun, stabbing at her face and hands as she walked. She never remembered being this cold. She couldn't feel her toes or her fingertips; the cuffs of her frozen pants scratched at her shins. Jogging in place, she tried to force some feeling in her feet, then took a left on the busy street, having no idea where she was or how to get to Stafford. She began to run full tilt again, flagging down cars. They sped by her, dousing her each time with a fresh assault of icy slush.

It was 6:58. Back in the locked psych ward, tucked away in her office, Astra sat at her desk, lit only by the greenish glow of her desk lamp. Satisfied with what she'd written, she capped her pen, closed the folder she was working on and filed it away in a drawer. She pulled out her pencil drawer and, reaching far to the back of it, extricated a syringe. After slipping on her winter coat, she tucked the syringe in her pocket and left her office, deadbolting the door behind her.

At precisely 7 o'clock, Astra unlocked Lucy's door.

A fat yellow cab slowed and pulled over a few yards ahead of Lucy, fishtailing on the icy road. She ran to it and jumped in the back. The driver, a small brown man in his sixties who looked like he'd seen every ugliness life has to offer, glared back at her.

"Where you goin'?"

"I'm...I'm – " she stuttered, drinking in the warmth of the cab as she struggled to get the sodden wallet out of her wet pants. "Can you just give me a second?" With stiff fingers she opened the wallet and counted out ten ones, some change, and a thick wad of soggy cat food coupons. The cabbie watched her, expressionless.

D ining room, rec room, therapy rooms, patient rooms, labs, kitchen, electroshock. Lucy was nowhere. Face set hard, Astra strode back to her office and locked the door behind her.

Perspiring heavily under her Burberry coat, she crossed to her closet and reached up to a high shelf where she pulled down a bottle of Glenfiddich and a tumbler. Hands shaking with rage, she filled the glass and knocked it back as if it were weak Kool-Aid, then filled it again.

This was bad, she thought. Very, very bad. How had she let this *happen*? That girl was too drugged up to think, much less get away. Shuddering, Astra put the glass down. She gripped the back of her chair with thin strong hands and squeezed her eyes shut, enduring the slight wave of nausea that always preceded slipping back. Her brow shone with sweat.

I will not slip back. I will not...

Teeth chattering, she willed herself to open her eyes and look at her hands.

Human, normal hands.

Whimpering with relief, she finished the rest of her drink, dropped down in the overstuffed patient's chair, and thought.

Thought of who Lucy might visit first.

The taxi driver stared at Lucy with oily eyes. "Is that your wallet, or did you 'find' it somewhere?"

"It's mine."

He turned back to the snow-filled road in front of them. "Ten bucks won't get you to Stafford, missy."

Lucy tried to smile into the rear view mirror. "Please, it's all I have."

He pulled the car away from the curb. "Where is your coat?"

"It's at home, I mean school…"

"Never mind," he said, turning up the volume on his talk radio program.

· NINETY-FIVE ·

Carmella checked her Braille watch again with quick, dry hands. Seven fifteen. She clicked the crystal shut and began to make her way from the second floor children's ward to the long hall which led to the stairs and the lobby. She wanted to be downstairs and waiting for Lucy at the front of the building when she arrived.

She took small steps down the hallway, her hand grazing the wooden bar built in at waist height – shoulder for her – along the walls. The old wooden floors creaked under her, a familiar music that comforted her over the years. But just as she reached the top of the stairs, she heard a rustling sound and stopped short.

Her sightless eyes grew wide, deep brown under milky white.

"Who's there?"

The rustling continued, like a rodent crawling under dead leaves.

A wave of cloying perfume, a million dying roses.

Her hand fluttered on the rail.

Then came a short silence, quelled by the high, thin laughter of the night nurse, Thelma.

Shaking her head and grasping the banister, Carmella stepped down to the first stair.

Sitting all the way forward in her seat, Lucy watched the meter tick higher and higher: 5.75...6.25...7.00. "Are we almost there?" she yelled over the screech of the radio.

"Nope. I wouldn't say so."

The snow slanted sideways into the cab. She still had no feeling in her feet, and her hands ached as they thawed. 8.15...9.25...10.00. Snapping his gum, the cabbie pulled over to the curb and switched off the radio. Windshield wipers slapped noisily back and forth, throwing small curtains of white to either side of the car.

"Time to settle up."

"...but we're not at Stafford."

"No kidding."

"Couldn't you just – you know, this one time – "

"Look, Missy, if I gave everyone a break who asked me to, I wouldn't be in business any more. Every night, ten times a night, some kid just like you asks me to cut them a break, usually to get to the square to buy whatever crap they smoke these days."

"But I don't – "

Not looking at her, he turned the radio back up and reached back with an open hand. She put the money in it, opened the door against a hard wind and stepped out into shin-deep slush.

He yelled out at her. "It's about a half mile down the road."

She watched him do a U-turn, then disappear into the whiteness.

Head into the wind, she made her way down the sidewalk in the direction he told her, crossing street after street. Bundled up pedestrians passed by, their conversations muffled by the snow. She ran until she thought her chest would burst.

When she stopped to catch her breath, she looked up to see ambulance lights flashing pink through the snow. She forced herself to run toward them. The craggy silhouette of the Stafford School rose in front of her.

An ambulance and police car were parked at an angle to each other in the circular drive in front of the school. Thelma, shivering in a thin sweater, held two hysterically crying blind children close to her chest as a body, covered with a sheet, was lifted into the ambulance.

Lucy sprinted to the stretcher, brushing by a burly police officer.

Startled, he took her by the shoulder.

"You shouldn't be here."

"Who is that? Is she dead?"

The cop looked from Lucy to Thelma, who shook her head. "You need to get back home, young lady."

Lucy shook out of his grip and ran to Thelma. "Who is it? Is it Carmella?"

The blind kids started a fresh round of keening. Through tears, Thelma nodded. Snow whipped at their faces.

Lucy stared at the small figure under the sheet. "What happened?"

"She fell down the stairs," Thelma said. "She broke her neck."

· NINETY-SIX ·

Soaked to her skin, copper hair shining wet under streetlamps, Lucy wandered through the now deserted square. A few cabs stood waiting for snowbound travelers. Otherwise, the streets were abandoned to the storm.

She passed under the yawning gothic arches into the quad. Constantin's light still burned in his corner office, a tiny star in the distance. She ran soundlessly across the snow.

The building was unlocked. She took the stairs three at a time, then slowed when she reached the second floor landing, stepping cautiously to his door. Everything rests on the next few minutes, she thought, gathering herself. She wrung out her hair in a puddle on the floor and tied it back with a rubberband she found in her pocket, but after glancing at herself in the reflection of an office window, gave up on improving her appearance any further.

She tapped at his door, glancing nervously all around her.

Constantin jumped when he heard the sound, nearly knocking over his reading lamp. Since the storm had emptied the campus, he'd been enjoying several hours of uninterrupted work time. Another knock, then the sound of someone rattling the door. He threw his pen down on the blotter and got up to see who was there.

He gasped when he saw her, ghostly pale, dripping wet, eyes wide with exhaustion.

"You have to let me in," she said.

"Lucy?"

She brushed by him into his office. "Lock the door, Constantin, please!"

He did so. "What are you doing here?"

She threw her arms around him and began to sob. For a few moments he let her hold him, her clothes soaking him through. Her whole body shook uncontrollably.

"Hey," he said, pulling her away. "Calm down and tell me what's going on." He took his jacket from a hook behind the door and handed it to her. "Put this on."

Stiffly, she put her arms through the sleeves of the tweed jacket. She was engulfed by it. "Promise me you won't tell me to leave until you've given me a chance to explain."

"Just tell me why you're here."

"Promise me."

He leaned against his desk and crossed his arms. "I promise."

"I'm here because, God, there's no easy way...I'm here because I'm Kim."

Constantin sighed, looked at the floor and massaged his neck. "You know, I really don't think you're dangerous, so I'm not going to call campus police, but I do think we should get you home and – "

She stood dripping in his huge jacket, holding her arms out to him. "Constantin, look at me. You used to say I was brilliant, that I was your best student, even though I was blind, because I was curious, because I never stopped asking questions."

He stared at her. "What is this, some kind of parlor trick?"

She took a step toward him, her pupils huge in the dim light. "You told me it was wrong to fall in love with one of your students, but you couldn't help yourself. We went to New York one weekend, you took me to the Bronx zoo, you described every animal to me. You drew them in the palm of my hand – "

"Jesus Christ," he said hoarsely, his eyes widening as he stood, stumbling backwards into a bookshelf. "Who *are* you?"

"You have three moles on your back, in a row, just below your left shoulder blade. I said they were like ellipses, and you laughed and said, 'then where is the rest of me' – "

He backed up further behind his desk. "Who the fuck are you – who have you been talking to – "

" – don't be afraid of me C – "

" – don't come any – "

" – I'm not the one you should be afraid of." She took a step closer to him, reaching out and touching the soft wool of his sleeve.

He knocked her hand away. "Get away from me! This is some sick game, Lucy, and you have to know how...how damaging it is to do this to people – "

"I'm your BC," she said, sobbing. "Your babycakes." She fell to her knees. "I'm Kim, I'm *Kim*," she cried, again and again.

He watched her cry. "Lucy, get up," he said in a low voice.

"No, no, I won't, I can't," she said, her head in her hands.

"Get – "

"I have nowhere to go – "

"Well, you better think of someplace – "

She lifted her head to look at him. They stared at each other for several seconds. Her eyes glittered grey. "Have you seen her body, Constantin?"

"What are you talking about?"

"Have you seen Astra's body?"

He walked out from behind the desk and stood over her. "Of course I have. She's my wife."

"You're lying!"

"Keep your voice down – "

"That's why she won't let you see, don't you understand?"

"What the hell do *you* know about my wife's body that *I* don't know?"

"Have you seen it?" Her voice was raw.

He looked away. "Of course I have."

"She's a Repeater, like me, but she's come back a hundred times. She's covered with scars! She says she can control it but I'm not so – "

"She's...she's shy about her body. Always has been. Look, this – "

"She killed me, Constantin. Look." She pulled the collar of her sweater away from her neck. The scar raged red. "That night – we should have gone home, but you wanted to stay for dinner. Don't you remember?"

The room thickened with silence. Lucy got to her feet and stepped back.

"Yes, I do," he said, his voice almost a whisper.

"And after dinner, we made love, and you fell asleep."

He shook his head and looked away. "This is absurd."

"She came after me – " Lucy said, her voice breaking. "What can I say to make you believe me?"

He stared at the books on the floor. "What happened on the way...to see Astra?"

"Lightning hit a tree! It was Carmella, sending us..." Her voice trailed off.

"Sending us what?"

"A warning, C."

"Good God, who *are* you? This is insane."

"We have to get out of here. She's coming. I know it!"

He took her by the shoulders and held her. His voice cracked open. "I didn't protect you, Jesus – "

"It's not your fault – "

"Why didn't you find me? Christ, all these years – "

A quick sharp rap at the door.

Constantin and Lucy froze.

The office door rattled. Another knock, this one echoed down the hall.

· NINETY-SEVEN ·

Lucy glanced around the room; the tiny window, a small closet in the corner. "Does she have a key?" she whispered.

"No, but she knows I'm here – get in here," he said, pointing toward the closet. He wrenched the door open; it was crammed with books. Frantically, they pulled them out, tossing them aside. Lucy crawled in and he threw his winter coat on top of her and shut the door.

From the dark closet, Lucy listened to Constantin go to the hall and open the door. Astra's high heeled boots clicked down the hallway and into the office. Lucy heard something tossed on his desk, a purse perhaps, and the creak of her long leather coat.

"What took you so long to answer the door?" she asked Constantin, looking him in the eye.

"I tripped over this huge pile of books, see?" He gestured at the cascading stacks near the closet door.

She looked over at the jumbled heap, then back at the relatively clear path from his desk to the hallway. "Is everything all right?"

He was aware of the layer of tacky sweat on his forehead, his shirt still damp from Lucy's embrace. "Everything's fine. I've been cleaning up, for once."

She walked around him, looking him up and down as if studying a shot for a movie. "Am I your first visitor of the evening?"

"Well, actually, an old student of mine dropped by earlier to say hello. Before the storm got bad."

"Really. Has she left yet?"

"It was a he. Hours ago."

She scanned the walls of books for any secrets hidden there.

"So what brings you out in all this? I thought we were going to meet up at home – "

"I was restless. Wanted to get out." She tucked a stray black curl behind one ear.

He leaned back on his desk, arms folded. "You look very sexy tonight, Astra."

"What?" she said, caught off guard.

"Maybe it's the coat." He playfully pulled her in to him by her belt.

She pushed his hand away, at the same time softening to him. "What are you doing?"

He smiled tightly. "I'm seducing you, but I guess I'm not very good at it."

Her expression relaxed. She glanced around the room again and took a small step toward him. "You actually started to clean up this place? You always said you wanted at least one place where you could be a complete slob."

"Yeah, well," he said, successfully reeling her in by the belt, "maybe I'm finally learning something from you."

She rested against his chest, leaning between his legs, back arched seductively. Her hair fell back like black water. "Did you eat?"

"Wasn't hungry." He pulled her closer to him. "Until now." He kissed her softly, then more deeply as she began to move against him. Slowly, he untied her belt and let the coat fall open, caressing her breasts under her cashmere sweater.

"This is kinky – your office," she said smiling, lips hovering near his.

He drew his hand up her stockinged thigh, lifting her skirt to her waist. She moved against his hand, breathing into his ear.

"Take this off," he said, pulling her coat from her shoulders. It dropped to the floor and she stepped back, looking at him, his face in shadow from the light behind him.

"Where are you going? Get back here," he said, pulling her into his arms again. He unzipped her skirt and slipped his hand down to her ass. She held him, stretching one arm behind him for the light switch.

She couldn't quite reach it.

"Constantin," she said poutily, pulling back a moment. "The light."

"No." He kissed her neck. "Tired of that."

"Come on, sweetie," she murmured, "you know how I feel about it."

"I *do* know how you feel about it." He held her gaze, as, one by one, he unbuttoned the small pearl buttons at the neck of her sweater. "And you know how *I* feel about it."

A flicker of fear crossed her face.

"Some other place then," she said, gently pushing him away.

"No, not some other place."

She stared at him, her eyes black holes, one hand fluttering at her throat.

"I want you here, now." He grabbed her tightly around the waist and kissed her hard, pulling at the buttons.

"The – the light, then, Constantin, and we'll – "

He clutched a handful of sweater and yanked it toward him. Her body slammed against his, her breath shallow and hot on his face. "Fuck the light, Astra. The light stays on."

Her pupils grew huge, her hair loose like lava around her shoulders. Gently she wrapped her hands around his two fists that held her sweater, practically lifting her off the floor.

"Constantin, let go of me."

"You will fuck me in the light or I will – "

"Please, Constantin, what are you *doing?*"

"You need to take your clothes off, *now* – "

"Stop it! You're frightening me!" She wrenched his hands away and staggered backwards.

"You're not afraid of anything. Take off your clothes."

She looked around frantically, for what she wasn't sure. "Why are you doing this to me? To us? Constantin, you are my love. I would die for you. Do you know that? Do you?" She melted back into his arms, stroked his hair from his forehead, kissed it. "I would die a thousand times for y – "

"Then take off your clothes."

"I can't."

"Do it."

"Do you love me, Constantin? Do you?"

"Or I'll take them off myself."

Weeping, she caressed his face one more time. Mascara ran in black rivulets down her chalky face. Never taking her eyes off him, she unbuttoned the first two buttons, then stopped. "I thought you loved me, Constantin, all this time. Did you? I need to know. Don't you love me now?"

She sank down to her knees. With badly shaking fingers, she reached up to his fly and began to unzip it.

He caught her by the wrist and yanked her to her feet, grabbed hold of the collar of her sweater and tore it all the way down the front. The buttons flew off. Shrieking, Astra turned away from him and ran toward the hallway but he caught her by the back of the sweater. With both hands, he pulled it all the way off.

Breathing hard, she stood facing away from him in the brightly lit hall.

He let out a choked scream.

· NINETY-EIGHT ·

She stood still.

Centuries of violent death raked across her back.

Constantin stumbled, crawling backwards over his desk.

Astra fell forward, her hands against the wall.

"Turn around," he said.

She didn't move.

"I said, turn around!"

With deathly slowness, she turned toward him. Hellish cuts criss-crossed her stomach. Bulletholes pocked her breasts, shining burn scars mangled the flesh of her pelvis. Tears poured soundlessly from her eyes. She took a few steps forward, eyes pleading, then halted when she saw the horror in his face.

It was over.

She broke.

She let loose a howl like an animal in a trap, collapsing into a heap against the piles of books behind her, the light in her eyes like sparks in black wells. Moaning, she turned her head away from him.

Then she began to change.

A black forked tongue hissed in and out of her still human mouth as her limbs zipped into her body. Her head flattened into a scaly triangle and disappeared under a pile of clothes. Six feet of fat copperhead snake slithered out from under her skirt and undulated among the books and along the wall where it stopped, lifted its head and looked at him with shining, bottomless eyes.

Then the snake was gone.

Constantin blinked, stared.

A slim adolescent boy in a torn T-shirt and jeans stood in the middle of the room, a gun in one hand. He began to turn, as if trying to comprehend his surroundings.

And he was gone.

A '50s housewife in a daisy-patterned apron stood sadly on a chair, a noose around her neck.

And she was gone.

A hugely pregnant Indian girl with kohled eyes sat on the floor against the bookshelves, blood running from between her legs.

Gone.

Shrieking and cawing, an enormous crow lay dying on the floor, an arrow through its shoulder. It flew up, banged against the ceiling, and disappeared. Blue-black feathers rained down.

A pale blond woman in seventeenth-century dress stood in a ring of fire, screaming as it engulfed her.

Ninety-nine incarnations appeared before Constantin, one by one, as fast as a beating heart. As he watched he made his way, inch by inch, along the wall to the closet.

His hand trembled at the closet door, scrambling for the knob as he watched the first incarnation.

It lingered for almost a minute in the room.

A newborn baby boy, sweetly pink and naked, lay on the rug, gurgling.

Constantin stole a split second to look behind him for the knob.

He found it and looked back. The baby was blue, a stiff cast of itself lying in a pool of water.

"No!" he cried, stepping toward the infant.

But it was gone. Gasping, he turned.

Astra stood between him and the closet door, naked, not human, an abomination.

· NINETY-NINE ·

Constantin lunged past her toward the closet, but she picked him up as if he were a child and threw him across the room. His body crashed on the desk with a horrific cracking sound, his legs hanging out the broken window. Moaning and clutching his thighs, he rolled over to his front, dragging his legs back through the jagged glass that scored his shins. He lay gasping, both legs at strange angles to his torso. Bright red patches of blood stained his corduroys.

Her voice a demonic blend of a hundred voices, Astra said, "I love you, Constantin."

She turned toward the closet door and stood there. She tilted her head.

In a singsong, hundred-person-voice, she said, "Oh Kimber-lee, your mommy's here. Time to come out now." She took a step closer to the door, turned the knob. The door creaked as it opened a few inches on its own. "Party's o-ver!" She grabbed the solid oak door, ripped it off its hinges and laid it neatly aside.

Lucy sat tucked back in the closet. Even when the light of the room shone on her face, she saw only darkness.

"Lucy, get up! Run!" Constantin cried. "My legs are broken!"

Lucy held herself in a tight bundle, teeth chattering, grey eyes wide.

Astra casually reached down and picked up her leather coat from the floor. She tossed it on and cinched the waist tight. "Looks like she's gone all freaky deaky on you, C."

"Lucy! Move! Now!"

Astra turned to him, flipping her collar up. "I never got it, Constantin. What *was* the big deal about this girl? I mean, please. What was so damned great about her? What's so great about her now?" As Astra spoke, Lucy pushed herself to her feet and felt her way out of the closet, her back to the wall as she stumbled over books and papers, making her way out of the room. Astra zipped on her boots and calmly followed her as she progressed.

She took the girl's chin in her cold hands. Lucy froze in place. "She's pretty, sure, but I'm prettier, don't you think? I'm definitely smarter. No contest there."

She let her chin go, but with a deceptively small gesture, took her by the back of the neck and propelled her forward. Lucy tumbled face first to the floor with a yelp.

"Look at her. So *ordinary*. She's vanilla pudding, sugar free."

Lucy crawled on her hands and knees. Gasping, she found the doorway to the hall but only hovered there, disoriented.

"What was it, Constantin? You wanted to *save* her because she was *blind*? Poor little blind girl. I think I'll *marry* her? What were you thinking? *I* at least have something to say, something to contribute to the conversation. But no," Astra kicked Lucy hard in the stomach; Lucy groaned and folded into herself. "You had to choose Miss Helen Keller over here, little Miss Barnesdale University I-can-be-a-marine-biologist-even-though-I've-never-even-*seen*-a-fish..."

She pummeled her again. Lucy rolled over on her back into the hallway, weeping and moaning.

"You're lucky I love you, Constantin, or I would kill you in *such* a horrible way – " She shook her head as if erasing an image. "We'll pick up on that later, but first..." Astra scooped up Lucy as if she were a small dog and tucked her under one arm. "I have some business to attend to."

The office door slammed behind them, drowning out Constantin's scream as he dragged himself across his desk and fell in a crumpled heap to the floor.

· ONE HUNDRED ·

Lucy thrashed and screamed as Astra carried her out into the hall, until Astra swung her to her feet and planted her down, slamming her against the wall and holding her by the neck.

"Listen to me, little girl," she hissed. "If you don't *shut up*, I will kill you here and now. Do you understand?"

Lucy's sightless eyes swam in her head. She nodded as much as she could.

"You will walk alongside me like a normal human being, do you hear me?"

Lucy nodded again, dropping to the floor when Astra released her.

"Take my arm."

Lucy scrambled to her feet and reached out. Astra's cold fingers wrapped Lucy's hand around her elbow. They walked together in silence to the end of the hall and down a flight of stairs. Astra pushed open the heavy back door. A blast of cold air smacked at them. Gripping Lucy around the shoulders, Astra led her along the sidewalk and into the parking lot.

A few yards from the car, Lucy lost her footing and fell, pulling Astra down with her to the slick pavement.

Lucy lost no time. She kicked and smacked at Astra as she got to her feet, then tore off into the cold blackness, shrieking. Arms out, she sprinted over icy pavement until she stumbled onto snow-covered ground that sloped slightly downward. She kept on running, the snow packing into her jeans past her ankles, her bangs frozen on her forehead.

She ran headlong into a tree. Dazed, gasping, she wrapped her arms around the rough bark and made her way past it; felt her way around another tree a few feet away, and another. She reached out again and there was nothing, no trees, just air, stillness. Her head spun with sharp stars, visions of teeth and blood. Her breath roared in her ears as she turned a slow circle in the vicious cold, waiting.

The roar subsided; she heard only the wind rustling in dead tree limbs, the sound of distant traffic.

Reaching out with frozen fingers, she stumbled a few steps forward down an embankment, a strangled cry for help stillborn in her throat as an inhumanly strong arm roped around her waist and lifted her, dragging her through the forest. She grasped at trees, the bark scraping and bloodying her hands. The smell of pine, a distant fire, warm leather. In moments they were out of the woods and back in the parking lot.

Astra wrenched open the door and hurled her into the front seat of a car, smacking her knees against the dash. Lucy wept from deep inside her cage of darkness.

Jerking the car to life, Astra slammed it into reverse and screeched out of the lot.

In a minute she was flying down side streets, raving. Lucy braced herself in the seat, her frozen sneakers jammed into the floor, arms straight out, hands flat against the dashboard. What are my powers, where are my powers, she asked herself, repeating the words again and again under her breath like a mantra to block out Astra's voice. Tears burned icy streams from her sightless eyes.

"He never loved you, you know. He felt sorry for you, little blind girl. He's got too big of a heart, that's his problem – "

Astra took a hard right, flinging both of them left. Lucy righted herself, rigid fingers scrambling for a seatbelt.

Crying, Astra slammed her boot on the accelerator. "He loved me and you've *ruined* it! *He loved me!*"

For a moment she let her head rest on the steering wheel – car horns blared until she almost casually looked up, swerving back into her lane. "The *centuries* I spent looking for this man...goddammit, I should get rid of you right now, but it would be too messy. Christ! It was hard enough the first time. I don't know what I'm going to do – "

A limning of light appeared at the periphery of Lucy's vision. Streetlights flickered by.

"You took him from me, you bitch!" With her free hand, Astra smacked Lucy across the face, splitting her lip.

Blood coursed down her chin and soaked into her sweater. Lucy let the pain go, like a red balloon floating away, concentrating only on shrinking her circle of darkness. Under her baggy sweater, she held both ends of the seatbelt with trembling hands.

"What difference does anything make any more? My life is over! My love," she moaned, "you took away my *love*, don't you understand? And look at me. Do you think I have a chance with this incarnation? I'm too old. *Look at me*! I'm old and ugly!"

Lucy could make out the jagged arms of trees flying by on either side of them, lights in buildings, everything except for the black circle opaquing the road ahead.

They roared down the highway.

"The fact is, my dear child, I have no reason to be here, and neither do you! We're leaving this life together, you and I. This is all going to end forever – "

Astra shot across two lanes of traffic toward the median strip. Cars screeched, careening out of the way as Astra and Lucy burst through a guard rail and sailed off the highway.

Utter silence as they lifted up, airborne, mother and reincarnated daughter, broken only by the sound of Lucy's seatbelt clicking shut. At once the circle of blackness cleared and Lucy saw everything: the metal grey sky swollen with snow, the city lights sparkling beneath them, Astra's saucer-eyed, tear-ruined face, arms flown back from the wheel; their descent past the horizon and down, plummeting into the dark grove of trees hurtling toward them. Lucy, lashed in by her belt, watched Astra leave her seat and burst through the windshield, the glass glittering around her like a shower of diamonds as she flew across the field and landed, a black stain on the brilliant white slope.

· ONE HUNDRED AND ONE ·

Nine months later, in steamy August sunshine, Lucy walked with Peter along the shore. He ran in front of her, skipping stones on rippling tidal pools. Low tide seemed to stretch out for miles.

"Come on, Lucy, come see this thing," he said, nudging something around in the sand with a stick. The waning sun glowed orange on his little sunburned shoulders.

"You know I can't run these days." Lucy strolled toward him, her very pregnant belly filling out her flowered sundress.

"Yeah, but this thing is cool," he said, bringing it to her.

It was a dead crab, half decayed and legless. "Peter, honey, I don't want that."

"Oh, all right." He threw it away with a plop, took her hand and peered up at her. "Is Constantin my father?"

She stroked his head of red curls. "No, Peter, you have a father."

"I guess so." He frowned and squinted at the sun. "Then who is Constantin to me?"

Lucy took his hand and led him to a dune where she eased herself down. Silvery beach grass whispered across her calves. She patted the sand next to her for him to sit. He didn't. He folded his arms across his sparrow chest, waiting for his answer.

"Well, he's like an uncle."

"Uncle C?"

She laughed. "Yeah, Uncle C. He'll like that. And this baby will be your nephew, or niece."

He reached out and placed his small hand flat on her stomach, then quickly took it away. "But I'm still your only brother, right?"

"My only brother, ever." Lucy watched the sweet curve of his back as he sat, his little belly pooching out over his madras shorts.

"So is your head all better?"

"My head is great."

Peter drew circles in the sand. "I just hope no more bad things happen."

"Don't worry, Peter. I really think the bad things are over with."

· ONE HUNDRED AND TWO ·

That evening Lucy lay in Constantin's arms, moonlight washing gently over them.

He smiled in the darkness. "So, what's it like being with such an old man?"

"Stop it, C, you know I love you."

"I can't wait till the baby comes. I want to have another and another and another – "

Lucy laughed. "Please, no. Let's see how this one works out first." She paused, adjusting herself on the bed. "C, do you ever wonder how long she'll live...like that?"

"She could stay that way the rest of her life."

"You mean, just lying there, staring up at nothing?"

"She could."

She turned again, pulling the sheets tighter around her. "I know this is going to sound crazy, but sometimes I feel like maybe I should visit her."

He was silent a moment. "You're kidding, right?"

"No I'm not. I just – "

He got up on his elbows. "You're not going to that hospital, Lucy, for any reason, ever."

"She's in a coma, she wouldn't even know I was – "

"Of course she would! My God, this is not your ordinary – "

"Okay, okay, it was just a thought. If it makes you feel any better, I won't go."

Constantin sighed and pulled her close, cradling her. "Just get some rest, all right, honey? That's what you need. That's what we both need."

Lucy pushed the heavy hospital door open a crack, glanced behind her at the dark hallway, and crept in the room. The whoosh and clamp of the vent filled the room, along with the vague smell of urine and antiseptic.

Astra's bed was in the center of the room, all of which was bathed in a bluish light. Lucy tiptoed to the bed and looked at her. Her still radiant hair was fanned out on the pillow, her arms free from the covers and straight down at her sides, her torso tilted slightly up in the bed. Her eyes were open but glazed-looking, the pupils wide and dark. A bit of drool had dried in the corner of her mouth. She looked pale and bloodless, her skin almost translucently white. A blue vein pulsed at her temple like a tiny fist.

Lucy pulled up a chair and sat, gazing at her. She still didn't understand why she had come. Was it curiosity? Spite? She couldn't fathom it.

"Hi, Astra," she said, her voice oddly loud in her ears though she felt she was almost whispering. "I bet you never thought you'd see me here. I don't have a good explanation, even for myself. Maybe I feel sorry for you, I don't know. Maybe it's that mother-daughter thing. I don't th – "

Lucy had no time to react. Astra's mouth opened obscenely wide, the fangs of a snake glistening in the deathly light. She lunged at Lucy's shoulder, sinking her teeth to the marrow, pumping her poison into Lucy's veins.

Lucy burst awake, her hair and nightgown soaked in sweat. She turned to look at Constantin, who snored softly beside her. Shuddering, she pulled her blankets close to her chin and fell back into a fitful sleep.

Considering her night, she woke in good spirits, singing goofy songs in the shower as she planned a pancake breakfast for her and Constantin. As she soaped up her body and touched her swollen belly, she pictured for the thousandth time how this boy or girl would look like both herself and

Constantin. This baby was a present she couldn't wait to unwrap.

The phone rang as she towel-dried her long hair. Tossing on her green terry robe, she grinned when she saw she could barely tie it around her middle any longer.

A stunning pain shot across her belly as she reached for the door to leave the bathroom. Breathless, she backed up and sat on the edge of the tub. She held herself, rocking slightly, eyes squeezed shut. Something gave inside her. She looked down. What seemed like quarts of warm water poured from between her legs.

A knock. "Luce, can I come in? There's something – " Without waiting, Constantin opened the door and stepped in. "That was the hospital," he said, then finally looked at her. Doubled over, she clutched her belly, gasping at quick sips of air. He ran over and kneeled by her. "Luce – "

"It's coming," she whispered. "It's coming."

"Oh my God, let's get you – "

Momentarily recovering, Lucy sat up, still holding her belly. "I'm okay, for the time being," she said, lines of pain still creasing her forehead. "What, C, you said the hospital called."

He sat next to her, wrapping his arm around her narrow shoulders. "She passed away early this morning. Astra is dead, Lucy."

"Oh, Christ," Lucy said, as unexpected tears flooded her eyes. They held each other, crying and rocking.

"We're free," Constantin said. "Finally free."

"What time was it...what time did she die?"

"Three-seventeen, I think he said."

A whip of pain lashed across her torso. She slid to the floor. "I don't think I can – "

"Stay where you are," Constantin said, covering her with his sweater. "I'm calling an ambulance."

· ONE HUNDRED AND THREE ·

Six hours into her labor, Lucy lay on the hospital bed, glistening with sweat, clutching Constantin's hand. She was almost fully dilated, but the baby wouldn't come.

Morning slipped into afternoon, afternoon into a long summer evening. She heard the cries of other babies being born on the floor, but all her pushing got her nowhere. In a daze, she lay on the bed watching the garish purple and orange sunset. Ellen and Peter had already come and gone, leaving instructions to call the moment "anything happened."

After a macaroni and cheese dinner from the cafeteria, Constantin lay down next to her on the narrow bed and promptly fell asleep.

Seconds later, Lucy's scream ripped at the darkness, pushing Constantin out of bed.

Lights blazed on, machines whirred to life and nurses arrived in seconds, prepping her, as Constantin donned a surgical outfit and gloves.

Once it started, it happened very quickly. In minutes the child was born. A high, keening cry. Applause and laughter from the nurses, doctors.

"It's a girl," Constantin said, his eyes squinting in a smile over his masked mouth.

Lucy's head swam with pain killers, an exhaustion like she'd never known flooding over her.

"Let me see her," she said hoarsely.

"In one second," her doctor said. "We're cleaning her up a bit..." His voice trailed off. The chitchat and exuberance died down. Lucy heard only the sound of splashing water, someone clearing their throat. She smelled her own blood in the room.

In a flash of white, a couple of nurses left the room, the doors swinging back and forth behind them. Heavy surgical instruments clattered on a tray.

"Get the, uh, better get some more lights over here," someone said.

Lucy got to her elbows, peering over at the scene at the other end of the room. A crush of doctors and Constantin huddled over a small, well lit table. They were silent, the room an airless box.

"Let me see her," Lucy said. She felt faint, the buzz of fluorescent lights above her throbbing in her skull.

Whispering to the doctors, Constantin bent over the table and picked up the child, wrapped tight in a small blanket, and brought her over to Lucy's bedside.

Lucy wedged a pillow behind her back, struggling to finally sit up. Constantin sat by her on the bed with the baby. She looked at him, at the tears in his eyes. She thought she understood their meaning, and smiled. With trembling hands she lifted the soft cotton wrap that partially obscured the little girl's face.

"She's beautiful," Lucy said, studying Constantin, the doctors standing awkwardly around them.

"She is." Constantin took Lucy's hand.

Tenderly, Lucy nestled the girl in the crook of her arm. Her eyes were shut tight, her features pinched and blotchy but Lucy thought she could see the shape of Constantin's nose as well as her own full lips. She laughed a little, crying at the same time.

With great gentleness, Lucy began to draw back the pink coverlet from the infant's neck and body.

Every gruesome mark and gash, scar and welt Astra had worn on her body was replicated on the baby's tiny one. The infant gurgled and squirmed, nosing closer to Lucy's breast.

For several moments she stared at its small, ravaged torso without comprehension. The doctors and nurses stood motionless in the back of the room.

"Get it away from me!" Lucy screamed, jerking the baby back to Constantin, who handed it quickly over to the doctors. She broke into sobs as she threw her arms around Constantin, who waved everyone out of the room.

· ONE HUNDRED AND FOUR ·

They stared at each other with haunted eyes. Disheveled and haggard, Constantin leaned against the door to her room. Lucy sat propped up by several pillows, still in her faded paisley hospital gown. Her hair hung down in damp strings.

"My God," she said. "What have we done?"

Constantin walked over to the window which was sealed against a balmy summer night. Air conditioning blew up at him, shellacking the sweat dry on his face.

"We should have known."

"Should have known? *Should have known?*"

Constantin pulled the curtains shut against the blackness and collapsed in a chair next to her bed, dropping his head in his hands.

"Do you know the chances of this happening? She could have repeated anywhere in this world, come back as any living thing, and she comes back through me, as our child, through *my body?*"

"Through our bodies, Lucy. And how do we know she doesn't have the power, now, after all this time, to come back when and where and how she wants? How do we know?"

Lucy started to cry, roping a sheet in her hands. "I don't know. Oh, God help us, I don't know."

Night nurses passed like ghosts outside their door as Constantin stared at the blank wall in front of him. "My little girl is...not my little girl."

Lucy hugged herself, rocking. "I can't believe that thing was inside me all this time..."

Tears flooded Constantin's eyes as he looked at her. His voice broke. "Her face is beautiful, though. Did you see her face?"

"Yes, she would be beautiful – "

"She's our child."

"I don't know what she is, C."

He pushed himself to his feet and began to pace. "I don't know if I want to find out."

"What are you saying?"

He turned to her. "You know what I'm saying."

She began to sob. "This is not what – I wanted a life with you. This is a nightmare."

He went to sit by her on the bed. "Yes, it is. It's a nightmare that's happening to us in our waking life. It's real, Lucy, absolutely real."

"But that's our baby out there, Constantin, our baby!"

"No," he said, rocking her in his arms. "No, my darling, that's not our baby."

She cried into his shoulder, her hysteria growing. "What are we going to do? How are we going to – "

"Shh, Lucy, let's calm down, we have to calm down and think."

"God, I'm so tired. I could sleep for a million years."

"Me too."

She gathered herself a bit, pulling her gown tighter around her. "We have to do something, don't we? *I* have to do something – "

"No, you don't. You just need to sleep tonight. I'll be right here with you."

She held him a moment longer, tighter, before she let him go. "You should go home, C, just for a few hours to sleep, and come back. You're right. What can we possibly do tonight?"

He tucked her hair behind her ears. "I don't want to leave you."

"This bed isn't big enough for both of us to really sleep. Besides, the cats must be starving."

"Are you sure you're going to be all right?"

"I'm in a hospital. I'll be all right." She managed a weak smile. "In the morning we can talk about what to do. In the morning this will seem less...less bad. We'll be clearer, really."

"Call me right away if anything – "

"Just give me a kiss and go," she said, wrapping her arms one last time around his wide back.

For hours she lay staring into the darkness, reliving every horror she had ever known. A nurse came by every so often to check on her. Each time she pretended to be asleep.

She turned toward the window, curled in a ball in her terry robe. Tears dried on her face, tightening the skin around her eyes. Little by little, dawn diluted the blackness of her room to shades of watercolor grey. Outside her window, the morning fog shifted like spirits floating across the fields, unveiling green hills in the distance. The day was going to be perfect, beautiful, utterly unlike what she knew she had to do.

With great effort, she swung her legs off the bed and got to her feet. Her muscles and joints ached as if she had been beaten. A headache stabbed at her eyes. Tying her robe around her waist, she padded barefoot on the cool linoleum to the bathroom.

The cold water felt good on her face. She stared at her eyes in the mirror, puffy from crying and lack of sleep.

The thing she was going to do tasted like bile in her throat, but it was a task that had to be done, in all its ugliness. The scar on her neck throbbed. She flipped up the collar of her robe and left the room.

As she made her way down the brightly lit corridors to the nursery, no one seemed to pay much attention to her; the sparse early morning staff going on their rounds, the orderlies cleaning rooms and changing linens.

The nursery was behind a wall of glass, a large, well lit room with dozens of babies in long rows of bassinets. Lucy watched a young male nurse attend to one of them as she rapped on the window. He looked up at her and came to the door.

"Hello, Mrs. – "

"I came to see my baby."

He unlocked the door and let her in. "I was expecting you sooner than this – "

"I was very tired."

"Sure, no doubt." He checked the ID tag on her wrist. "Sorry, just a formality. Anyway, follow me. I'm sure she'll be happy to see you."

As if moving through cold mud, Lucy walked down the aisle toward her child, passing small but otherwise normal looking babies. They waved their tiny hands in the air, toothless mouths opening and closing, or slept curled up like small fleshy knots.

The nurse checked her wrist band against that of the baby's, then excused himself. At last Lucy stood above her baby's bassinet. She was awake, stuffing her balled up fists in her mouth, her little legs kicking up. Purplish scars and welts looked even more hideous in the garish glow of the room. Her eyes were shut, as if fighting the light.

Shaking, Lucy reached down and lifted the clear plexiglass cover. She wrapped the baby tight in her blankets, closed the cover and began to push the bassinet toward the door.

With quick steps, she passed the nurse who was occupied with another new mother, and almost ran into the hall. The baby stayed surprisingly calm as Lucy wheeled her back to her room, the overhead lights of the hospital strobing across her tiny face.

Her heart beat furiously as she lay the baby down near the head of the bed. She stood back and stared at its pinched face and tuft of reddish hair under the swath of pink blanket.

She thought of Peter, how squinched up he'd looked on his first day back from the hospital after he was born, then the wave of desperate love that washed over her the moment she held him.

367

Suddenly sick, she closed her eyes tight and gulped the air, waiting for the nausea to pass.

She turned and ran to the bathroom where she stopped up the deep basin and jammed on both spigots. The water rushed out hard.

Lucy stepped back into the room. The hospital bed dwarfed the pink bundle. She walked over and stared down at it. She could smell its baby skin, the newness of its life. As she watched, the baby kicked herself free of her little blanket and lay there just in a tiny diaper, a portrait of helplessness.

Water churned in the sink. Lucy ran back to the bathroom and turned off the spigots with two sharp squeaks. The basin was brimming. She touched the water; it was as warm as the milk that filled her breasts.

The baby began to whimper, a sound that started thin and reedy, but quickly grew into a loud, rhythmic cry.

Lucy ran out to her. "Be quiet," she said hoarsely. "You have to be quiet!"

But she continued to wail.

"This is something I have to do. Please forgive me."

Arms shaking violently, she reached down and picked her up. She felt her tiny ribcage, her little chest expand and contract with each gasping cry. Holding her straight out from her body, Lucy carried her into the bathroom to the sink.

The baby quieted a little, suspended over the basin. Lucy could barely breathe, as if all the air had been sucked from the room. A drop fell from the spigot into the pool of water with a loud plop. The baby burped softly, a bit of chalky formula oozing down her chin, then stuffed her little hand in her mouth. Lucy held her there, arms rigid and outstretched, watching the baby's tiny limbs churn in space.

Lucy's face twisted with horror as she lowered the baby toward the brimming sink, down and down and down.

The moment the baby's toe touched the water, she shrieked as if she had been burned, drawing her legs up to her belly. Lucy watched as her tiny eyes opened. They were pale blue, like her own.

The baby looked at her, then wailed as Lucy submerged half her body in the water.

Lucy began to sob as she watched the baby thrash, her small face reddening as she screamed.

Held her under water to her chest, her neck.

Lucy's scar raged in the mirror.

The baby squirmed and beat at the water, her eyes tight with tears, the tuft of red hair plastered to her tiny head.

A full minute went by, until Lucy understood one thing only.

That she couldn't do it.

She pulled the baby up and out.

Water splashed off her like tiny jewels in the light.

Lucy unlocked the bathroom door and carried her, arms still out straight, into the room where she gently laid her down on her soft blanket. As the baby continued to cry, its tiny chest heaving, she tucked the blanket loosely around her and picked her up, holding her against her shoulder.

The weight of her baby on her, for the first time.

Still the baby screamed.

Lucy walked slowly to the window, patting her on her little back and making small sounds of comfort.

As the minutes went by, the baby's cries died down, and she gurgled softly against Lucy's terry robe.

· ONE HUNDRED AND FIVE ·

Lucy faced the window, holding the baby with one arm. With her free hand, she reached and drew her hair back and away from her face and neck. The scar across her neck had begun to fade, and as she stood swaying with the child in her arms, it grew lighter and lighter until it disappeared, blending perfectly into her own skin, radiant under the warmth and light of the morning sun.

Someone tapped lightly on her door. Lucy walked over with the baby to open it. A thickset Haitian woman stood there with a bucket and mop. She broke out in a blinding white smile as she looked at the baby.

"I'm not disturbing you, Miss?"

Lucy stepped back into the room.

"It's all right. Come in."

The woman took a few steps toward her, pulling her bucket and mop behind her. "You had your baby girl last evening, is that right?"

Lucy nodded.

"Well then, what's her name?"

"We don't...have one yet."

"Ah, she's so pretty, though. Can I hold her?"

"Of course."

As Lucy held the baby out to her, the blanket came undone and fell to the floor. The baby's skin was flawless, clear and sweet.

"She's beautiful," the woman said, cradling her. "Such beautiful baby skin."

370

Lucy watched as the woman cooed and gently stroked the baby's forehead, her hands pocked with small white scars as if they had been dipped in broken glass.

Interior design by Nancy W. Grossman of Back
Channel Press. Text set in Adobe Garamond Pro,
with headings and footers in Minion Pro. Layout
performed in Serif Page Plus. ❧